THE DOXIES PENALTY

A Sarah Tolerance Mystery

MADELEINE E. ROBINS

For Ann, and for Bernice, many years later.

With love and so many thanks.

October 1811. Another London

Chapter One

The family of Brereton had long been settled in Buckinghamshire. Their estate was large, and the residence was at Briary Park, where they had, for the most part, lived in so respectable a manner as to engage the good opinion of their surrounding acquaintance. Only twice had the reputation of the Breretons been threatened: once, nearly forty years before when a daughter of the house had had the poor judgment to elope with a half-pay lieutenant of good family and poor morals, and a second time some five-and-twenty years later, when that lady's niece had run off with her brother's fencing master. In both cases the family had closed ranks, deeming the lost children ungrateful and their reputations unsalvageable. The first Miss Brereton had, as is often the case, gone from man to man until, being a woman of intelligence and enterprise, she became the owner of the most expensive brothel in London.

The second Miss Brereton, more fortunate in her lover, had fled with him to the continent where, despite the war, they had taught fence and lived happily until the man's death some years later. In a daze of grief, she had returned to England and taken refuge with the only relative who would have her: that same aunt whose ruin had presaged her own. But despite her aunt's urgings the girl had proved unwilling to join her aunt's enterprise. Instead, using the skills available to her—a ready wit, a facility for puzzles, and the swordplay which she had learned and taught, Sarah Brereton changed her name and set herself up in a profession all her own, as an Agent of Inquiry.

Thus it was that on a chilly September evening, Miss Sarah Tolerance, formerly Brereton, found herself impersonating Destiny, or perhaps Nemesis. She had been about a client's business since very early that morning, making visits to many of London's less savory neighborhoods and interviewing a number of suspect characters. Now she was prepared for the final act of the day's drama. She sat in the parlor of a retired courtesan, upon a chair that seemed to have been stuffed with dried peas. Her client, Mrs. Caroline Jones, reclined upon the more comfortable divan with a scented kerchief over her eyes and her smelling salts to hand; from time to time she made a noise which might have been characterized as a tragic sigh. An instinct for drama went far to explain why Mrs. Jones, thirty years before, had been a popular actress and a more popular *fille du joie*, rejoicing in the *nom d'amour* of Caro Bawdy.

Also in the room, but seated well to the rear by the heavily draped window, was a pawnbroker, Mr. Varsey, a tall, raw-boned man of middle years with a large nose and dense blond whiskers, dressed with neat shabbiness in an old-fashioned skirted coat of brown broadcloth.

Mrs. Jones sighed again. "Why does he not come?

"There was no urgency in the message you sent," Miss Tolerance pointed out. "But I am sure he will come soon. We are in agreement? I shall talk, and Mr. Varsey, if it is necessary. You need do nothing but tell your nephew, if he asks, that we are here at your request. He will very likely resent our interference."

Mrs. Jones nodded beneath the kerchief, releasing a burst of rose scent into the room.

There was a stir in the hallway. Mrs. Jones's maid-of-all-work appeared at the door.

"Mr. Hasbrow, ma'am."

The girl stepped back and her place was taken by a tall young man in a tightly-fitted coat of bright blue superfine wool with large brass buttons. His neckcloth was high enough to scrape his ears, his watch had two fobs, and his boots shone with blacking. He came into the room smiling, very sure of his welcome.

"Good afternoon, aunt!"

Mrs. Jones, at the sound of her nephew's arrival, righted herself upon the divan and pulled the kerchief from her eyes. Her face was round and much lined, but it was possible to discern how very pretty a young woman she had been. Her lips trembled but she said nothing. If Mr. Hasbrow was disturbed by her silence he was not long stopped.

"How do you do, ma'am?" Hasbrow approached his aunt and bowed and kissed the air above the hand she extended to him with a practiced air. "And who is your charming companion?" He turned to smile upon Miss Tolerance. He was very certain of his power to please.

"Mr. Walter Hasbrow?" Miss Tolerance rose.

"I am entirely at your service, ma'am." Mr. Hasbrow bowed. When Miss Tolerance did not return the courtesy, his smile dimmed. He looked from Miss Tolerance to his aunt and back again.

"You have the advantage of me, ma'am. You know my name, but I have no idea how I should address you."

"My name is Tolerance, Mr. Hasbrow. I have been helping your aunt to discover the whereabouts of several pieces—"

"Treasured pieces," Mrs. Jones said, tremulously.

"Several pieces of jewelry which she has lately missed."

"Jewelry, ma'am?" Hasbrow's expression was so bland as

to compel suspicion. "Where have you looked? I am sure I could have helped you to find them. My aunt—" he spoke confidingly to Miss Tolerance. "Her eyes are not what they once were, and—"

"It is difficult for even the sharpest eyes to discover a necklace that has been removed from the house and is not to be found in Clapham, Mr. Hasbrow."

The skin on Mr. Hasbrow's jaw just above his neckcloth was suddenly a mottled red. "Not in the house?" After a moment's pause, he laughed. "Oh, of course. Aunt, we have both forgotten that you asked me to have some of your jewelry cleaned. I owe you an apology; I ought to have fetched it back to you from Asprey's—"

Miss Tolerance placed a leather wallet that had been resting beside her onto the table. "We have saved you that trouble, Mr. Hasbrow." She unfolded the wallet and poured from it three necklaces, a pair of earrings, and a bracelet. "However, none of these were found at Asprey's."

Hasbrow coughed. He meant to play the game to the end, Miss Tolerance realized. She did not know whether to admire his nerve or dislike him more.

"Did you inquire at Asprey's how they came to be elsewhere? I took my aunt's jewelry there because of their reputation, but by God, if they can lose property in this fashion—" as he warmed to his lie Hasbrow's tone became self-righteous. Miss Tolerance interrupted.

"You have not greeted Mr. Varsey, sir."

The pawnbroker had been sitting so quiet that Miss Tolerance thought Mr. Hasbrow must not have noticed him at all. Hasbrow looked up, took in the man by the window, and nodded in Varsey's direction with the brisk, blank courtesy of a gentleman to a person of inferior standing. "Good evening, sir. Now, to this misunderstanding—"

"Mr. Hasbrow, there is no misunderstanding, and you will try your aunt's patience very much if you continue with this pretense. Mr. Varsey is a pawnbroker. It was to his shop that you brought jewelry—"

"I never saw that man in my life!" Hasbrow sputtered.

"But I seen you," Varsey said. He had a deep, resonant voice that was loud in the small room. "Gents don't generally look at a man when they comes in to pawn their pretties—they takes their money and hoofs it. But I got yer name in me book." Mr. Varsey stroked a ledger lying on his lap with long, red-knuckled fingers.

"He's lying." Hasbrow smiled at his aunt. "I am certain I can discover where—"

"You need not trouble yourself, Mr. Hasbrow. Your aunt, Mr. Varsey, and I have already satisfied ourselves upon the matter. The only question—"

"Who the Devil *are* you? What business is all this of yours? You dress respectably, but from your name, I'd hazard you were—"

"Fallen? I am." Miss Tolerance agreed. "That has nothing to do with the matter currently before us, sir. I earn my living assisting people with inquiries such as your aunt's. To return to Mr. Varsey—"

"I told you, the fellow is a stranger to me!"

"You may say so, but Mr. Varsey has your signature in his book, and your aunt has verified it. Too, Mr. Varsey had possession of the jewelry. It would be much quicker and more pleasant for everyone if we could turn our attention to resolving the situation. I believe your aunt has no wish to involve the authorities since her jewelry has been returned to her. But Mr. Varsey requires to be paid."

At the mention of the authorities, Hasbrow's bluster deserted him and he became sullen. "He may whistle for it, then. I've no money to give."

Miss Tolerance smiled. "We understand that, sir, else you would not have found yourself stealing your aunt's jewelry and pawning it."

For a moment it appeared that Hasbrow would object to this characterization, but he sank back in his chair and Miss Tolerance turned to Mr. Varsey.

"How much is owed you to redeem the jewelry, sir?"

Varsey stroked his fair whiskers with one large hand. "Matter of thirty pound ten shillin'," he said at last.

Hasbrow sneered. "Might as well ask for the moon in a silver basket."

"There is my fee to be added in," Miss Tolerance said thoughtfully. "I do not feel that your aunt should be made to bear that cost, do you, sir? That's an additional three guineas, plus—" she took a small notebook from her reticule, consulted it, and returned it. "Two shillings ninepence halfpenny in expenses." She rose and gestured Mr. Varsey forward. "How do you reckon we should get our money, sir?"

Mr. Varsey had come around the divan so that he now stood between Hasbrow and the door. He looked the younger man up and down consideringly.

Miss Tolerance nodded. "How much is that gold pin worth, do you think?"

"Just a minute!" Hasbrow looked from Varsey to Miss Tolerance in horror. Unmoved, Mr. Varsey leaned forward and pinched the gold stickpin set in Mr. Hasbrow's reckcloth between his thumb and forefinger. The younger man was pulled forward into a half-bow. "That's fine work. I'd say it might fetch six guineas."

"This is thievery! The Law—"

"The Law will reckon that we are within our rights as creditors, Mr. Hasbrow. And summoning the Law would doubtless expose your financial situation to the bailiffs and others who might not be as sympathetic even as Mr. Varsey and myself."

"But I bought that pin for twelve guineas!"

Varsey clicked his tongue against his teeth. "Matter of the market, mister. Ye don't get what ye paid, ye get what ye're offered. Now, about that ring." Miss Tolerance suspected the pawnbroker was enjoying himself. He kept one hand upon the gold pin; with the other, he circled Hawbrow's right wrist and raised the hand up to examine a signet ring set with a green stone. "Maybe ten guineas."

"Ten!" Hasbrow's voice ascended an octave. "That was my father's!"

"Can't eat sentiment." Varsey tugged the ring off Hasbrow's finger, then loosed the pin as well and laid both on the table by Mrs. Jones's elbow.

"Aunt, will you permit this?"

The old woman pursed her lips and said nothing.

"That makes—" Miss Tolerance mimed calculation. "Sixteen guineas from a total of 33 pounds, 10 shillings, ninepence halfpenny. The balance still outstanding is sixteen guineas, fifteen shillings, ninepence halfpenny. What else have we, sir?"

In a quarter hour, Mr. Hasbrow had been divested of his fobs, coat, boots, hat, and waistcoat. Mr. Varsey and Miss Tolerance decided they were satisfied before the man was forced to strip off his shirt and breeches. Varsey, taking possession of Mr. Hasbrow's goods, paid Miss Tolerance her fee and bowed to Mrs. Jones. "A pleasure doing business with you, madam. And you, miss." He bowed to Miss Tolerance. "Ever you're needful to dispose of a trinket or so, you just let me know."

Miss Tolerance thanked the pawnbroker and escorted him to the door. When he was gone, Mrs. Jones, who had been dead to her nephew's entreaties and insults during his ordeal, now looked him up and down. "I am *very* disappointed, Walter," she said. "I had thought you were different from the rest of the family, and I was foolishly eager to mend fences with them through you. I see now that I permitted sentiment to outweigh good business sense."

This was apparently too much for Mr. Hasbrow. "Business! What does an old *whore* know about business?"

Mrs. Jones tilted her head and smiled. Her eyes glittered. "A woman who survives to be an *old* whore keeps her wits about her, Walter. You may think, sometime, of what you have lost. I had meant to make you my heir; you would have had my fortune, soon or late. But I will see my solicitor and leave my money elsewhere—"

"Your *fortune*! What will that be? Earbobs and a box of letters from your fancy men?"

The old woman had become steely. "I loved you because I thought that you, out of all our family, were able to see past my lapses of so many years ago. How do you imagine I live, stupid boy? My *whore's fortune* is safe in the Navy Funds, and if I live quiet it is because I live upon the interest. The capital—well, whether I leave it to a reformatory or a school for sailor boys, you will never see a farthing of it." Mrs. Jones rose shakily to her feet, less affected by age, Miss Tolerance thought, than by grief. There were tears in the old woman's eyes.

"Ma'am, shall I show your nephew out?"

Mrs. Jones nodded. "Good-bye, Walter. Thank you, Miss Tolerance."

"It has been my pleasure to assist you, ma'am."

"No, wait, Aunt—" too late, Mr. Hasbrow extended a conciliatory hand, ignoring Miss Tolerance's gesture toward the door. Recognizing that he would not leave except under compulsion, Miss Tolerance took his outstretched hand, twisted his arm behind his back, and marched the man out of the house.

Outside, Miss Tolerance released her hold and Hasbrow shook himself like a wetted cat. He shivered in the evening air and shifted from one stockinged foot to the other. Miss Tolerance, for the first time that day, felt a little pity for the man.

"Would you like to share a carriage back to town, sir?"

"Go to Hell."

"For this day's work? I think not. Come, Mr. Hasbrow. It is chilly, you are bootless, coatless, and without money. It would take you several hours to walk back to your lodgings."

"Why would you assist me? *You* think I am a thief."

A carriage rattled down the street. Miss Tolerance raised a hand to hail it, noting that a stitch had come loose on her glove "Are you not one?"

The carriage halted. Miss Tolerance raised her skirts out of danger from the mud and crossed the road. "Are you coming, sir?"

She had climbed into the carriage and was about to close the door when Hasbrow dashed across the road and jumped in beside her.

Miss Tolerance gave the address of Mr. Hasbrow's lodgings in Charles Street and sat back.

"It wasn't my fault! It's the damned duns, if I had known—"

Miss Tolerance leaned forward and put her finger to his lips. "Hush. I will talk about politics or art or commerce, but not your innocence."

"My aunt—" Mr. Hasbrow began a muttered catalogue of insults directed at the absent Mrs. Jones.

"None of that either, sir. You are the author of your problems, not your aunt. As a matter of fact, you might do well to emulate her."

"Emulate her!" Hasbrow's eyes, wide with outrage, shone in the dim light.

"Consider, sir. Your aunt has done what you have not. However you may despise her moral lapses, she found a way to support herself, selling only what was hers to sell."

"You suggest I should prostitute myself?"

"Not in the least. 'Tis a difficult profession, not one I could contemplate. But you have an advantage Mrs. Jones did not. You are a man. There are many opportunities open to you by virtue of your sex. You might consider selling your energy and your wits; you might find occupation."

Hasbrow drew himself up. "I am a gentleman."

"And a thief." Miss Tolerance reminded him without rancor. "Hardly gentlemanly behavior, is it?"

There was silence for several minutes. At last, barely audible over the creaks and rattles of the carriage, Hasbrow muttered sullenly that he would have no idea how to find employment.

"You have family, sir. Ask for advice. There is honest work to be had, and I imagine you have at least one relative who will be happy to help you to it."

Mr. Hasbrow shivered and sank back against the seat. Miss Tolerance watched out the window as the carriage rattled through the silky gray dusk. At Charles Street the carriage pulled up and Hasbrow descended, shivering, into the frankly chilly air. He said nothing to Miss Tolerance but did sketch a bow before he turned toward his lodgings with as much dignity as a bootless, coatless man can muster on a public street. Perhaps he would take her words to heart; she was unlikely to know if he did so. Still, pleased with her evening's work, Miss Tolerance rapped on the roof of the carriage and gave the driver directions to Manchester Square.

She alighted at the meeting of the Square and Spanish Place; here she saw a cluster of people gathered on the green to observe the immeasurably slow progress of the Great Comet across the sky. Miss Tolerance had viewed the Comet often enough; it was cold and she wanted to be indoors. A few paces along Spanish Place and she reached a gate set in the ivied wall; she unlocked the gate, stepped through into the moonlit garden, and looked to her left, at the great house to which the garden belonged. Yellow candlelight shone from the windows of Mrs. Brereton's brothel—for such it was— and filled the garden with light to rival the rising moon. The sounds of conversation, a pianoforte, and voices raised in song, drifted over on the autumn breeze, the civilized prelude to the evening's less civilized activities. Miss Tolerance locked the gate behind her and turned toward the small house half-way down the garden. This structure was no more than a cottage, one room above and one below, whitewashed and ivied; it belonged to the larger house and had been Miss Tolerance's home for the past five years. She was always pleased to return here; as her work often took her to the foulest and most hazardous precincts of the city, the cottage was her haven from dirt, disorder, and danger. Miss Tolerance unlocked the door and made her way through the darkness to the fireplace, where she stirred up the banked coals and caught a light for her candle.

Within a few minutes she was comfortable, with the kettle on for tea, a plate of cold ham and a sliced apple beside her, and her 'counts book at her elbow. The music across the way stopped and she heard increased laughter, by which Miss Tolerance gathered that the girl playing the pianoforte had been solicited for some other activity. She rinsed out her teapot, set the tea to steeping, and began composing a letter to a former client who had been for months promising faithfully to pay her fee "at my earliest opportunity," but had thus far failed to do so.

She picked up her pen, sharpened it, and began to write.

Dear Mr. Cartmare:

You will recollect that it has been some time since I completed the service for which you engaged me...

The next morning Miss Tolerance, at liberty with the conclusion of Mrs. Jones's business, stopped at Mrs. Brereton's house to see if her friend Marianne Touchwell was likewise free and wished to accompany her to Bond Street.

Mrs. Touchwell approved the outing and went up to fetch her pelisse.

"Is today for looking or buying?" As with all Mrs. Dorothea Brereton's whores when venturing away from the house, Mrs. Touchwell was dressed with a propriety that would have done credit to a bishop's wife; behind them, a maid followed to lend them consequence and carry their parcels.

"Today is emphatically for buying. I have only one decent pair of gloves to my name," Miss Tolerance admitted. "My work seems to be particularly hard upon them."

Mrs. Touchwell grinned. "Assume an air of disinterest or the glovers will double the price." As they stepped out of the gate Miss Tolerance observed a spare older woman in a coat and hat from the last century, waiting at the servants' door to the kitchen. She raised an eyebrow in query at Mrs. Touchwell.

"One of Cook's friends, I imagine." Mrs. Touchwell was incurious. "She keeps up with a number of women who left Mrs. Brereton's service."

"What do they do when they leave here? Do they cease —" Miss Tolerance faltered.

"Working as whores?" Marianne was unconcerned. "Some set up in business for themselves as madams. Some take their savings—if they've been clever enough to have savings—and assume a new name and retire quietly. My first year with Mrs. B—that was before you returned to England, Sarah—we had a girl who married her favorite client. All respectability she is now; they live in the North, and never come to London. Well, that's rare, of course. As for the rest—" Marianne shrugged. "It's hard to know. A woman who leaves Mrs. Brereton's without the intention to retire must find work somewhere else."

Somewhere else, Miss Tolerance knew, meant somewhere meaner, where the prostitutes were likely to be ill-treated, diseased, and drunk. Although Mrs. Brereton did not run her house for the convenience of her employees, she had told both Miss Tolerance and Marianne that treating the staff fairly was, in the long run, worth the money it cost her.

Miss Tolerance considered the retired courtesans she knew personally; many of them, like Mrs. Jones, took a new name and lived the quiet, respectable lives that had eluded them in their youth, with perhaps fine embroidery or china-painting to eke out their savings. As many, she suspected, died within a very short time of quitting the life.

"I trust you have money saved against such a day," Miss Tolerance said.

"Me? I keep my money locked away tight, never fear it."

"The Funds?"

Marianne shook her head. "Nothing so fancy for me. I've a box in my room I put my money in."

"In a box?" Miss Tolerance disapproved on professional grounds, but Marianne would not be scolded.

"I suppose I ought to take it to a bank, but I don't like the risk of them funds and investments. No, not even if 'tis in the Navy and supporting our sailors. The Navy won't support me when I'm too old to please. What d'you do with your earnings, then?"

Miss Tolerance admitted that her savings were earning five per cent per annum in the same Navy funds that Marianne so disdained.

"Well, you must tell me, some day, how that investment worked for you," Mrs. Touchwell said, as they turned the corner onto Oxford Street.

Miss Tolerance invested in two pairs of gloves. Mrs. Touchwell found a length of silk for a new gown. They refreshed themselves with a cup of tea and biscuits at a shop on Bond Street and made their way companionably back to Manchester Square.

The door to Mrs. Brereton's house was opened by Cole, the junior of the two porters. "Miss Marianne."

"I trust all is well?" Marianne was Mrs. Brereton's second, and the first to hear—from the employees or her employer—if anything was out of order.

"All's right and tight, miss." He took Marianne's parcel and turned to Miss Tolerance. "Good afternoon, Miss Sarah."

"How do you do, Cole?"

"Tolerable well, thank you, miss. Oh, Cook was wishful to have a word with you when it's convenient."

"Did she say why?"

The porter shook his head. "Not Cook, miss. If it was just, she had gooseberry tarts or some other treat she knows you favor, she'd have told me. Ah, if you'll excuse me, miss?" The knocker on the front door had dropped. Cole turned to admit a patron.

Miss Tolerance bid Marianne adieu and made her way through the green baize door that represented the division of the upstairs and belowstairs precincts of the house. Cook she found standing over the stove, instructing the kitchen maid in proper whisking technique.

"You mind careful at that, Jessie Cleese. If I find there's lumps in that saucing there'll be lumps on your brow!" Cook, a massive woman, tall, broad, and of respectable years, might have made four of Jess; the girl stirred her sauce with an eye upon her mistress, but Miss Tolerance had come to believe that Cook's threats were merest bluster.

"Good afternoon, Cook. Cole said you wanted a word?"

Cook turned away from the heat and wiped the sheen of sweat from her forehead with the back of her arm. "Miss Sarah! Deed I do. Are you hungry? Jess, when that custard's smooth, put it aside to cool, and you get me a plate of cakes for Miss Sarah—"

"No, please, I entreat you!" Miss Tolerance laughed.

"Marianne and I had tea while we were out. I cannot possibly eat more."

"You're all skin and bone!" Cook shook her head. "'Ow can you do your work proper with no food upon your stomach?"

"I promise you faithfully: when I am hungry I will apply to you. I have a great appreciation for the excellence of your kitchen. But now: how may I help you?"

Cook admonished Jess to keep whisking the custard without fail until it was 'just so,' then took Miss Tolerance's arm and drew her out of the kitchen, past the doors to the still room and pantry, and out into the tiny kitchen garden, where a cold breeze was stirring the herbs. "You just get me a handful of that thyme, Miss Sarah, will you?"

Miss Tolerance bent, obedient, and picked a dozen wiry sprigs of thyme. Cook took them into her plump red hand and looked from side to side.

"I know I can trust you, miss," she said at last. "Do you remember a girl name of Annie Pouter?"

"Annie Pouter?" Miss Tolerance shook her head. "Not by that name. I collect, from the styling, that she is Fallen?"

Cook nodded. "Oh, yes, Miss Sarah. Fallen for years, Annie is. Worked for your auntie for almost ten years, and left —" she held out the hand that did not have thyme in it and wiggled her fingers as if counting upon them. "Ah, well. A' course, she left before you come to us. See, Annie and I is friends," Cook went on. "Some of Mrs. B's girls hold theyselves too high, thinkin' because they work with the custom and I'm in the kitchen that they's better than I am. Not Annie, though. Annie and I got to be very good friends indeed." Cook looked over the garden, shading her eyes as if from a forceful recollection.

"And?"

Recalled to the present, Cook continued. "Annie needs

some 'elp, miss, and I tol' 'er you was the one would be able to take care of the matter."

"And what *is* the matter?" There was an edge to Miss Tolerance's voice; between the glare of sun in her eyes and the chilly wind, she was aware of a strong desire to be in her cottage with her bonnet off.

"Someone's stole 'er nest egg," Cook said. "Left 'er with naught. She come round 'ere today 'oping there might be work for her. Happen five year ago she might 'ave squeaked back into the 'ouse—there's some gennelmen like a older woman, I'm told. Mrs. B might 'ave found something for 'er to do out of sentiment and such—"

Miss Tolerance, who had never known her aunt to permit sentiment to interfere with her very acute business sense, considered the problem. "Is there nothing else she could do to sustain herself but—"

"Cept whorin'?" Cook shook her head. "Annie 'as 'er standards, like. 'Avin been rather a favorite of the gennelmen when she was younger, she sees anything' else as a step down."

Miss Tolerance had encountered this attitude before and, regardless of how inexplicable she found it personally, she did not debate the matter.

"Do you know the details of the theft?" She entertained the image of Marianne's box beneath her bed.

"Not I, miss. I tol' Annie she must talk with you. She's going to come 'round tonight—you ain't going out, are you, miss?"

"I have no plans to do so." There had been a time not long past when she had often gone to the theatre with her friend, the magistrate Sir Walter Mandif. But since the day when Sir Walter had laid proposals before her—honorable proposals of a sort Miss Tolerance had never expected to hear, but which she had felt herself honor bound to refuse—their friendship had been much reduced. Miss Tolerance, when not working, stayed at home.

"Then I'll just 'ave 'er come knock upon your door," Cook suggested.

"No, please." At Cook's look of surprise, she explained, "I prefer to keep business out of my cottage when I can. Do you think she could come to Tarsio's Club instead? Is there a time convenient for her this evening?"

Cook allowed that this was possible. "I don't know when she means to come, but when she does I'll direct her there. What street's the club in?"

"Henry Street. The white building with columns. I shall tell the porter there to look for her. Any time after six?"

"That'd be fine, Miss Sarah. I'll tell Annie when she comes. And I thank you. Now, cannot I give you just a wee plate of something to eat?"

Miss Tolerance smiled. "No, no. I promise you, Cook: I am not likely to starve between here and my own door. And you must return to see how Jess's custard has turned out."

Cook, with an oath, turned and hurried back to the kitchen, brandishing the thyme in her fist like a pennon. Miss Tolerance retreated to her cottage.

Chapter Two

At three-quarters past the hour of seven, Mrs. Annie Pouter was escorted into the Ladies Salon at Tarsio's Club by Steen, the senior of the club's porters. Mrs. Pouter had clearly dressed with care, in a gown and bonnet that had been of good quality several years before, and were clean and neatly maintained. There was nothing vulgar in her appearance save perhaps for her hair, a shade of dark brown given the lie by the silver at her parting. Miss Tolerance recognized her as the short, wizened woman she had seen waiting at the kitchen entrance to Mrs. Brereton's house earlier that day. The porter observed Mrs. Pouter with suspicion that seemed, to Miss Tolerance, excessive. But Mrs. Pouter clearly disdained Steen quite as much as he did her.

"You needn't give me your airs," the woman said loudly. "Just point me direct to that Miss Tolerance."

Miss Tolerance was on her feet at once, detecting the possibility of calamity and determined to head it off. The relief upon Steen's face was comical. "Mrs.—"

"I told you, Mrs. Pouter." The woman waved her fingers in dismissal. "And you'll be Miss Tolerance. Laurie Gordon has told me all about you, you may be sure." She offered her hand. Miss Tolerance shook it.

"I beg your pardon, Mrs. Pouter—who is Laurie Gordon?"

"Cook! Mrs. Brereton's cook! I don't suppose anyone but me recalls her name, she's been there that long." Mrs. Pouter spoke loudly, as if to claim the space around her through sheer volume, since she could not do so by size. "She thinks the world of you, does Mrs. Gordon. What did she tell you about me?"

Two women who had been engaged in a quiet conversation nearby rose and moved further away. Miss Tolerance beckoned to Steen, who had hovered anxiously in the doorway. "Are any of the parlors available, Steen?"

With a look eloquent of approval, Steen answered that there were indeed several open.

"We will be very much more comfortable and private there," Miss Tolerance told her visitor. "My guests usually prefer to keep their business to themselves. May I offer you some refreshment?" Mrs. Pouter's eyes lit as Miss Tolerance ordered Jerez wine and a plate of cakes.

When the two women had been settled in the parlor—a room just large enough to hold a pair of armchairs and two side tables set before a grate in which a small fire glowed—and Miss Tolerance had provided a glass of wine and a plate of the ginger biscuits for which Tarsio's was justly famed, Mrs. Pouter came to the point. Her savings had not been stolen from a box beneath her bed. "Swindled," she said flatly. "Mrs. Gordon says you're the one to help me, though for the life of me, I can't see how. I give my money over to be invested, and them I give it to has gone and left me with nothing. Frankly, my dear, I'm more in need of employment than of a what-d'ye call it."

"A *what-do-you-call-it*?" Miss Tolerance was mystified.

"An inquirer. That's what Mrs. Gordon called you."

"An Agent of Inquiry?"

"If you like. You can poke all you like into the matter—"

"Suppose you tell me the history of your problem," Miss Tolerance suggested. "I may be able to help you, or I may not."

"Well, there's honest. Can't say fairer than that." Mrs. Pouter paused to select one of the ginger biscuits. "I shan't mince words, and I suppose you'll know as well as any what our life is like. I retired from whoring three years ago. I'm not so young as I look. Even when I was working for your auntie I wasn't in my first blush. And custom begins to thin, and unless you wish to manage a house, which don't pay unless you've a stake in the business, which I couldn't afford, and beside, I don't think I'd have cared for the work —well, the long and short is, I've worked hard since I was a girl, and I thought I was entitled to a little peace before I die. I was at my bank to ask for the name of a good manager for annuities when I fell into conversation with a woman—too young to be a *retired* woman like myself, but that's neither here nor there—who told me about a miraculous fellow named Marvell, who could promise nine per-cent return on my money."

"*Nine* per-cent?" The Navy funds promised no more than five at best.

Mrs. Pouter nodded. "At the least. She said it might even be more. Well, in course I asked where I might find this Mr. Marvell: I ain't greedy, my dear, but a difference of a hundred pound a year is the difference between scraping by and being comfortable for an older woman. I got this Marvell's direction and wrote him straight away; he was in Bruton Street, with everything proper about him. I thought certain when I saw his place that he must be on the square. An address like that—and no, you needn't look disapproving at me, miss. I know better now. So Mr. Marvell begged that I come visit him, and I did, and he took my money and there you are."

Mrs. Pouter folded her hands in her lap and regarded Miss

Tolerance as if she might start into action at once. Miss Tolerance shook her head.

"I think there must be more to the story than that, Mrs. Pouter. You visited him in Bruton Street. Was he in a shop? Rooms? A house?"

The older woman looked as if the questions made no sense to her, but, "Rooms. Over one of them expensive bootmakers, Cavall and Sons. Brought me into a tidy little book room, furnished neat as two pins, and sat me down and talked to me about the fund. Investments in the Americas: sugar and cotton and tobacco. All safe as houses. All I had to do was give him my nest egg and my return would be paid quarterly to my banker."

"And did you ask for references?" Miss Tolerance did not wish to aggravate the woman with criticism, but nor could she imagine handing over savings so hard won to a stranger, simply because his lodgings were in a fashionable part of town and his manner was polished.

"References? 'A course I did! I wasn't born yesterday! And he handed 'em over, quick as you please. Aside from that Mrs. Brown, he directed me to a Mrs. White and a Mrs. Black."

"Mrs. Brown was the woman who first mentioned Mr. Marvell to you."

"That's right. And Mr. Marvell was most particular I should not invest with him until I had spoke with the other two and felt perfectly at ease. A funny-looking little man, but such an open, pleasant manner. If he'd been one of those too-handsome-by-half fellows p'raps I'd have fretted more. I wrote Mrs. White and received a note from her by return. I met Mrs. Black in the public room of the inn where she lives."

"It is likely, if these women are not Mr. Marvell's confederates—"

"Confederates? In league with 'im, you mean?" Mrs. Pouter appeared genuinely startled by the notion.

Miss Tolerance nodded. "It is a possibility we must consider. If they are not, they may be as aggrieved as you and might be very useful allies. Do you remember where you wrote to Mrs. White?"

"I got better." Mrs. Pouter took a paper from her reticule and laid it before Miss Tolerance with a click of the wax seal against the marble tabletop. "This is her letter to me."

Miss Tolerance unfolded the letter and scanned it. Small, cramped letters and ornamented capitals; flowery praise, and spelling of the most creative sort. Deciphered, Mrs. White wrote that she had been fortunate indeed to find *"the amazing churming Mr. Marvel, who has so wunderfly lived up to his promises and made my life a dream of comfort."*

Miss Tolerance was less interested in Mrs. White's encomiums than in her address. The letter had been written from Lisson Grove, almost two years prior.

"Is there anything else you can tell me about Mrs. White, ma'am?"

Mrs. Pouter shook her head; a scrap of feather detached from her bonnet and drifted slowly downward. "White ain't the name she'd ha' worked under, in course. I don't know what that would ha' been. The other one, Mrs. Black, I know she was called Arabella Twitchit when she was working. She and I had a glass of gin at the place she was living, an inn called the Dog and Tiger, cross the river near Horsemongers Lane Gaol."

"And she, too, sang Mr. Marvell's praises."

"Oh, aye, she did. So I give 'im my money, and all went along fine, payments every quarter day—until one day the payment didn't come. I wrote Mr. Marvell, and when I didn't hear from him I went back to his rooms, only to be told he'd been gone for months. Then I went across the river to 'ave a word with Mrs. Black—I'm not stupid, miss, no matter what you might think—but she'd died a month before."

Miss Tolerance's head went up. "Died, ma'am? How?"

Mrs. Pouter shrugged. "Run down in the street by a carriage, I think they said. Poor old thing."

"So you cannot say if anyone else suffered the same sort of losses?"

"What if they did? It's *my* money I'm concerned for."

Miss Tolerance sipped her wine. "Quite understandable, but the more people I can find who know Mr. Marvell, the more likely I am to find a clue to the whereabouts of the man himself, and the more chance that we shall have some luck prising your money out of his fund. Is there more you can tell me about him?"

"About him? Odd little fellow, short and bandy-legged, with yellow hair and a funny nose."

"Funny nose? Large?"

"Not large. Like… like God put his thumb on the bridge of the poor fellow's neb and pushed it clear up against his brainbox. Not comical. More as if he'd been dropped on 'is face as a tyke. But a cheery fellow for all of that. Good dresser, and 'is boots was particularly fine, but in course, he had a bootmaker just downstairs, hadn't he? A little hard of hearing, but bustling. Told me 'e regarded it as a blessing to be able to do something to help women situated like me."

I imagine so, Miss Tolerance thought, but this she did not say. "Well, thank you for the description. If I come upon him using another name I shall be better able to recognize him."

Mrs. Pouter nodded. "But in the meantime, what am I to do for money now is what I want to know?"

Miss Tolerance was not certain if the question was rhetorical or not. She was certain that Cook had not represented her as some sort of charitable agency. "I do not know what to tell you, ma'am. I will ask—"

"I can't go back to the old life. The sort of men you get when you're my age ain't worth the having." Mrs. Pouter wrinkled her nose. "But there ain't much else left to me."

"Many of the retired women I know augment their incomes with—"

"What? Tatting or china-painting or some such? I never learnt." Mrs. Pouter dismissed the idea as if to admit to such a skill would be to devalue herself. Miss Tolerance found this willful incompetence unappealing.

"Employment is outside my scope, Mrs. Pouter. If we are agreed that I should try to find Mr. Marvell for you, I had best let you know my terms."

"Terms?" Mrs. Pouter's voice slid upward an octave.

"Yes, ma'am. I generally charge three guineas a day and expenses—"

"*Three guineas!*" Mrs. Pouter was on her feet. "I didn't charge so much for a whole night with a man, not even when I was a girl! Laurie Gordon said you'd *help* me!"

Miss Tolerance made a little play of drinking the last drops of her wine, giving the older woman a moment to compose herself. Then, "Mrs. Pouter, if a man had come to you in the old days and asked for a night's pleasure, gratis, because he was needful, would you have granted it to him?"

The older woman sputtered. "I ain't got that kind of money—it was taken from me—"

"I understand. That is a different matter entirely." Miss Tolerance did not like to work for nothing. Still, some day she would be old, and might be in need, and would hope someone would extend kindness to her then. "Ma'am, if you will undertake to cover my expenses, I will agree to seek Mr. Marvell upon contingency."

"'Pon what?"

"If I find Mr. Marvell and am able to shake your money loose from him, you will pay me my fee. If I do not find him, I shall not charge you beyond the monies disbursed on your behalf."

Mrs. Pouter sat again. "That's fair, I spose. And I imagine the promise of pay will encourage you to work the harder."

Miss Tolerance agreed that this might be so.

"Well, all right then. If there is aught else you're needful to know from me?"

"A number of particulars, if you don't mind. The dates when you first heard of Mr. Marvell, when you met him, when you spoke with Mrs. Black, when you first realized there might be a problem with this fund, and what caused you to believe that."

"Oh. Particulars." It was evident from her demeanor that Mrs. Pouter did not have the sort of orderly mind that revels in particulars. She held out one gloved hand and counted on the fingers. "This is October. I must ha' met that Mrs. Brown at the bank in September of the year Nine. I remember that in particular, because she and I talked about the dreadful news from Walcheren. I went home directly and wrote to Mr. Marvell that very day. Must ha' heard from him within another day or so, so I'd have gone round to Bruton Street to meet him—say, within the week."

"All in September of '09, then."

Mrs. Pouter nodded. "And I give him my money within a few weeks—"

"How did you transfer the funds, ma'am?"

"Draught upon my bank. They wasn't best pleased to see the back of such a sum; I wish I'd listened to their cautions, I must say. I made the draught payable to Mr. Marvell in the amount of—" The older woman leaned forward as if fearful that the tarnished portraits on the walls of the small room might be listening. "It was a thousand, eight hundred and seventy pounds. I kept a hundred in the bank against emergencies. I brought Mr. Marvell the draught to his rooms and signed a paper, and that was that."

"A paper, ma'am? Did you bring that with you?"

Mrs. Pouter shrugged. "I've no idea where it got to, if I'm honest. Might well ha' gone to kindlin.'

Miss Tolerance suppressed a strong desire to shake the other woman. "Do you recall what it said?"

Again Mrs. Pouter shrugged as if to say that matters consigned to paper interested her very little. "Some mumblyjum lawyer's stuff." Her vowels were beginning to relax into what Miss Tolerance inferred was their native state. "That I was givin' Mr. Marvell the money of my own free will, without co—without being forced to it. That 'e'd pay me on behalf of the fund a sum each quarter, January, April, July, and October, by the tenth of the month. I remember that part but beyond it? Nothing much."

"But there was more?"

"I told you. Lawyer's mumblyjum. And no use tellin' me I ought to 'ave read it more particular. I know that now. Scoldin' won't change the thing. So I signed it—"

"Only the one copy?"

"Only the one, but Marvell took it and sent me a fair copy a day or two later. But what good would it be to me now?"

"It might have served as a receipt." She wondered how Mrs. Pouter had survived in her business well enough to save up a sum near to two thousand pounds. "If I find this Mr. Marvell, what is there to prevent him saying there was no payment, or that it was a gift, or—"

"What on God's earth would I pay near to two thousand quid for?"

Miss Tolerance dropped the subject as one likely to lead to aggravation. "And when did Mr. Marvell first default on the payments?"

"I was paid all in January of the year Ten, and all through that year and through April in this year."

"That would be six payments of—"

"Forty-one pounds." Mrs. Pouter produced the sum quickly. "On quarter day in July I went to the bank, expecting to have the money ready like always, and—pfut!" She made a flicking gesture with her fingers. "Nothing, not that day nor the next, nor the one after. And then I went straight to Bruton Street, only to be told Mr. Marvell had not lived there for a six-month. Well, I thought sure that he had only moved from that address and didn't intend to be out of touch, so I give the matter another week or two—"

Miss Tolerance was astonished. "You waited? What did you expect the delay to accomplish?"

"I don't know!" the woman snapped. "What was I to do? I didn't know where Marvell had got to. All I could do was hope that it was a mistake. And I had some money in the bank to hold me until I found out where he'd ha' got to. Only, in course, I'd no idea how to discover it and—well, Laurie Gordon says you're a bright girl and will find him for me."

Miss Tolerance found herself torn between impatience and pity. What sort of fool would give over the proceeds of a lifetime's work to a man with the improbable name of Marvell, expecting a clearly impossible rate of return?

"Ma'am, I cannot promise that I will find this man Marvell for you, but I will attempt it. Now, you say you have Mrs. White's address?"

Mrs. Pouter fished a piece of paper from her reticule. It was grubby and thrice folded. "Here it is."

"And Mrs. Black—Mrs. Twitchit that was—lived at the Dog and Tiger in Bermondsey?"

"La, what a memory you got. That's right."

"Well, ma'am, I shall see what I can discover. Where may I reach you if I have questions?"

Mrs. Pouter ducked her head as if embarrassed. "You ask Laurie Gordon. She'll know." She eyed the biscuits that remained on the plate. "You'll not be eating those, will you?" When Miss Tolerance shook her head, the other woman swept them into her reticule, crumbs and all. "That's our business, then, is it?" She got to her feet and fixed Miss Tolerance with an evaluative gaze. "You 'ave a way with you. Laurie weren't wrong in that. I don't generally trust women, but I shall trust you. I think you'll see me right."

Miss Tolerance was touched and amused by this straightforward encomium. "I shall do my best, ma'am."

Mrs. Pouter shook out her skirts and patted her reticule, full of biscuits. Miss Tolerance escorted her to the head of the stairs and watched as the older woman left the house. The expression of relief on Steen's face as he held open the door was not lost upon her.

Miss Tolerance was by no means an expert in matters of financial malfeasance, but she had several acquaintances who could make that claim. The evening was not far advanced; it was possible she could find the most reliable among them still at work. Accordingly, she desired Steen to hire a hackney carriage, and once installed therein, gave the direction of Savoy Court and the public house called The Wheat Sheaf. In addition to the usual provisions available at such establishments, the Wheat Sheaf served as an office of sorts for Mr. Joshua Glebb, whose business it was to know all the money lenders, bankers, and money men in the City, licit or otherwise. Mr. Glebb chose to work from the Wheat Sheaf, Miss Tolerance understood, because it was located in the Liberty of Savoy, one of the few neighborhoods still existing where, by law, a debtor could find sanctuary from the bailiff's staff—and the bailiff himself.

The barman of the house was wrestling with a tun upon which someone had writ in chalk: DARK. Miss Tolerance watched from the door to the taproom as the bluff, ruddy fellow rolled the barrel behind the counter, called for assistance, and raised the barrel into its place among several others along the wall. The ostler who had come to his aid returned to the stable, and the barman stood, catching his breath and wiping his palms on his apron.

"Good evening, Mr. Boddick." The taproom was noisy;

Miss Tolerance was not certain at first that he heard her. Then he turned, smiling.

"D'in't see you there, miss. Good evening. What might your pleasure be?"

"As always, a short meeting with Mr. Glebb. But I do not see him here. Did I miss him?"

"No, miss. 'Tis 'is daughter's wedding day, and Mr. Glebb put off all business until 'e'd seen the girl safely stowed."

"A daughter?" Miss Tolerance had some trouble imagining Mr. Glebb, whose personal charms were not obvious to her, married, let alone the father of a marriageable daughter.

"Oh, aye. Third daughter of five, Miss Gertrude. First two was married off last year, together—that is, on the same day. I expect Mr. Glebb found it economical that way."

Miss Tolerance was amused. "Well, then. We must drink to the health of the bride and groom."

"There's a 'appy thought. I've some madeira come just last week; will you sample it?"

"If you will join me, Mr. Boddick."

Boddick drew off two small beakers of wine. Miss Tolerance slid a coin across the bar to pay for the drinks and raised her glass. "To—" she looked at Boddick. "Do you know the groom's name?"

Boddick shrugged and shook his head.

"Well, to Miss Gertrude and her new husband. Long life and happiness."

"And prosperity," Boddick suggested. "Mr. Glebb wou'nt want that forgot."

"Assuredly, prosperity." They touched their glasses and drank. The madeira was a little sweet for Miss Tolerance's taste. "What time do you expect that Mr. Glebb will appear, Boddick?"

"I'd say any time, now. Within the hour, certain."

Miss Tolerance looked about her at the crowded room. "I

must wait, it seems. Tell me, Mr. Boddick: how does your family?"

Boddick launched into the tale of his wife's confinement with his fine new son; about his daughter's ear-ache, which no number of boiled onion poultices had relieved, and about his brother Bob's attempts to hold employment despite the ill-health that had dogged him since his service at Walcheren. Miss Tolerance made appropriately sympathetic noises, particularly at the trials of Bob Boddick, with whom she was a little acquainted. Boddick paused to draw ale for other patrons; when he returned his conversation moved from the personal to the public. He had served under General Lord Lake in Ireland, had been invalided out, and had nothing good to say about the current prosecution of the war. Miss Tolerance, who had lived in countries occupied by the French, was equally concerned with matters on the continent.

At last Mr. Joshua Glebb appeared. He was an elderly man, bald but for a fringe of yellowing white hair that spilled over his collar. He wore today a well-cut suit of black superfine wool with a highly starched collar and neckcloth. This finery did not disguise his pear-shaped body and substantial gut, but it did give him unaccustomed dignity.

"I am to wish you joy, Mr. Glebb."

Glebb smiled thinly. "That's three daughters of the five turned off in style, and an expensive business it is. But I thank you for your good wishes. You've come wanting information?" Glebb took a seat and tapped a finger at the side of his nose, which signal would bring Mr. Boddick over with a tankard of ale.

"You know me well, sir." Miss Tolerance took her own seat at the table.

"Well, I've spent the day making merry; time to recoup my coin." Glebb took a long draught of ale, shifted uncomfortably in his chair, belched fragrantly, and patted his stomach. "Beg pardon, Miss T. Let's to it, then."

Miss Tolerance, by force of will, did not wave her hand in front of her face. "Have you heard of a man named Marvell, sir?"

"Marvell?" Glebb pulled a face. "Half-a-dozen. It's a family sort of name, you'd say."

"I beg your pardon?" Mr. Glebb was rarely oracular.

"Never expect good from a man named Marvell, miss. It's a name commonly took by folk on the mace—fortune-tellers, swindlers, cheats. There's families that pass their secrets, father to son and mother to daughter, along of the name Marvell."

An alias. Well, she had feared no better. "I am seeking a particular Mr. Marvell, sir. One who preys upon older women."

"Breach of promise suit?" Mr. Glebb was obviously still in a matrimonial humor.

"No, sir. Not that I know of. This Mr. Marvell has convinced retired *dames de joie* to invest their savings with him, paid a few quarters' worth of dividend, and absconded with the balance."

Mr. Glebb took another long, deep draught of ale. "Marrying off is a thirsty business." He wiped the corner of his mouth with the back of his hand, leaving a smear of foam on the cuff of his good coat. "So you're lookin' for the sort of Marvell as does impures out of their jointures, as it might be said." Glebb twitched his nose thoughtfully. "You know nothing else about him?"

"I know that until some time last spring, he had rooms in Bruton Street and received his clients there."

Glebb gulped the rest of his ale, spilled some upon his neckcloth, and sponged busily at the mess with a kerchief. "Well, that's something. Not much, though."

"I know of two women other than my client who reportedly had funds invested with him but I do not yet know whether they were victims or accomplices."

"Well, you'll have to hunt them down, won't you?" Done with the kerchief, Glebb left it in a sodden wad on the table and peered into his tankard. "I don't off-hand know of the specific Marvell you're huntin' of, Miss T. Give me a day or so and a bit to be goin' on with and I'll tell you what I learn."

Miss Tolerance took from her reticule a half-crown, which she slid across the table. Upon consideration, she added another sixpence. "To drink the health of your daughter and new son."

Mr. Glebb slid the money to him with a stubby finger; his ears were red. "That's mightily kind of you, Miss Tolerance."

"So I may call again tomorrow?"

Glebb shook his head. "Day after, I'm thinking. It could take me a bit of time to sort the cheatin' Marvells from the potion-sellers and card readers. I've my normal business to be about as well, remember. Daughters is expensive things."

"I have heard it said so." Miss Tolerance rose to take her leave. "I will call upon you the day after tomorrow. Thank you, Mr. Glebb. And again, my felicitations." She curtsied and left him to his ale.

Outside the Wheat Sheaf, full darkness had fallen. Miss Tolerance gave a boy ha'penny to find her a hackney carriage and rode home to Manchester Square. The night air was damp and smelled of the Thames—the familiar blend of fish, ordure, and sulfur that penetrated the carriage and mingled with the scents of sweat and onion from earlier occupants. The carriage reached Manchester Square just before the smell had become unbearable; she alighted, entered the garden by the door on Spanish Place, and found upon her doorstep the day's newspapers and a note with her name writ in her aunt's hand.

Sarah—

I am taken again by this tedious complaint and expect to be confined to my room for the next day or so. I hope you will forgive me if I cry off from our engagement to dine tomorrow.

Your affectionate, DB

The tedious complaint of which Mrs. Brereton wrote was a recent development, a periodic attack of stomach pain debilitating enough to confine her to her bed. Her physician had diagnosed intermittent cachexy with colic, and prescribed laudanum. This latest spell must be a relatively mild one if her aunt could write of it so composedly. When she was well, Mrs. Brereton attempted to pass off illness as an inconvenience, but even she acknowledged that her formerly abundant health was somewhat reduced since the apoplectic stroke she had suffered the year before.

Miss Tolerance regretted the dinner; she enjoyed her aunt's company. But it might be as well, she thought. When she was at work upon an investigation it was often difficult to keep social engagements, and Mrs. Brereton, while requiring that business come first in her own household, had little sympathy when her niece missed a promised appointment.

Miss Tolerance took up the decanter and poured herself a glass of wine; took a heel of bread that sat in a box on the dresser and, judging it too stale for any other use, toasted it on the fire and completed her supper with some sausage and an apple. As she ate, she took out the slate she used for notes when puzzling out questions in her work, and made a list of what she knew.

Mr. Marvell: Bruton Street, over Cavall Bootmakers
Mrs. Brown, whereabouts unknown
Mrs. Black, deceased. Dog and Tiger, Bermondsey
Mrs. White, Great Quebeck Street
Bank?

As she wrote the last, Miss Tolerance sighed. She had

forgotten to ask Mrs. Pouter where she banked. It was sadly possible that a clerk there might have tipped Mrs. Pouter to a confederate as a candidate for fleecing.

By the battered watch she kept upon her mantel it was barely ten o'clock. The evening was well under way across the garden, but it was possible that Cook was still presiding in her kitchen. Miss Tolerance left her cottage and stepped across hoping to find her. Jess, setting out dishes to replenish the supper commonly offered upstairs, indicated that Cook was in her 'office' down the hall.

"I beg your pardon, Cook," she began, but paused when she realized that Cook was not alone. Mrs. Pouter herself sat at a deal table covered with neat stacks of paper—bills from victualers, Miss Tolerance surmised—with her face drawn in a mask of tragedy. Cook loomed over her, one large hand cradling the other woman's cheek as if in comfort. Both women looked up, startled by the interruption.

"Oh, Miss Sarah! Have you news?"

Miss Tolerance found Cook's faith in her both endearing and exasperating. "I have barely begun, Cook. But I am happy to find you here, Mrs. Pouter. There was a question I had forgot to ask. Who was your banker when you met Mrs. Brown?"

"My—Oh, Child's Bank, dear, near my last house—it's in Child's Place, just south of Fleet Street. Though I've no money there anymore, so what good will come of talking to them I'm sure I don't know."

Again Cook put her hand on her friend's shoulder. "You trust Miss Sarah to 'ave 'er reasons, Annie love."

"Well, that bank and I, we din't part on what you'd call friendly terms, what with me takin' the last of my funds out."

Miss Tolerance envisioned a scene in the hushed precincts of Child's Bank. She thanked her client for the information and took her leave before Cook could offer her some delicacy intended for the custom upstairs. She crossed the garden again, tidied away her supper things and her work, and retired to her bed to listen to the stirring of ivy against her cottage walls until, at last, she fell asleep.

Chapter Three

Once she had risen and washed and broken her fast, Miss Tolerance mapped out an ambitious day of activity. Her first goal was the Dog and Tiger in Bermondsey, home of the late Mrs. Black. The inn being considerably more than an easy walk from Manchester Square, she asked Cole to arrange the hire of a hackney carriage, and within a short time was rattling southward through London at the best speed possible in a city where it seemed all her fellow creatures—human, equine, and otherwise—had taken to the streets.

Swan Street was not far removed from the Horsemonger Lane Gaol, and the Dog and Tiger clearly derived much of its custom from visitors to the prison and spectators at hangings. With no entertainment of that sort occurring today, the inn was dour and quiet. Even the horses stabled there appeared sullen; the ostler who brushed past her as she made to enter the inn had a fixed scowl, and the woman behind the bar in the taproom looked as though her feet hurt her. The room was dim and meager in its appointments, as uncongenial as the barmaid. When Miss Tolerance began her inquiry the woman was all dull silence; the appearance of a sixpence in Miss Tolerance's hand only slightly improved her volubility.

"Mrs. Black? Got kilt last—" the tapwoman leaned over the bar and twisted to call to someone out of Miss Tolerance's sight. "Lijah! When'd yer old bunter die?"

A man's voice answered from somewhere beyond the taproom. "Mind yer tongue and don't speak ill o' the dead. Just after we 'eard of Wellin'ton's victory at Funtis Donrowrow."

"*Fuentes d'Onoro?*" Miss Tolerance suggested.

"Foo-wentees de Honor-o?" the barmaid called back. When she heard an affirmative noise she jerked her head in the direction of the voice. "There. Y'see."

"That would make it May." The barmaid had said, *got kilt*. She recalled Mrs. Pouter had suggested an accident. "How did Mrs. Black die?"

"Run down in the street by a charnel cart." The barmaid shook her head. She was a gaunt woman with reddish hair and crepey jowls, perhaps twenty years Miss Tolerance's senior. "Drunk, I spec' the driver was. Din' even stop to see what 'e'd done. Poor ol' Mrs. B—" the woman leaned over the bar and muttered "She'd been a whore, see, but was retired and tryin' to live respectable, like. Sad."

Miss Tolerance agreed that it was, indeed, sad. "How long had she lived here?"

"'Ere at the Dog?" The woman shrugged. Her jowls danced. "Some years, she 'ad. P'raps around about Warsaw year. Ought-six? She knew Lijah in 'er younger days, so 'e let 'er stay even when she 'adn't the coin." She raised an eyebrow knowingly.

"Do you think Mr. Elijah could spare a word for me?"

"I could maybe ask." The woman eyed the sixpence that peeked between Miss Tolerance's gloved fingers. Miss Tolerance put the coin on the bar and slid it toward the barmaid.

"If you would be so kind?"

The woman placed her finger on the coin firmly, as if she feared that Miss Tolerance might attempt to reclaim it. "Lijah!" She yelled with enough force that Miss Tolerance felt her own bonnet strings stir. "Lady to 'ave a word of you."

The barmaid turned away abruptly. Miss Tolerance surmised, from her subsequent shimmy, that she was tucking the sixpence somewhere private upon her person. A moment later a man quite as gaunt as the barmaid, but considerably older, appeared blinking in the doorway.

"Yah?"

"Are you Mr. Elijah?"

"I'm Mr. Sutt. 'Lijah's my Christian name. To what d'I owe the honor, miss?" He leaned heavily upon the aitch.

"I was inquiring about a Mrs. Black who lived here for a time, sir."

"Oh, aye. Belle, rest 'er pore soul. She did live 'ere for a piece, right up to 'er untimely passing."

Mr. Sutt ought to have been an undertaker. He appeared to have not only the demeanor but the humor for it. He looked at Miss Tolerance, pressed his fingers together in a little steeple, and shook his head sadly. "I know Belle since we was bantlin's. She strayed from the path 'pon which she ought to 'ave stayed, but we never lost touch. In 'er later years, when she give up the whorin'—beg your pardon for the language, Miss, but I'm a plain-spoke man—I give 'er a room 'ere."

Miss Tolerance did not follow up upon the barmaid's hint that Mrs. Black had exchanged services for the roof over her head. "I understand that she had an annuity—"

"Ooo tol' you that?" the man asked, surprised. "Not what *I'd* call a 'nuity, now. Little bit o' something she'd put by. And even then, in the end, pore Belle adn't barely a brace of pennies to rub together."

"At the end, sir. But I was told that at some time before her death Mrs. Black invested her money—"

"Oh." The syllable was expelled on a long breath. "Bad idee, but you couldn't tell our Belle naught when she was taken with a notion. Took 'er money out of the Navy funds and put it all in some new-fangled scheme. Like backin' the dark 'orse, I told 'er. She got money for a sixmonth, then the payments stopped cold wivvout a word. She was lef' worse off than before."

"Did she try to contact the man with whom she had invested her money, sir?"

Mr. Sutt nodded. His left eye was rheumy; the other was clear and bright with moisture. "She didn't 'ear naught for a while, then she got a letter and tol' me confidential that she expected th' 'ole misunderstanding to be mended. Tol' me she'd pay me back 'er rent an all. Went off to meet wiv—" Sutt shrugged. "Wiv whoever. But never got to the meetin' on account o' that wagon."

Miss Tolerance felt her spine straighten. "She was on her way to meet someone in regard to this investment when she was killed?" Mr. Sutt nodded again. "The coroner's court ruled her death accidental?"

"What call 'ad 'e to think else, miss?"

"I see. Did she mention the name of the person she was meeting? Or where?"

"Goin' to see a Mr. Wonder. Or Glory. Sommat like that. The note she got was from 'im, I think." Sutt stuck out his lower lip. "This 'ere's a mortal lot of questions. Who'd you say you was, miss?"

Miss Tolerance produced a genial mixture of truth and fiction. "A friend of Mrs. Black's from her working days was alarmed that she had not heard from her, and asked me to inquire."

Mr. Sutt examined Miss Tolerance, took in the respectability of her costume, but was still suspicious. "Why din't this friend come and ask 'isself?"

"*She* is bed-ridden, Mr. Sutt. The result of an illness which is a hazard of that occupation shared by herself and Mrs. Black." Miss Tolerance assumed an expression of sorrowful gravity to match Sutt's own. "She will be very sad indeed to hear this news. Mr. Sutt, I thank you for your time." She made to take her pocket book from her reticule, but Sutt waved her away as if outraged by the idea of payment.

"Then, sir, may I ask that you take a drink in Mrs. Black's memory?"

This was a different matter, and Sutt professed himself much touched by the gesture. Miss Tolerance emerged from the Dog and Tiger into the late-morning light and bid the dozy post-boy to secure a hackney carriage for her. She gave the direction of Great Quebeck Street in Lisson Grove.

If the statements of the barmaid and Mr. Sutt were correct, Mrs. Black was no accomplice of Marvell's but rather his victim. Should she attach significance to the fact that the woman had been killed on her way to a meeting with Mr. Marvell—for so she thought "Mr. Wonder" must be— The coroner's court had not done so

Great Quebeck Street proved to be a pleasant thoroughfare a little removed from a church surrounded by a knot of shops. The houses that lined the road were neat but small, not much larger than Miss Tolerance's own cottage, each with a kerchief-sized plot of garden before; the road was so little traveled that weeds sprang up between the carriage ruts. Miss Tolerance had the hackney carriage wait by a grocer's, where she inquired for Mrs. White's house. She was directed along the street to a house near the far end on the right side of the street, shadowed by an elm tree. The small yard was ill-tended and the paint on the shutters was chipped and distressed. If Mrs. White was a confederate of the mysterious Mr. Marvell, she did not derive much benefit from the association. Miss Tolerance put a gloved hand on the gate; it squeaked when opened, and her glove came away smutted with rust.

Her knock was answered by a woman, short, round-faced,

and smiling, wearing a green dress and a heavily-laced widow's cap. It was not the sort of cap a servant would wear; was this Mrs. White herself?

"Yes, my dear?" Her voice was breathy, her intonation redolent of the Scots lowlands.

"Good afternoon, ma'am. I am looking for Mrs. White."

The woman's smile broadened. "Then you have found her! Now, who would ye be? No, let us not stand here on the doorstep for every oud hen in the road to see. Come inside. You shall tell me all by-and-by."

In five steps Miss Tolerance had followed Mrs. White into house and parlor. Mrs. White moved with a bouncy step as if, despite her age, she would prefer to be dancing. Miss Tolerance thought she must have been a very jolly sort of whore in her youth.

"Sit, my dear, if ye will."

Miss Tolerance looked about her at the pleasant clutter of the room: three armchairs, one holding a work-basket that trailed tatting; another occupied by a very large, hairy gray cat that snored audibly. She saw a straight chair set a few feet to the side of a small table strewn with papers and sat there. Mrs. White took the unoccupied armchair and leaned toward her guest. Her feet, childlike, dangled above the floor. "Now, how may I be of service to ye?"

"I wonder, ma'am, if you remember a correspondence with either a Mrs. Black or a Mrs. Pouter?"

"A Mrs.—" Mrs. White raised one sandy eyebrow in a delightful mime of concern. "My dear, I know I look tame enough now, but are ye aware that I was once a very disreputable woman? I was known as Mattie Cumwell in those days. And at least one of the ladies whose names ye gave sounds like she must be in the same profession herself." Mrs. White appeared undismayed by her tarnished status. Miss Tolerance could only respond in kind.

"I am called Tolerance, ma'am, but that is not the name to which I was born. I am Fallen, likewise."

"Are ye, indeed? With a name like that, it's clear ye're not hanging out for custom. Ye're young to have retired, but I suppose it takes just one wealthy man to set one up in style." Mrs. White smiled knowingly. "Still, young as you are, perhaps you miss the excitement of—"

Miss Tolerance cut her off before the other woman could suggest possible re-employment. "In fact, I have never been a *fille de joie*, Mrs. White. I do not believe I am suited to the work. I undertake to ask questions and take on commissions as a way of earning my bread and butter. My work provides me with more than enough excitement. And my latest commission has been to find you."

"About a letter from a Mrs. Poxer, did ye say? That's an unlucky name."

"Mrs. Pouter, ma'am. She wrote a letter to you and has a letter written by you to her. I do not know if Mrs. Black contacted you—"

"Pouter. When would this have been?"

"September of '09, I believe. She wrote to ask you for a reference for a gentleman who told her he had invested some money for you."

"Ah." Mrs. White let the word out on a sigh. "Mrs. Pouter. Well, to be entirely honest with you, my dear—and now I'm retired I am all honesty, you may believe! — I dunna recall such a correspondent. And I do not get so many letters, nor write so many, that I would forget. Are you certain that the letter was writ to me?"

"I have seen your reply, Mrs. White." Miss Tolerance was a little stern.

"Have ye?" Mrs. White appeared unfazed.

Miss Tolerance inclined her head. "I have. The direction given was yours, ma'am."

"Well, anyone may write a direction, lassie. Have ye the letter?"

"I have it at my offices."

"Ah, well. You'll not know whether it was writ in my hand or not," Mrs. White pointed out. "I will tell you, my dear, I have no recollection of this Mrs. Pouter."

"What of a Mr. Marvell, then?"

"Is that your investment gentleman? I'd not leave a coin of mine with a man so named. But I'll tell you what. I'll give ye a sample of my fist and ye may take it away and compare it with the letter ye're holding. I cannot offer fairer than that, can I?"

The woman bounced from her chair to the desk, rummaged for a minute or so, and made a production of writing something on a scrap of paper, which she then waved before her until the ink had dried. "Here, my dear. Take this back and compare it with the note ye hold. For I swear, if I've been a-writing of letters I dunna recall to a woman I've never met, they'd as well lock me up in Bedlam straight away."

Miss Tolerance received the paper and tucked it into her reticule.

"I suppose you have never heard of Mrs. Black? Her *nom d'amour* was Twitchit, Mrs. Arabella Twitchit."

"Don't know her by either name, dearie." Mrs. White's voice was all regret, but her demeanor was still rosily jovial. "I am sorry ye've come so far for naught."

"Did I say I had come far, ma'am?"

"My dear, there's nowhere Lisson Grove is much convenient to except it be St. John's Wood. Did ye come from St. John's Wood?"

"No, ma'am, I did not." Miss Tolerance rose. "Thank you for your time, Mrs. White."

"T'was my pleasure to give ye what poor help I could." Mrs. White waved the thanks away. "I see very few people, and to tell the truth I get a mite lonely some days. If ye had told me when I was a working woman that the day would come when I would miss the goings and comings—ye'll pardon the pun! —of my younger life, I'd have laughed. Aye, laughed to hear it. But now—" She tucked her hand into Miss Tolerance's arm. "Well, this visit, mistake though it might be, is quite the highlight of my day." Without seeming to apply any pressure at all, Mrs. White guided Miss Tolerance out of the room and to the door. "If ye have any further inquiries, my dear, feel free to come again. I should be interested to hear how a Fallen women fares outside of pleasin' a man."

Miss Tolerance curtsied and thanked her hostess again. "I shall let you know how my career progresses, Mrs. White. Thus far I have managed to stay alive." She waved to the driver of her carriage, who nodded sleepily and nearly fell from his perch leaning backward to open the door for her.

Miss Tolerance directed the driver to Fleet Street and Childs Place, then sat back, her mind troubled. She had never been an enthusiastic proficient of arithmetic, but she knew when the sum of her information did not add up. Mrs. White had been so blandly jolly, had given no indication of anxiety at Miss Tolerance's questions, nor even a convincing evidence of bewilderment. Had she been too accommodating? To have volunteered a sample of her own handwriting—there existed two possibilities: That Mrs. White had received a letter from Mrs. Pouter and answered it and was now lying about the matter and hoping her writing would be dissimilar enough to persuade; or that Mrs. Pouter had written a letter to Mrs. White which had been intercepted and answered by some other person. This seemed like an inordinately chancy effort if it was meant merely to convince one not-very-clever whore that Mr. Marvell was on the square.

Childs Place was a small court dominated by the squat, stone-faced structure which housed the Messers Child's bank. Miss Tolerance dismissed her carriage. The outer office of the bank was a whitewashed room with large arched windows facing on to the street. On entering, Miss Tolerance was greeted by a young man, in need of a shave but otherwise of gentlemanly appearance, whom she took to be a junior clerk.

On the ride from Lisson Grove to the City, Miss Tolerance had studied how to approach this visit. She doubted that the management of Child & Company would take kindly to questions suggesting that someone among their staff might be in league with a swindler. It was therefore best to come at her inquiries sidewise and in the person of some other character. Squinting just enough to suggest near-sightedness, and allowing her voice to rise half an octave, she explained to the clerk that her late aunt had said she banked with the Messers Child. This aunt had left her affairs "all in a muddle" and left it to her heirs to determine "what was what."

The clerk urged Miss Tolerance to take a seat and asked the name of her aunt, and whether she had—he paused delicately—provided for a distribution of her assets.

Miss Tolerance used the tone of a woman used to managing others for their own good. "Oh, there's a will, and all of Aunt's worldly possessions left between me and my sister Tess, but if I should leave it up to the lawyers to discover what-all Auntie owned, I'll be in my dotage before we see the good of it. I don't mind telling you I've got my eye on a neat little millinery shop, and—what?"

The clerk, taken aback by the stream of words, asked again for the deceased aunt's name.

"Her name?" Miss Tolerance leaned forward and lowered her voice as one divulging a dire secret. "Annie Pouter. That's not her born name, of course, but the one she—you understand, sir.”

The clerk looked as though his neckcloth had inexplicably shrunk, nodded, and assured her that he did, and if the lady would be so kind as to wait a moment— He darted toward an enormous case of ledgers at the far end of the room. Miss Tolerance folded her hands, aware that she enjoyed discomfiting pompous young men more than was either seemly or kind. She watched as the clerk ran a practiced finger along the spines of the ledgers, took one down, turned the pages until he found the one he sought, and then looked up blindly. After a moment he closed the ledger, tucked it into his arm, and vanished through a door at the side of the room. After a few minutes, the clerk reappeared in the doorway, followed by a very spare elderly man in a black coat and cravat who moved with magisterial authority. The clerk quietly indicated the source of his concern: Miss Tolerance herself. The elderly man made his way across the room to her.

“Madam?” The gentleman’s bow was the sort calculated to the quarter-inch to express his notion of the visitor’s importance: he clearly did not think Miss Tolerance worth his time. “You were inquiring about a former patron of Child’s Bank?”

Miss Tolerance, in character as meddling heiress, rose to her feet. “*Former* patron, sir?”

“Former, madam. Mrs.—er—Pouter withdrew the last of her funds—” The elderly man snapped his finger at the clerk, who stood just behind him, an anxious shadow.

“More than two years ago. Twenty-seventh September, Ought-Nine,” the clerk supplied.

“Twenty-seven September,” the elderly man repeated. “I am afraid we cannot be of further—”

“Oh, indeed you can, sir!” Miss Tolerance was firm. “*All* her funds? I was under the impression that Auntie had a hundred pounds with Childs as late as five months ago! If you cannot keep your accounts straight, I do not wonder that she removed her funds from this establishment. Where's the funds she left here, I ask you?"

The clerk swallowed audibly in the silence. After a long pause, the old man turned and asked, "Is there any annotation on the account?"

The clerk fumbled through the ledger until he found the page he wanted. "It was all withdrawn, sir. For investment, it says. Sir."

"Withdrawn for investment," the old man repeated. Miss Tolerance's imposture was calculated to inspire discomfort in a man of his position; still, she considered it very unmannerly that he had neither introduced himself nor asked for her name. Bad business. And his poor clerk was clearly terrified of him. She therefore felt no hesitation in enlarging upon the scene she had created.

"Investment, sir? Auntie never had any more idea of investments that she had of flying to the moon! This is a very strange business, I'm sure. P'raps I had ought to call upon the magistrate and ask him to investigate what becomes of a woman's money when it's entrusted—" Her volume rose with each word.

"Madam!" The old man's voice, paper-dry, cut through Miss Tolerance's. "The law does not require that we interview our clients if they wish—however misguidedly—to remove their money from our bank."

"So it was misguided, then?"

"I beg your—"

"Why do you say it was misguided?"

Before the old man could respond, yet another clerk appeared at his side. He murmured something into his senior's ear. The senior raised an eyebrow, then nodded. Without taking his leave he turned his back on Miss Tolerance and departed.

The new clerk had a square, snub-nosed face and a curl of

light brown hair that defied pomade to tumble over his brow. "That'll do, Willis," he said to the first clerk, who bobbed his head in lieu of a bow and departed with speed.

"Perhaps you will give me the favor of a few minutes, ma'am? Please, come sit." He led her to a bench at the side of the office. "I am Mr. Perry. It was I who spoke with your aunt at the time when she withdrew her funds."

Miss Tolerance looked up at Perry, who still stood. "Then she did withdraw the money? All of it? That goes against what Auntie told me. What sort of investment? With whom, sir?"

"Your aunt said she meant to give it to a broker who promised a very good return."

"A broker? Auntie? Where'd she hear of such a man is what I'd like to know."

"I believe she may have been referred to him by another patron of Child's, ma'am. Mrs. Pouter was awaiting the opportunity to speak with someone when she fell into a conversation and left with the other woman."

"And she come back and took it all from Child's?"

Perry nodded.

"Well, you see how this places me, Mr. Perry. All my expectations are tied up in my aunt's property, and I've no idea who this broker-person might be. Did you hear a name?"

"I overheard only a little of their conversation, and I do not recall a name."

"What about the woman as recommended the broker to Auntie?"

Mr. Perry appeared to make an honest attempt to remember. "I believe her name is Pilgrim, ma'am. Mrs. Jane Pilgrim. Whatever her faith in this investment scheme, I do know that *she* did not close out her account with Child's."

Miss Tolerance gave an inward sigh. "And can you tell me where this Mrs. Pilgrim is to be found, sir? If I cannot find her I do not see how I shall ever learn what became of

Auntie's funds. My poor sister Tess is relying upon me to—"

"Quite. If you will excuse me for a moment, ma'am?" Perry stepped to a drawer of cards, rifled through it, and returned with one. "At the time she opened her account with Child's, Mrs. Pilgrim resided in Paradise Row in Bethnal Green. Number 7."

"Well, sir." Miss Tolerance got to her feet and offered her hand. "You are a gentleman, indeed. I see no reason to trouble you further." Moved by the spirit of mischief, she raised her voice again. "Since *you*, at least, have seen fit to treat decently with me."

Perry showed no sign of dismay at his visitor's manner. He politely escorted her to the door and wished her a good day. If, once she was gone, he and his colleagues breathed a sigh of relief, Miss Tolerance was not to know it.

Miss Tolerance hailed a hackney carriage to Manchester Square. She had much to consider. She regarded the visit to Child's Bank as a success: she had learned an alternate name for the woman identified to her by Mrs. Pouter as Mrs. Brown, and she had an address for her, as well. A drive to Bethnal Green would be a pleasant way to spend a morning.

Once home, Miss Tolerance took from her writing box the letter Mrs. Pouter had given her the day before. Lighting a lamp—for afternoon was drawing to a close, and her house was generally rather dark—she took Mrs. White's writing sample from her pocket and laid it beside the letter. The letter was written in a cramped back-slanted fist, closely lined, with fancified capitals. The spelling, as Miss Tolerance had noted before, was more evocative than correct, but the note was an emphatic endorsement of Mr. Marvell's financial acumen. The sample of writing Mrs. White had given her today was blotchy, as if her pen needed mending, but the handwriting was clearly different. The letters were round and open, a good, plain hand. The sample itself was brief: *I am very pleased to meet you, Mrs. Mehetibel White.*

It seemed Mrs. Pouter's letter had not been written by Mrs. White.

The sense of accomplishment that Miss Tolerance had briefly enjoyed vanished. She was aware of some annoyance: a chore that had begun as a favor to Cook was rapidly becoming complex. Mrs. White seemed to be absolved of any connection to the matter, but there was something in her very helpfulness that made Miss Tolerance suspicious. The whole case was a tangle. Mrs. Pouter's story had been corroborated, in the main, by Mr. Perry at Child's, but why had her client insisted that she held back some part of her money from the investment with Marvell if she had, in fact, withdrawn it all from Child's Bank?

Miss Tolerance put both pieces of paper into her writing box and locked it. Then she crossed the garden to inquire of Cook for Mrs. Pouter's whereabouts.

"Didn't Annie tell you, Miss Sarah?" Cook was sitting on a stool by the door to the kitchen garden, rotating first one swollen slippered foot and then the other, and drinking a cup of tea. Jess sat just outside the door, shelling peas, shivering slightly despite the afternoon sun. "Annie's staying with me."

"With you? No, she did not tell me so." *Here in my aunt's house*? Then Miss Tolerance recalled that Cook did not live in the house, although from the hours she kept she might as well have done.

"Since I'm not there so regular, it was no problem for me to let Annie stay in my lodgin's." Cook took a noisy sip of her tea and smacked her lips. "I've rooms in Castle Street over a pie shop. Cozy as can be. That's where you'll find Annie, Miss Sarah, tucked up neat in my place."

Miss Tolerance was surprised to hear any lodgings in the infamous neighborhood of Seven Dials pronounced "cozy," but she did not like to argue. She thanked Cook again and took her leave.

Before she departed, Miss Tolerance returned to her cottage and assumed the trousers, coat, and greatcoat of masculine garb. Seven Dials was home to a significant segment of London's criminal element, and she wanted whatever advantage—and weaponry—she could bring. She took her small sword and hat, checked the pocket of her Gunnard greatcoat and found her pistol there, primed it, and thus armed, went off to Castle Street.

The chair she had hired let her down at the meeting of Castle and Little White Lion Streets. At late afternoon, Seven Dials looked no worse than any other of London's slums; it was shadowed and busy, and clusters of men stood on each corner, talking urgently. She had taken the precaution of tucking the money she carried into an inner waistcoat pocket, and so felt herself reasonably secure against pick-thieves. Still, she kept her eyes open. On her side of the street a crowd of drunkards clustered in the doorway of a gin shop, and two hedge-whores fawned and flirted on the corner.

On the opposite side of the street the crowd was dense; as they moved Miss Tolerance saw there was indeed a pie shop. The smells that wafted to meet her as she crossed were not appetizing; her first thought was to wonder how Cook, that excellent practitioner of the culinary arts, could bear to live here? Then the throng before the shop dispersed a little, and Miss Tolerance realized that the crowd was all men, and most of them were smudged and grimy far beyond the London norm. Many carried buckets, and all wore expressions of grim exhaustion. There had been a fire. She looked up, saw the tell-tale marks of charring above the right-most window on the upper floor, and felt a frisson of alarm.

She timed her dash across the street between a procession

of drays, and reached out to grab a boy on the edge of the crowd.

"Whot! I an't touched you, mister." The boy looked side-to-side as if gauging his best route to escape.

"I know it," she said shortly. "What happened here?" She pointed her chin in the direction of the pie shop.

The boy's eyes lit. "Fire. Right nice one too. They put 'er out too soon, but there *is* a ol' lady dead." He offered the last as if it confirmed the fire's superiority.

Miss Tolerance loosed him, and the boy ran off.

Chapter Four

"Yor pardon, gents, yor pardon!" A large, roughly dressed man stepped in
front of her, arms outstretched to bar the way. "Respec' for the dead n'all."

Behind him came two more men of equal size and rough mien, carrying a stretcher. And on the stretcher, as Miss Tolerance had feared, Mrs. Pouter lay unmoving.

"Let me through," she demanded.

The big man looked down at her, seeing only her clothes and not her gender. "Can't do that, sir—body must be got out the 'ouse."

The body.

Miss Tolerance had a hearty respect for the forces of coincidence, and in the rickety wooden slums of the city fire was a daily hazard. But how likely was it that a client of hers should die by fire at the same time that she was asking questions on the woman's behalf?

"I must see. It might be my aunt!" The much-rehearsed lie came easily to her lips.

The man paused, holding out a hand to signal the

stretcher-bearers to halt. "Yer aunt? Then you'll be wantin' to take charge of the body yerself, sir?"

That was a burden she did not want. She temporized. "How could this have happened?"

"Yer nose'll tell you t'was fire. Not much of a blaze—poor old thing must ha' been took by the smoke."

"Let me see her."

"I'll do better, mister. You tell me where you want yer auntie brung, me and my boys'll cart 'er round to you."

This was little short of a nightmare. Miss Tolerance wanted to examine the corpse, but taking charge of a body—and perhaps having to provide burial—was not something she had planned for. "Let me see," she said once more.

The big man stood aside. The men carrying the stretcher put their burden down and settled themselves in attitudes properly respectful of death, with their heads bowed and feet braced apart. Annie Pouter had been laid upon the stretcher with her hands folded across her breast in the traditionally prayerful attitude. Her fine-boned, wrinkled face was smirched with smuts and soot, and she smelled powerfully of charred wood and smoke. Her face was oddly rosy; on closer inspection, Miss Tolerance saw that this appearance was created by tiny red dots on her nose and cheeks, like the face of an habitual drunkard. She had had no such marks when Miss Tolerance had met her before, but perhaps it was a consequence of suffocation by smoke. Mrs. Pouter had been dressed in a plain gown of light brown wool with an old-fashioned scarf twisted every which way about her neck; the light cambric was singed in places with tiny holes. Miss Tolerance slid the fichu down an inch or so and saw what she had feared to find: marks of bruising on her neck. Mrs. Pouter might very well have been killed by the poisonous effects of smoke, but not before she had been choked to insensibility by an entirely human hand.

"Were there signs of arson?"

"Signs o' whot?"

Clearly, she would get little information from this quarter. Miss Tolerance thought rapidly. "Where is the Watch?"

The man shrugged. "Sleepin' it off, most like. Watchman got no love for our neighborhood—lest it be the aleshops." He grinned. He was missing two bottom teeth in front.

If no one claimed the body and no question was raised as to the cause of death, the responsibility would likely be thrown upon the parish, and Mrs. Pouter would be buried in a pauper's grave. Miss Tolerance had no reason to love Mrs. Pouter, but she rebelled at consigning even a stranger to such a fate. Further, she was morally certain the woman had been murdered, and it seemed unlikely that official notice would be taken unless she undertook to make that happen. Deeply unhappy, Miss Tolerance gave the direction of her aunt's house, instructing the men to go round to the gate on Spanish Place and deliver Mrs. Pouter's remains to her cottage.

"You will speak to the porter in the front of the house and he will instruct you what to do. You are on no account to bring the body into the house itself, do you understand?"

"Deed I do, sir. Talk to the porter, aye."

Miss Tolerance liberated her purse from her waistcoat pocket and gave the man a few coins. He saluted and gave that toothless grin again; the stretcher bearers picked up the body again, and the three of them started off down the street at a trot with the leader bawling "Make way! 'Spect for the dead! Make way!" at the top of his lungs. Miss Tolerance hoped that whichever porter was on duty—Cole or Keefe— would have the presence of mind to deal appropriately with this unexpected development. She could only imagine with what outrage her aunt and Marianne Touchwell would regard the introduction of a corpse into the brothel.

Before she could return home, she must see the scene of the fire.

The crowd had largely dispersed, some following after the

body in an informal parade. Miss Tolerance pushed past the remaining bystanders (with a hand on her waistcoat pocket) and entered the shadowed door next to the pie shop. She groped along in near-darkness until she found the stairs, made her way upstairs, and found the door to Cook's rooms had been left open, spilling a little light onto the landing. There were puddles of water and grimy footprints; the smell of water and burnt wood was foul, and while the fire had been extinguished, the charred wall to the right of the door still gave off heat and vapor; a pile of ash and charred refuse lay at the base of the wall. Miss Tolerance stepped into the room. It was small, perhaps four paces across in either direction; there was a door to the left leading to what she presumed was a second chamber; the furnishings were or had been, neat, spare, and well-worn. There was a small grate across from the burned wall. It was empty of ash or the residue of fire.

Miss Tolerance was certain that Mrs. Pouter had been throttled first and the fire set after. She was no expert, however. She saw nothing in the room that confirmed her belief except that empty grate. What reason was there for a fire to break out with no sign of candle or lamp, and so far from the grate? She inspected the room for several minutes, gaining no information of particular utility, and at last left, closing the door behind her, to return to Manchester Square.

S he had been right to mistrust the man and his porters. Not more than ten minutes later Mrs. Pouter's remains, with their escort, were brought to the door of Mrs. Brereton's establishment.

Miss Tolerance was in the kitchen, where she had broken the news of Mrs. Pouter's death to Cook and was now attempting comfort. Mrs. Gordon's round, red face had drained of blood, and she had sat with a suddenness that made her stool rock and creak. She had wept a little on Miss Tolerance's breast but was now sitting upright—much to Miss Tolerance's relief—and drinking a restorative tot of gin from Jess's hand. When the commotion from the front of the house filtered down through the service entrance, Miss Tolerance excused herself to Cook and sped to the gate on Spanish Place to unlock it. Cole had escorted the bearers to that gate, arguing with their toothless leader about what his orders had been. When he saw Miss Tolerance he ceded place to her with an expression of relief. "Thank God."

The toothless man spat after Cole's retreating back, then turned to smile at Miss Tolerance. "Well, mister, 'ere's yer auntie, right n' tight, no thanks to that catchfart round the front—" He jerked his head in the direction of Manchester Square. "If you'll be showin' us where you want 'er stowed? Me mates is powerful worn." For a moment his glance wandered across her face, then he shook off the question of her gender—or so Miss Tolerance perceived it to be—and waved the bearers forward. They had not thought to cover Mrs. Pouter's corpse with so much as a scarf; no wonder Cole had looked so dismayed.

In a few minutes, Mrs. Pouter's body had been covered with a sheet and left on the stretcher by the stair in Miss Tolerance's cottage, and Miss Tolerance had supplied a shilling to soothe their wounded sensibilities and escorted the trio to the gate, thence off Mrs. Brereton's property. Then she returned to her cottage and her ghastly company to write a letter.

Dear Sir Walter:

I find myself in an original dilemma. A client for whom I had undertaken an investigation has died under circumstances I find distinctly suspicious.

She outlined the manner of Mrs. Pouter's death and the reason why she had herself taken charge of the body.

I am not perfectly clear what I must do in this instance:

surely a Coroner's Court should be called? But as the men in Seven Dials seemed ready to take the corpse who knows where, I volunteered that it could be removed to my cottage. You will appreciate that this is no perfect solution. May I ask your advice as to what action I should take to see that the matter is handled properly?

She subscribed herself his humble servant with a sigh. Once this expression would have conveyed uncomplicated collegiality and friendship. Now any contact with Sir Walter was tinged with apprehension and regret. If she could not accept his proposal of marriage, ought she not to leave the man in peace? Yet Sir Walter was the best resource she had for such unusual queries; there was nothing to be done but to let him do his work. Miss Tolerance sanded the letter, sealed it, and, leaving Mrs. Pouter to lie in solitude, sought out Cole to have the message delivered.

Until the matter of the corpse had been settled, her cottage held no charm for her. Instead of returning there straightaway, Miss Tolerance decided to call upon her aunt. She climbed the stairs to the second floor and Mrs. Brereton's apartments, to find Frost, Mrs. Brereton's dresser, zealously controlling access to her mistress.

"She's not well, miss." The woman stood in the door and fixed Miss Tolerance with a look that could have quelled a bevy of subalterns. Miss Tolerance, who understood that Frost was intractably jealous of her mistress's attention to her niece, responded without heat.

"She wrote me so yesterday, Frost. I do not mean to tax her, merely to inquire if the complaint is improved."

"Not hardly at all, miss. She takes a little broth and restorative jelly, but beyond that, barely a mouthful. And yesterday, a rash—"

"Frost!" The voice that called from behind the door gave no impression of weakness. "Do not make my ailments a gift to the entire house. For God's sake, Sarah, come in."

Her lips compressed in an expression of disapproval, Frost stood aside to admit Miss Tolerance to the room. She found her aunt, not in bed as she had imagined, but sitting on the sofa in her drawing room, wearing an elaborate beribboned dressing gown, laced cap, and mitts. She shared the sofa with a small writing desk and a pile of newspapers. Mrs. Brereton had evidently felt well enough to apply the maquillage that obliterated any flaws in her complexion, and while she appeared tired, she was clearly not bedridden.

From the door Frost fired one last shot. "Don't you stay too long, miss. Madame needs her rest, as I keep saying to her."

Miss Tolerance turned to smile at the dresser. "I won't tire her, Frost. Thank you." She took a chair opposite the sofa. "How do you go on, ma'am?"

"Vilely." As Mrs. Brereton spoke the word, a grimace of pain so quickly suppressed that it might have been imagined, passed over her face. "I cannot imagine what I could have eaten to occasion this—" Mrs. Brereton gestured vaguely toward herself. "In one moment I have such pain I think I shall die, and in the next, I merely feel as if I should be ill."

"Frost said you have a rash as well?"

"I don't regard it," Mrs. Brereton said flatly. "Tis just a little reddening on my arms and hands. I have a salve which I imagine will cure it shortly. I cannot stay locked away upstairs, you know. I must think of the business."

"You are not … I thought, since Mr. Tickenor's departure —I had believed you had ceased to receive gentlemen, aunt." Her aunt's brief affiancement in the spring had ended with Gerald Tickenor being dismissed from the house, but under such circumstances that Miss Tolerance almost feared to mention him. There was no doubt in her mind that the man had intended upon marrying into, and taking over, Mrs. Brereton's business.

"Just because I no longer entertain men in my bed

—*receive*, as you call it, Sarah—does not mean that it is not important that I appear in the salon and make my presence known. The house runs better for it. But enough of this tedious malady. I understand you had a body delivered to the house today?" The expression on Mrs. Brereton's face was one of polite interest.

"I am afraid I did, aunt." Better to own it at once and be scolded for it. "I did not arrange it so deliberately—in fact, I gave clear instructions to bring the — the corpse around to my cottage directly, but their leader seemed determined that he should bring it straight into your parlor. I am very sorry for the inconvenience, and to the wear-and-tear upon Cole's patience."

"You do not intend to make a habit of it, I trust?"

"Good God, no, ma'am. It was only circumstance forced my hand in this case. Believe me, I am no happier about having the late Mrs. Pouter in my house—"

Mrs. Brereton's eyes widened. "Pouter? Not *Annie*? But she was one of *mine*."

Miss Tolerance nodded. "I regret to tell you so, Aunt Thea."

"But how did you even know her? I let her go years ago, before even you came to me here. Where did she go after she left us? How did she—I presume, since you were so hot to have the body here, that she must be part of one of your—"

"My investigations. Yes." Miss Tolerance regarded her aunt with concern: suddenly her color was high and her voice shaking. "I did not mean to distress you. I believe, yes, that Mrs. Pouter was murdered, but since no one in Seven Dials would lend the notion enough credence to call the Watch, I had her brought here. As for where she's been these last years, perhaps Mrs. Gordon can tell you."

"Mrs. Gordon?"

"Your cook, aunt."

"I know her name, girl. But how should she know what—oh, of course. *That*. Still."

"*That*? Of course? Take me with you, Aunt Thea."

"Cook and Annie Pouter were—oh, years ago." Mrs. Brereton. The flush in her skin had receded, leaving her pale beneath her powder and paint. For a moment Miss Tolerance thought she might faint, but then, as she watched, her aunt gathered her strength and seemed to shake herself free of the spasm of pain that had interrupted her.

"In the days when Mrs. Pouter worked here, she and Cook were lovers, my dear."

Miss Tolerance absorbed this information thoughtfully. She knew such relationships existed, but it had never occurred to her to find one under her nose, as it were. Particularly as Mrs. Brereton discouraged any liaison that did not provide revenue to the house. "Poor Cook," she said at last. "Had I only known…"

"Well, I don't think they advertised it—I spoke with them more than once about it—it was part of why I let Annie go. Had they been in touch all these years? Fancy that. Sarah, I wish you will tell Cook that when it comes time to bury Mrs. Pouter the house will underwrite the expense. No woman who has worked for me should go into an unmarked grave. Go now, my dear. I am a little fatigued."

If Miss Tolerance was surprised by her usually frugal aunt's generosity, she did not say so. She rose, kissed her aunt on one scented cheek, and went out past Frost, who nodded at her and swept back into the room, magnificently dismissive.

Miss Tolerance made her way downstairs through the public rooms and thence to the kitchen, where she found Cook grimly supervising the removal of a joint from the spit. Her round, red face was more flushed even that usual, and seemed curiously flaccid. Tear tracks showed on the cheek nearest Miss Tolerance.

"Aye, Miss Sarah, what is it?"

"Mrs. Brereton has asked me to tell you—but perhaps you would prefer I come back later?" she finished, as the joint was freed from the spit and Cook bent to catch it on a huge carving trencher.

"No, no, miss. Here, you." Cook shoved the trencher and its fragrant burden at Jess. "Slices thin as you can make 'em, girl. We'll sauce 'em when I come back from talking with Miss Sarah." She wiped her hands on the towel that hung from her apron, then put her hand through Miss Tolerance's arm and steered her toward the kitchen door. "Now, miss, what does ma'am want?"

"Only to tell you that the household will—Mrs. Brereton hopes it will be acceptable if the house covers the expense of Mrs. Pouter's funeral."

Cook's face began to loosen, as if she would be crying shortly. "I would ha' done it. I've money saved—" She gave herself a shake. "Well, we won't be needin' that, shall we? Annie and me was going to find a place in the country together when I left service. She and I—"

Miss Tolerance nodded. "I am so sorry."

"It's kind in Mrs. B to make the offer, and I'll accept on Annie's behalf, as she h'aint nothing much left to 'er. I still 'ave my old age to think on."

"I think that is wise, Cook." Miss Tolerance put her hand on the other woman's shoulder.

"You are a good lass, Miss Sarah. If it's not a 'pert'nance to say it. Yes, Cole?"

The porter was hovering in the kitchen wearing the expression of mixed anxiety and concern with which proximity to grief seems to afflict some people. "Beg your pardon Cook. Miss Sarah, magistrate come to see you."

"Sir Walter? Is he here now? Cole, will you show him through to my cottage, please?" Miss Tolerance squeezed Cook's shoulder one more time. "We may speak more on this later, if you wish."

She left the woman standing in the doorway, staring blankly at the herb garden. Miss Tolerance made her way across the garden to her own door, considering the revelations of the last hour.

S ir Walter Mandif was not a tall man. Slight, with none of the extravagances of fashion common to gentlemen of his age and class, he might have been a scholar or natural philosopher. But to see Sir Walter in his magistrate's court, as Miss Tolerance had done on more than one occasion, was to perceive an entirely different facet of his character. She had seen him quell a chamber of unruly witnesses with a word, unpick a tangle of lies while maintaining a tone of quiet courtesy, and rule intelligently in cases where emotions ran high. Miss Tolerance knew he was well-read—far better than she—and thoughtful. She knew how fortunate she was to have earned his regard and yet, for his sake as well as her own, she would not return those feelings.

At the door, Sir Walter bowed. Miss Tolerance stood to return the courtesy, aware that she was still in her breeches and coat.

"You have been at work, I see." Sir Walter took the chair nearest the fire.

"I had no idea of your coming so quickly. To be frank, I expected Hook or Penryn or another Runner."

The magistrate inclined his head toward the stretcher lying by the stair. "I did not think any delay was advisable. Hook and Penryn are in Cornwall, looking into a death there. And it seemed to me that a possible murder should be investigated without delay. May I?" He gestured toward Mrs. Pouter's body.

Miss Tolerance inclined her head. "Please."

Sir Walter rose, inspected the corpse with attention to the

face, hands, and finally the neck. At last, he draped the sheet carefully over the corpse and returned to sit again.

"Murder," he agreed. "At least, it has the seeming of it. Where did you say she died?"

"In Castle Street in Seven Dials."

One of Sir Walter's brows quirked upward.

"Yes, I know." She answered his unspoken concern. "'Tis why you see me in my working clothes. I am less likely to be troubled so."

"Your friends must always wish you to be untroubled anywhere, of course. But I do not mean to oppress you with my concern."

It seemed churlish to dismiss so mild an expression of anxiety. "I am grateful for it. Still, you see I am here and hale. Unlike poor Mrs. Pouter."

"What do you know of her?"

Miss Tolerance recited the few facts she had at her disposal: the dead woman's age, her former occupation, and the problem for which she had sought Miss Tolerance's help. "This is the second death connected to the matter of which I know," she said. "And given the circumstances of the first death, I find it hard to believe them unrelated."

"Run down by a charnel cart? Not a dignified death, I agree."

"Run down by a charnel cart on the way to meet with this Mr. Marvell, who would have known where she lived and when she was likely to be going to their appointment."

Sir Walter was pensive. "The first thing to do, then, is to have a doctor examine the remains, and—"

"When he has done so, may I make arrangements to have her taken elsewhere?"

"Certainly. I suggest we summon the doctor and the undertaker in tandem; the one is accustomed to await the pleasure of the other. 'Tis a pity I had no chance to view the scene before Mrs. Pouter was removed from it."

"I will tell you what I saw of it." Miss Tolerance described the sooty, burnt interior of Mrs. Gordon's apartment. "The grate was empty, and there is no stove. The wall opposite the grate was charred and smoking. I saw what appeared to be small kindling and rags at its base."

"Not even a pretense of a normal fire," Sir Walter agreed "I don't doubt that the man who set it expected the whole room to go up in flames, or indeed the building, else I would be insulted by such lack of effort. This villain seems to think very little of the deductive powers of Bow Street."

Miss Tolerance smiled. "You will teach him to know better, I am sure. Sir Walter, what is best to do now?"

"If it is not too great an imposition, perhaps someone from your aunt's household can take a note for me? It will summon a doctor and an undertaker."

"I should, I admit, very much like to have poor Mrs. Pouter removed." Miss Tolerance took up her writing desk and offered it to Sir Walter.

For a few minutes, there was silence in the cottage save for the scratch of pen on paper. When he had finished the note, addressed and sanded it, Miss Tolerance excused herself to cross the garden and request that Keefe see the missive to its recipient. When she returned to the cottage she found Sir Walter on his feet by the mantel, examining the pocket watch she kept there. It was old, made for utility rather than display, and had several deep dents in its silver cover.

"It was *his*?"

"Yes." Suppressing a desire to snatch the watch from Sir Walter's fingers, Miss Tolerance sat. The watch had belonged to her first lover, Charles Connell, dead almost seven years ago; she had little but the watch by which to remember him.

"What was he like?" Sir Walter asked. "He must have been an interesting fellow who could win your heart."

"He was kind. Quiet. Does that surprise you in a fencing master?" Why tell him anything about Connell? And yet she kept on. "He was stocky and much my height, but light on his feet. He had a deep voice and a sense of humor and—" she cleared her throat. "He was twenty-three when we met—it seemed very old to me at the time. With nothing to offer me, which he felt very much. Even in Holland, when I had cast my lot with his, he would fret that I should return to my family. As if that were possible! He worried that he had ruined me, but did I not ruin him as well? If you have imagined me, Sir Walter, as the girlish victim of a brutal seduction—"

"I had not, as it happens. Even at sixteen, I imagine you were too much the woman you are now to have been a victim."

Miss Tolerance was struck with an unsettling sense of being understood as no one—other than perhaps Charles Connell—had ever done. She could not think what to do; tears stood in her eyes for a moment.

She cleared her throat and retreated to talk of work.

"Sir Walter, I imagine your office has made you acquainted from time to time with swindlers—"

It was a testimony to the nature of their friendship that Sir Walter took the question without pause. "A good number have passed before my bench, yes. Was there any particular swindler in whom you are interested?"

"The man whose swindle began my inquiries called himself Marvell."

Now Sir Walter raised an eyebrow. "That's a name sometimes taken by fortune tellers and medicine peddlers, particularly among the Travelers and other itinerants. You do not think Mrs. Pouter—Pouter? Yes—you do not believe that her death might be laid at the door of one of the Travelers? In my experience, any criminal charge justly laid at their door is more likely to be pick-pocketing, shell-games, fortune-telling, or quackery. Crimes that are—"

"Highly portable?"

"You might say so." Sir Walter ran a hand back over his

smooth, tow-colored hair. "The trick you described to me would require resources and time, the ability to rent rooms in a fashionable part of town. It is not in character for the Travelers I know. But you do say the fellow called himself Marvell."

"He did."

"If he is not one of the Travelers, I doubt they will be happy to hear that the man has been using a name that implicates them in some business not theirs. I wonder—I might have a friend who would speak to you."

Like most country-bred children Miss Tolerance had often been scolded into compliance with threats that the Travelers would steal away disobedient children. She was no longer so naïve as to believe that—but the mention gave her a frisson of distaste, and of surprise. Sir Walter Mandif, arbiter of the law, had a *friend* among the Travelers? But why not? she thought a moment later. His work brought him into contact with all manner of questionable persons—including her own self. She smiled. "I would very much appreciate that."

"Shall I direct him to Tarsio's?"

Miss Tolerance briefly imagined the horror of that club's staff if a Traveler called upon her there. From the smile that played upon his lips, she thought Sir Walter had a similar notion.

"Perhaps I will ask him to appoint a meeting place and get word to you at your club?"

"I would appreciate that greatly, Sir Walter. I wonder if—"

What she wondered was lost to a firm rap on the door. Keefe accompanied an amiably rumpled man with the round, cheerful face of a cherub and the nose of the habitual drinker. He wore a dark wig, ill-fitted and showing some cropped fair hair beneath it, as the sign of his office.

"Sir Walter." The doctor went at once to the magistrate. "What have you for me today?"

Sir Walter first introduced Miss Tolerance, before

gesturing to the body by the stairs. The doctor—by name Hardesty—spared hardly a glance for her; his attention was all for Mrs. Pouter. Approaching the stretcher, he pulled the sheet from her face and peered closely at the dead woman's face. Miss Tolerance, realizing that at this hour his examination would be aided by very little natural light, took up a lamp and went to stand at the head of the stretcher. In the improved light, Hardesty pulled back Mrs. Pouter's eyelids. He untangled the scarf from her neck completely and put it to one side, then ran his fingers along the darkened flesh of her throat.

"Throttled, aye. But not, I think, to death. Was the neck like this when you found her?" He directed the question to Sir Walter.

Miss Tolerance took it upon herself to answer. "The bruising has darkened in the last several hours."

Hardesty nodded. "Then it is not from some earlier attack. From the smell of her—and her color—I would give my oath that smoke is what killed her. After she'd been handled in such a way as to keep her quiet." He made his remarks to Sir Walter as he got to his feet, took a handkerchief from his pocket, and methodically wiped his hands.

Sir Walter, glancing first at Miss Tolerance, was curt. "You'll make a report to the Coroner's Court?"

"If asked, aye." Hardesty took up his hat—a short-crowned beaver that perched awkwardly upon his wig. "If that will be all, Sir Walter?"

Sir Walter nodded. "If you see Gibney on your way out, tell him we are ready for him."

The doctor bowed to the room in general and departed.

Sir Walter cleared his throat. "I am sorry. Hardesty is a blunt fellow, but his manner toward you was unconscionably rude."

Miss Tolerance returned the lamp to her dresser. "Unconscionably? He encountered a woman in men's dress in highly unusual circumstances. Most men would be taken aback."

Sir Walter shook his head and frowned. "You are generous to say so, but—"

"My dear Sir Walter, there are things that you, as a man and a gentleman, are unlikely to encounter. The doctor's attitude is not, I assure you, unusual. But—" a thought occurred to her. "You did not think he ignored me because I am Fallen, did you?"

The expression on his face suggested that he had.

"No, I think not. It is kind of you to be mindful of my feelings, but I assure you, in this instance, I was neither hurt nor surprised."

Sir Walter looked as though he would have said more but at last, did not. "Is there any other service I can render you?"

"Only if you will let me know if someone from the Travelers will consent to speak with me. Come, let me take you out."

She did not propose to make Sir Walter walk through her aunt's hallways. As they left the cottage a man hurried toward them, dressed all in black and wearing a professionally lugubrious expression: the undertaker, missing only the black veil upon his hat. Miss Tolerance acknowledged him with a nod: "Will you wait here for me, sir?"

Turning away, she led Sir Walter to the ivied gate that let onto Spanish Place.

"Thank you for your help."

He still looked troubled.

"I beg you will not refine upon the doctor's manner. It is the fate of all women, Fallen or not, that some men will consider them as naught. I am grateful that you are not one such."

She unlocked the gate and let him out.

Chapter Five

Miss Tolerance passed an uneasy night in her empty cottage. Annie Pouter's face—eyes vacant and bloodshot, mouth twisted in a gasp for air—appeared everywhere in her dreams, intruding in situations and among people Mrs. Pouter could never have known in life. When at last she abandoned hope of further sleep, Miss Tolerance rose, hung the kettle over the fire, and attempted some book-keeping. When the kettle boiled, she left her ledger and its unsatisfactory column of figures and made tea. Waiting for the tea to steep, fragrant fingers of steam rising in the chilly morning air, she put in order her plans for the day. First to Bruton Street, to see if by some miracle the owner of the building could shed light upon Mr. Marvell's tenancy there. Then, perhaps, to the Wheat Sheaf, to see if Joshua Glebb had intelligence for her.

Sometime in the midst of making these plans, she realized that she no longer had a client on whose behalf she was acting. Any further action in the case would be done for her own satisfaction and without hope of payment.

Logic—and her hard-headed Aunt Thea—would suggest that she end the inquiry. With no hope of payment, or even of reimbursement for the monies she had expended so far, it was foolish to continue. Yet Miss Tolerance found herself strongly reluctant to abandon an investigation that clearly had stirred alarm in some quarter. Poor Annie Pouter had been murdered, and it was impossible to believe that the investigation was not the cause of it.

Miss Tolerance turned the matter over until her tea was cold and bitter. She had no other work before her or prospect thereof. Well, then, she would continue with Mrs. Pouter's business until paying work presented itself. With a decision that satisfied her, Miss Tolerance tossed out the contents of her teapot, made a fresh pot and, when she had drunk her cup, called over to Mrs. Brereton's for hot water and began her day in earnest.

Bruton Street, lined with neat, modern brick and limestone buildings, was predominantly residential. Four of the structures on the northern side of the street housed businesses on the ground floor. Of those, Cavall and Sons was the western-most, a prosperous-looking establishment with a newly painted sign above the door. A bell suspended from a spring above the door tinkled when Miss Tolerance entered. The shop smelled richly of leather: men's boots, ready-made, were on display. At the rear of the shop, a clerk in a long apron was dusting a pair of Hessian boots, making the tassels dance. No women's footwear was in evidence; the store was clearly intended to cater to a wealthy and fashionable male clientele. In a green silk-twill walking dress and spencer, Miss Tolerance might be mistaken for the former, but never the later.

"May I help you, madam?"

The clerk advanced. He was shorter than Miss Tolerance, with a fall of black and gray curls over his forehead and a rich shadow on his jaw. His eyes were bloodshot, and there was a whiff of brandy about him.

"Thank you, yes." Miss Tolerance flattened her vowels a touch and spoke with a bustling sort of quickness. "Can you tell me who the landlord of this building is?"

The man screwed up his face in a mime of perplexity. "Landlord, madam?"

"The building's owner," she confirmed.

The clerk shook his head. "I couldn't say, madam." His cordiality and his diction had slipped a notch with the suspicion that she did not mean to buy anything.

"May I speak to the owner of the shop, then?"

This simple request appeared to distress the clerk. "The owner, madam?" He cast a sidewise glance at the rear of the shop.

"To the person who pays the rent on quarter day? The person who would know who the landlord, or the landlord's agent, might be."

The clerk looked left and right, as if assistance might come from those directions. Then, doubtless reading resolve in his visitor's face, he turned and disappeared into the back of the shop. A few moments later he returned, followed by a man who might have been his twin, thirty years on. From this Miss Tolerance understood the owner to be Cavall and the clerk to be the Son. The father reeled unbalanced against a counter, righted himself, and arrived in front of Miss Tolerance. She nodded in acknowledgement and repeated her inquiry.

Mr. Cavall cocked his head to one side and begged her to say again.

"Can you give me the name and direction of the landlord or agent for this building?"

Miss Tolerance watched as the older man unscrambled the meaning of her request. Judging from the fumes that emanated from him, he was not only slightly deaf but very jug-bitten; where the younger man carried the scent of brandy, the father moved in a cloud of it.

"Landlord doesn't come around here much, madam."

"Does he not? His agent, then. To whom do you pay your quarter's rent?"

The father cupped his hand round his ear. Miss Tolerance repeated herself.

"You looking to take rooms?"

"My brother is," Miss Tolerance lied smoothly. "He has been abroad, but he had taken a liking to this building and asked me to inquire."

This idea was clearly foreign to the experience of the men she spoke to. They looked at each other, then back at her. "Where'd he go, then?" the son asked, at the same moment as his father said "Eh?"

"Jamaica!" Miss Tolerance was beginning to wonder if the bootmakers were stupid as well as drunk. "He asked me to make inquiries."

Mr. Cavall looked out the window, wrestling with the ideas presented to him. "Agent's name is Quilt." He squinted and produced further information. "Office in Marylebone Road, number 21. Though I misdoubt your brother will find any rooms to let here. We usually hears it first if there is."

"If that should prove to be the case, I shall tell my brother so. My commission was merely to make the inquiry; it will be fulfilled whether he elects to live here or not." Miss Tolerance nodded decisively, as if to end the discussion, and turned toward the door.

"You don't want boots, then." Cavall *pere* asked.

"I do not. Although the work is very handsome," she added in justice. Despite the inebriation of the craftsmen, there was no question that anyone coming to the shop for footwear rather than conversation would leave delighted.

Cavall junior whispered something in his father's ear. The older man brightened. "Agent? Agent's name is Quilt, madam. But I doubt you'll find rooms to let this time a' year…" his words trailed off.

"Come on, Dad," the younger Cavall said loudly. He had his hand on the older man's shoulder and pushed him gently toward the rear of the shop. "You've an order half-made on the last."

Mr. Cavall turned without apology toward his work. Cavall junior shrugged as some sort of sign of dismissal and followed after. Miss Tolerance exited the shop, followed by the merry jingling of the bell.

Marylebone Street is one of those corridors that extend through the city, along which traffic commercial and residential moves sluggishly. Miss Tolerance, taken up by a hackney carriage, had just begun to wonder if the two-mile journey might have been quicker on foot, when her carriage drew up and she descended.

In contrast to the neat, prosperous exterior of the building on Bruton Street, number 21 Marylebone Road was not ramshackle, precisely, but down-at-heel. The front had not been painted in recent memory, and the step creaked and shifted as she stepped upon it. No porter admitted her to the building, although there were lamps in the hallway that shed a dim yellow light. Without further information, Miss Tolerance did not know behind which door to find Mr. Quilt. She sighed in resignation and knocked upon the first, then the second, with no result. The third door was opened by an elderly woman with a scowl etched bone-deep in her face, who sent her to the first floor, "second in from the stairs, an' tell 'im I sent you wiv the Devil's compliments."

Wondering idly what history lay between Quilt and his downstairs neighbor, Miss Tolerance ascended and knocked upon the second door.

The man who answered was short and solid, with a long face that descended , column-like, from brow to shoulder, and a nose that overshadowed all. He was plainly dressed, his brown hair gathered in an old-fashioned queue; in fact, everything about him, from the cut of his coat to his square-toed buckled shoes, harkened to an earlier time, a time he seemed too young to remember. He stood in the door, blinking, and did not ask her to enter.

"Mr. Quilt?"

"I am he." His voice was deep.

"I was given your name by Mr. Caval, of the bootmakers that occupy—"

"The property at Bruton Street," he finished for her. "How may I assist you?"

"I am seeking urgently to find the tenant who lived on the second floor there some months ago, a Mr. Marvell."

The flesh on Quilt's neck wobbled as he nodded. "I remember him. But he left almost a year ago."

"As long ago as that, sir? Did he leave you a new direction in case—"

"No." Quilt was polite but definite.

Miss Tolerance expressed surprise. "No, sir? That is a handsome property and was let, as I understand it, furnished. Perhaps you required that he give his bank as a reference? Perhaps he was sent there by someone already known to you?"

Quilt shook his head; his neck wobbled frantically. "I would remember it."

With an inward sigh—no monies she expended now would ever be reimbursed, and she had only her own stubborn curiosity to satisfy—Miss Tolerance reached for her reticule. "I would be happy to provide a token of my appreciation for any assistance—"

Quilt put a finger to his upper lip, then to his temple, as if hoping to prod information from it. Then he stood aside, a mute invitation to walk in.

The room Miss Tolerance entered was dark, although it was not much after noon. The walls were lined with bookcases, the cases filled with bound ledgers. A large desk, empty but for an inkwell and a neatly squared stack of foolscap, stood in the center. Mr. Quilt stepped around the desk to take a ledger from the left-most bookcase. The book was large enough to hide the man's upper torso entirely when he held it in front of him. He put it on the desk, licked his thumb and forefinger absently, and began to flip through the marble-edged pages.

At last he ran a short, ink-stained finger down the page. "I see him here. George Marvell, an open term at five pounds the quarter."

"And he stayed for how long?

"Three quarters and a matter of days. Beyond that, I have no intelligence. I was not concerned in arranging the lease, only in collecting the payment."

Miss Tolerance was beginning to feel very much annoyed. "Not concerned for the lease? Is that not your job, to concern yourself with the property? Surely if the owner confides a building to your care—"

Quilt's mouth flattened. "As it was the owner's son who arranged the lease, I do not think *I* will be found derelict."

"*And?*"

Quilt regarded her blankly.

"Who is that owner? Who is that owner's son?"

Now the agent looked uneasy. "I am retained as agent particularly because the owner does not wish to have business intrude upon—"

"Mr. Quilt, I am not an annoyance. I am not a difficulty from which you are rescuing your client. I am a woman with a very considerable need to find this Mr. Marvell. I mean no one —not your employer or his son or you—any mischief.

Please." Again she fingered her reticule, as if she would draw her pocket book from it the instant she had the information she sought.

"Why is it so important that you find this Marvell? If it is a matter of business, surely a man would be better—"

"There is no man available to make the inquiry. Indeed, I believe Marvell to be a swindler and a thief—"

"And what sort of woman goes chasing after swindlers and thieves on her own? More like you're a *friend* of his. Or some such." His emphasis on the word friend was entirely unsubtle.

"I have never met the man in my life, but I know others he has treated very ill. I should think this a thing it might benefit your client to know, lest he become a target himself."

That argument distracted Quilt. After another moment of wobbling indecision, he capitulated. "The owner's name is Kent. *Mrs*. Kent. But it isn't she would know about this Marvell, it is the son I spoke of, Mr.—ah—George Kent." He pulled the name as if snatching it from the air above his head.

"Where will I find Mr. Kent, sir?"

Again Quilt sighed, as if having begun to provide information, it was no longer in his power to stop. "I cannot think of any other place than his mother's house. Hans Place."

Miss Tolerance completed the act of withdrawing her pocket book from her reticule, removed a banknote, and offered it to Quilt. The man looked at the money dubiously.

"There is nothing wrong with the note, Mr. Quilt." He might have preferred to receive the bribe in less obvious fashion, but Miss Tolerance was in no mood to indulge his nicety. She held the note out until Quilt took it between thumb and forefinger.

An unpleasant ride from Marylebone Street in a carriage with moth-eaten cushions and a strong smell of sweat brought Miss Tolerance an hour or so later to Hans Place. This part of Kensington was an oval of modern residences of black or red brick, circling a little park of greensward, trees, and a brackish pond. It was a comfortably wealthy neighborhood, its occupants likely in the upper reaches of the gentry or minor nobility but not part of fashionable London. Unlike nearby thoroughfares such as Sloane Street, there were few passers-by of whom to inquire for Mrs. Kent's house. A handy crossing-sweep would have been an excellent thing; Miss Tolerance had found in the past that such boys were a good source of neighborhood intelligence. Lacking that, when a cloaked and bonneted maid passed, Miss Tolerance enacted one of her favorite roles: the near-sighted, anxious spinster fretting over a lost direction. She was at once pointed to number 45, and the maid departed, a ha'penny better for her assistance.

Like its fellows, number 45 was a tidy building of black brick picked out in white and green paint, with a marble step and burnished brass knocker. She utilized the latter and continued in the role of flustered spinster, asking if Mr. Kent was to be found at home.

The young manservant who had opened the door answered in the negative and would have closed the door, but Miss Tolerance, licensed by her imposture, pushed forward until she was within the front hallway, and began a lengthy and deliberately nonsensical explanation of why it was particularly crucial that she locate this Mr. Kent. The manservant, flustered and unsure what to do—he was, Miss Tolerance thought, new to his position—looked about as if for rescue. It came, after a moment, in the shape of a maid who approached and murmured something in the man's ear.

"If I cannot locate him then my poor brother will never be able—"

Miss Tolerance kept up her prattling until the manservant, with a nod to the maid, stood away from the door.

"If you will follow Milston, madam?" He gestured at the maid who was already ascending the stairs as if certain she would pull the visitor with her like the tide.

Miss Tolerance nodded and smiled and followed, all the while wondering where she was going and what she must say when she got there. Her plan had been merely to try the porter's patience until he produced Mr. George Kent or his address. To explain to someone in the family why a strange woman had come calling in search of Mr. Kent—and hope to gain any information—would require less glib fabrication and more quick logic.

The maid, Milston, brought her to a curtained parlor in the back of the house. The person awaiting her was a woman well struck in years, but handsome and very much in the mode. Her dress and cap were neatly made and expensive. She had been a beauty, Miss Tolerance thought: her blue eyes were faded, but the brows above them were still dark and well-marked, and despite papery skin her features were clean cast and expressive.

"How may I help you?" When she spoke a dimple played at the corner of the woman's mouth, but her tone was cautious. She clearly reserved judgement of single females calling without introduction.

Miss Tolerance curtsied. "I am so very sorry to disturb you, dear madam," she began, still in the pinched and hurried character of the spinster she had been playing. "And without so much as an acquaintance in common. What you must think of me! But if the fellow below had only directed me to your son—I imagine he must be your son, ma'am—"

"My son?" Mrs. Kent's expression grew even more distant and her brows drew together.

"Is Mr. George Kent not your son, ma'am? It is he I am seeking, on my brother's behalf, but if I was sent here in error, I do very heartily apologize."

The hitch of tension in Mrs. Kent's face eased at the question. "George Kent is... my son." There was a definite pause. "But what does anyone want with *him*?" A moment before the older woman had been cautious, even suspicious. Now she was puzzled.

"My brother, whose agent I am, badly needs to locate a tenant who once lodged in a property of his in Bruton Street."

"You must address your questions to the agent, Mr. Quilt—"

"But it was Mr. Quilt who referred me to Mr. Kent, ma'am."

"Nonsense." Mrs. Kent shook her head adamantly. "My son has nothing to do with the property. He is not the owner, I am."

"Mr. Quilt was very clear that it was Mr. Kent who had arranged for this particular lease, else I would not trouble him or you. I am seeking to find the tenant who lived for some months on the second story, above the bootmaker's."

"Those rooms are frequently re-let. I do not believe my son will be able to assist you." Mrs. Kent's chin came up. "Nor can I. I am not concerned with the day-to-day business of that property. If Mr. Quilt cannot direct you, I am afraid your brother will be disappointed."

"There is no possibility that I may speak with Mr. Kent, then?"

The civility of tone with which Mrs. Kent had greeted her visitor was wholly departed. "None at all. Please believe me. George has no more idea of what goes on with any of my properties than he has of—" she waved a hand. "Anything. He has no head for business." The older woman raised her head further, apparently for the sole purpose of being able to look down her nose at her guest.

"I am very sorry to have troubled you, then," Miss Tolerance said mildly. "You will understand the natural concern of a sister for her brother, and in truth, ma'am, Mr. Kent was my last hope."

If she had hoped that her guest's distress would soften Mrs. Kent's adamancy Miss Tolerance was disappointed. It seemed rather to anger the woman.

"If you have placed any sort of reliance upon George, you have hoped in vain—or never met my son. And where is this brother of yours? Why is he not attending to his own business? You are genteel-seeming enough, but you might well be one of those—those women. Those sluts. Harpies." Mrs. Kent's tone became more strident, the words spilling out faster. "Harpies. Invading my home. I thought I was done with that, that I should have a little peace, but no, they are a plague—"

"I *beg* your pardon, Mrs. Kent." Miss Tolerance attempted to stem the tidal flow of words. *Sluts? Harpies. Invading her home?* If she had not had business to accomplish, Miss Tolerance would have been curious about the origin of those expressive phrases.

"—without shame, bringing their corruption into a house that once kept only the best..." Mrs. Kent continued without pause; the longer she spoke, the angrier she appeared to be, as if her words were fanning coals of a rage concealed until this moment. Miss Tolerance saw no option but to leave.

She rose and curtsied. "I am very sorry to have disturbed you, Mrs. Kent."

As suddenly as it had arisen, the older woman's rage abated. "No, wait, I—I beg your pardon." She extended a hand as if to stop her guest. "If there is any topic upon which I am hot, it is that of— No, I must not continue with that. Perhaps I was too quick to believe the worst. Come, Miss—I am sorry, I do not know your name. Sit down, please, and tell me about your brother's trouble."

Miss Tolerance thanked her mildly and gave her name as Bennet. Concern that she might further distress Mrs. Kent warred with her belief that the mystery of Mr. Marvell required her to find Mr. Kent. She proceeded carefully with the story she had begun for the footman's benefit earlier, that her brother needed to find the former tenant of the Bruton Street rooms, who had borrowed money from him which he could not now afford to have outstanding.

"So you see, ma'am, if I cannot assist my brother in finding this Mr. Marvell he will be unable to make the payment that is being demanded of him, and—"

Mrs. Kent took Miss Tolerance's gloved hand in her own. "I feel very much for your brother, Miss Bennet, but I am afraid you would disappointed even if I could direct you to my son. As I said, he knows nothing of my business affairs and very little of anything else. George is—it is hard for a mother to say such a thing, but George was born to disappoint. It is his only gift."

What could a son do to so thoroughly turn his own mother against him? "You have quarreled, ma'am?"

"Quarreled?" Mrs. Kent's mouth twisted. "I should as soon quarrel with this footstool." She pushed at the ottoman with one slippered foot. "I have not spoken to George these two years."

A moment before Miss Tolerance had felt sorry for Mrs. Kent. Now she felt a reciprocal sympathy for Mr. George Kent.

"I am sorry if I have called up some painful feelings, ma'am. Were it not—"

"Not for your brother, yes. I understand."

Miss Tolerance rose, curtsied, and turned to leave. At the door, a thought occurred to her. "Does Mr. Kent belong to any clubs, sir?"

"Clubs? One of those houses where men go to gamble and whore?" Mrs. Kent's voice lowered. "Like his father? It may well be, but even George would not speak of such things to me."

"I was thinking of gentlemen's clubs, ma'am. Watiers or Boodles or the like." This was not to say that whoring and gambling were unknown in the men's clubs of St. James's, but the clubs also provided a meeting place for gentlemen in the city. It was not impossible on the face of the thing that Mr. Kent would belong to a club.

"I cannot imagine that a club that admitted *gentlemen* would accept George," Mrs. Kent said.

"Perhaps your footman would know?" Miss Tolerance suggested mildly.

"I told you that George and I have not spoken in several years," Mrs. Kent repeated. Her tone was so definite that it begged exploration.

"What was the cause of this estrangement?" The question escaped her lips before Miss Tolerance could call it back, and she fully expected another explosion from the older woman.

Mrs. Kent appeared untroubled. "Miss Bennet, my marriage to Mr. Kent was not a happy one. He was my second husband. After the death of my first—my William—I felt his loss very keenly indeed, and when Mr. Kent offered for me I thought—foolishly I believed—I had a child who needed a father. I did not know there were worse things than to be alone. Too late I learned it. Kent was addicted to the company of vile wantons—and every time I look at his son I am reminded of his father."

"Are they so alike, ma'am?"

Mrs. Kent shook her head. "The very sight of him puts me in mind—the humiliation. Even when he was a child I could barely look at him. When he came of age I insisted he set up his own establishment. So you see, Miss Bennett, there is no way for anyone here to know where he has gone."

It was time to end this interview. "I understand, ma'am. And I am sorry to have awakened painful memories. I can only beg your pardon most heartily, and take my leave of you."

Mrs. Kent leaned forward as if to confide in her visitor. "Miss Bennet, I have spoken of some things I have kept very close for many years. I beg that you will not mention them abroad—I am not usually so indiscreet."

"Perhaps it was something that needed to be spoken aloud to a sympathetic ear, Mrs. Kent. But you may rely that I will not share this with anyone. Indeed, I suspect that by the time I reach your doorstep, I will have forgotten it entirely."

Mrs. Kent smiled sadly. "Good bye, Miss Bennet. For your brother's sake, I wish you good luck."

Miss Tolerance curtsied again. She still intended to have a word with any of the staff she met on her way to the street.

She was disappointed in the hope that someone among the servants at Mrs. Kent's house would be able to offer a clue to George Kent's whereabouts. Neither the maid nor Cates, the footman at her door, appeared to know anything about him— indeed, George Kent's very name inspired expressions of aversion. It was merely a gesture when Miss Tolerance pressed her card and a coin into Cates's hand and desired him to let her know if he recalled anything.

Once on the street Miss Tolerance paid a crossing-sweep a farthing to hail a hackney coach for her and returned to Manchester Square. She wanted to ask her aunt a question.

To Miss Tolerance's gratification, she discovered her aunt so far recovered from her illness as to be found in the yellow salon, trimming a hat and listening to complaints from one of her *filles de joie*. The contrast between the domestic quality of the former activity and the necessarily salty nature of the latter struck Miss Tolerance forcefully.

Anne-Josephe, eyes wide in a dark face, was finishing the

end of a tirade, the Caribbean music in her voice at war with the outrage of her words. "—and if he cannot be bothered to clean himself when he comes to me from the necessary, I will *not* see him!"

Mrs. Brereton pinned a bit of braid on the brim of her hat before she spoke. "You may dismiss him from your following, of course. But before you do so, perhaps there is another way? Make a game of washing, perhaps? And let him see your pleasure in his, um, cleaner self? I should dislike to see you deprived of his very handsome contributions."

Anne-Josephe considered. "A game. He might like that—he is the sort that likes games."

"Well, then." Mrs. Brereton inserted another pin. "The next time you receive him, see what you can do, *ma chere*." Mrs. Brereton held the hat up and tweaked the placement of a feather. "What do you think, Sarah?" She turned the straw and silk confection to afford her niece the fullest view.

"Of the advice or the hat, ma'am? They are both very clever. The hat is not quite in your usual style, is it?"

"Why can I not wear something dashing when I choose? What is the good of being Fallen if I cannot dress as I like?" Still, Mrs. Brereton looked at a spray of silk cherries in her hand, then put it aside.

Miss Tolerance sat, removing first her gloves and then her bonnet. "Aunt, I wonder if I might ask you a question?"

"You may always ask, Sarah," the older woman began.

"Whether you will answer is always another matter," Miss Tolerance finished for her. It was a statement she had heard before. "Very well. Do you recall a man who might have been a patron—oh, years ago. A man named Kent."

"Kent?" Mrs. Brereton considered. "'Tisn't a remarkable name. How many years ago?"

"That, I do not know." Mrs. Kent had implied that her second husband's habits had been well established by the time their son was born, but without knowing George Kent's age it was difficult to provide an answer. "Perhaps twenty years ago?"

"Twenty years ago?" Mrs. Brereton scoffed. "My dear, this establishment was only three years open, and we were very select, perhaps more so even than now. The few mere *misters* who graced the beds here were of such status that I remember them all. Brummel, Fox… I do not recall a Kent. Why should you think I would?"

"I met his wife today. She suggested that her husband was partial to the sort of entertainment which you and your ladies provide."

"London has no shortage of establishments that offer entertainment, Sarah. This Kent does not recall himself to me."

"It was worth the asking, aunt. Have you finished your hat?"

"Oh, my dear, one never finishes with a hat. One only abandons further attempts to perfect it." Mrs. Brereton took up the bonnet again. Miss Tolerance took up her own bonnet and gloves, kissed Mrs. Brereton on her smooth, cool cheek, and left, intending to take advantage of what daylight remained to her.

She meant to go to the Wheat Sheaf. Joshua Glebb had promised results to her inquiry. But when she reached her cottage to change into masculine garb, Miss Tolerance found two messages waiting for her. The first was a note from Sir Walter Mandif.

You will have wondered about the result of your actions yesterday in the matter of the deceased Mrs. Pouter. The coroner, agreeing with our assessment and Doctor Hardesty's statement, believes the death to be suspicious—

"As I should think he would," Miss Tolerance sniffed.

—and has called an inquest for tomorrow morning. You will doubtless be summoned to give testimony, as it was you who found the poor woman.

Well, that was not strictly true, but she had seen the site of the woman's death in a relatively untouched state.

In the meantime, I have got word to an acquaintance who has offered to speak with you about the fellow you seek. His name is Joe Boswell. While his appearance is unprepossessing, I think you will find him in a position to be of some assistance to you. I have recommended that he reach you through Tarsio's, and hope he will be quick to let you hear from him.

As always, if there is any other way in which I can be of service to you, I beg you will call upon me.

Yours, WM

She felt a pang: was he, indeed, still hers? She would not ask but could not say she was unaffected by the question.

She shook her head to dispel these thoughts and took up the second piece of mail. This was a form, completed in an elegant clerk's hand: a summons calling her to a coroner's inquest at eleven of the clock the next day, warning of the considerable penalties likely should she fail to appear.

All this changed Miss Tolerance's plans. Mr. Glebb's information would wait until after the inquest upon Mrs. Pouter's death. Now she must take herself to Tarsio's and hold herself in readiness for an interview with the mysterious Joe Boswell.

Chapter Six

<hr>

As she no longer contemplated a return to the Liberty of
Savoy, Miss Tolerance did not bother to change from
her twill dress. She asked Cole to find a chair for her
and was carried through the traffic to Henry Street. So jolting was
the ride that by the time she reached her destination she had
arrived as well at the belief that one of the chairmen was peg-
legged; alighting, she saw that both men had the usual
complement of limbs. She paid the fare agreed upon, but no more.

Corton, the senior of Tarsio's porters, opened the door and
greeted her pleasantly. He was an older man, portly, with the
demeanor of a churchman and an expression that hinted at
toothache. He had more than once done her a good turn, and
Miss Tolerance was warm in returning the greeting.

"Anyone I should be on the look-out for, miss?"

"It is possible that a man may inquire for me, by the name
of Boswell. I do not know for certain, but I suspect that he
will be the sort of man you would prefer not to welcome
through the front door."

Corton pursed his lips. "Kitchen, then, miss?"

Imagining that the hubbub of Tarsio's kitchen would not

conduce to conversation, Miss Tolerance made a counter-proposal. "Perhaps you will ask him to meet me at the Duke of Sussex, and inform me so that I may join him there?"

"I will, miss. And thank you. Do you wish anything sent up for now?"

"A glass of claret, if you will be so kind."

Having demonstrated to Corton that, while she intended to take her visitor to another establishment, Tarsio's had first claim upon her heart and pocketbook, Miss Tolerance ascended to the first floor and the Ladies' Salon. This was a large, well-appointed chamber where, at this hour, those women who had sought a restorative cup of tea after the labors of shopping or gossip were beginning to disperse. The women who would hold court later—actresses and more acknowledged women of expensive frailty—had not yet begun to arrive. The Salon was quiet. Miss Tolerance sipped at her wine and read a number of the *Gazette* that had been left on the table.

When she had finished with that paper, she took up the *Times* and then the *Post*; she was reading the third set of Dueling Notices—similar but not identical between the three papers—when Corton appeared in the doorway and gestured to her. His brows were steepled with concern.

"Is it my guest, Corton?"

"Yes, miss. Just the sort of fellow I cannot admit here, and thank you for your thoughtfulness. But he says he will not be sent away unless it is with you. 'Tis full dark out, now. I don't feel right sending you off alone with him; I can send one of the waiters to walk with you."

Miss Tolerance was amused by the porter's concern. He was not to know that she carried a pistol in her reticule and was confident of her ability to defend herself against one man on a well-traveled London street.

"If you will tell the fellow I will be with him directly?"

Miss Tolerance pressed a penny into the porter's hand and turned to take up her bonnet.

Corton waited in the doorway, clearly intending to make sure that her visitor did not immediately attempt to overpower her. Miss Tolerance thanked him and turned to confirm that the man was, indeed, Joe Boswell.

"Aye, that's the name I was christened wiv." By his accent Boswell was London-bred, but there was a slight, pleasing music to his speech. "And you will be Miss Tolerance? Magistrate's friend?"

"I will. That is, I am. I thought we might be comfortable at the Duke of Sussex. Do you know it? It is only two streets away."

"I don't know much in this part of town, but I'm happy to follow." Boswell touched his forelock, the ancient gesture of respect, but his eyes reserved judgment. Miss Tolerance did as well until they reached the Duke of Sussex. There, settled under a flyspecked window that spilled cold air down upon them, Miss Tolerance ordered ale for Joe Boswell and brandy and water for herself.

From Corton's manner, Miss Tolerance had expected a man who radiated menace, but in the yellow lantern light of the tavern, Joe Boswell did not appear at all a monster. He was compact and lithe, with a bony, clever face and dark, curly hair above it. His skin was weathered, his eyes a deep brown, and his smile, which he displayed often, disclosed several missing teeth. Despite that lack, there was something charming and attractive about him; certainly, he did not look markedly different from any other man at the Duke.

"Now, our friend Sir Walter said you was wishful to talk to..." Joe paused to take his drink from the barmaid's hand. "Thank you, my love. You was wishful to talk to someone from my family, like."

"To a representative of your community, in any case. Are

you such?" Miss Tolerance took a scant sip of her watered brandy.

"Not official-like. I could bring you to one who is. But I'd need to know a mortal lot more of the why before I brung you there."

"Fair enough. I have recently learned of a man who has been running a swindle, using a name which might reflect discredit upon the—upon your people."

Boswell's eyes narrowed a fraction. "Trying to lay something off on the Travelers, is he?" His brows drew down and he regarded her with doubt. "Wouldn't be the first. And why is this a matter for you? In the general way, the *gadje* aren't so very concerned when my folk is fingered for some business or other."

It had not occurred to Miss Tolerance that her guest might be as wary of her as she was of him. She collected her thoughts. "I am trying to find this fellow; he has used a friend of mine very ill. It was suggested to me that your folk might have heard of him or—if you had not before—that you might be moved to seek him out and get him to cease his tricks."

"Want us to do your seeking for you? T'would help to see the color of your money, miss. I could go back to my folk and tell them you was on the straight."

Miss Tolerance began to reach for her pocketbook, then stopped. "Perhaps I should explain the circumstances of the matter and you may judge if your folk will want to know more."

Joe tasted his ale and made a waving motion which she took for encouragement.

Miss Tolerance briefly recounted Mrs. Pouter's tale, leaving her name out of it. "Sir Walter told me this is not the sort of business that even the most aggressive of your folk would be involved in; still, the man doing it is calling himself Marvell, a name I'm told is sometimes used by—"

"The Travelers."

"The Travelers. My thought was that he meant to lay the blame for his actions on your people."

"Wouldn't be the first. You think it is in our interest to find this Marvell and set him straight—"

"Or turn him in."

"What if he *is* one of ours?" Joe grinned and his eyes glittered in the lamplight.

"If he is one of yours, I think he is serving your people very ill, calling attention of the sort that an ignorant public might take seriously. I would think you'd prefer to hand him to Sir Walter—"

"In the general way, we'd find 'im some justice from our own—*if* 'e's one of ours. Look, I cannot promise to look out for the fellow, nor give him up, without I ask a blessing to it."

"I understand." Miss Tolerance put her tankard down. "May I ask that you seek that blessing on my behalf?" Now she did reach for the pocket-book and slid the sixpence she removed therefrom across the table until it tapped Joe's tankard. At the tiny clink, Joe's eyes flickered, then his lids dropped. Joe Boswell kept his own counsel.

"I should know tomorrow night, I 'spect. Shall I come again to that place?" He jerked his head back and to the side as if pointing toward Tarsio's.

"I don't know that I will be there tomorrow night. Can you leave a note?"

He shook his head. "Tried learnin' to write, but it didn't take."

"In that case, leave word with one of the porters at Tarsio's and they will let me know of it. Does that suit?"

Joe brought his tankard to his lips again, drank deep, and wiped the foam from his upper lip before he answered. "Suits. What I don't know is why, if Marvell h'aint taken none of your blunt, you're so hot to find him."

"I made a promise."

"A promise." He examined her for a few long moments, as

if weighing the word. At last, "Well." Finishing the last drops of his ale, Joe put his tankard back on the table with a smack and rose to his feet. "Thank you for the ale, miss. Y'may expect t' hear from me."

"I look forward to it," Miss Tolerance said politely. She watched as the Traveler left, took another sip of brandy, and rose to go herself.

The Coroner's inquest was held in Upper Thames Street; Miss Tolerance rose early, bathed and dressed in her steel-blue wool walking dress and spencer, which were just shy of severe in their appearance. A Coroner's inquest in London was a more formal business than one held in a country inn, and aside from the solemnity of the occasion, she had once or twice got employment as a result of an appearance in court. It made sense to present herself as both business-like and genteel.

If she had hoped that the courts might be quiet at this early hour, Miss Tolerance was disappointed. The street around the building thronged with people, either those come to participate in the business of the court or those come to make sport of it. A girl with a wen the size of a cherry above her eye was selling the wizened last of the season's flowers from a basket; an elderly man was hawking little tin horns which were meant to be used to express the crowd's appreciation or dismay at a ruling. Miss Tolerance, her elbows well out to keep pickpockets at bay, threaded her way through the crowd and entered the building.

The inquest would be held in one of the smaller rooms upstairs, "It not bein' of much interest," the clerk informed her. Miss Tolerance extended her elbows again and climbed the stair, surrounded by a small parade of men, soberly dressed, their eyes full of business. Miss Tolerance made herself one of the progress and shortly found herself in a small, well-lighted room on the first floor which overlooked the street. She was early; the inquest for Mrs. Pouter's death was not the first of the cases scheduled to be heard that morning. A harassed-looking clerk, his neckcloth coming untied and flapping with each word, came to inquire if she meant to watch or was there to give testimony, and if the latter, in which case? He ticked her name off on a list in a small book and turned away without further instruction. Miss Tolerance took a seat and settled in to wait.

The jury was brought in, and then the coroner arrived and introduced himself. Mr. Younge was a short, square man with a bald head, a broad, full-lipped mouth, and an important manner. The first case was of a child who had been run over by a carriage in the street; the death was ruled misadventure, and Mr. Younge addressed a short lecture to the mother of the girl, saying a parent who let children run wild in the streets must expect no good to come of it. The mother stood silent, tears streaming down her frozen face, until the coroner declared the matter closed. As the next case was brought, Miss Tolerance heard a stir and turned to see Mrs. Gordon attempting to join her. *Of course, she is here. The fire was in her home. I ought to have asked her to come with me.*

Mrs. Gordon reached Miss Tolerance, who moved as far as the oaken bench would permit to give the woman room. "It's kind in you to be here, Miss Sarah," she wheezed. Her face was blotched red and white, and her brow and upper lip were damp with exertion. "Will it be soon, d'you think?"

"After this case is heard," Miss Tolerance whispered.

The second case was a matter of a man shot by a friend while both were drunk. Sober now, the survivor insisted that he and Jacko had been wrestling all in fun; another witness suggested there had been a woman under dispute, and the tone not friendly in the least. In the end, the jury brought in a verdict of manslaughter and the protesting friend was bound over for trial.

The clerk called for the case of Mrs. Annie Pouter, born Annabel Ebbets, and urged all having knowledge of the matter to come forward and be heard.

Miss Tolerance was an early witness, giving testimony that she had arrived to speak with Mrs. Pouter only to find her body being carried from a building in which a fire had recently been extinguished.

"Then it is your belief that Mrs. Pouter died from the effects of the fire?"

"Not in the least," Miss Tolerance said firmly. "The woman had marks about her throat which suggested she had been throttled."

There was a good deal of curiosity on the part of Mr. Younge as to how Miss Tolerance would know the marks of throttling. He scolded her for having removed the body from its site, although she made it clear that it was others who had done so, and she who had given them a place to take the corpse. Younge thanked her, grudgingly, for her quick thinking, and released her from testimony. Doctor Hardesty was called and confirmed Miss Tolerance's assessment that neither smoke nor fire had been the sole cause of Mrs. Pouter's death. Unsurprisingly, Younge appeared to weigh the doctor's opinion more heavily than her own. Mrs. Gordon was called to assure the court that the deceased was indeed Mrs. Annie Pouter and to explain how she came to be in the rooms on Castle Street. "She was a little down on her luck, was Annie, so I invited her to stay with me." Cook's lips were pursed, the lower one trembling, but she did not weep.

The Watch was called, in the person of a stringy elderly man with a red nose and one arm. He reported having inspected the premises and seen nothing to suggest that the fire was anything but accidental. Hearing this, Miss Tolerance rose to her feet. "May I ask a question, sir?"

The coroner glared at her. There was no rule against an onlooker asking a question of witnesses, but it was rarely done. After a moment Younge nodded, but warned her in no uncertain terms not to waste his time or the jury's.

"I am curious to know if Mr. Hanwell—" that was the Watch— "noted that the site of the fire was across the room from the grate, and how he thought a fire might have started in a spot that seemed so unlikely.'

The coroner turned back to Hanwell, who hemmed and looked guilty and admitted, at last, that he had not in fact inspected the premises of the fire, owing to the fact that climbing stairs troubled his gamy leg, and he had deputed a boy to "take a look round and tell me if anything seemed as it oughtn't."

Mr. Younge pinched his nose as if he had a headache starting, and dismissed Hanwell. He did not issue either thanks or an apology to Miss Tolerance.

Lacking more evidence to be presented, the jury was charged with the case.

Very shortly a verdict was returned: death by homicide, by person or persons unknown. Miss Tolerance felt a grim satisfaction; poor Annie Pouter had died alone and unprotected, but the law would not permit the matter to be ignored. She turned to assist Cook to get to her feet, and together they left the courtroom.

Miss Tolerance sent Cook back to Manchester Square in a carriage and continued on to the Wheat Sheaf. She found Mr. Joshua Glebb at work at his table in the taproom; a line of folk with anxiety writ in their gestures and expressions stood waiting for a moment when he could meet with them and suggest a source—licit or not—from which to borrow cash. Miss Tolerance went to the bar and asked

Boddick for coffee and the paper and settled in to wait until such time as Mr. Glebb had disposed of all his prior clients.

When at last the procession of butchers and bakers (judging by their attire) and younger sons (judging by their jug-bitten and repentant miens) had learned from Mr. Glebb who was lending and at what price, Miss Tolerance folded the paper and joined him at his table. Glebb's long face brightened at the sight of her, then fell.

"Have a seat, miss, but know I've come up empty as a leaky pisspot." Glebb generally resorted to vulgarity only when he felt he was disappointing her.

"Nothing about Mr. Marvell?"

Glebb shook his head; his jowls danced. "Only that I'm ready to swear that Marvell ain't the name he was born with. There's Marvells about town, aye, but they're mostly tinkers running little maces, small cons, fortune-telling, or selling potions to the gulls. Travelers and the like. And they's all easily found by other, born names. *Your* Marvell, may I call him so, might ha' been born full-grown, dressed and shod, and put out on the street. No one knows aught of 'im before 'e took them rooms in Bruton Street, nor what 'appened to 'im after. I'm powerful sorry, miss."

"Surely a man cannot so easily invent himself in such a fashion? Or disappear so easily?"

Glebb dabbed at his nose with a much-used kerchief and considered. "Fact of it is, I'm surprised there ain't more as does it. All Bob Smith 'as to do is move from one town to the next—in London that's one nebberhood to another—and tell the folk he meets that 'e's John Taylor, and who's to know? You changed your own name, miss. If you'll pardon me mentioning it."

"But I make no secret of who I had been." Miss Tolerance did not think of herself as having changed her name so much as having adopted the identity under which she worked. She had been Sarah Brereton when she returned to England; it was only when she joined Mrs. Brereton's household, attained the legal status of *feme sole*, and set herself up in business, that she had taken "Tolerance." By now the name was hers, by use if not by official process. "So it is not difficult. And there is no way to trace who he was before, or who he is now?"

"None I can tell you." Glebb's expression showed genuine dismay; she was not certain whether he regretted more his failure or his inability to charge for it. Notwithstanding, Miss Tolerance took a coin from her pocket-book and slid it across the table; it was worth the money to keep Joshua Glebb well-disposed.

"I call that handsome of you, Miss T. Another time, I vow I'll be more help."

"I rely upon it, Mr. Glebb. Now, I see your custom is lining up. I must not keep you." She ceded her place to an anxious-looking matron and bid Mr. Boddick good day on her way out.

She was as sorry as Joshua Glebb that his inquiries had gained nothing. Her experience insisted that the deaths of Mrs. Pouter and Mrs. Black were related to each other and to the matter of Mr. Marvell, but she had no evidence, and evidence was what the Crown would require if a prosecution was to take place. Assuming that Marvell could be found at all.

Miss Tolerance shook her head at the ruffian boy who offered to sweep the streets for her to cross. She had relied more heavily than she should have upon Joshua Glebb finding some trace of Marvell. She must use other resources. She believed that the man who had taken Mrs. Pouter's savings and the man who had taken her life must be one and the same. Her attendance at the inquest had suggested that without a gadfly to provoke investigation, the Law would be just as happy to ignore the matter of a retired whore's death. *I must be the gadfly, then*, she thought. She turned her steps toward Tarsio's.

Corton, very much on his dignity, reported that the tinker-man had come and asked him to pass along his words, "being as how he don't write, miss." The message was that Joe would return to Tarsio's at five of the evening, and if Miss Tolerance would hire a hackney carriage he would take her to meet someone who could assist in her inquiry.

Thus, a little past six in the evening Miss Tolerance was in a rattle-trap carriage with Joe Boswell slouched in the corner opposite, heading north toward Highbury to meet a woman Joe called Mother Ella.

Miss Tolerance had hired the carriage in which she rode, and had invited Joe Boswell to enter it. She was as certain as she was of anything that Sir Walter Mandif would not have arranged for her to talk with the man had he believed he posed a danger to her. Yet the memory of her nurserymaid's hints coupling Travelers with unspecified but darkly unsavory doings, arose in her as the carriage wheeled onward. Rising thirty and accustomed to confronting the lowest sort of criminals and libertines, she was surprised to feel anxiety at the prospect of meeting Mother Ella among her people. Even the weight of the pistol in her reticule did not wholly assuage her unease.

The carriage clattered through close-packed streets into the suburbs, arriving just at dark on a countrified road with a stretch of green park on one side and a field on the other. In the field there was what seemed like a small town made up of elaborate tents and wagons, all lit with lanterns. It should have looked ramshackle and sinister, Miss Tolerance thought. Instead, it looked warm, comfortable, and welcoming. When they alit, Joe led her between tidily cultivated frames of herbs, pointing to a structure that was half wood-frame and half tent, with more planted frames before it. In the lantern-light, Miss Tolerance recognized plants from her country childhood: comfrey, chamomile, mint, rue, and burdock.

"Mother makes tonic." Joe had stopped and turned to her,

startling Miss Tolerance. She did not permit herself to step back, but his sudden nearness, the loudness of his voice in the still dark, disconcerted her. "Good for all manner of ills, is Mother's tonic."

Miss Tolerance took a breath. Her instinct was to trust the man, but she was still on edge. At least, he was not between herself and a rapid retreat, should such become necessary. And at least the carriage had been instructed to wait for the return fare.

Joe grinned as if he divined her thoughts. "Coming, then?" He stepped forward and swept aside the flap of a tent, which revealed a small room, warm with rugs upon the ground and hanging from the walls, and a lantern hanging from a joist. Seated in a circle in the center was a seethe of small children, all with the same lustrous dark hair and eyes as Joe's, all dressed in clothes which had seen hard wear but were clean and well-tended. One child—a girl with her curls subdued into a long plait—jumped to her feet, smiling broadly. "Our Joe!"

He was a clear favorite with the children, who echoed the pleased greeting; two of the smallest girls grasped his legs and stood upon the toes of his boots, confidently expecting to be carried forward this way.

"None of that. I've brung Mother a guest. I'll come back to play with you later. Now!" He leaned down to gently disengage the toddlers from his legs and sent them back to the circle with gentle swats on their posteriors. "Ellora, is Mother in the great room?"

"She is, Joe." Ellora was the girl who had first greeted him. "I'll tell 'er you've called, shall I?"

"You do that, lass." He made a gesture as if he would send her off with a swat as well. He turned to Miss Tolerance. "Had as well come along, miss. Unless you're afeared of the little 'uns."

"Only afraid I might step upon one of them," Miss Tolerance answered. "You are well-liked, I see."

"Comes of scarcity, I reckon. I'm not here as oft as 'Lora's mam would like." Before he could expand upon this, Ellora came back, took Joe's hand, and began to tug him through the tent flap. Miss Tolerance followed.

The chamber they entered was larger than the first, a pavilion of sorts with a high tented ceiling. The walls were tightly packed with shelves and baskets. Rugs and more baskets hung from the ceiling round the edges. Whatever her upbringing had led her to expect, all was tidy and clean; the only scents she could discern were beeswax and a slight smell of lambswool. Near the center of the room a large brazier put forth both light and warmth; close by it was a deep wing chair draped in brightly colored shawls. It was only when the shawls moved that Miss Tolerance perceived, settled among them, a very old woman.

Miss Tolerance curtsied, youth reverencing age. The old woman laughed. "'Ave manners, do ye?" She had the shrunken frame of a woman who had been tall and buxom and was now neither; her face resembled in color and wrinkles a walnut shell. She wore no cap, and her scalp shone through sparse white hair parted and pulled into a tight knot. "Your like don't generally bow to mine."

"Perhaps you mistake my like, ma'am." Miss Tolerance waited for Joe Boswell to introduce her. After a long, awkward pause, Joe appeared to realize what his role was. "Mother, this is Miss Tolerance, as is looking to find a fellow I 'spect is making inroads upon our good name. Miss Tolerance, this is Mother Sophonia Gray."

"No one calls me that. Mother Ella will do." The old woman reached to take a clay pipe from the table beside her. Her hand was skeletal, but even in the dim light, Miss Tolerance could read the play of sinew and bone beneath the skin. She thought the old woman must have a good deal of strength in those hands still.

Mother Ella noted her gaze. "Used to wring the chickens' necks for 'em," she said. "Joe, find the girl a seat, do ye. And you, miss, tell me what the boy means by 'making inroads on our good name,' if you please."

Miss Tolerance perched on the high four-legged stool Joe brought her and began her explanation while Mother Ella went through the business of lighting her pipe and drawing upon it thoughtfully. Miss Tolerance suspected the pipe was merely a prop to let the old woman listen without reaction.

At the end of Miss Tolerance's story, "Marvell, you say? I must call the man a fool if he thinks we'd permit 'im to go on with that for long. And anyone of sense 'd know that messing with anni-yuitees ain't our sort of rig. So what do you want of us, miss?"

"At this point, ma'am—"

"Mother."

"At this point, Mother, I only need to confirm that the business was not being run by one of your folk. Joe said he thought not, but that you would know for certain."

The look the old woman gave Joe suggested that there would be a further discussion of his disclosures, but she only said "None of my folk, that's certain. Nor any other Travelers in the city. Most of us do regular work—Joe's in movables, his dad and his brother work with horses. The sort of game y'er talking of—I can't think of anyone among our folk would have the first idea of it. I'll take money for tellin' a fortune or liftin' a curse, or for a bottle o' tonic, but that's value for value, you might say. This—preyin' on women my age, in so cold a style?" She shook her head.

Miss Tolerance nodded. She found the old woman compelling. "It would certainly bring the wrong sort of notice to you. May I ask, Mother, that if any one of your folk should

discover this man, you will let me know? Before any…
summary action is taken?"

"Summary action?" Mother Ella cackled. "No gilded airs
about you, is there? If this feller shows 'is 'ead, I promise I
will not keep 'im from talkin' to you before we try 'im."

Miss Tolerance briefly imagined a magistrate's court with
Mother Ella at the bench and felt a pang of sympathy for the
elusive Mr. Marvell. "Ma'am—Mother—you have been very
generous with your time. May I offer you some recompense?"
She took her pocket-book from her reticule.

Mother Ella held out her hand to receive the emolument.

"Should I cross your palm?" Miss Tolerance held a
sixpence between her gloved thumb and forefinger.

The old woman snorted. "That's for the trade, dearie. Not
for friends."

Miss Tolerance dropped the coin into Mother Ella's hand
and sat again, watching the woman's sinewy fingers close
over the coin.

"Aught about this gent you an't shared with me?"

"My client said he was short and sturdily built, with fair
hair and a flat nose, as if he'd been in a fight. He seemed well
to do—flush with cash, as the phrase goes. He has been gone
from his rooms in Bruton Street for several months."

"What of 'is movables?"

"The rooms were let furnished. The surroundings that
looked so prosperous and respectable belong to the landlord,
not Mr. Marvell."

Mother Ella took a deep draw at her pipe, expelled the
smoke, and spat into a kerchief that appeared in her hand.
"Well, then, yer man travels light—and thought to put the
blame for 'is game upon my people. If 'e can be turned up,
we'll find 'im."

Miss Tolerance rose. "Thank you, Mother."

The old woman held out her hand. Thinking she meant to
shake upon their agreement, Miss Tolerance extended her

hand in return. When Mother Ella grasped her wrist in a strong grip she felt a stab of anxiety. Then the old woman turned her hand over and, with a practiced motion, stripped the glove from Miss Tolerance's hand. She held it, palm up, studying it. When Miss Tolerance would have pulled her hand away, Mother Ella redoubled her grasp.

"Don't pull," she scolded. "'Alf a Lunnon would pay dear to 'ave me read their palms. I like to be sure who I'm dealin' with, dearie."

Miss Tolerance found the notion of being pawed at to ascertain her reliability distasteful, but she stood still, enduring the scrutiny for the sake of this loose partnership. She waited, looking down at Mother Ella's pink scalp while Mother *hmmmed* and *tsssked* as if the hand told her something. She tilted her head one way, the other, tucked her chin in like an ancient tortoise, and at last smacked her lips and loosened her grip.

"Well?" Miss Tolerance's tone was not without amusement.

Mother Ella shrugged. "I don't give away my secrets, dearie." She half extended her palm as if to accept further payment.

Miss Tolerance laughed and tugged her glove on. "I have survived thus far without knowing what my future holds, ma'am. This was for your satisfaction, not mine. Now, if you have anything to communicate, ma'am, Joe Boswell knows how to find me. Or a message sent to Tarsio's on Henry Street—"

"I don't put things to paper," Mother Ella said. Her lips quirked in a half-smile. "Terrible 'abit."

Miss Tolerance curtsied again and took her leave. Joe Boswell, who had waited silently by the tent's exit through the entire interview, stepped forward, saluted Mother Ella, and fell in behind Miss Tolerance. They were silent as they watched the carriage execute an awkward series of maneuvers to turn back toward the city.

"Mother took a right shine to you," Joe said at last.

"Did she?"

The dark man nodded and smiled. The missing teeth gave him an amiably raffish look. "'Ad she not, she'd 'ave called in one of the others to sit with 'er and given 'em the sign to get rid of you. Send you away," he added, as if she might fear something more permanent was intended. "Don't know if we'll find this man Marvell for you, but Mother'll see that we try."

He handed Miss Tolerance into the carriage carriage, closed the door, and watched as it rattled away.

Chapter Seven

On her return the night before, Miss Tolerance had found a plate of dainty meat pies and a branch of grapes which Cook had sent over for her refreshment. In the morning she returned the plate to the kitchen and found Cook, Jess, and Tim in the midst of morning preparations: breads had been withdrawn from the oven and stood in fragrant rows; Jess broke eggs into a vast iron skillet, and Tim had been set to slicing rashers from a marbled slab of bacon. Cook alternately scolded the boy and dispatched fresh baskets of rolls to the Little Salon, where a morning collation was laid out for the replenishment of gentlemen after their amours.

"Take another bread, Miss Sarah. We've greengage jam from last summer to go with. No? Nor a—" Cook cut short her solicitousness. "You, Jess, stop worryin' them eggs, give 'em a stir and salt 'em and 'ave done before they're tough as old boots! That bacon ain't going to fry itself. And you—" she turned her attention to Tim. "You'll chop yer thumb off do you keep at it that way. That'd be a fine thing to serve Ma'am's guests, I don't think."

Miss Tolerance, watching the movement of the great

chopper in Tim's hands, thought it miraculous that the boy had not taken his whole hand off before this.

"You'll be there this afternoon, Miss Sarah? For Annie's funeral?"

"At what o'clock?"

"Three, at St. Giles's. Mrs. B is doing everything proper, even hired a carriage to go to the service and the buryin'. You could ride along of me if you'd a mind to."

Miss Tolerance thanked Cook and promised her attendance at both the church and the burial. "I've an errand this morning, but if I am able to return here before the service, I will be happy to ride with you."

She touched Cook's shoulder in a gesture of comfort before she left the kitchen for the servants' door, where she almost collided with Cole. "Miss Sarah, a letter come for you," the porter said over a tray of dirty crockery. "Mr. Keefe has it."

Miss Tolerance found Keefe at his usual post for the hour in the entry hall, handing hats and walking sticks to their departing owners. Most of the gentlemen were bleary and disheveled. It occurred to Miss Tolerance to wonder why Mrs. Brereton did not retain a valet to attend to departing clients.

She waited unnoticed until the last of the group had taken their leave. She disliked in general to mix with the house's clientele. When Keefe closed the door on the last of them, she stepped forward to claim her letter. Keefe wished her good morning, handed her the missive, then turned away as a fresh wave of gentlemen emerged from the Little Salon. Miss Tolerance made her retreat.

The letter was from Joshua Glebb.

Dear Miss T: a late bit of word from an associate, who says there's a fellow calls himself Miracle is working a game in Battersea. I can't say that this is your Marvell by another name, but I thought you'd be wishful to know. This Miracle holds his court, as you might say, just outside the village. It

*sounds as if he might be set up more as bawd than swindler,
but in any case, I thought I would just say a word in your ear.
You know best how you wish to proceed.*

Glebb subscribed himself her very humble servant. Miss
Tolerance recalled that she had paid Mr. Glebb in despite of a
lack of results; it seemed now she might have the worth of her
money in hand.

She had intended to call upon Mrs. Jane Pilgrim of
Bethnal Green, from whom Annie Pouter's death had
distracted her. But this new piece of intelligence gave Miss
Tolerance pause. Bethnal Green was a quicker, easier trip, just
to the eastern outskirts of the city, but would Mrs. Pilgrim
herself provide more than a single flag in the path to Marvell?
Battersea was decidedly less convenient, and Mr. Glebb had
not provided either street or house number—but should this
Miracle prove to be Marvell himself it would bring her to the
verge of discharging her obligation to Mrs. Pouter.

Miss Tolerance decided upon Battersea. Given the hour of
Mrs. Pouter's funeral, there was no time to waste in starting.

Miss Tolerance's general experience with neighborhoods
south of the Thames was that they were sometimes rough, if
not outright dangerous. She changed into breeches, boots, and
her Gunnard greatcoat, slipped her pistol into her pocket and
clasped her sword hangar around her hips, and made her way
to the stable to hire a hack for the morning. Shortly, she was
riding toward Chelsea.

The Battersea Bridge was only forty-odd years old, but it
had aged very ill. Constructed of timber, it appeared rickety,
as if it had been built by a child in his nursery. Miss Tolerance
paid the toll and urged her reluctant horse along the gravel
road, riding slowly, threading her way through the wagon
traffic heading northward. Twice the bridge shuddered when a
boat slammed into one of the pilings.

The southern shore was marshy and dull green, the
prospect broken by a tall wooden mill tower and, just a little

beyond, a church. She had expected to find tenements of the sort she had encountered in Southwark and Bermondsey, but Miss Tolerance saw instead small farms and forcing houses along the road that took her into the village, and one or two larger industrial structures. Now and then she passed a pedestrian or a smocked farmer driving a cart, but Battersea was startlingly quiet for a place so close by the capital.

The village was a cluster of buildings centered round the town pump: a large inn and public house, a church, a few shops, and a scattering of whitewashed houses. *If I were a man hopeful to encourage business from retired whores, this is not where I should make a beginning*, she thought, and very nearly turned her horse round to return to London. This had been a gamble; Joshua Glebb had only said "a man named Miracle." But she was in no hurry to cross that bridge so soon again, and it seemed a waste to have come so far without investigating a little further. She tied her hack up and entered the public house.

Despite the hour—it was not yet noon—the place was busy. Miss Tolerance stepped to the bar and ordered ale. The barman gave her no second look; he drew off a pint and put it before her amiably. Miss Tolerance put a coin on the bar, gestured to the man to keep any change, and asked, as casual-seeming as possible, if he knew of a man named Miracle or Marvell.

"Which is it, then?" The barman studiedly polished a tankard with his apron. He was bald, with only a fringe of short curling gray hair about his ears, and a round, ruddy face.

"Do you mean you know men by both names?

The tapster shook his head. "Nah. I know of a Miracle, but —" he raised his eyes from the tankard, looked at her, looked again, and his amiable mien changed. "I was going to say 'e warn't the sort of man I'd recommend anyone 'ave truck with, but *your sort*..." He had discerned her gender and made an assumption about what it meant.

"I imagine he is not the sort of man I wish to associate with, but I have business with him nonetheless." Miss Tolerance took another draught of ale; she saw no reason to explain herself.

"We-el, if you're wishful to find 'im, 'e keeps a 'ouse up York Street, a bit ways from the old 'namelware manufactory." The barman rolled his shoulder as if to indicate a direction. "Drink up and go. I keep a Christian 'ouse. Your like'd be more comfortable there than 'ere."

Miss Tolerance left her ale unfinished. She untied her horse and cast a look about for someone who could direct her to York Street. There was only a cluster of children at the pump, two older girls taking turns drinking from the common tin cup, and a scatter of toddlers in petticoats, their genders indeterminate. What were their mothers about, to let such babies loose in the street? There was not an adult in sight.

She was startled from the thought by a voice at her elbow. "Kin' I 'elp you, sir?"

The speaker was a girl of eight or nine years, sun-browned, her hair a nimbus of tight curls around her head, eyes bright and curious. She wore a cut-down dress of faded Calicut and carried a basket of onions.

"Can you direct me to York Street?" She thought back to what the tapman had said. "To the enamelware factory?"

"The 'namelware factory ain't been open since I been alive, sir. What you want with it?"

Miss Tolerance let her horse drink from the trough by the pump. "I don't want the factory—just a house I'm told stands near it."

"Oh." The child gave a knowing inflection to the word.

"I'm told there's a Mr. Miracle there?"

The girl nodded. "That's our house, an' 'e's my da. Come along of me, sir. I'll show you where it is."

The child waved good-bye to her playmates, hitched the basket up on her arm, and gestured forward.

Miss Tolerance led her horse—it seemed neither mannerly nor safe to ride while the child walked along beside her—and they struck off westward.

After walking a few minutes in silence Miss Tolerance asked, "So then you are Miss Miracle?"

The child gave a snort. "I'm just Rosie, sir. I won't be *Miss* 'til I'm one of the girls."

Miss Tolerance regarded the girl with surprise. "Are you not a girl now?"

"Not that sort of girl. In a few years, when I'm takin' men like the big 'uns do."

Miss Tolerance was momentarily bereft of speech. Prostitution, even of children, was not unusual in London, but this child seemed to regard it as a quite natural, perhaps even desirable, fate.

"I'll 'ave a new dress, and a room of me own, an' gennelman will bring me presents."

"Will they?"

"Oh, not all of 'em. Mos' gennelmen's right hunks, Izzie says. Won't spend a farthin' more'n they must. But Izzie says if I keep myself nice and mind me manners..." the girl went on, speaking very practically of what she must do, when she was grown enough to take custom, to attract the more free-and-easy spenders. She chattered as the road became a rural lane surrounded by a drying lavender field on one side and a rank of beehives on the other. "...I'd 'ave silk an' maybe ribbons, Izzie says. Do you like my hair, sir?"

The girl went on without pause for a reply.

At last, they arrived at a ramshackle fence of unpainted pickets, with a flagged path that led to a large, wooden house whose original color had faded to gray.

"'Ere we are, sir." Rosie gave a shove and the gate swung open. At the same moment, the door of the house slammed open and a man exited, reeling drunk, his breeches half buttoned. He turned and blew a kiss to a woman who stood in the door, her bodice unlaced and one breast exposed. The drunk staggered to the gate, pushed past Miss Tolerance, and turned toward the town. While his attention had been on the woman, she grinned; once his back turned the grin disappeared.

"Now ye're here, sir, will you come take yer ease?" Rosie grinned. "Looks like Grace's free, an' maybe Maggie."

"Neither of them will do for me, Rosie. I need a word with Mr. Miracle," Miss Tolerance said firmly. She was by this time fairly certain that the man would not be Mr. Marvell; it would be only the work of a moment to be sure of it. But she was aware of a powerful desire to tell the man as well what she thought of a father grooming his daughter so he could pimp her out.

"It truly *was* Da you was lookin' for all along?" The girl screwed her face up, perplexed and disappointed. "What ye want with 'im?"

"Just a few words," Miss Tolerance assured her.

"I thought you was looking for a quiff. Woulda been worth ha'penny to fetch you for a quiff."

Miss Tolerance took out her pocket book, found a ha-penny bit, and offered it gravely to the girl. "I did not mean you to lose anything. I am happy to pay for your directions."

Rose's face lit. "You *are* a gennelman! You come along 'a me, sir." When Miss Tolerance had tied up her horse the child took her hand and half-pulled her into the house.

The doxy she had seen from the road sat in the front parlor, sprawled across a sofa with a blue bottle in her hand. At the sound of Miss Tolerance's arrival, she attempted to sit upright, spilling gin upon her skirt, which she then tried to mop with a soiled fichu. Without looking up she asked what her visitor's pleasure might be.

"I would like a word with Mr. Miracle."

"A word?" The woman looked up from her mopping, her

eyes red-rimmed and unfocused. "You ain't here for a quiff, then?"

This was a question of which Miss Tolerance was already wearying. "No, I—"

The woman put the fichu in her mouth to suck the gin it had absorbed. It was clear her attention was already elsewhere.

"You *sure* you don't want a quiff, sir?" Rose asked again. "Mags could do you fast, like—" Her tone cajoled.

"I am quite sure." Miss Tolerance used the most repressive tone of which she was capable. "Where is your father?"

The child darted down the dim hallway toward the rear of the house, through a door from which a dazzle of light suggested windows in the chamber beyond. It occurred to Miss Tolerance to turn and leave, but the beginning of sounds of enthusiastic rutting from the floor above, and the sight of Rosie, who had returned to the hall and beckoned to her, reminded her that she wanted a word or two with the proprietor on his daughter's behalf.

"Come on, then!" Rose assured herself that Miss Tolerance followed, and turned back into the room beyond. When she reached the door Miss Tolerance found herself in a crowded pantry that gave on to the kitchen on the left and another chamber on the right. She followed Rose into the latter. It would have been a pleasantly bright room in contrast to the front of the house, but someone had hung a miscellany of shawls and rugs over the windows; the room was as dim as a cave. Against the far wall there was a sofa draped in more shawls; nearer the door was a man sprawled in a low-set armchair, legs extended. He was ruddy, blue-eyed, with a spill of curls much the color of Rose's over his forehead. He had been dozing, and a long-stemmed clay pipe dangled from his hand. The musty scent of the smoke that curled upward from the bowl made it clear that Rose's Da was an opium smoker.

Rose darted across the room, threw herself on the floor by

his knee, and smiled upward with an attitude of worship. "This 'ere man, Da, 'e come to talk with ye."

The man's eyes slid open, and he studied Miss Tolerance as he made an attempt to sit more upright. "What business 'ave you and me?"

A mingling smell of unwashed flesh, beer, and opium made Miss Tolerance's stomach turn. "I was looking for a man named Marvell. It was suggested you might be he, working under a different name, but—"

"No different than what I was born with. Cyrus Miracle. My pa was Welsh. They's lots of Miracles in Wales. I'm not your man, then?"

"It appears not, sir. I am sorry to have troubled you." Miss Tolerance was rethinking her desire to give Rose's father a piece of her mind for involving the child in his business. What did it matter to her? Except that she had seen the life the girl aspired to.

"Is Rose your daughter, sir?"

Miracle laughed coarsely. "S'what 'er mother says."

"And you send her out to drive custom to your house?

He reached to take a handful of the girl's dense curls and turn her face up to his. She showed no surprise or dislike of the treatment. "That what you done, Rosie? Brung this gennleman for a gig?"

"I ast 'im if he wanted one, but 'e said no, Da."

He released the girl's hair and grinned. "Well good on ye for trying, Rosie girl." He regarded his visitor critically. "What's wrong with our quim, then? You too goo—" he stopped, tilted his head to one side, then shook it as if to clear away the fog. "Damme, ye're a woman."

Rose looked up at him. "No, Da, see? It's a gent." Her tone suggested that he must be very far gone in intoxication to make such an error.

He cuffed her casually. "Girl, if you're going to work

upstairs by and by, ye'll need sharper eyes. There's no prick in them britches, nor never 'as been."

Rose sniggered but was at once upon her feet, one hand cupped around the ear Miracle had smacked and the other outstretched as if she meant to test her father's observation. Miss Tolerance stepped back to avoid those inquisitive fingers, nearly falling backward as her heel came down on a discarded bottle. She caught herself against the door jamb.

"Is Da right? Ye're a woman?" Where Miracle's tone had been one of amusement, Rose's was impressed. "Nellie! Come see!"

Miss Tolerance heard a stir in the pantry behind her, and a girl a few years older than Rose pushed past. The two girls put their heads together, Rose pointed, Nellie whispered some question to her, and the two of them threw back their heads with laughter.

"If Miss Rose is your daughter, Mr. Miracle, do you really want her on the road seeking custom for your house? How old is she?"

"I'm ten!"

Nellie poked her "Ye're never ten! Nine last Michaelmas, you are!"

The two girls began to quarrel in a fashion that suggested this was a frequent pastime.

"Mr. Miracle, do you see nothing wrong in a child of ten shipping for a bawdy house?"

Miracle shrugged. "What else should she be doing, then? Broidery? Dancin' lessons? That ain't going to suit 'er for the future, is it?"

In a moment, Miss Tolerance understood the only argument that might conceivably work. "Dancing and embroidery would better suit her to a higher class sort of establishment, Mr. Miracle. One at which she could charge far more than I imagine the women upstairs can bring in."

"An' 'ow'd you know?"

"I know because—" she hesitated, then went on. "I know because my aunt runs the most exclusive house of accommodation in London, and you may well believe that she does not send the ladies in her employment out on the street to draw in custom."

"What *does* she do, then?" The question came from behind Miss Tolerance, and the speaker was a woman. Miss Tolerance turned enough to see a young woman, slender, slight, and neatly dressed, with a clean fichu across her breast and sandy brown hair plaited and pinned into a crown on her head. "What does your aunt do, sir?" she asked again.

"There's the joke of it, Iz." Miracle waved a hand at Miss Tolerance as if she were an exhibit in the Tower Menagerie. "T'ain't a man at all. It's a woman."

"*No.*" Izzie came around Miss Tolerance and turned to examine her, her hand momentarily outreached in much the same way that Rosie's had been. Miss Tolerance put her hand out to block it, as she might have parried a sword thrust.

"And your aunt runs a house in London and don't mind you traipsing around like that?" The woman's speech was as crisp as Miracle's was drawling, and only lightly accented. North of London, Miss Tolerance thought, but not much. "She don't have *you* drawing in custom then as if you was one of the fellows?"

"Not at all. The ladies draw in their own custom by report. And I dress this way to avoid being accosted in the streets."

"By report, then? What's that?" Izzie appeared to have taken over the interview; Cyrus Miracle had found a spill and caught it at the candle to light his pipe again. Izzie saw this and made bold to take Miss Tolerance by the elbow. "Come into the kitchen where we can talk."

Miss Tolerance had no interest in talking. She had attempted, against better judgment, to intercede on Rosie's behalf. It was clearly of no use. She was very aware that Annie Pouter's funeral was that afternoon, and that she had wasted a morning in traveling to Battersea. She shook her elbow from the other woman's grasp.

"Don't leave! Please! I've so many things to ask!" Izzie held out her hand in supplication, a gesture Miss Tolerance suspected was well rehearsed.

"I have business to attend to, and nothing I can tell you."

"But you do! How'm I going to help them girls if I can't get advice from one as knows? If I leave 'it to Cyrus they'll never be naught than common cracks!"

"Do I understand that you, as well as Mr. Miracle, are grooming these children to become part of a covey?"

Izzie could not have missed the outrage in Miss Tolerance's voice. She lifted her chin. "Best thing for 'em, if we can give them some polish. Them upstairs—" She jerked her head toward the stairway in the hall. "Them upstairs is common drabs, but Cy and me, we have plans for a better place than this. Girls with quality."

"Best thing for them?" Dear God. "I'm afraid I must go. Mr. Miracle? Ladies?" She bowed in the general direction of the company.

"Ladies!" Nellie and Rosie snickered, heads together, at the word.

Izzie scowled. "See? If you mean to be fine game and able to have the pick of the gents and charge high, you need to *act* like ladies. Learn to talk nice and dress pretty. Wash your ears. Set some value on yourselves."

Rose rolled her eyes. "No'un'd take my like for a la-a-a-ady."

"Not if you don't act like one," Izzie scolded. "Did you see, girls? Manners, that's the thing. Act like a lady and you get treated like one. You can charge more. They'll treat you better, ain't that right, miss?" She looked to Miss Tolerance as one appealing to unassailable authority.

"Manners, yes," Miss Tolerance agreed, looking over

Izzie's shoulder toward the front of the house. "I really must go."

"I'll show you out," Izzie offered.

"I can find my way."

Nonetheless, Izzie followed her down the hall and out the door. As they stepped into the daylight Izzie caught her arm. "You could *help* them girls."

"How would I do so?" Miss Tolerance briefly imagined taking Rose, Nellie, and the others away with her—but to where? Even if Mrs. Brereton was willing, taking the girls back to Manchester Square would solve nothing.

"I can tell you're a lady. You know things, things that'd help them fly higher, have the better sort of men."

"My best help would be to tell them on no account to become whores."

"Better than being a scullery slut or washerwoman and jigged will or nil she: shoved against a wall by the master or the master's son. Rosie calls Cyrus her Da, but it wasn't him. It was one of 'em at the house where I was a respectable laundress—"

"That is iniquitous, and I am heartily sorry for it," Miss Tolerance said. "But I should think that after your experience you would not have turned to whoredom, nor—"

Izzie straightened. "I'm not a whore no more. I done my time at it. Lucky enough, too: didn't take the pox or fall afoul of some brute. I look after the house and the girls and help with raisin' the children. When we open a *good* house, I'll be the manager*ess*." She squinted against the sunlight. "You got no advice for me? For the girls?"

What was she to say? Her best advice would not be taken. "Clean linen. On the beds and for the girls. Daily." Miss Tolerance took up the reins of her hired horse. Another thought came to her. "Can you read?"

Izzie stared at her. "Read? Why would I?"

"If you want advice, Miss Izzie, learn to read. Teach the

girls to read so that it will be harder for others to cheat them—and so they can talk about something other than—than sex. That—and clean linen—will set your establishment apart from other houses better than satin gowns." She swung up into the saddle and touched the brim of her hat.

"Reading." Izzie was thoughtful. "Reading and clean linen. Wait'll I tell Cyrus."

Miss Tolerance reached home in time to change into clothing more suited to a funeral, and joined Cook on the ride to St. Giles's Church. The coffin was met and greeted prayerfully by the minister and brought down the aisle. The mourners were not a large group; there were only a few whom Miss Tolerance did not recognize. She was surprised to see two of the men who had carried Mrs. Pouter's body from Castle Street to Manchester Square, heads bowed respectfully through the hymn, the prayer of penitence, and the sermon. There were two men and a woman who Cook identified as neighbors at her Castle Street rooms; two older woman who Miss Tolerance privately characterized as retired colleagues of Mrs. Pouter sat together in the back.

The minister, a man of considerable years who had doubtless buried many of less virtue than Mrs. Pouter, trod lightly upon the ground of her sins, noting that they were known to God, and more hopefully upon the Almighty's capacity for forgiveness.

From the corner of her eye, Miss Tolerance saw Mrs. Gordon nodding; tears rolled over the round of her cheeks and dropped onto her black pelisse.

Miss Tolerance put a hand out to pat Cook's; the older woman took it firmly in her own and held it there through the final hymn and the Lord's Prayer.

At the end of the service, Cook and Miss Tolerance rode

with Mr. Henkes, the curate, in the hackney carriage Mrs. Brereton had provided, to St. Pancras, where Mrs. Pouter would be laid to rest (the churchyard at St. Giles having long ago become too full to accommodate the dead of Seven Dials). Mr. Henkes attempted a few vague words of comfort, being not perfectly certain in what relation Mrs. Gordon and Miss Tolerance stood to the deceased, before his eyes fluttered closed and he slept.

The coffin arrived in the churchyard before they did, and had been lowered into its resting place. It was small and plainly made; a large bundle of lilies lay atop it.

"From us girls at Mrs. B's." Marianne Touchwell waited at graveside for them, wearing a mourning coat, her maid trailing behind her. She offered her hand to Cook. "I am so sorry I could not be at the church, Mrs. Gordon."

Cook nodded and bit her lip as though such kindness might cause her to weep anew.

Mr. Henkes had begun to speak. Miss Tolerance attended with only half an ear to the familiar words: "the sure and certain hope of the resurrection to eternal life." The greater part of her attention was given to the observation of others in the churchyard. Cook's three neighbors had come; the retired whores had clearly felt their duty done at the church door and had departed. Halfway across the yard, a tall man in a dusty black greatcoat watched from behind a monument; she could not discern if he was a participant in the burial, a mourner, or simply a curious bystander.

Once the business in the churchyard was concluded and the sexton and gravedigger had stepped forward to conclude the last business of the burial, Miss Tolerance and Marianne took Mrs. Gordon away for tea.

In a small confectioners' shop off Bond Street, the three women had a desultory and somber meal, although Miss Tolerance noted that Cook could not refrain from taking professional notice of the scones and jam they were served.

They spoke first of Mrs. Pouter and then touched upon Cook's plans for the future, a subject she addressed quite literally.

"There's dinner to be got, and that Jess can't do it all on her own. Not for so many and to Ma'am's standard."

Marianne protested that assistance had already been retained in the matter of that night's collation. "We thought that after today's events you might prefer—"

"To sit about doing naught and dwelling on what's happened? Bless your dear heart, Miss Marianne, and Ma'am's as well, but work's the tonic I need, so you can go un-retain them assistants. Nor I won't want Jess giving 'erself airs that she's in charge of my kitchen."

But when the party arrived back in Manchester Square and Mrs. Gordon made to return to her fiefdom in the kitchen, she was intercepted by Keefe, who told her that Mrs. Brereton required her presence upstairs. Cook looked from Marianne to Miss Tolerance with an expression eloquent of panic. "Ma'am wants to see *me*?"

"She likely wishes to condole with you in person," Miss Tolerance said reassuringly. She took Cook's arm. "Come, I'll go up with you."

Cook was not used to climbing the three flights from the servants' hall to Mrs. Brereton's rooms, and the back stairs were steep and narrow. But no one who had seen her beating cream to a fine soft peak could be surprised that she attacked the stairs with energy. When she reached the second floor she was red of face, but after a moment to settle her bonnet and catch her breath, Cook straightened her shoulders and went forward.

Mrs. Brereton was at her table with a substantial tea set before her. She wore a dressing gown so lavishly laced that it might have been mistaken for a court dress, and a matching cap, and looked very much her usual self. The minute Cook entered the room she rose and extended her hands.

"My dear Mrs. Gordon, please let me offer you my utmost sympathy and a glass of wine."

"Wine?" Cook appeared flustered. "I should be—"

"You should be here and nowhere else." Mrs. Brereton's tone was firm but kind. "Now, sit. Sarah, if you would like to stay, please ask Frost to bring another glass. As you see, I have a great deal of food to eat, and there is no way I can finish it myself."

Miss Tolerance watched with no little awe as her aunt drew Cook in, helped her take off her bonnet and pelisse, and sat her down at the table. Mrs. Brereton was not, in her niece's estimation, a motherly or comforting woman; her kindness was more usually acerbic and impatient. But she was all patience now, and under her care, Cook relaxed and drank first one glass of madeira and then another, and ate several of the dainty cakes that were on offer without pausing to decide whether she could have made them better. After a time Miss Tolerance, heeding an unspoken directive from her aunt, rose to go.

When she looked back from the doorway Mrs. Brereton had seated herself beside the cook, and the other woman was weeping into the expensive lace of her employer's robe and being comforted with pats and a murmured "I know, I know, my dear."

Chapter Eight

Paradise Row, in Bethnal Green, was a modern road that faced upon the Green itself. Terraced houses of brick and stone, quite new, looked out upon a pretty park with a small pond at the northern end. It was a pleasant neighborhood, not far removed from the days when it had been farmland, and had about it an air of prosperity. Miss Tolerance imagined that doctors, lawyers, Naval officers, merchants, and other worthies lived here for the salubrious air and proximity to the excitement of the city

She left her hackney carriage at the foot of the street and walked toward her object, number 7, enjoying the sunshine which cut a little into the sharp chill of the October morning. Across the street, a cluster of nursery maids and children were making their way into the park; once their clamor had diminished, the street was as quiet as a country lane, and Miss Tolerance the only person in it. Number 7 was a neat brick house of three stories, the windows freshly picked out in white paint, the door green, with a polished knocker in the whimsical shape of a hedgehog.

Before she could avail herself of the knocker the door was flung open by a boy of perhaps ten years, fair-haired and snub-nosed. Miss Tolerance assumed, from his lack of livery and formality, that he was a member of the family rather than a servant. He had an armful of books and appeared much surprised to find someone on the other side of the door.

"Oh! I beg your pardon!"

"I beg yours," Miss Tolerance said. "Does Mrs. Jane Pilgrim live here?"

Without answering her the boy turned and bawled into the interior house, "Aunt Jane! There's a caller here for you!" Then, with easy cordiality and no ceremony whatsoever, he turned back to invite Miss Tolerance in. "Come sit in the parlor," he suggested. "I'm sure my aunt will be down directly."

He saw her seated and excused himself, saying something about the parson's dictionary. She was left alone.

The room to which she had been directed was square and light; a white fireplace stood opposite the door and a small pianoforte in the corner had been placed more for use than display. Miss Tolerance was favorably impressed; the chairs were pretty without being fussy, and the sofa on which she sat was comfortable. She had considerable time to examine the comforts of the room, for she sat, unattended, for some time: if the timepiece that stood upon the mantel was to be believed, more than a quarter hour. When she was discovered, it was by a buxom woman in a blue stuff gown and pretty cap who bustled past the open door, stopped, and returned to peer in. She recoiled as if genuinely startled to find someone there.

"Mrs. Pilgrim?" Miss Tolerance rose and curtseyed.

"I? No, that's my sister. I did not realize that Jane had a visitor." If the woman wondered how a stranger came to be sitting in her parlor, she did not speak the words aloud.

"I am sorry to have startled you, ma'am. A young man let me in and called for Mrs. Pilgrim, but she has not come."

The other woman closed her eyes and shook her head, as if all were become clear to her. "Martin. I am so sorry. I'm afraid that my son has more enthusiasm than propriety. I am Mrs. Pilgrim's sister, Mrs. Graham."

"And I am Miss Tolerance, and was hoping to have a few minutes of conversation with Mrs. Pilgrim, if she is in."

"Of course, of course." Mrs. Graham nodded. "And she did not hear, I am sure. I shall fetch her at once." She left the room with much the same energetic enthusiasm as young Martin had shown.

A few minutes later, Miss Tolerance heard a rustling in the hallway and a murmured exchange, then a different woman entered. She was tall and handsomely made, with light brown hair contained in a cap of lace and fine lawn. Her dress was as simple as her sister's, but more subtly tailored. Her face was rounded, her features delicate, her eyes a pale blue; she might have given an impression of docility had her expression not been vigorously intelligent. She certainly had no look about her of a retired courtesan. Miss Tolerance thought that this was a woman she would like to know.

"You wished to speak to me?"

Miss Tolerance rose; the two women exchanged curtsies.

"Thank you for seeing me, Mrs. Pilgrim."

As Miss Tolerance spoke the words, Mrs. Pilgrim raised a small black ear-trumpet to her left ear. "I beg your pardon. I am a little hard of hearing. To whom do I have the honor of speaking?"

"I am Miss Tolerance. I beg you will forgive a stranger intruding upon you with neither notice nor ceremony, but I have several questions to put to you to which I very much desire answers."

"This is very mysterious. Why do you believe I would know the answers you seek? Do please sit down, Mrs. Tolerance."

"Miss."

"Sit, *Miss* Tolerance, and tell me what brings you to me."

"Thank you. I realize how unusual it is for a stranger to

apply at your door without introduction, but I have been endeavoring, on behalf of a friend, to locate someone. I was told at Child's Bank that you might be able to help me. Do you remember meeting a woman at the bank to whom you recommended an investment?"

The look on Mrs. Pilgrim's face recalled to Miss Tolerance what a peculiar question she was asking. "A woman at Child's?"

"Yes. It was quite two years ago, I am afraid. The woman's name was Annie Pouter. The gentleman at Child's was quite certain that it was you who spoke to her about a Mr. Marvell."

Mrs. Pilgrim's brows drew together thoughtfully. "Annie Pouter. Is it she you wish to find? I take it by her name that she is—" Mrs. Pilgrim paused delicately.

"Fallen? She was. Now she is dead."

"Dead!" Mrs. Pilgrim's eyes widened. "Bless my soul." She put her fingers to her lips as if to contain her shock. After a moment of silence, "Mrs. Pouter. Was she a little woman, somewhat struck in years?"

"You remember her?"

"I do. She and I fell into a conversation about annuities."

"And you recommended Mr. Marvell to her?"

"I beg your pardon?" The ear trumpet came up.

Miss Tolerance repeated herself. "Mr. Marvell. It is he I am seeking, ma'am."

"Yes, Mr. Marvell. A very talented man with money—but surely he can be found in his office? Why do you not seek him there?"

"Where was that office, ma'am?"

"Oh, in Bruton Street. I remember because there is a tea-seller nearby that I particularly like."

"He has not been in the Bruton Street lodgings for some time," Miss Tolerance said. "Nor have I been able to find where he removed to."

Mrs. Pilgrim shook her head. "That is very strange."

"How is it that you were not aware of it? You strike me as too sensible a woman to leave money with a man whose whereabouts you do not know."

"Leave money—Oh, but Mr. Marvell no longer has my funds, nor has for more than a year. When I took the lease on this house, it necessitated that I withdraw my money from his fund."

Miss Tolerance's heart fell. "Did you, ma'am? And when was that?"

"A year in December."

"And you have had no contact with Mr. Marvell since that time?"

Mrs. Pilgrim's eyes were on Miss Tolerance's lips as she spoke. "None," she said at last. "I am very sorry I cannot help you."

Miss Tolerance had arrived believing that Mrs. Pilgrim must be a confederate of Marvell's, but she now had to consider that perhaps she had been a prospective victim who had the luck to escape in time. Still, "Mrs. Pilgrim, Mrs. Pouter gave me your name as Brown. It was only by great luck that the man at Child's was able to identify you by your right name. Can you explain why you gave her a false one?"

Mrs. Pilgrim colored. "You met the late Mrs. Pouter, I apprehend?"

"I did, ma'am."

"I dislike to speak ill of anyone, Miss Tolerance, but in a few minutes' conversation with Mrs. Pouter, she struck me as a... as an encroaching sort of person. I was happy to do her a good turn by directing her to Mr. Marvell, but I did not want —" Mrs. Pilgrim's blush deepened.

"You did not want to find her on your doorstep," Miss Tolerance finished. She thought of Mrs. Pouter and her insinuating, needy manner, and acknowledged to herself that the other woman's assessment was not far wrong.

Mrs. Pilgrim, hands in her lap, fidgeted with her ear trumpet. "Miss Tolerance, I hope you will understand. I was widowed young, and there are certain... prejudices which society can bring to bear upon a young woman living without the protection of a husband. Any appearance of transgression, keeping the wrong sort of company—it might affect my sister and her son, as well—"

"I do understand."

Mrs. Pilgrim's eyes were lowered, and it seemed she had not heard her guest. After a few minutes of awkward silence, "So you are hoping to find Mr. Marvell, Miss Tolerance? I am heartily sorry that I cannot help you."

"I appreciate your kindness. There are still a few other questions I would like to put to you, if you will permit me. Are you acquainted with a Mrs. Mehetibel White?"

"No." The answer was unequivocable but delivered without force.

"Or a Mrs. Arabella Black?"

"Again, I am not. Ought I to be?"

"They were both given by Mr. Marvell as references for his fund. I regret that Mrs. Black died several months ago." If Miss Tolerance had hoped for a tell-tale response to this revelation, she was disappointed. "Mr. Marvell gave Mrs. Pouter their names as reference; she spoke directly to Mrs. Black, and wrote to Mrs. White, from whom she received a letter of endorsement. However, Mrs. White says—and offered proof—that she did not write or send the letter that Mrs. Pouter received."

Mrs. Pilgrim had returned the ear trumpet to her ear and watched Miss Tolerance's lips carefully as she repeated what she had said.

"Did not send the letter? How is that possible? Who else would have done so?"

"That is one of the several questions I am attempting to answer, ma'am."

"But I thought you were looking for Mr. Marvell."

"I am indeed—but as he is not in Bruton Street, I sought out the people who recommended him in hopes that someone would know his whereabouts. It is a curious thing that a letter writ endorsing Marvell and purporting to come from Mrs. White was not written in her hand."

Mrs. Pilgrim looked uncomprehending.

"Ma'am, if, as it seems to be the case that Mrs. White did not know Marvell and did not write the letter, perhaps the person who did write it can be persuaded to tell me where to find him."

"Ah." The woman toyed with her ear trumpet. "I understand. It is clearly a very vexing business. Still, I cannot think how I can be of assistance to you."

"I will be frank and say that this case is tied in as many knots as a bonnet string. But you might do a favor for me if you would."

"If it will serve to assist you, ask anything of me, Miss Tolerance."

"May I ask for a sample of your handwriting, ma'am?"

"My handwriting?" Mrs. Pilgrim appeared baffled. "What good will that do you?"

"The letter written to Mrs. Pouter, supposedly by Mrs. White, was not in her fist. I think I must talk with her again, and it would be useful to be able to show her that the letter was not written by the only other person I've found among Marvell's acquaintance who is still living."

Mrs. Pilgrim considered, then rose from her chair. "I will give you something at once." She rose to fetch a plain writing case of white-painted wood from a bookcase, took out paper, pen, and inkwell, and in a matter of a few seconds had written several lines. "Here." She proffered the paper to Miss Tolerance.

"Excellent. Ma'am, I cannot thank you enough for your help." Miss Tolerance fanned the paper a few times to make certain that the ink had dried and folded it away in her reticule. "I must not take up any more of your time." She got to her feet.

"If I can provide any help, Miss Tolerance, I hope you will call on me."

Miss Tolerance looked about the quiet, sunny room and felt loath to disturb its comfort any further. "I am hopeful that I will not need to, Mrs. Pilgrim." She curtsied.

Mrs. Pilgrim returned the courtesy and led the way to the front door. "Goodbye, Miss Tolerance. Godspeed."

I t took Miss Tolerance some time, in this quiet neighborhood, to find a hackney carriage to carry her back to Manchester Square. As the carriage wheeled toward the center of London, she laid out the contradictions in her inquiry as she knew them. Mrs. White had assured her that she knew neither Mrs. Pouter or Mr. Marvell, and she had demonstrably *not* written the letter that had purported to come from her. However, Mrs. White was to Miss Tolerance's mind the sort of woman who might lie if it suited her purpose.

Mrs. Pilgrim—here Miss Tolerance had to make an effort to untangle her own instinctive liking for the woman from her judgement regarding her trustworthiness. She had gone to Bethnal Green believing that Mrs. Pilgrim, like the other women in this case, had been a courtesan. Instead, she appeared to be a young widow living respectably with members of her family. Her link to Mrs. Pouter was only through a chance meeting at Child's Bank.

How to proceed from this point? *Could* she proceed from this point?

When the carriage had deposited her in Spanish Place Miss Tolerance went at once to her cottage and opened the paper Mrs. Pilgrim had written for her. She was amused to see that the woman had taken the First Psalm for her text: *Blessed is the man that walketh not in the counsel of the ungodly, nor standeth in the way of sinners, nor sitteth in the seat of the scornful.*

"Blessed, perhaps, but not very useful," she murmured. "I must discern which of you is walking in step with the wicked." She took the paper Mrs. Pilgrim had given her, Mrs. White's brief note, and Mrs. Pouter's letter, and laid them side-by-side.

All three appeared to have been written by different hands.

For a long moment, Miss Tolerance was overcome by the impulse to wash her hands of the whole business. She had no client; her expenses would be borne by no one but herself, and the injured party was beyond having her loss made good. Why continue? Yet, it was good to have a use for her time and energy until paying work came her way.

She folded the three papers and put them away. Her client had been murdered; finding Marvell was the only way she could begin to assist in seeing the killer brought to justice. And doing that would remove one more hazard to the elderly and credulous of London's *demimonde.*

She locked her cottage door and went out again, bound this time for Lisson Grove and Mrs. Mehetibel White's cottage.

The sky, which had been bright and full of scudding clouds when she left Manchester Square, was gray and lowering when she stepped from her carriage in Lisson Grove. It had not been easy to find a carriage to hire at the finish of her last conversation with Mrs. White; mindful of this, Miss Tolerance instructed the driver to wait for her and went to knock upon Mrs. White's door.

Again the door was opened by the woman herself, dressed

today in a creamy muslin gown with a plaid shawl clutched across her shoulders. Her reddish hair, shot with gray, was pinned up off her face, uncovered by a cap.

"Aye? Oh, are you here to call again?" The old woman appeared as pleased to see Miss Tolerance as she had been on her first visit. "Come in from the chill, my dear, and take something warming." She took Miss Tolerance's arm and brought her into the parlor. "Now, sit. Would you take tea, or something stronger? There's a bite in the air."

Miss Tolerance read her demeanor and requested wine, if that was quite convenient. The old woman smiled with pleasure.

"I've just the thing. If ye'll let me catch the fire, we'll be cozy in no time." For a few minutes, Mrs. White bustled, lighting the previously-laid fire and fanning it until it caught, then departing the room to return with a tray, a bottle, and two glasses. "I rarely have the excuse of a visitor."

She poured Miss Tolerance a glass and one for herself, and sniffed at the wine appreciatively before taking a sip. Miss Tolerance raised her own glass and was surprised to find not a sweet, homemade wine or a light claret but a good, strong Burgundy. She drank a little with appreciation.

"Well, now." Mrs. White had drunk half her glass and sat in an attitude of attention. "How can I be of help today, dearie?"

Miss Tolerance put her own glass aside. "The last time I visited, ma'am, you were so good as to tell me that both a Mrs. Black and Mr. Marvell were unknown to you."

"So they were and so they are," Mrs. White said firmly.

"I wonder, ma'am, if a Mrs. Brown is also a stranger to you?"

"Brown? I used to know a Maisie Brown when I was a girl in Ayr, but that was long ago, dearie."

"Mrs. Brown is an alias taken by a Jane Pilgrim, ma'am."

The old woman cackled. "Pilgrim! That's a name as bad

as yer own! Is this the fashion, these days, to take a name that makes ye sound as temptin' as an old boot?"

Miss Tolerance shook her head. "I do not believe Mrs. Pilgrim to be Fallen, Mrs. White, but only a widow. There must have been a Mr. Pilgrim at some time."

"Well, either I've lost my head to a good wine—which I *don't* think—or I'm at a loss to understand why ye've visited today. D'ye mean to ask me if I'm acquainted with every person in the city? Some I am, more I am not."

Miss Tolerance took another sip of the Burgundy and put her glass down. "You have told me you do not know Mr. Marvell, the late Mrs. Black, or Mrs. Pouter, and now, Mrs. Pilgrim-Brown. Yet Mrs. Pouter had a letter that purported to come from you—which I know you did not write," she added, to forestall any protest from Mrs. White. "But Mrs. Pilgrim did not write it either, as you see." She took Mrs. Pilgrim's note from her reticule and spread it, and the original note that purported to come from Mrs. Brown, together.

"So neither this Mrs. Pilgrim nor I wrote the letter, and as for Mrs. Brown—" Mrs. White's expression of twinkling cheer faded. "I don't know aught of either of them. If they say else, they're lying."

"It is a puzzle," Miss Tolerance said. "And it appears, at the very best, that someone is mistaken. To sum the matter up, you have never met Mrs. Pilgrim, and neither Mr. Marvell nor the late Mrs. Pouter are known to you."

"The late!" This news seemed to distract Mrs. White from her dismay. "She's deid, then?"

"I am sorry to say that she is," Miss Tolerance agreed. "Murdered. The finding of Mr. Marvell has become even more imperative, ma'am."

"Murthered." Mrs. White went as pale as the muslin of her gown, then, with effort, she attempted to regain her poise. "But there's nothing new in an old whore bein' done to death, is there? Why d'ye believe the one thing has aught to do wi' the other?"

"Mrs. Pouter was murdered after I began to inquire into Mr. Marvell's whereabouts; some months before that, at least one other woman died after making similar inquiries. Until I learn otherwise, I must regard the two events as linked."

Mrs. White nodded, but cautioned, "I'd fear for mysel' if I was you, lassie."

Miss Tolerance smiled thinly. "I am careful, ma'am. I am well aware that prodding a hidden monster is a dangerous pastime."

"An' is he a monster?"

"Someone who kills an elderly woman—whatever her past occupation—sounds monstrous to me, Mrs. White."

"And ye've brought all this to my door. Am I to thank ye' for it?"

"I am sorry to have done so. When I began this matter, I had no idea that any danger attached to it. Now I think that the only way to restore matters is to find the person who killed Mrs. Pouter. And for that, I must find this Marvell. May I ask you one last question, Mrs. White?"

The other woman nodded, but she toyed with the fabric of her gown at her knee, as if to discharge anxiety the conversation had raised.

"I know that you did not write the letter that Mrs. Pouter received. But she sent a letter to this address, in your name. Did you receive it?"

Mrs. White pursed her lips. "I canna remember it."

"Please, ma'am. Answer this one question and I will leave in peace. Surely such a letter would have surprised you, coming unexpected as it would have done."

Mrs. White took a deep breath. "I might have, once or twice, received letters from persons I did not know, written about I knew not what. I might even have got a letter from your Mrs. Pouter, but I swear I have no memory of it."

Miss Tolerance felt a pulse of excitement. "Do you have any of those letters, ma'am?"

"No, I used them for kindlin'." The old woman spoke irritably. "What was I to make of a stranger writing to me by name, speaking of things I'd never heard of? I thought someone mistook me for another Mrs. White—the name ain't unco'."

"No, it is not, ma'am." Miss Tolerance had a moment of inspiration. "I am sorry to hear that you destroyed those letters; they might have had some value, had I only been able to put my hands on them."

"Value?" Head down, Mrs. White looked upward through her eyelashes as if she had no particular interest in the answer.

"Perhaps, ma'am. They would bring me closer to untangling this puzzle, you see. Well," Miss Tolerance arose and took up her reticule. "Thank you so much for your time. And your excellent wine." She curtseyed. "Please do not bother to see me out."

Something had changed in Mrs. White's demeanor at the suggestion that the letters she had received might have value. She could not magically reconstitute them from ashes; she would need at least enough time to miraculously discover them.

Regretting she had not found the lever that would loosen the old woman's tongue immediately, Miss Tolerance said "If you do think of anything you believe might be useful, I can always be reached at Tarsio's Club in Henry Street."

"Tarsio's Club in Henry Street," Mrs. White repeated. Then, with energy, she bounced to her feet. "Well, I'll walk out wi' you, regardless. I've an errand to do at the end of the street. If ye'll be kind enough to wait for a moment?" She banked the fire quickly. "Now, my bonnet."

A few minutes later, as they stepped from the house, Miss Tolerance suggested that an umbrella or rain shield might be of use.

"If it rains, what of it?" Mrs. White pulled her shawl tight to her throat. "I've had worse done to me than a little water."

Privily Miss Tolerance thought that a woman of Mrs. White's years should have respect for the hazard that a good soaking represented on a cold day, but she said nothing. They walked toward the cluster of shops visible ahead on Great Quebeck Street, where Miss Tolerance's hired carriage awaited her.

"Well, here's me," Mrs. White said when they drew even with the door of an apothecary shop. "If I think of anything more, I'll write you at—what was it?"

"Tarsio's in Henry Street, ma'am."

The older woman nodded. "In the meanwhile, I'll wish ye well."

Miss Tolerance bowed; Mrs. White bowed in return, and Miss Tolerance went on to her carriage.

By one of the coincidences of the London Streets, the first street down which her driver turned was blocked at its end by the collision of two wagons; one was full of gilded furniture under half-fallen canvas covers, the other of crates of poultry, and the noise and chaos were considerable. With no consideration for the respectable sensibilities of the neighborhood, the two carters were swearing furiously at each other and making no attempt to untangle their wagons. After briefly adding his own invective to that of the waggoners, Miss Tolerance's coachman leaned down to instruct his passenger to hold tight. "I'm going to 'ave to back the rig down the road."

Such a procedure is generally best performed by at least two people, but for once Miss Tolerance did not offer to assist. It had begun to rain in earnest, and after all, was she not paying the driver to deal with just this sort of inconvenience?

It took some minutes before the carriage had emerged back on Great Quebeck Street. Just ahead of the carriage,

Miss Tolerance could see Mrs. White, who had apparently finished her business in the time it took to turn the carriage around and was trudging in the downpour, her shawl pulled up over her bonnet.

As Miss Tolerance watched, Mrs. White arrived on her own doorstep and reached for the latch of her door—only to have the door swing open before her and a man's arm extend to pull the old woman roughly into the house.

Muttering a curse, Miss Tolerance rapped on the carriage roof, demanding the driver stop. It took a moment before the man heard, then another before the carriage drew up. Before the driver could descend to help her down, Miss Tolerance had leapt from the carriage—a clumsy business in petticoats and half-boots—and began to run for the cottage, calling over her shoulder to make certain the driver would wait for her.

The door to Mrs. White's cottage stood open, and the rain had already soaked the rag rug at the doorsill.

"Mrs. White?" Miss Tolerance called as loudly as she could, hoping that volume would discourage assailants; she was no elderly woman, and she was accustomed to the hazards of her profession, but she was unarmed and saw no reason to confront a stranger if she could scare him away. "Mrs. White?"

There was a small, animal sound from further down the hall, then a crash and the sound of breaking glass. Miss Tolerance reached the parlor to find Mrs. White prostrate upon the sofa, arms splayed, unconscious, a ring of bruises already empurpling her throat. A flicker of light made Miss Tolerance turn to see that the fire had been stirred ablaze and coals scattered by the curtains. One lacy curtain had already caught fire.

Miss Tolerance raised Mrs. White almost to standing and dragged her from the room, then from the house, and finally to the door of her waiting carriage.

"Put her in and keep her there," she instructed her driver brusquely.

Miss Tolerance ran back to the house. By now one curtain had catched another, and the parlor was full of dancing orange light and smoky haze. She laid hands upon the fire shovel and used it to paw the burning drapes to the ground, beat the flame out, then tried to push and sweep the live embers back toward the fireplace hearth. Too late, she realized that a tasseled pillow had also catched and fire was spreading, fingers of orange flame dancing upward.

She abandoned her attempt to extinguish the fire on her own and ran from the house.

People from the houses nearby had emerged onto the street with buckets of water, heedless of the rain that served to douse them all but as yet had no effect upon the fire. Grateful, and coughing grittily, Miss Tolerance stood back and let them work.

"You awright, miss?" The driver of her hired carriage was sitting inside his vehicle, attention divided between the burning house and his unconscious passenger.

"I'll do, thank you. What about the old woman?"

"She's alive, but someone like to choke the daylights from 'er. If she was *my* ol' mother, I'd 'ave a doctor to physic 'er."

"She is not—" Miss Tolerance abandoned explanation. "You're quite right." She cast a look at Mrs. White's house, where the crowd had evidently vanquished the fire and was now dispersing. After a moment, she called to the nearest man, hoping that his sober mien meant an equal probity.

"Sir, can you direct me to a doctor? Mrs. White is overcome."

"The woman who lives here? I don't know who usually physics her, but Doctor Broadax in Bell Street saw to my Jemmy when he had the flux—"

"Thank you. And may we rely upon you to see that Mrs. White's home is shut up well?"

He agreed that he would do so. "She won't want to come home and find some Jack a' Legs has done a job on her movables. My name's Polley. I live in the next house but one. When you're done with the doctor you apply to me and I'll see your—" he paused expectantly.

"My aunt," Miss Tolerance supplied. She had gained a number of aunts in this fashion.

"I'll see your aunt back in her house again."

The carriage driver, who was now comporting himself more like a retainer of some duration than a man hired for the afternoon, handed Miss Tolerance into the carriage, climbed up to his rain-sodden seat, and started his team toward Bell Street.

Mrs. White was alive, but in what Dr. Broadax termed a state of "stubborn unconsciousness." When he pinched her arm, she flinched, but no amount of calling her name seemed to rouse her, nor the deployment of a vinaigrette, and the doctor admitted that he was concerned that the throttling she had suffered would cause a swelling in her neck that might stop her breathing entirely.

"She must be kept warm and safe until she regains consciousness." He was a tall, stocky man with a pair of spectacles perched crookedly upon his nose, which he several times took off and wiped with a kerchief. His manner was professionally grave.

Miss Tolerance considered. She did not want to return Mrs. White to her house; attacked once, she could be attacked again. Nor did she want to bring the old woman to her cottage; Mrs. Brereton's household had already had one dead elderly impure delivered there, another in a state of coma would try Mrs. Brereton's patience. What to do with the woman? After a moment she took Dr. Broadax into her confidence—after a fashion. Sooty and rain-soaked, she was well aware that she did not present a reliable appearance, but she threw herself upon his kindness.

"I am at a loss to know what to do, sir. There was a fire at her house, started by the same villain who did this to her—" she stopped to gesture at Mrs. White's throat. "I do not believe it is safe to return her there."

"Has she no friends or family?" The doctor looked meaningfully at Miss Tolerance, who scrambled for a story that would both satisfy the doctor and put an end to further questions.

"I am a schoolroom teacher for a family in the city, sir. I cannot bring her there, it would be the end of my employment did I attempt it. If there was an inn nearby—"

Doctor Broadax sighed meatily. "We have a room where she may rest—only until she wakes and can make her own plans, mind. And neither my wife nor I will be able to wait upon her."

Miss Tolerance seized upon the suggestion eagerly. "If you will permit it, sir, I can do so. I will arrange to take a day from my duties. You think she will not stay long in this condition?"

Broadax shook his head. "She is old, and given the insult she has suffered, I cannot say how long it might take for her to awaken—or if she will do so." He was not encouraging, nor particularly pleased with their plan. His wife, when informed of it, was even less delighted. A compromise, Miss Tolerance reflected as Mrs. White was settled in the doctor's spare room, by its nature leaves no one happy.

Chapter Nine

Miss Tolerance wrote a note to Marianne Touchwell explaining her absence, paid her much-enduring carriage driver to deliver it, and settled herself in as nurse to Mrs. White. The Broadax's spare room was prettily appointed but small and airless. The only seat available was a ladderback chair with a thin cushion. Mrs. Broadax, having given permission for the invasion of her household, appeared to have decided to do the thing as well as possible; she sent up tea and a light meal for Miss Tolerance, and begged her visitor to ask for anything else that might be needful. Miss Tolerance in turn thanked her very sincerely and resolved to ask as little of the Broadaxes as possible.

In truth, she required nothing. Mrs. White lay as one sleeping; only the stirring of the folds of her gown as she breathed gave any sign that she was alive. She did not stir unless in response to a touch but at least, Miss Tolerance thought, there were no particularly ominous signs to be concerned with. It was likely to be an uncomfortable but uneventful night. She saw several books on a dresser by the window, one a novel and two, poetry. Miss Tolerance chose the novel, turned up the oil lamp Mrs. Broadax had provided, and began to read.

It took no great time for her to doze. She was awakened in near darkness by a dreadful noise from the bed. Mrs. White's eyes were open, her back arched and rigid, and she was scrabbling at her throat with both hands.

"Mrs. White! Be calm, you are quite safe!" Miss Tolerance took both the woman's hands in her own, sustaining several scratches as she did so. "No one will harm you. Please be calm."

At last, the old woman relaxed into the bed, and her breathing, while labored, ceased to be accompanied by the awful rattling sound. She moaned a little. Miss Tolerance smoothed the faded red hair from the old woman's brow.

"You are quite safe," she said again. "You are in the house of a doctor. We brought you here after you were attacked."

Mrs. White's gaze darted around the shadowy room; she attempted to speak, but the sounds made no sense.

"Rest," Miss Tolerance urged. It took considerable self-restraint to do so, as her desire to ask questions was powerful. "You may tell us all in the morning."

The old woman stared into Miss Tolerance's eyes as if it were possible to convey information by such means. Then she slept, and Miss Tolerance did so as well.

In the morning, Mrs. White took some thin gruel, which was all her bruised and swollen throat could manage, and a good quantity of weak tea, generously sugared. The irritation in the old woman's throat had begun to subside, and she was able to speak, although with considerable distress.

Doctor Broadax assessed the state of the patient, appearing when Mrs. White was attempting to question Miss Tolerance on the events of the day before. Her speech was labored, not so much because of the rawness of her throat, but because of a curious, frustrating inability to find the words she sought. "Was she struck upon the head?" the doctor asked Miss Tolerance, as if Mrs. White were not lying propped upon the bed only an arm's length away.

"I do not think so, but I am not certain of it." Miss Tolerance wondered why the doctor, who had examined his patient thoroughly the night before, could not say with more certainty than herself. "Ma'am, were you struck on the head?"

Mrs. White shook her head in the negative and gestured with both hands at her neck. "Hee'r."

"You were struck—no, you were throttled?"

Mrs. White nodded. "Wwh whh whh—" she looked agitatedly from Doctor Broadax to Miss Tolerance. "P-p-peh!"

Doctor Broadax tutted and patted Mrs. White's hand. "You shall have something for the pain, ma'am, but I beg you will not exercise yourself." He turned to Miss Tolerance and the genial expression vanished. "I do not understand why her speech should be affected," he murmured. From his tone, the doctor considered his patient at fault. "She is well recovered, given the state I first saw her in. She can speak and has sustained no other lasting harm."

From the silence that followed this declaration, Miss Tolerance apprehended that Mrs. Broadax had asked her husband to encourage Mrs. White to go elsewhere.

"If you will give me a little time to learn where Mrs. White wishes to be taken, sir, I do not think she will need to make further claims upon your time or your hospitality."

The doctor made a noise of assent and embarrassment, told Mrs. White he was delighted to see her out of her slumber, and left them alone.

Miss Tolerance turned to the invalid. "It was kind of him to permit you to stay here, but I think we must not abuse the hospitality of the house. If you wish to return home—"

Mrs. White shook her head vigorously—and winced as if

the gesture hurt her. Her expression was panicked; she was unmistakably opposed to returning to her home.

"Where else might I take you, ma'am?"

By a long series of questions, nods, halting words, and at last a pencil and paper, Miss Tolerance was able to obtain the name of a friend to whom Mrs. White wished to go, and her direction. She thought it cost the voluble old woman dearly not to be able to chatter as fluidly as she had the day before. She could only counsel patience and more sweet tea.

They departed the Broadaxes' house with many protestations of gratitude and a promise that Mrs. White would settle her account with the doctor as soon as might be. Miss Tolerance sat with Mrs. White in a hired carriage bound for Paddington and her friend. If she did not ask questions now, she might not have the opportunity again.

"Who attacked you, Mrs. White?"

The old woman gestured helplessly.

"You do not know who. Do you know *why*?"

Mrs. White screwed up her mouth with effort. "Pp-p-pa." She shook her head and tried again. "Papapa."

"I do not wish to distress you when you are still recovering, but your best hope of safety is for your assailant to be found and made to answer for what he has done. You did not know him, but there anything particular about him?" She had a moment of inspiration. "Was it a short man?" She repeated Mrs. Pouter's description. "A short, fair-haired man with an odd, flat nose?"

Mrs. White shook her head and raised her hand to indicate a person substantially taller than herself. "Bannnnnk," she said.

Bank. Had not Mrs. Pouter learned of Marvell at Child's Bank? "A man from Child's Bank?"

The old woman shook her head again and slumped against the seat, clearly exhausted. "Pa-pannnn."

Pain. Miss Tolerance was ashamed of pushing so hard. "I am sorry, ma'am. I am asking more of you than I should. When we reach Mrs. Edward's house you may have some of the laudanum draught the doctor prepared, and a rest."

Which bank? What man? She did not ask further questions; it was plain to see that Mrs. White was fragile and exhausted. Miss Tolerance delivered the woman to her friend Mrs. Doughty's house in the Edgware Road, suggested a dose of laudanum and a nap, and promised to see them both soon. Of Mrs. Doughty she asked that if Mrs. White should recall anything helpful, a note would be sent to her. The woman fluttered over her friend and Miss Tolerance returned to Manchester Square.

She celebrated her homecoming with a bath, fresh clothes, and a leisurely scan of the newspapers that had been left on her doorstep. Only one entry in the Dueling Notices, she saw, and nothing else that hinted at the possibility of paying clientele. At last, with reluctance, she took up the slate and chalk she kept for the purpose and began to make notes of what she knew. The notes she had begun a se'ennight before reminded her that she still wished to talk to Mrs. Kent's son.

"I let that poor woman put me off pursuit. That will not do." She put aside the slate, sought her pelisse and bonnet, and left the house to return to the house of Mrs. Kent of Hans Place. She kept a sharp eye out as she entered the carriage Cole had hired for her—the attack on Mrs. White reminded her that two women had died in this business. She had no interest in becoming a third. The weight of her pistol in her reticule was a comfort.

The sky was a bleak, dull white, and the air was damp and cold. Miss Tolerance eyed the lap-robe provided against chill in her hackney carriage; she suspected it would have fleas. The trees in the park that faced Mrs. Kent's home were bare, and the little pond less appealing than ever.

Miss Tolerance rapped at the door and asked the footman —Cates, she recalled—if Mrs. Kent was at home. The man shook his head; Mrs. Kent was making a call elsewhere.

"And is her son with her?"

"Which son, madam?"

Miss Tolerance cursed her own blind stupidity: it had not occurred to her that there might be more than one Mr. Kent. "Mr. George Kent, I believe."

"Ah." A curious expression passed over the footman's face, quickly banished, at the speaking of that name. "Mr. George don't live here. Ain't done for years."

Miss Tolerance pursed her lips. "Can I prevail upon you to tell me where he resides?" She mimed reaching for her pocketbook.

The footman shook his head. "Not without I have instruction to do so from Mrs. Kent, madam."

A reasonable response from a man whose livelihood depended upon his employer, and yet entirely unsatisfactory. Miss Tolerance thanked the man, turned to take her leave, then turned back. "I beg your pardon, may I ask the name of Mr. Kent's brothers?"

"Only the one, and that—" Miss Tolerance realized the maid, Milston, stood well back in the hallway, observing them. Cates swallowed. "I can't say nothing more, madam." He closed the door upon further questions.

It was only an hour or so past noon but the sky was darkening. Miss Tolerance turned toward Sloane Street in search of a carriage. The street was momentarily empty of passers-by; it appeared that the local tradesmen had made their visits earlier in the day. It was precisely the sort of circumstance that created a sense of caution in Miss Tolerance, but she saw no one, and aside from holding her reticule, and the uncharged pistol within it, closer, all she could do was hurry away from the Kent house.

She had not gained Sloane Street when she felt, rather than heard, someone behind her. She had begun to turn when hands closed upon her neck from behind. *Stupid, stupid, all my care for naught.*

Even as she struggled to pull the pistol from her reticule her attacker pressed close from behind, his elbows tight over her own arms, tangling her in a coat that smelled of sweat, rum, and wet wool. He wore leather gloves, cold against the skin of her throat; his thumbs ground into the base of her neck, and the stitching of one glove burst as he tightened his fingers. His flesh was warm against her own and his nail scraped the underside of her jaw. The man at her back was tall and strong.

Tasting coppery blood in her mouth, she twisted, trying to duck out from under her assailant's grasp. His arms tightened. She thought of Mrs. White and Mrs. Pouter and the purple bruises about their necks. Fear gave her new strength: she raised her foot and drove her heel down where she thought his foot must be; she struck only the paving stone. It hurt.

"Try that, will ye? I'll soon teach you manners. You won't be meddling no more." The man's voice was low and gravelly, the accent coarse. Not a Londoner, she thought. Midlands. She felt a shift in his position as her assailant stepped back away from her feet while keeping his arms tight atop her own, so that their two bodies were arranged steeple-like.

She raised her foot again and struck, not down this time, but up and back. She felt her heel connect with his leg, just below the knee.

The man swore, half-fell, and shoved her away. Miss Tolerance flew toward a set of stone steps and landed hard, the air knocked from her. Someone cried out across the street: "Oi, what're you about!"

The arrival of a witness sent her assailant hobbling off at

speed toward Sloane Street. From her position, draped across the steps, Miss Tolerance watched him go. He wore a rusty black greatcoat and an undistinguished low-crowned hat; there was nothing other than his height to identify him.

The man who had cried out—a footman, by his livery— appeared at Miss Tolerance's side and helped her to sit, panting, on the cold step. Her hand still clenched her useless pistol through the fabric of her reticule. After a moment, with her would-be rescuer's assistance, she got to her feet. She thanked the man and waited until he had returned to his house before she swore, low and fluently, and started for Sloane Street again.

When she reached the corner she scanned the passers-by, but there was no sign of the man she sought. Limping from the hurt to her heel, Miss Tolerance hailed a carriage and, just as the first snow of the winter began to fall, gave orders to return to Manchester Square.

Her cottage was cold and it took some time to catch the fire, add a few sticks of wood, and fan it into a satisfactory blaze; even then the warmth extended only a few feet from the fender. Miss Tolerance, stiff with cold and tension, hung away her pelisse and draped a shawl around her shoulders. Then she set the kettle on to boil and sat before the fire, removing her boot and stocking to examine the damage done to her foot. No bone had been broken that she could tell; still, a gentle massaging of her heel made her catch her breath. She sacrificed most of the hot water she had intended for tea to make a poultice of arnica and chamomile, wrapped her foot in a clean rag, and put it up on a cushion. A series of shudders went through her, gradually fading as the warmth of the fire loosed her tight muscles and the tumult in her blood dissipated.

I am alive, she told herself. Then, honestly, *but I could as easily not be*. There was a brassy aftertaste of fear in her mouth. *But what could I do? I cannot walk the streets of London with pistols drawn!* She sank back in her chair and closed her eyes. *I was lucky.*

She fell into an exhausted doze.

"Sarah?"

Miss Tolerance woke in near darkness. Marianne stood in the doorway, round face ruddy with cold and the rosy light of the dying fire.

"Marianne! Come in. What hour is it?" As Miss Tolerance straightened in her chair the bruises consequent upon the attack she had sustained made themselves felt. She took a sharp inward breath.

"T'ain't so late as it looks," Mrs. Touchwell told her. "The snow came on to fall fast. Mrs. B and I were thinking you'd be freezing in here tonight, and I was sent over to invite you to stay in the house."

Miss Tolerance shook her head. "I shall be fine here, thank you. I've weathered the cold here before."

"I never know how. Don't be stupid, Sarah. Do you mean to sleep in front of the fire all night? With no grate upstairs you'll surely wake with icicles on your nose—"

Miss Tolerance laughed, then gasped.

"And you're hurt again. As any idiot could see. Come, Sarah. We'll put you in a room away from all the doings and —what have you done to yourself?" Mrs. Touchwell looked disapprovingly at Miss Tolerance's bandaged foot.

"I stamped my foot like a nursery-child in a tantrum." Miss Tolerance shook her head at the stupidity of the tactic. "I should know: kick back, not down."

Marianne said nothing, but shook her head.

"It *is* cold," Miss Tolerance allowed.

"And looks to be colder still after the sun sets. And you in pain. I'll fetch your nightrobe, shall I?"

Miss Tolerance fully intended to refuse this kindly-meant

concern. But it *was* cold, she *was* hurt, and she could not deny that a night's sleep in Mrs. Brereton's larger, warmer, and better-attended house was not likely to harm her autonomy, but was likely to add to her comfort.

"Thank you." She rose gingerly from her chair, stepped lightly on her foot, and determined she could pull a slipper over the bandaged heel. By the time Mrs. Touchwell had brought a bundle down from the upstairs room, Miss Tolerance had banked the fire, taken up her workbag, wrapped a second shawl about her shoulders for the brief trip across to Mrs. Brereton's house, and was ready to depart. Mrs. Touchwell saw her into the house and up to a room she had used before, on the floor above her aunt's apartments.

"Mrs. B asks you to dine, if that's quite convenient." She stopped in the doorway. "What shall I say?"

"I haven't a dress—" Miss Tolerance began, but stopped at the sight of her friend's smile. "You brought one with my nightrobe?"

"Aye. Put that foot up again, Sarah. I'll send a maid to help you dress."

Mrs. Brereton was in an acerbic mood, although she forebore to mention her niece's limp. She and Miss Tolerance amused themselves for a while by reading bits from the day's newspapers aloud; Mrs. Brereton followed politics avidly, and in particular enjoyed reading accounts of the same events as they appeared in both the Tory and Whig papers, the better to inveigh upon the disingenuousness of the Tories and the fecklessness of the Whigs.

"Do you love no one, aunt?"

"Love? I partake of a liberal sensibility, I think, but that does not mean I am not fully alive to the lollypoops among my party. At least, the Tories show some enterprise in their venality—"

Miss Tolerance scoffed. "Such praise."

"In my youth, Sarah, it was all different. This stupid, endless war draws everyone's attention—Tory and Whig alike—away from the situation here at home. When poor Fox was with us—" Miss Tolerance had heard her aunt's anecdotes about Charles Fox and frankly did not pay close attention to what followed, until she realized that Mrs. Brereton was awaiting a response.

"I beg pardon, Aunt?"

"I asked how you came to injure yourself this time, Sarah. Surely you did not think to keep it a secret."

"Injure?" It took her a moment to recall the damage. "My foot? Oh, I stepped down too hard coming out of a carriage—"

"That won't wash." Mrs. Brereton shook her head. "In a full lifetime of stepping into and out of carriages, *I* have never injured myself so that it required arnica and wrapping to mend it. You were hurt; you might as well tell me how."

"I did not want to bring my problems into your parlor, Aunt Thea. I stomped on a man's foot—and missed and hit a cobblestone. I shall be entirely recovered by tomorrow."

"Stomping on a man's foot is a necessary part of the business in your trade? What is it now? Has the Prince sent you to find loose diamonds, or a dowager dispatched you to retrieve her erring son from the stews?"

"Neither one. I'm still trying to sort Mrs. Pouter's business."

Mrs. Brereton put down the newspaper she had been holding. "Surely that is over. The poor woman is in her grave, and I'll be sworn she left nothing to pay you with—"

Miss Tolerance smiled. "I have no other inquiries at present. And I promised Mrs. Gordon—"

"Is *Laurie Gordon* paying you to continue?"

"No, ma'am. But I could not tell her that I would not seek to find who had murdered her sweetheart."

Mrs. Brereton pursed her lips. "Sentiment. For the love of heaven, Sarah, why are you pursuing an inquiry which results in injury for you, for a client who can neither pay you nor—nor thank you? It makes no sense."

"Did it make sense that this house bore the expense of burying Mrs. Pouter? Or that you spent an hour comforting Mrs. Gordon in her loss?"

"An entirely different matter. Mrs. Gordon has worked in this house for nearly as long as I have owned it, and Mrs. Pouter, for some years, worked here as well. But neither has any claim upon you—"

"The claim of kindness, aunt. Mrs. Gordon has never failed to act kindly toward me. And the claim of sympathy, for a woman as lost as you or I, who had bad judgment and worse luck. It might have been me, or you, or any of the women downstairs doing the work of this house."

"But what do you *gain*?"

"Gain? In coin, nothing. Unless you wish to pay my fee, aunt?" Miss Tolerance raised an eyebrow. "No, I thought not. Some gains are simply for the soul, not the purse. And here," she observed with a considerable feeling of relief, "is our dinner."

Cook, under the ongoing impression that Mrs. Brereton's invalid state required feeding up, had provided more food than two women might reasonably be supposed to consume. What was left over from the hare roasted with apples and the pigeon and onion pie would, Miss Tolerance knew, make up the servants' supper or be turned into some savory which would tomorrow grace the buffet table in the salon downstairs.

"What I do not understand is how this Marvell thought he could manage to get woman after woman to participate in the fund if he had no intention of paying them."

"Were all of his clients retired?" Mrs. Brereton asked. "He might have hoped they'd die swiftly." At Miss Tolerance's reaction, "'Tis not an unreasonable thought—if you don't know how early some girls are forced out of the game or tire or sicken." The older woman took a sip of wine and, after a moment, pushed her plate from her with a gesture of finality. "You are too young to remember the Fordyce affair—"

"I beg your pardon, Aunt: the what?"

"Oh, I was little more than a child myself. A banker named Fordyce ran off to Europe to escape his debts, and caused a rush—no, a run—first on his bank and then on many others."

"A run?" It was not a term familiar to Miss Tolerance.

"All the bank's depositors descending at once to withdraw their funds." Mrs. Brereton gave a dry chuckle. "My father— your grandfather, Sarah—sat at the breakfast table with the London papers, talking of how the world was coming to an end, what with people rushing the banks to demand their money."

"But if it was only Fordyce's bank which was involved, how could this affect the other banks?"

"My dear, as near as I have been able to fathom it, the greater world of finance is all a fiction based upon trust and confidence. So long as no one examines it too closely, it works. But let one investor lose faith and the others panic. It isn't the banks that go bad, Sarah, but the investors."

Miss Tolerance nodded, thinking with disquiet of her own savings. "What of the Navy Funds? Were they affected by this loss of confidence?"

"That is His Majesty's Navy, my dear. If the government is ruined, we shall have more to worry about than a run upon the banks."

"I suppose you are right—but what connection is there between this Fordyce affair and Mrs. Pouter's misfortune?"

"I wondered if perhaps this Marvell, or whatever his true

name is, might have been doing what Fordyce did: taking money from one source, paying the interest from another, then looking for a third source to pay interest to the first."

"It makes one's head spin."

"So it does. I have told you more than once that my business is far more savory than many others." As if this thought led to another, "I have sent for my lawyer."

"Have you, Aunt?"

"With my health so chancy, I need to make my will."

"Again?" Miss Tolerance regarded comments about Mrs. Brereton's will as an attempt to drag her into involvement in Mrs. Brereton's business. She considered diverting the topic to winter boots.

"You make it sound as if I did so every month. I need to make some changes." Mrs. Brereton looked sideways at Miss Tolerance, one immaculately shaped eyebrow raised.

Miss Tolerance refused to be baited. "I hope you will remember Marianne and the other women who work for you."

Mrs. Brereton's lips tightened. "You want nothing for yourself, Sarah? Nothing? Truly? You cannot be so foolish as to imagine an old age resting on the proceeds of your employment."

"I can and I do, Aunt Thea." Miss Tolerance smiled to belie the flat contradiction of her aunt's words. "I live quiet and careful, to save for that same old age."

Mrs. Brereton shook her head. "You cannot live so quiet and careful as to be certain—"

"And yet I do. Living with Connell on the continent, I learned how little I need to be happy. I would have regarded my life now as a paradise of comfort."

Mrs. Brereton shook her head again. "You are setting yourself up for a mean old age."

"I must hope you are wrong," Miss Tolerance said but without heat. Suspecting that her aunt would not abandon her argument without considerable distraction, she inquired as to her aunt's thoughts on rabbit-skin gloves.

Mrs. Brereton permitted the diversion but gave her niece a glance which plainly said the subject would be revisited.

The room Miss Tolerance slept in that night was warm—almost too warm, by her hardier standards. She reflected as she dressed the next morning that heat was undoubtedly an important consideration in an establishment where so many parties spent their time in states of undress.

The swelling in her heel had gone down, and unless she stepped down very hard there was no pain. Miss Tolerance put on her slipper, took up her shawls, and made her way down the stairs.

Although every attempt had been made, through construction and the later use of drapes, to ensure that sounds of lascivious activity did not intrude upon the polite quiet of the brothel's hallway, it was impossible to walk down the two flights of stairs from Mrs. Brereton's rooms to the foyer without hearing some noises which hinted at activities behind the doors. As a matter of habit, Miss Tolerance generally hummed as she went past the doors, which gave her an air of abstraction.

"Sarah!" Marianne Touchwell stood in the open doorway of the salon, where several of the house's ladies were taking tea and conversing with a gentleman who appeared not to have made his choice among them yet. "Have you been with your aunt?"

"Not since dinner last night. Is there a problem?" Miss Tolerance stopped a few steps short of the salon doorway; her aunt forbade gossip, particularly about herself. She had no qualms about discussing Mrs. Brereton with Marianne, but she did not wish to make a gift of their conversation to anyone nearby.

"No, no, I've heard nothing from Frost, and you may believe she'd come tell me the first thing if she suspicioned any problem with Mrs. B. No, Sarah, what I called you over for is, there's Nan—the second upstairs maid—is in a family way. Not by one of the gentlemen, she assures me. But she's fearful that Mrs. B will want her turned off."

"Turned off?" Miss Tolerance did not give rein to a first, instinctive denial that her aunt would do such a thing. After a moment's thought, "I imagine that so long as the girl can perform the work for which she was hired, there's no need to fret about it, although perhaps, when she is very large, you might find work for her that is not so... public. Surely Aunt Thea did not tell you to dismiss her."

That would have been so much out of Mrs. Brereton's character that Miss Tolerance felt a stab of concern: in the spring her aunt's behavior had been erratic, ending with a disastrous, short-lived engagement.

"I ain't spoken to Mrs. B about it yet. I wanted to have a plan in place to put before her. But I never had a sense of what her sympathies would be toward a girl—she's very strict that we all use the Precautions, and it ain't happened, a pregnancy that is, among any of us since I've been here."

The Precautions, Miss Tolerance knew, were the diligent use of sea-sponges liberally soaked in vinegar as a contraceptive measure.

"Tell her what you have told me, and tell Nan that she must make sure to complete her work, and we will see if it serves. Did she mention who the father was?"

"I take it he's some lad she walks out with on her way to Chapel." Marianne sniffed. "Or rather on her way home."

"Has this lad any notion of taking responsibility for her?"

"He's in service as well, and quite unable to care for her until he has some preferment in his post. Well, we've a plan that will do for now. Thank you, Sarah. Come have some tea; 'tis a quiet morning."

"I don't like to intrude," Miss Tolerance began. Then a murmur of conversation from the salon caught her attention and she changed her mind. "Very well. Thank you."

She and Mrs. Touchwell found that the lone gentleman seated in the salon appeared to have narrowed his selection to two of the five women present. The other three had withdrawn to the fire and were talking over a plate of muffins. Miss Tolerance supplied herself with a cup and a plate of eggs and toast and joined them, with Mrs. Touchwell. After a few minutes, when the gentleman had retired with the girl he favored, she spoke up.

"I beg your pardon, but did I hear that one of you had found an excellent investment?"

"That was me." Chloe said. "Marianne, you asking last week where I keep my money made me think of putting my savings to better use. I was telling Lisette I found a gentleman will give me a better return on my savings than the Navy funds or anything else I heard of." She bit daintily into her muffin as if to punctuate her satisfaction.

"And what is this return? Who is the gentleman?"

"As to the return, he says I might see as high as ten percent. His name is Marvell, and I'm planning upon putting my money with him, as you may best believe."

Miss Tolerance was shocked and dismayed. A week earlier, no one at her aunt's establishment had had any thought of investment beyond the Navy Funds. And safe in the belief that Marvell only preyed upon the elderly, she had not thought to warn Mrs. Brereton's employees.

"I beg you will not do so," she said firmly. "I know a little something of this Mr. Marvell. He has been swindling money from women with this scheme of his."

"Swindling? How is it possible? I've a letter from a woman said she's been getting her money right along—"

"And one does so, for a year or so. Do you recall Mrs. Pouter, who worked here some years ago? She lost her savings to this man, and when she attempted to find him—"

"Oh, there is no difficulty in finding him," Lisette broke in. "Set up as fine as you please in an office in Stafford Street."

"Have you been to see him?" Had *two* of Mrs. Brereton's ladies fallen prey to the man?

"No, I ain't. Just saying what *you* told me, Chloe."

Chloe scowled at Lisette, who stuck her tongue out. Miss Tolerance ignored these hostilities. "When Mrs. Pouter met him, Marvell did business from rooms in Bruton Street, but when she went back later to discover why her payments had ceased, he had vacated those premises. I beg you will believe me. Your money will be safer in the bank, or in the Navy funds. Chloe, may I see the letter you received?"

"I might have known it was too sweet to be real." Chloe was sullen. "I suppose I ought to thank you."

"You may thank me by letting me see the letter of reference of which you spoke."

When Chloe appeared unwilling to rise and fetch the paper, "Come, Chloe, Miss Sarah has saved you from a great loss." Marianne looked meaningfully at her.

With bad grace, Chloe summoned Keefe to ask a maid to bring the letter down to her. Miss Tolerance thought the woman was less relieved to have avoided a great harm than angered to have lost the promise of imagined gain.

"Where did you hear about Marvell?" Miss Tolerance asked.

"The woman as told me about him is a girl I knew from before I come—came—to Mrs. B's: Sadie Handy, as she was then. Keeps a hat shop now. And this Marvell's place of business is upstairs, just across from the Goat Tavern on Stafford Street, number 12, I think."

When Keefe returned with the letter Chloe gestured to

Miss Tolerance. Miss Tolerance resolved to buy the woman a new pair of gloves by way of a thank you.

She was unsurprised to find the handwriting and the spelling familiar, the author grateful for the efforts of "the amazing churming Mr. Marvel." The letter was signed by the same Mehetibel White whom Miss Tolerance knew for certain could not have written it. Stafford Street, clearly, was meant to be her destination.

Chapter Ten

It is not difficult to impersonate the lowest sort of prostitute: even a woman with a full set of teeth and no florid marks of disease may dress herself in a cheap, revealing gown, scent herself liberally with gin, and carry off the imposture. To present oneself as a whore with aspirations to something greater requires more thought and an eye for detail. From the small collection of third-hand garments she kept for the purpose, Miss Tolerance chose a muslin gown that was more decorative than suited to the weather, a spencer cut slightly too tight across the breast, broken-down half-boots, and a pair of twice-mended gloves. She pinned two silk flowers among the cherries that already decorated her bonnet, then applied soot from a burnt cork on her eyelashes and enough rouge to her cheeks to hint at lack of skill and lack of taste without expressing outright vulgarity. Thus accoutered, she desired Keefe to summon a chair and was shortly carried off in questionable style to Stafford Street.

Number 12 was a tall, narrow, whitewashed building of four stories with a tall, narrow door. The hatmaker's shop on the ground floor had not yet opened, and there was thus no one to ask for Mr. Marvell's whereabouts. Needs must: Miss Tolerance knocked.

She was surprised when the door was opened immediately by an elderly man built as tall and narrow as the building itself, wearing a rusty-black skirted coat and knee breeches and leaning heavily upon a dark wood cane.

"Aye?"

Miss Tolerance began her imposture. "Oi do beg your pardon. I am looking to foind a Mr. Marvell?"

The man twisted his mouth as if the answer required prodigious thought. After a moment, during which she offered him a ha'penny, he nodded and stepped back to permit Miss Tolerance entry. She found herself in a dim hallway; just before her, a set of stairs climbed steeply upward. Beside the stair and blocking access to the hallway that stretched beyond it were a chair and a table on which a candle burned in a pewter candle-lamp. A book lay open on the chair seat. It appeared that the elderly man's sole occupation was to open the door for visitors.

"Marvell, up to the second floor, second door of three," he said. "You'll find lamps on the landin's."

This information shared, the old man returned to his chair and picked up his book with an air of finality.

Miss Tolerance climbed one flight of stairs and the second. On the second floor, she found the second door, which had a small, brightly polished brass plate fixed to the frame with an iron nail. In the flickering light, she made out the word *Marvell*.

For a man who had been so difficult to find, Mr. Marvell had not scrupled to disguise his name.

She tapped at the door. After a moment it swung open onto a room so much brighter than the hallway that Miss Tolerance was briefly dazzled. When she had blinked away the glare, she made out a chamber neatly furnished as an office: a desk, chairs, a short case of books, and drapes at the windows, which had been drawn back to allow the full of the sun's light in. The man who had opened the door and stood with an expression of inquiry was young, gentlemanly dressed, and perhaps the ugliest man she had ever met. He was a full head less than Miss Tolerance's height, with a square brow, a nose peculiarly flattened across the bridge, and staring brown eyes. His well-formed mouth displayed teeth like aged ivory pegs when he smiled, which he did with no apparent self-consciousness.

"Yes? How may I assist?" His voice was oddly flat, but as gentlemanly as his dress.

"Oi'm looking for a Mr. Marvell?" Miss Tolerance pitched her voice upward, loosened her vowels, and softened her consonants to suggest a country upbringing and an attempt at gentility.

The man smiled with every evidence of delight. "You have found him, madam. Please walk in." He bowed.

Miss Tolerance curtsied, advanced into the room, and was waved to one of a pair of chairs that faced the desk. Rather than seat himself behind the desk, however, Marvell spread his coattails with a flourish and sat in the chair next to hers, leaning forward confidingly as if he might at any moment seize her hand. There was something curiously guileless about the ugly young man's pleasure in her visit.

"My name is Mrs. Rosie Lipper." Miss Tolerance had furnished herself with a *nom d'amour* and a story beforehand, and brought them out now with ease.

"I am charmed to meet you, Mrs. Lipper. May I ask how you found me?"

"Oh, I've a friend told me all about you. Said you was a proper wizard with the shillin's and pence."

Marvell beamed. "That is very pleasing to hear. And how may I assist you? A matter of money, of course?"

Miss Tolerance batted her corked eyelashes and admitted that he had hit upon the root of the matter. "I'm thinking of me old age, if I live that long. Want to put a mite by, if you see. My friend Chloe said you was the gentleman would know what to do."

She had pitched her voice to suggest confidential conversation, but Marvell frowned apologetically. "I beg your pardon; I'm a little hard of hearing."

"A mite put by," Miss Tolerance repeated a little more loudly. "For me old age."

Marvell nodded. "Very sensible, madam, very sensible. Just what I like to hear. Have you money already saved?"

"Oh, aye. I try to save where I can, though a woman in my position's got expenses."

"Of course. I hope that you have your money safe in a bank, and not—" the ugly little man grinned conspiratorially. "Not under the bed, as some ladies keep it?"

"Oh, what I got is in banks. I've some of my saving at Coutts, some with Hammersley, some with a little bank in the Fleet—Jones and Wilkes, I think it is. Didn't seem smart to 'ave it all in one place."

Marvell shook his head. "Those are all fine institutions, but not one of them are what I would recommend for you. For a man of fortune they do well enough, but for a lady like yourself—have you approached any other banker?"

Miss Tolerance thought rapidly of all the banks she knew. "I didn't care for the clerk at Pitt and Son. Nor Bolt and Retifer. I thought perhaps Pennantine, a little there—"

This last name appeared to electrify Mr. Marvell.

"If you have money with Pennantine I would not for the world have you move it. The Fund makes its payments through the Pennantine bank. For the rest of them—well, as I said before, they are well enough for a gentleman of means, but for a *lady*—" There was no breath of satire or condescension in the word. No wonder Mrs. Pouter had been so pleased with the odd-looking Mr. Marvell. "If you choose to invest with our Fund, I am certain that we will do better for you than those other banks."

"'Ow much better?"

Marvell smiled. "We commonly produce for our clients a return of nine percent. The Navy funds, of course, promise only five percent at best, and banks—"

Miss Tolerance permitted herself a low whistle. "I don't mean disrespect, Mr. Marvell, but how is it your fund can pay so high?"

If she had thought to put the man out of countenance, Miss Tolerance was disappointed. He grinned more broadly, as if that was the very question he had hoped she would ask.

"T'is a special fund, Mrs. Lipper. Invested in ventures which are more speculative in nature—"

"Specky-lative? Don't that mean risky?"

Marvell shook his head, and a fair curl drooped over his wide brow. "Not in the least, my dear lady. Because we have so many ventures, and such a number of investors, the speculation is spread broadly enough that there is virtually no risk at all."

This sounded like criminal nonsense to Miss Tolerance, but would not to Mrs. Rosie Lipper. "What would you need from me to begin?" Miss Tolerance took care to sound eager but not too eager. "Is there papers an' such to sign?"

"Only one or two. All we need from you is your signature and the money you wish to invest, Mrs. Lipper. When we meet next, you bring me a draft for your funds, and I'll have the papers ready for your signature."

"And what sort of papers would they be?"

"Oh, an authorization for me to act as your representative in the matter of investment—a businesswoman such as yourself will see the importance of such a thing."

"Oh, aye, certain-sure."

"May I ask what sum I should expect for your investment with us?"

Miss Tolerance mimed considering. "Round about two hundred?"

Marvell's smile broadened. "That is hardly a *mite*, Mrs. Lipper. You have done well for yourself, I see. And you shall see how that is turned to a fine sum for your retirement."

"When should I bring you the money? Or should I bring it round to Pennantine's bank, as you're so keen on working with them?"

If she had hoped to panic the young man by attempting to make a connection between himself and the bank, the tactic failed. "No, dear lady, you will pay your money to me, so that I may give you a receipt at the same time that you sign the authorization. Pennantine is merely my agent in paying funds into your bank."

"But will they only pay if I've an account there? What if I—"

"They will make payments to any other institution you stipulate, madam. Request," he added, when Miss Tolerance wrinkled her brow over 'stipulate'. "I only say that I have the greatest respect for Pennantine's bank."

Miss Tolerance nodded with feigned relief. "Well, now I see it. And to whom should the draft be made out? To yourself?"

Marvell shook his head. "Payable to cash, if you please. It is simpler and less expensive for you, as the Fund must charge you a fee to convert a draft from my name."

Miss Tolerance nodded. It was a very polished business: all of the questions she had prepared had been met with answers that would sound plausible to an unsophisticated woman. And Marvell himself was so amiable, so earnest, she could almost think that he believed what he said.

"Well, sir," Miss Tolerance rose and offered her hand to the gentleman. "You put my mind at ease considerable. I should return here, then, with my savings?"

"Indeed, ma'am. What time shall I expect to see you?"

"I don't want to incommode you, sir. I imagine a gennelman such as yourself is mightily busy—"

"You will always find me here, Mrs. Lipper."

"Well, then, I shall come tomorrow in the after-noon, if that's quite convenient."

Marvell bowed over her hand. "I shall look forward to it. A great pleasure to have made your acquaintance, Mrs. Lipper."

"For me as well, Mr. Marvell. Until tomorrow, then." She spoke the words with a suggestion of rote flirtation, curtsied, and left.

So the man Marvell existed and, if this interview was any proof, was up to the same game that had entangled Annie Pouter and Mrs. Black. But while she stood ready to swear that the odd, ugly man was indeed the Marvell who had swindled away their money, Miss Tolerance had yet no evidence that he was responsible for their deaths. The connection might be logical, but a court would require something more evidentiary than mere logic.

She made her way along Stafford Street, dodging a fishmonger's cart to cross to Albemarle Street, deep enough in thought that she only barely avoided a pile of horse dung as she reached the far curb. She had believed that the hunt for Marvell was the hunt for Annie Pouter's killer, but now she found it difficult to imagine that odd, fantastical man was a murderer.

Odd, fantastical *little* man.

Miss Tolerance stopped in the middle of the sidewalk, much struck. If, as she believed, the man who had murdered Annie Pouter and the late Mrs. Arabella Black was the same man who had attacked her the day before—it could not be Marvell. However culpable the man she had just met might be in the swindle that had taken Annie Pouter's money, he was too short to be her own assailant. He was too short—she did not think he could reach far enough up to attempt to throttle her, let alone to wrap his arms around her arms to keep her from breaking free.

He must have an accomplice. Or—it was possible that the deaths were unrelated to the swindle—but these coincident deaths and assaults seemed unlikely. Could she have been following the wrong trail all along?

Miss Tolerance stepped out of the path of oncoming pedestrians, trying to think. If she was to pursue her livelihood it was necessary that she have faith in her powers of ratiocination. The tangle of possibilities before her shook that faith. She needed to talk with someone. The thought of speaking with someone of common sense who could help her see her way through the tangle made her heart lift.

Miss Tolerance turned eastward, toward Bow Street.

The Bow Street public office was a large granite structure that dated from the last century; the anteroom to the court itself was that afternoon bursting with people waiting upon the mercy of the court, giving witness, or come to be entertained by the sight of justice being dispensed. The ground floor rooms were high-ceilinged and open, which was, Miss Tolerance thought, a great mercy given the number of Londoners who packed themselves into them. Fresh air might circulate near the ceiling, but the air nearer the ground stank of unwashed humanity. The clerk informed Miss Tolerance that Sir Walter Mandif was in the process of finishing up the day's business. He took a second look at Miss Tolerance, with her thin dress and corked eyelashes, and was clearly ready to send her about her business, when she spied a familiar face. Mr. Penryn, Sir Walter's Cornish-born constable, appeared beside her and told the clerk "Zor Walter'll be wanting to zee 'er, Mr. Mack. I'll take 'er back to 'is chambers," and led her away without further discussion.

Miss Tolerance thanked him for his intervention. "I look disreputable, I fear."

"I 'ave seen you lookin' finer," Penryn agreed. "'Ave a seat and Zor Walter'll coom right to ye soon enough."

Within a quarter hour, Sir Walter appeared at the door to his chamber. Miss Tolerance's spirits lifted at the sight of him —then her pleasure faltered. His usually imperturbable countenance was weary, and Miss Tolerance remembered unhappily that they were no longer on such terms as to encourage a casual visit. "I should have made an appointment," she began.

"Why should you?" The fatigue on the magistrate's face seemed to melt away. "Never apologize for an unexpected pleasure. How may I help you?"

"But I am interrupting," Miss Tolerance said. "Would you not prefer that I go—"

"Not in the least. Come, S—Miss Tolerance. Am I correct that this is not a social call? How may I be of assistance?" He observed Miss Tolerance's appearance without visible qualm. "And may I offer you refreshment?"

"I beg you won't trouble yourself, Sir Walter. I thought, since I brought you in to the matter of Mrs. Pouter's death, that I should let you know what I have learnt of the matter. I have found the man I sought, but I confess he is not at all what I expected."

"This is the man Marvell you told me of? The murderer?"

"I am quite certain that he is the man who took Mrs. Pouter's money." She outlined her meeting with Marvell. "He cannot be the murderer, however."

"Why do you think not?"

Miss Tolerance attempted to explain. "First, it makes no sense to me that two women should make violent ends after complaining about a swindle, and a third be attacked, and the swindler *not* be involved. And yet... If he *is* the swindler, I can hardly believe he knows what he is doing. I wish you might meet him. He is—there is almost a childish enthusiasm for his scheme, as if he truly believes he is doing good. Such an odd, funny little—" Miss Tolerance straightened against the back of her chair. "But I am taking the wrong way around to explain."

"I beg you will take me with you. Why can he not?" Sir Walter's mouth crooked in a half smile.

"He's too short to have throttled anyone."

"How short is too short to throttle someone?"

"Neither Mrs. Pouter nor Mrs. Black was tall, but Marvell is shorter still." She mimed reaching up with both hands. "Unless they were seated, he would be reaching up. And if the murderer is the same man who attacked me—" the moment the words left her mouth Miss Tolerance regretted them, but she continued, hoping to distract her auditor from his inevitable objection. "The man who accosted me was considerably taller than I. Mr. Marvell must have a confederate."

"When were you accosted?" Sir Walter might have been asking when she had last been to the theatre.

"Yesterday afternoon."

"Attacked yesterday and despite that, you met with Mr. Marvell—alone, I apprehend?—today. Was that entirely prudent?"

Miss Tolerance frowned. "I cannot say for certain that what happened to me connects to Mrs. Pouter's death. Yesterday I was dressed ladylike and calling upon a respectable widow in Hans Place. Today I went as you see me, in the guise of Mrs. Lipper, a new client, and did not feel a moment's unease." This conversation was exactly what she had hoped to avoid. "Sir Walter, you know that I am well able to protect myself, but if it will make you feel better, I will go armed when I return tomorrow—"

"Return?" Sir Walter regarded her with great seriousness. "Please do not imagine that I think you defenseless. I know better. But I recall a time not distant when you were hurt—"

"By a blow from behind, in the street!" Sir Walter had given Miss Tolerance refuge after that attack—a period of enforced intimacy which had been unsettling to both parties. That, on another occasion, it was Sir Walter who had found her at the site of a crime, bleeding from an unlucky wound, made the magistrate's concern damnably reasonable, given that Miss Tolerance had no intention of assuaging his anxiety. "It might have happened to anyone!"

Sir Walter quirked an eyebrow.

"Oh, my work entails risk. I suppose it is a wonder that I am not struck down from behind on a weekly basis." If she had hoped that humor would defuse Sir Walter's concern, this sally fell flat.

"I would be much happier if you would permit me to send Penryn or Hook with you—"

"Bring a Runner? Even if you could get one of them to put aside the red waistcoats they take such pride in, what role would I present them in? Financial advisor? Pimp? I have great respect for your associates' gifts, but they are blunt instruments. It would only take one of them calling me "miss" —she growled in imitation of Mr. Hook. "I appreciate your concern, but I cannot consult your happiness in order to do my work."

"You have made that plain," he said. For the first time in their acquaintance, Miss Tolerance heard real bitterness in his tone.

"Sir Walter—"

"Do not mind it." Sir Walter ran his hand over his face as if to wipe away a strong emotion he did not wish to reveal. "If you will not permit me to offer assistance or protection, may I ask why you came to me today?"

"I thought—I believed that the information I had gleaned would be useful to Bow Street. I needed someone whose judgment I trust to talk with. An exchange of ideas—"

"My *idea* is that you know you are doing a dangerous thing and wish to let someone know of it. Let *me* know of it," Sir Walter corrected himself. "I wonder why, as you have made it plain you do not wish to be stopped. Is there some assistance that you require—and will accept?"

Miss Tolerance bit her lip and thought. Did she want assistance? She had turned to Sir Walter instinctively. "I wanted your counsel," she began. "When I—when we used to meet more easily, I could unpack a question and you would help me sort through it."

"If it is just that, I imagine your friend Mrs. Touchwell would do as well."

"You are already aware of the matter of Mrs. Pouter's death—and Marianne is not a magistrate, nor is she familiar with the requirements of law." She struggled to put into words what she meant, without giving way to sentiment. "I know I do not value the judgment of any other magistrate as highly."

"You flatter me." His tone was dry. "But you have refused to consider my judgment regarding the hazard in which you place yourself."

That is a different matter! She did not say it aloud. Her heart was beating strongly, tears stood in her eyes, and Miss Tolerance could not say what first came to her lips: when she had refused his offer of marriage, she had refused him the right to be concerned for her. But if she had refused him that right, had she forfeited the right to come to him for counsel?

She rose from her seat. "I should not have troubled you. I apologize for my intrusion on a busy afternoon."

"Sarah—" Sir Walter stood and extended his hand. "Miss Tolerance. Please sit again. We have both become rather hot. You came for advice. Let me attempt to assist you. Are you certain that I cannot offer you a glass of wine?"

"No, I thank you." But she sat again, close to the edge of

her seat. Mandif sat as well. For several minutes neither one said anything, as if both wished to let the heat between them dissipate.

"Well." There was another silence that lay heavy between them. "What *legal* advice can I provide to you?"

Miss Tolerance marshalled her thoughts. "I told Marvell I would bring him my money—in this guise. So we know where he will be found. Can the Law arrest him for his investment scheme without a victim to prefer charges? Were I to give him money and wait until it was lost to me—well, that could take months or years, and he might well disappear again."

"It is difficult of proof," Mandif agreed. "The Law may arrest him on any charge at all, but I dislike to have no proof in hand, and if he was arrested, the only course I see would be to press him for the name of his confederates."

"Press him?" Miss Tolerance was horrified by the thought of Marvell—or anyone—stripped and laid upon a stone slab with stones piled upon his body until he confessed or died.

"I do not like it, myself," Mandif agreed. "Particularly as you do not believe he is the murderer. But the only other path I see is for you to make yourself a target, and you know my feelings upon the matter."

"If I go as Mrs. Lipper—without money, but with questions of the sort she might think to ask—perhaps I could learn something from him. But I cannot simply say—" Miss Tolerance dropped into Mrs. Lipper's soft country accent—"I don't suppose you're that same Marvell as took me friend Annie Pouter's mite and disappeared with it and what 'surance do I 'ave that you won't be doin' it again?"

Sir Walter raised an eyebrow. "That is quite remarkable."

Miss Tolerance managed a one-sided smile. "I am blessed with an imitative ear."

"Among many gifts. Well, as to what questions Mrs. Lipper might ask—I suppose she is suspicious by nature?

Perhaps she has heard about another woman—a friend of a friend?—who has lost her money in an investment scheme. Perhaps pressing just a little will get the man or his confederate to show his hand?"

"I can only make the attempt."

"And be wary on your way home."

"And be wary," she agreed. "I should leave you to your work." She had established that the Law was unlikely to arrest Marvell without a complainant or the proof she was able to offer. What reason was there for her to linger, except the pleasure of Sir Walter's company?

She rose and curtsied. "Thank you for your help, Sir Walter."

He bowed. "I hope you will always feel free to request it."

As she left the office, Miss Tolerance thought she heard the magistrate say again, "Be wary." She did not turn to see if it was so.

Despite the chill, which she felt very much in her skimpy spencer, Miss Tolerance decided to walk back to Manchester Square. She had found on more than one occasion that a walk could provide inspiration, or at least distraction. Inspiration regarding Mr. Marvell would be welcome; distraction from the subject of Sir Walter Mandif would be equally so. But this usual remedy did not yield satisfaction. As Miss Tolerance threaded her way through the Covent Garden market stalls, along Long Acre and north on Wardour Street, she came to the conclusion that she had gone to Bow Street simply because she missed Sir Walter and had made Marvell her excuse to see him. No wonder the magistrate had been irritated with her.

When a voice at her elbow spoke her name, it was almost a relief to greet Joe Boswell. "I'm surprised to see you here, miss" he said pleasantly. What he thought of her appearance, she could not tell.

"On Wardour Street?"

"Afoot in a rough part 'o town."

"I am often afoot, and often in rougher parts of the city than this." She looked around her. "Although I will admit I am not so often dressed this way."

"Took me a moment to be sure it was you. Shall I offer you my arm?" Joe Boswell's expression suggested that he expected her to refuse. Instead, Miss Tolerance tucked her hand through his crooked elbow.

"That is very kind in you," she said. "Unless, of course, you dislike to have yourself seen in the company of a woman of… inadequate virtue."

Boswell's smile broadened into a laugh. "There's my favorite sort, miss. I was thinking more that you wouldn't care to be seen with *my* sort."

"Let us acquit each other of condescension," Miss Tolerance said. "How is Mother Ella?"

"Mother's tolerable well. I'll tell her you asked after 'er, shall I?"

"Please do. And what brings you to Wardour Street?"

"Just good fortune. I looked up and thought, could that be Sir Walter's friend, Miss Tolerance?" Miss Tolerance winced at the characterization. "So I made bold to greet you and ask how you did."

"I am happy you did so. As it happens, I have news. I have found Mr. Marvell's whereabouts."

"'Ave you? Given 'm to Watch, 'ave you?"

"Not yet. It appears that just finding the man won't be enough to see him tried. I need more evidence. His game has become a little more complex since you and I spoke, and I want to make sure that I understand the scheme—and who his accomplices are—before I do that."

"So what shall I tell Mother?"

"Tell her that I do not think the man took the name he took in order to point blame at the—to your folk. Why he took it, I am not yet certain. But I also do not believe it is the name he was born with. In any case, I do not think there is any cause for Mother Ella to believe he means you harm."

"Ummm." They stopped at the corner of Oxford Street to watch a perilously top-heavy wagon rumble past while a beggar, marked as blind by the black scarf tied round his eyes, was pulled out of harm's way by a little girl in a dirty gown and knitted shawl. As they began to cross the street themselves, "I'll leave that to Mother to suss. There's 'arm meant and there's 'arm done."

"I understand. But in a day or two, I hope that Mr. Marvell will be the Law's problem and neither yours nor mine."

"A day or two? I suppose Mother'll wait to order any action needs to be t'uk."

Miss Tolerance was dismayed. "What sort of action might she take?"

Joe Boswell shrugged. "S'up to Mother Ella. We can't 'ave folk thinking they can lay things off upon us, see, and if we let it pass, well, that only means other folk might be the more ready to do it again."

"If *folk* planned the imposture to cause trouble for your people, perhaps," Miss Tolerance said firmly.

"Like I said: that's up to Mother Ella. If the Law don't take up your Mr. Marvell first."

Another reason to press the matter and provide Sir Walter with information upon which he could act.

"And here is Duke Street," she said. "I can make my way from here, if you are busy. But I do thank you again for your escort."

Joe bowed, still grinning. Miss Tolerance made him a curtsey in the same mocking spirit, and they parted cordially.

Chapter Eleven

When Miss Tolerance returned to Mr. Marvell's rooms the next morning, having donned the appearance and manner of Mrs. Rosie Lipper, the little man all but capered with delight.

"What a pleasure, what a pleasure! I had not hoped to see you again so soon. Come in, dear lady. May I offer you a glass of wine? Or perhaps a tot of gin?"

It was close on noon, and Miss Tolerance did not generally take spirits so early. She declined in Mrs. Lipper's arch tones. "I cannot touch the stuff, Mr. Marvell, it muddles my insides terrible."

"Then tea, perhaps?" He moved about the room with his curious bow-legged gait as if his eagerness to please could not be contained. "No? I cannot persuade you? Well, then, may I hope your presence indicates you have decided to go forward with an investment?"

He spread the tails of his coat and perched on the chair opposite hers, smiling with apparent pleasure.

"The givin' over of so much money's a weighty matter, and I must take it serious," Miss Tolerance began. She had spent a good part of the prior evening thinking, and had at last decided, against her earlier inclination, to bring the names of Annie Pouter and Belle Black into the conversation as early as she could. "I've heard tell of them as was done out of their savings by men on the mace—that is, been cheated of their money. I'm minded to be careful-like."

Marvell nodded vigorously. "As well you should, my dear Mrs. Lipper."

"Now, I told you I was recommended to seek you out by an acquaintance called Chloe Climber as works in Manchester Square. But that's only one reference, and a woman in my position must be choice of where she rests her funds. You understand that, I hope."

"You wish the names of some other of the Fund's clients who might provide a reference?"

"You could give me some, I suppose. But I got some names on my own. Another woman used to work for Mrs. Brereton, a Mrs. Pouter?"

She watched the little man carefully, but Marvell gave no sign of anxiety at Annie Pouter's name. "Indeed, I recall her well. I hope you will give her my compliments when next you speak with her."

Miss Tolerance was surprised enough by this response that she almost forgot to answer in the character of Mrs. Lipper. "You know I cannot do that, sir!"

"Oh, do not say there has been a falling out between you! I know how ladies—"

"Nothing of the sort. I am just surprised to hear you ignorant of it, Mr. Marvell. Mrs. Pouter is dead."

"Dead!" Miss Tolerance would have taken her oath that the ugly little man was genuinely shocked. "I am grieved to hear it. A quick illness? She did not suffer, I hope."

"You truly 'adn't 'eard of it? No illness at all. She was done in. And as for suffering, you may judge for yourself, for she was throttled and 'alf burnt-up in a fire."

"My God." All animation left Marvell's face, and tears

stood in his eyes. "She was such a pleasant lady, and I was so happy to be able to help her to a little fortune."

"The perils of bein' a retired impure in Lunnon, I'd say. Why, I 'eard of a woman name of Belle Black of Bermondsey as was run down in the street by a charnel cart and killed straight away—another retired lady." Miss Tolerance injected a tone of relish suited to her character as Rosie Lipper.

"Mrs. Black, too?" Marvell rose from his chair and once more strode rapidly about the room as if the action could discharge his distress.

"Why, did you know 'er, sir?"

"If it is the same woman—surely there cannot be two!—Mrs. Black was another beneficiary of the Fund. I am most distressed."

"Do all the beneficiaries of your fund wind up deceased, Mr. Marvell? If that's the case, I don't think I—"

"This is nothing to do with the Fund, Mrs. Lipper. It is a horrid coincidence, that is all, and very saddening. Horrible. They were both such lively ladies."

Lively was not, perhaps, the first word that would have come to Miss Tolerance to describe Annie Pouter, but she agreed that the deaths were horrible. "What I heard, Mr. Marvell, was that before they died your Fund stopped paying 'em. In point of fact, I'm told they didn't die 'til after they complained of it."

"To whom did they complain? I heard nothing, and I assure you, if there had been any problem I should have known at once and made all right."

"Do you tell me you had no idea of it?"

Now the little man looked horrified—and angry. "What are you suggesting? Of course, I had no idea! *If*—and I have nothing but your word upon it—if indeed there was a problem with the fund, Mrs. Pouter and Mrs. Black should have come to me. I do not manage the fund—I freely confess that I have no head for business of that sort—but I would have gone at once to the manager to learn where the problem lay, and seen it fixed. My part has always been to find persons who would benefit from the fund and persuade them to invest. As a kindness—"

"And who is this manager?" Miss Tolerance had abandoned the pretense of Mrs. Lipper, her vowels and vocabulary returned to normal, and she regarded Marvell with the eye of avenging justice.

"I—" Marvell swallowed and appeared to find his collar and neckcloth too tight. "I cannot say."

"Because you do not *know*? Or because you will not say? If you are not part of this fiddle, Mr. Marvell, it is very strange in you to protect a *manager* who swindles the savings from women who cannot look elsewhere for protection."

"There is no swindle, nor any thought of such a thing. The Fund has been ongoing for a decade or more, and I very much resent—"

"You may resent it all you wish, but both Mrs. Pouter and Mrs. Black died believing that this Fund was nothing more than a cheat—"

"I say again, why did they not speak to me direct?"

"Because they could not find you!" Miss Tolerance played this card with the attitude of one who has trumped the game. "Mr. Marvell, does it seem to you the action of an honest man, to disappear from a location without notice to the clients who might have wished to find him? Does it seem the action of an honest man to use a name not his own to conduct business?"

"My name—I have no underhanded intention in taking a business name! It was meant to—" he stopped.

"To what, sir?"

Marvell shook his head, his lips pressed tightly together.

"Whatever your intention, the seeming is that you meant to keep investors like Mrs. Pouter from being able to find you. When you disappeared from Bruton Street—"

"I did not disappear! The cost on those rooms was high,

and I decided to find new accommodation. Nothing in the least mysterious about the matter."

"And yet you left no forwarding instruction."

"Of course I did! I do not know to whom you have been speaking, Mrs. Lipper, but everything I have done has been accomplished in the most open manner possible."

"Appearences go against that assertion, Mr. Marvell. When I applied for your whereabouts, no one was able to direct me to you. And if no trickery was meant, why take a name that is so much identified with Travelers and sharpers—"

"*Sharpers?*" Marvell's eyebrows rose so high they almost disappeared into his hairline.

"Cheats, Mr. Marvell. The name is commonly used by swindlers."

"Is it really? We had no idea—*I* had no idea of it. T'was simply a name we—I—thought would encourage confidence."

"You and the manager of the Fund, sir? Why will you not name him?"

Marvell looked down, studying the toes of his boots. "I gave my word. I promised not to—not to name my partner. But I swear there is no intent to defraud. No nefarious reason. We thought if I used my own name, investors might believe the Fund to be too much in the pocket of one bank."

"You and your nameless partner. And which bank?"

Marvell shook his head. "I have said too much already. He will be very cross." The little man's lower lip quivered.

"I will have answers, Mr. Marvell. Two women are dead, and I am persuaded the matter has something to do with your Fund. If you are not involved in a crime, then it must be your partner—"

"Never! I swear to you, Mrs. Lipper!" The little man's voice was tremulous, panicky. "He would never! And he would tell you himself, if he—"

"If he were not well hidden behind all this falsity."

Mr. Marvell sat again, not bothering with the foppish gesture of spreading his coat tails, but leaning back in his chair, legs outstretched and head bent to study the stubby fingers of his hands. "There will be a perfectly good explanation," he said, low. He spoke to his hands, as if gaining counsel from them. "I must ask him. But he will be *so* angry—I don't know what to—I'm not clever." Marvell looked up, brows drawn together and lips tremulous. "My— the manager could explain matters better than I. Yes!— I will ask him to meet with you and explain. The—partner. Give me a few days to speak to him— the manager of the Fund—and learn what happened. I am certain he will be able to explain the problem with payments to poor Mrs. Pouter and Mrs. Black."

"You insist that the Fund is a legitimate one?"

"I believe it with the utmost faith," Marvell said. "Give me but a few days—a single day, even—to prove it to you."

Miss Tolerance had arrived in Stafford Street ready to charge Marvell with theft and as an accomplice to murder. This interview had shaken her certainty. The little man was, in his quivering distress, peculiarly convincing. His insistence upon the legitimacy, and his reference to the mysterious manager, suggested that he could be a dupe of someone else. She wanted very much to meet this person.

Dare she give him one day? "Can you bring this business partner of yours to explain all to me?" If Marvell would promise his confederate's attendance as well, the next time she would bring one of Sir Walter's Runners with her. Perhaps she should set someone to watch and follow the little man to the confederate himself. It was worth the gamble of leaving now, if she could be assured of catching the manager of the Fund. "If I leave now and return tomorrow, you must be here, Mr. Marvell. If you are not, I will lay evidence before Bow Street." What that evidence would be she was not certain; Sir Walter already knew most of what she had learned.

"I will be here," Marvell promised. "And I will bring him."

"Your mysterious partner."

He nodded eagerly. "You have my faithful promise. There is no reason to involve the Law, you will see. He will make it all clear to you."

"If he does not come—"

"He will. When I explain it to him, I know he will come."

Miss Tolerance thought that Marvell was less certain than he sounded, but he was her best chance to trace the scheme to its root. "Very well. It is just noon now, Mr. Marvell. I will return at this time tomorrow."

The Marvell who escorted Miss Tolerance to the door was chastened in his manner. "I will be here," he promised again. He bowed.

Miss Tolerance did not curtsey.

Once out upon Stafford Street, she turned her steps south toward Jermyn Street. There, at the crossing of Duke of York Street, a group of enterprising street sweeps loitered and worked. Miss Tolerance had used these lads before to keep watch upon the movement of persons when she could not do so herself.

The boy who headed the grubby crew was called Bart. He was a head taller than most of them but appeared to Miss Tolerance to rule over his mates by the force of his character rather than his size, and while cuffing and mockery were common language among the boys, Bart made it his business to keep it from becoming bullying. She found him in front of Paxton and Whitfield, examining an immense round of cheddar in the cheese-monger's window.

"Good afternoon." Miss Tolerance stopped beside him and studied the same cheese with absorption.

"Ullo, miss. You got a job o' work for us?" Bart did not look at her, but a dimple in his grimy cheek suggested he was grinning. Her disguise did not appear to have confounded him.

"I do. I need a few of you boys to keep watch on a place in Stafford Street, number 12. You are to let me know if a man there leaves and, if he does so, where he goes. Also, to keep an eye for anyone who comes and goes there."

"Us'al terms, miss?"

"Thruppence a day, per boy. You should not need more than three boys, I think. The boys keep the proceeds of any sweeping done while hanging about the place. And all of you must be home when your mothers expect you."

For a moment, it seemed that Bart would argue this last stipulation. Then he shrugged. "Who's the fella we're keeping peepers on?"

Miss Tolerance gave the boy Marvell's description. "Come round to my house tomorrow morning to make your report. I shall tell Mr. Keefe to expect you."

"Yes, miss. Mr. Keefe." Bart's tone was full of hero-worship: Mrs. Brereton's porter was a former prize-fighter, and his manner with the boys, when they visited Miss Tolerance, was one of man-to-man insult which had made them his slaves.

"At the kitchen door, mind."

"Yes, miss. Mr. Keefe been quite clear on that, miss."

"Very well, then. I shall leave you to it." Miss Tolerance departed; she had not stepped but a few paces before she heard the sharp whistle by which Bart summoned his troops. She turned her steps toward Manchester Square confident that her assignment was already underway.

Miss Tolerance returned to Manchester Square and shed Rosie Lipper's likeness. Having shown her true colors to Marvell, she did not plan to assume it again. Instead, she put on her men's guise, grateful for the warmth of her green Gunnard greatcoat, and hired a hack to visit Mrs. White in Paddington.

She found the old woman much recovered physically, but scattered and agitated in her manner. Her friend, Mrs. Doughty, was another Scotswoman but not, by her manner and appearance, another retired Fallen. Mrs. Doughty was tall, flat of bosom, and stoic of demeanor. She wore a plain cap over dark hair, and a businesslike fichu clearly intended for purposes of warmth and modesty, not decoration. For all that she appeared undisturbed by her visitor's unusual attire. Miss Tolerance had only met the woman briefly when she had brought Mrs. White there; now, at Mrs. Doughty's urging, she sat and took tea and listened as the older woman unpacked her concerns about her friend.

"She's better than she was when ye brought her, that's certain. Her voice is none sae hoarse as it was, and she's got her spirit back. But—she's addled. Just a wee bit," she added.

"How so?"

"Ye'll see. I've seen nothing like it except when Mr. Doughty was thrown from his horse in Cape St. Vincent year."

"I take it Mr. Doughty struck his head."

"Aye. Bloodied fine it was."

"But Mrs. White was not struck about the head."

Mrs. Doughty shrugged and poured out a little more tea. "Yet that's what she puts me in mind of. Ye'll see."

Fortified with tea and a small square of rock-hard shortbread, Miss Tolerance was taken up to speak to Mrs. White.

She found the older woman making lace with a bobbin

and needle, but the results where what Miss Tolerance might have expected from a child learning the craft.

"I hope I see you much improved," she said.

Mrs. White looked up from her work. "How nice ye've— ye've—" After a moment of searching after the word, she smiled.

"How do you?"

"Oh, well enough. Mrs. D-d-d—Mary is seeing to me kindly. And my neck is—" She hooked a finger into the kerchief which circled her throat to show Miss Tolerance the fading bruises there. "Bet-t-er."

"I am glad to see it. I was hoping to ask you about what happened when you were accosted."

Mrs. White's mouth began to tremble, and she looked down at the tangle of thread in her lap. "I don't—I canna recall."

"Do you recall that I came to call upon you? That we went up to York Street together, and it came on to rain? You returned to your house in the deluge without a rain shield or umbrella and were quite soaked when you got there."

Mrs. White shook her head and gazed up at Miss Tolerance. Her expression beseeched something, understanding, perhaps, or help. "Nothing."

"After you were attacked you attempted to say something about the man who hurt you. Something about a bank? Bank, you said."

The older woman looked bewildered. "Do I know a person named Bank? Did he do—" she gestured at her neck and tears started in her eyes. "I canna recall. I don't know." One tear slid from the inside of Mrs. White's eye and along her nose. She made no attempt to stop it.

Miss Tolerance leaned forward to pat the other woman's hand. "Perhaps with some rest it will come back to you."

"I hope," Mrs. White said sadly. But looking at the old woman's face, her round, rosy cheeks now pale and slack, the eyes faded and anxious, Miss Tolerance was certain that the return of that memory, however useful it might be to herself, would be no blessing for Mrs. White.

She stayed for a little while longer, and they spoke of Mrs. Doughty's kindness in taking Mrs. White in and of the lace Mrs. White was making. "It doesn't—I cannot—I used to—" Mrs. White regarded the mess of thread in her lap.

"And I am certain you will again. Did you make the lace on that cap? It is very handsome."

That won from Mrs. White the first genuine smile since Miss Tolerance's arrival, and Miss Tolerance judged it was time to take her leave.

Miss Tolerance returned the hack to the stable and decided to walk to Tarsio's to see if there was any hope of business there. She had spent more than a week on Mrs. Pouter's business, and while she was still determined to find the person responsible for her death, the necessity of paid employment had begun to gnaw at her attention. Perhaps someone had left word for her at the club.

Corton was on duty at Tarsio's door and pronounced himself gratified to see her. There were two messages, which he would bring up to the Ladies' Salon if Miss Tolerance would be so kind as to ascend, and was there anything she would like by way of refreshment?

She asked for tea and biscuits, and went up to the Ladies' Salon to peruse the announcements in the Gazette with half her attention: births, deaths, affiancements, bankruptcies, all the joys and calamities in the genteel nation published for anyone to see. A name caught her attention, and Miss Tolerance read the entire notice:

Whereas a Commission of Bankrupt is awarded and issued forth against Mark Wheelock Retifer of Fetter Lane, London,

Banker, and he being declared a Bankrupt is hereby required to surrender himself to the Commissioners in the same Commission named, or the major Part of them, on the 10th day of November instant, and on the 14th of December next, at Ten in the Forenoon, at Guildhall, London, and make a full Discovery of his Estate and Effects; when and where the Creditors are to come prepared to prove their Debts, and at the Second Sitting to chuse Assignees, and at the Last Sitting the said Bankrupt is required to finish his Examination and Creditors are to assent or dissent from the Allowance of his Certificate. All persons indebted to the said Bankrupt, or that have any of his Effects, are not to pay or deliver the same but to whom the Commissioners shall appoint, but give notice to Mr. Syddall, Alders-gate-Street.

Not a client, nor someone involved in a past case. No one who owed her money. *Retifer.* She had spoken the name aloud in the last day or so. Bolt and Retifer, Bankers, in whom Mr. Marvell had said—what? That he reposed no confidence? Well, it appeared he was not wrong in that. And Marvell's own true name would, he believed, draw a line from the Fund to a bank that his partner did not want implicated. Which bank?

Miss Tolerance made use of the appointments of the Ladies' Salon to take up a sheet of paper and a pen and sit at a desk near the fireplace, where she wrote down the names of every bank she could recall.

R *othschild*
    Coutts
Drummond's
Child's
Snow's
Jones and Wilkes
Pitt & Son

Bolt and Retifer
Pennantine
Wallpole & Sons
Ingraham, Bruce, Simpson & Co.
Brown, Shipley & Co.

Her pen faltered. There might be a hundred banks in London. Some—Coutts and Rothschild and Snow's—were both large and venerable. She thought perhaps she might start with an assumption that they were too large to be complicit in such a scheme. But the others? If Retifer of Bolt and Retifer was declared a bankrupt, did that make him more or less likely a suspect? And his partner, Bolt, if he existed, was by no means exonerated.

Of the rest of the names, were there any more likely to be entangled with an operation such as a false fund? Any which were less likely? Perhaps she could make another call upon Joshua Glebb, whose encyclopedic knowledge of the institutions of London finance would surely help her narrow her list to something manageable. The hour was not late, but dark had fallen. And there was still tea in the pot; she decided to finish it before she ventured from the warmth of the Ladies' Salon.

She turned her thoughts to Marvell's Fund. The women who had been targeted—elderly, gullible, Fallen, of a better class of impure but not by any means wealthy—suggested that the Fund was not a large operation. The amounts of money swindled from Mrs. Pouter and Mrs. Black, when multiplied by perhaps a dozen more victims, still amounted to... she did the figures in her head. Not much more than five thousand pounds. A considerable amount to an individual, but would a bank or banker risk the reputation of the establishment for such a sum?

She pushed the paper away and put down the pen. As if summoned by the gesture, a waiter appeared at her elbow.

"More hot water, miss? And what message for the fellow in the kitchen?"

"I beg your pardon? What fellow?"

"Didn't Mr. Corton tell you, miss? A man come to the kitchen half an hour ago asking for you. He may be there yet."

"Mr. Corton did not tell me." He had said there were two messages, but clearly had been distracted from their delivery; she would have some words for Mr. Corton later. "May I come down to the kitchen with you? To see if the man—he gave no name? To see if he is still waiting? As Corton did not bring him up, I presume he is not the sort that Mr. Jenkins would like to have speak with me here."

The slightly strangled expression on the waiter's face confirmed her presumption.

"Very well. If you will take me downstairs, I will appreciate it very much."

She followed into the narrow warren of halls and stairways that were the precincts of the club's staff, thence down through the kitchen to the back door. Miss Tolerance gave the waiter a coin, learned his name was also Jenkins—a nephew of Tarsio's manager—and went out to find Joe Boswell on the stairway up to the sidewalk, hands in pockets, hunched against the chill.

"I apologize—I understand you have been kept waiting here for me, and this is not the night for it." As she spoke her breath plumed up whitely. "I wasn't told until just now that you had called. May I at least buy you something warming to drink?"

Joe's smile flashed wide. "You may indeed, miss."

"Shall we go to the Duke of Sussex, where we spoke last time?"

"Suits me fine."

Shortly they were seated in the tavern at a table Miss

Tolerance chose because it was near the fire. Joe Boswell had spoken no word of complaint, but she thought she saw his jaw working with the effort of keeping his teeth from chattering. Joe asked for punch, Miss Tolerance for ale. When the punch was delivered, hot and fragrant, Joe cupped his hands over the steaming tankard and smiled.

"There's as does a body good," he admitted.

Miss Tolerance kept her curiosity in check, and they drank in companionable silence for a few minutes. At last, Joe looked up from his empty tankard. "Wouldn't mind the same again."

Miss Tolerance hailed a pot-boy, the order was given, and she decided that enough time had gone by that she could ask why he desired to speak with her.

"I've some news and questions for you."

"Questions?"

"And news. When you hear the gen I got for you, you'll feel it worth the second—ah, thank you, my darlin'." That was for the girl who brought his punch, and was accompanied by a smile that made the girl stammer her reply.

"If you are finished making that young woman fall in love with you," Miss Tolerance began, once the maid had returned to the bar.

"Just bein' polite, ain't I?" Joe Boswell grinned again, clearly enjoying his effect. "Now, about your Mr. Marvell. There's a slippery fellow. Hasn't much of a mark on the world, and no one that should know of 'im seems to want to speak of 'im. But I can tell you what 'is name is, anyroad. Mr. George Kent."

As she repeated the name to herself, the matter revealed itself to Miss Tolerance with enough force that she suddenly felt she had been stupid not to suspicion it. "The son of the woman who owns the building on Jermyn Street," she said.

"Might be," Joe allowed.

"Mrs. Kent owns the building where Marvell used to live.

The agent told me, and I spoke with her at her house. But she insisted she knew nothing of a Mr. Marvell—"

"Could be so. Stands to reason your man'd lie to 'er, specially if 'e's been carryin' on some sort of mace on 'er property."

"I suppose so. I had a very interesting conversation with him today."

"Met 'im face to face, did you? What'd 'e 'ave to say for 'imself?"

"A good deal. I found him by quite by accident and went to meet him in the guise of—of a potential victim. You saw me in that guise when we met yesterday in Covent Garden."

Joe nodded thoughtfully. "I didn't say at the time, but that struck me as not your usual style, miss. So, did 'e break down and spill?"

"On the contrary, he was all denials and professed himself shocked to hear that the Fund is not all it should be."

"Well, that's no surprise, is it?"

"No. But I wish you had heard him. I am almost convinced that he believes what he told me. He did go so far as to admit that Marvell was not his real name—a *nom d'enterprise*, he called it, but he argued that the Fund was a purely altruistic attempt to assist the elderly—"

"A purely what?"

"Altruistic. Selfless. Not criminal. He implied that he took his name so that his connection to a banking family would not be apparent. But I know of no banking family named Kent, do you?"

"History of the bankin' families of London ain't much in my line."

"Nor mine. But I do have an acquaintance in whose line it decidedly lies. I was planning to visit him until I heard that you were waiting. I will say, for your interest in the matter, that he told me the name was chosen without thought of any connection to your people. He was surprised to hear there was any connection at all."

Joe took a deep draught of punch, so that Miss Tolerance could not judge his reaction to this information. "So where'd this Marvell-Kent pike off to, once he left Jermyn Street?"

"Stafford Street. He said the Jermyn Street rooms were too expensive—although if his mother owns the building, why would cost be a problem?"

"Can't say." Joe shrugged.

"His mother swore that she did not know who rented the room, that her son had arranged the lease himself, so perhaps she did not know—" Miss Tolerance looked up. Joe Boswell was watching her with mingled amusement and curiosity. "I beg your pardon. Sometimes the only way for me to puzzle out a problem is to speak it aloud."

Joe grinned. He had finished his second tankard of punch, and the scents of wine, gin, fruit, and spice were on his breath. It was not unpleasant.

"Mother Ella does that."

Miss Tolerance was recalled to herself. "How is Mother Ella? Will you give her my compliments?"

"I will, that. So you've found the gent a-livin' in Stafford Street, and you've no more need t' track 'im down."

"Yes. Although the intelligence of his true name is very useful. Thank you. May I—" She slid her hand into the pocket of her greatcoat to find her purse.

"Mother'd skin me alive do I take yer silver. She took a likin' to you."

"Well, Joe, I am in your debt." As she spoke the words the admission gave her pause. Who knew what meaning a debt had among his folk?

As if he guessed what she was thinking, Joe shook his head. "Don't fret, miss. I shan't demand anything of you ye can't make good on."

This assurance Miss Tolerance found less than reassuring.

"If you need to get word to me for anything else, please leave word at Tarsio's."

"The catch-fart there won't be 'appy to see my face." The idea seemed to amuse him.

"I shall leave word with Mr. Corton and Mr. Steen that I am always interested in messages from you—passed along in a timely manner. Oh, I have just now recalled that Corton told me that there were two messages for me. I assume one was from you, but—"

Joe got to his feet. "But you're eager now to find out what the other was, I reckon."

Miss Tolerance put a few coins on the table to cover the cost of the drinks. "I am. I regret to leave so unceremoniously."

"I don't much stand upon ceremony." Still, Joe made her a bow with enough flourish to make Miss Tolerance laugh as she returned the courtesy.

Miss Tolerance's interview with Corton was accomplished in the foyer of Tarsio's, after the arrival of two separate parties of gentlemen whose coats and other requirements it was necessary for him to deal with. The porter apologized that he had forgotten the messages; she put them in her pocket and took a moment to make it very clear that, whatever his opinion of Joe Boswell or anyone who left a message for her, it was not Tarsio's business to keep those messages from her. Several expressions—of resentment, chagrin, and dismay—chased across his face before he managed to assume the face of imperturbability he normally wore.

"I hope we are clear on the matter?"

Corton bowed stiffly. "Yes, miss."

As a corrective for the harshnesss of her tone, Miss

Tolerance slipped him a coin and permitted him to hold the door for her when she went out into the night. On the Tarsio's step, by the light of the torch that illuminated it, she opened the papers Corton had passed to her. One was a slip that said, tersely, *A Traveler-fellow come asking for you.* The second was a note in Marianne Touchwell's hand.

Sarah, when you receive this, please return to Manchester Square as soon as you may.

Chapter Twelve

Miss Tolerance did not delay in returning to Mrs. Brereton's house; Mrs. Brereton's health had been unreliable enough of late to make that a matter without question. Joshua Glebb would certainly be holding court at the Wheat Sheaf in the morning, and happy to see her. Miss Tolerance went first to her cottage, left off her Gunnard coat and the rest of her masculine garb and, dressed in modest feminine attire, entered Mrs. Brereton's through the kitchen.

Mrs. Gordon, her slippers off, sat at the kitchen table with Jess, Tim, and one of the upstairs maids, in a moment of repose. The younger of the party had tankards of ale before them; Mrs. Gordon had a generous measure of gin in a chipped glass, and sat back heavily, rotating first one foot and then the other with an expression of relief.

"Miss Sarah! Come sit! Will you have a tot with us?"

"Thank you kindly, Cook, but the three of you are taking your ease after a long day; I won't interrupt that." Miss Tolerance noted the fleeting expression of relief on the younger faces; the thought of socializing with someone whose station was neither servant nor upstairs worker seemed to oppress them.

Mrs. Gordon had no such qualms and repeated her invitation. "I'd like to hear how you're getting on."

Miss Tolerance, reflecting that she was yet unsure what report to make, put off that evil hour by insisting that she must first call on her aunt and Marianne Touchwell.

"Well, should you come down afore I've punched my breads down for the last time, take a glass with me then."

Miss Tolerance promised that she would do so and made her way through the green baize door into the front hallway. Sounds of music and jollity issued from one of the parlors, but she encountered no one on her way up to her aunt's room. She was met at the door by Frost, who pressed a finger to her lips to make clear that her mistress was not to be bothered.

"How does my aunt, Frost? Mrs. Touchwell seemed concerned."

Frost sniffed. Although she had made common cause with Marianne and with Miss Tolerance over the matter of her mistress's health, she was jealous of any influence with Mrs. Brereton and believed that no one else could tend her as she did. "That Marianne gets upset over the least thing," she said. "Ma'am's just tired and has a bilious stomach. Nothing to be worried about."

Miss Tolerance took this to mean that if worrying was to be done, Miss Frost would get the first chance of it.

"I am sorry to hear Aunt Thea is unwell," she said gravely. "I am relieved to know she is in your good care, but if there is any way in which I might be of use—"

"Tell that Marianne not to worrit Ma'am over things." Frost sniffed again. "If she's been given the authority over all *that* downstairs—" her tone left no doubt of Frost's opinion of the activities of Mrs. Brereton's establishment— "let her use it and leave my poor lady alone!"

"I will tell her," Miss Tolerance promised. "Pray give my aunt my best love when she wakes."

Frost made no promises but nodded as she turned back into the room.

Mrs. Touchwell's diagnosis did not much vary from Miss Frost's. "She's got a touch of dyspepsia and perhaps a little fever. But her mood in the past few days has been rather low."

"Low?"

Mrs. Touchwell shrugged. "I think she's dwelling on the fact that man is mortal, as the vicar says. Woman, too."

"Indisputably. But my aunt is not ancient. Is there something that causes her to dwell heavily upon mortality?"

"It's since she stopped receiving callers. That was always—well, not that there was ever a question that she was fine-looking, not even in the last few years. Still, I think having men flocking round gave her the sense that she weren't so old as her years. Now that she stopped—and time enough, I'd say—she hasn't had that to buoy up her spirits."

Had she been asked, Miss Tolerance would have said she believed that relinquishing the relentless demands of the flesh by men for whom she had no fondness must be a relief to her aunt. It certainly would have been for herself in like circumstances. Mrs. Brereton assuredly had enough vanity to appreciate the admiration due her as a woman both handsome and clever, but why should she lack that?

"Surely my aunt still has company?"

"She don't come downstairs like she used to, to preside over the drawing room." Marianne pursed her lips. "I blame that bastard Tichenor—" she spoke of Mrs. Brereton's former suitor. "He was a blow to heart and head, if you take my meaning. I think it did Mrs. B a world of good to feel that she had one truly devoted follower, and then to find out he was reaching for the purse-strings—"

"Very lowering," Miss Tolerance agreed. "But surely she has had other callers."

Marianne shook her head. "Not since then. Not that I have seen. As I said, she don't come down to the salon as she used to."

"And no one calls merely for old time's sake?"

"I think Mrs. B discouraged it. Vanity, perhaps. Or maybe she didn't want custom to get in the habit of visiting without paying, if you take my meaning. Frost would know."

A brief conference with Miss Frost suggested that Mrs. Brereton indeed had callers but refused to see them, saying that now she had quitted as a woman of pleasure she would not stand to be seen as a figure of pathos.

"And so she stays in her room all day."

"She *does* go down," Frost insisted, "some days. Now and then. Not often."

Marianne shook her head. "I had thought she must be feeling poorly, or that she came downstairs when I was not there to see her there."

"No wonder if my aunt is melancholy." Miss Tolerance spoke quickly to forestall any demur from Frost. "And I am sure the business would be the better for having her make an appearance when she is well enough to do it. It is Mrs. Brereton's house, after all." She glanced at Mrs. Touchwell, begging her agreement.

"I should say it is. The girls mind me well enough, but I know both they and the gentlemen would be the better for casting an eye on the mistress of the house more often."

"Frost, how do you suppose we might convey this—"

But Miss Frost, her mistress's importance appealed to, was already considering the matter. "I'm sure ma'am has not considered things in that light, but you leave all to me."

Frost's expression of militant resolve gave Miss Tolerance pause. "If she truly is not well—" she began, but was instantly cut short.

"If she's needed, I know Ma'am won't shirk. She needn't

stay below all evening, but occupation will do her good. Tomorrow evening!"

Taking this, rightly, as dismissal, Miss Tolerance and Mrs. Touchwell went downstairs.

"I only hope Frost don't persuade your aunt that the business is suffering under my management," Marianne murmured. "We don't want her in a panic."

"Do you continue to show her the 'counts books? Then she can see that the finances of the house are not suffering, and you are not allowing the maids to drink the cream or forget to polish the brass. If she dares to fret over your management, tell me and I shall set her straight."

Marianne grinned. "And wouldn't I like to see that. But thank you, Sarah, for taking the time—"

"As if I would not! Any concerns over Aunt Thea's health are properly mine as well as yours. And Frost's, of course."

They parted in the hallway.

Miss Tolerance went down to the kitchen, where the brief period of relaxation had evidently ended. Jess was arranging tiny, elegant pastries upon a silver salver, and Tim, under Cook's supervision, was beating cream. When his arm began to flag, she poked him in his side, hard enough that the boy almost dropped the copper bowl he held.

"Go on, go on!" she exhorted. "Don't you stop until it holds a peak, boy!" She looked up long enough to greet Miss Tolerance. "Do you go into my little room, Miss Sarah. I poured you out a glass of wine, and I'll be with you directly the cream is whipped."

Miss Tolerance, judging that Mrs. Gordon had something to discuss beyond cream and hospitality, did as she was told. She perched upon a stool and took up her glass, which had a good measure of burgundy, and sipped it appreciatively. Mrs. Brereton did not stint the kitchen on wine and spirits.

"Well, Miss Sarah." Cook squeezed past her and sat in the rocking chair by the cot. Everything in the little room was neat and clean, but there was little Miss Tolerance could see that was personal to Mrs. Gordon herself. But of course, much of her belongings might have been lost in the fire in her rooms.

"Have you quite abandoned your lodgings in Castle Street?"

"I couldn't go back there no more. Nothing much lost, except it put paid to my poor Annie." Cook's lip trembled, which sent her jowls dancing momentarily. "I never was a one for keepsakes and bits o' stuff, that was more Annie's way. Whatever wan't taken by the neighbors I brung back here, but you can see it ain't much."

Miss Tolerance put her glass aside. "You'd like to know what progress I've made in finding Mrs. Pouter's killer, I imagine."

"To know if there's any point to going on wi' it. Now the funeral's over, and the first shock of it, I—with no Annie to take the money back, and nor I don't suppose you'll find much of anything—"

"In fact, as of today I had several very interesting leads. I spoke with the man I believe to be the Mr. Marvell who swindled her, and tomorrow I have an appointment to see him again, and, I hope, his partner."

"Partner?" Mrs. Gordon looked at Miss Tolerance her eyes wide. "I was sure, when I come to think on it, that there's be no chance your finding anything. And with Annie gone—"

"She was not the only one to be so taken advantage of, Cook. Another woman almost died a few days ago. You may rest assured that I am very interested in seeing the matter to conclusion."

"Are you?" It seemed to Miss Tolerance that Mrs. Gordon's tone was less than enthusiastic, but the hour was late. Perhaps she was merely tired. "You mean to go on, then?"

"While I can," Miss Tolerance agreed. "But it is late, and I must not keep you from your bed—"

"I've a way to go before I sleep, Miss Sarah, but thank you for the thought. I've got my jellies to go up, and the second batch of breads to punch down and leave to rise."

"Then I shall leave you to it."

As she passed through the kitchen, Miss Tolerance caught sight of several cloth-covered bread pans left by the hearth, Jess engaged in sugaring grapes, and Tim sweeping out ashes from the oven. She did not wish to be there to witness Cook's wrath if she saw the soot flying in proximity to her rising dough, so took herself back to her cottage and to bed.

Miss Tolerance rose early, breakfasted, dressed in breeches, boots, and her Gunnard greatcoat, and was on the way to the Wheat Sheaf before Manchester Square had had an opportunity to fill up with flower-sellers, knife-grinders, and the other hopeful vendors who populated it in the hours before noon. The sun shone brightly in an unaccustomedly clear sky, although it did little to cut the bite of the wind; Miss Tolerance nestled her chin further into the collar of her coat and started the walk to the Liberty of Savoy, the Wheat Sheaf, and Joshua Glebb.

That neighborhood was by no means as quiet as her aunt's had been. A victualer's cart stood at the door of the Wheat Sheaf, and a gaunt woman with a flyaway cap perched on a quantity of pale blond hair stood with her arms akimbo, in tense conversation with a man who had the corpse of some animal—a sheep, perhaps—hoist on his shoulder. Miss Tolerance dodged around them and made her way to the tap room, wondering if hostilities were about to break out. If they did, her money was upon the woman, who had a particularly ferocious demeanor.

No one was at the bar, but a beefy, square-set man sat near the fire, drowsing over a tankard. Miss Tolerance dared to hope that Mr. Boddick would arrive shortly and serve coffee. She took a seat near the fire, relishing the warmth, and looked about her for a newspaper. The drowsing man had the Times on his table; she did not scruple to take it up and was shortly involved reading a report about a battle in Bornos, somewhere on the Spanish peninsula.

"What will ye have, sir?"

Miss Tolerance looked up to see the fair-haired woman standing behind the bar, hands still upon her hips, expression of displeasure still upon her face.

"Coffee, please."

At the sound of Miss Tolerance's voice, the woman's brows drew together and she bustled away as if no other mode of locomotion was suited to express her disapproval. A few minutes later, Miss Tolerance heard raised voices from the room behind the bar; one she recognized as belonging to Boddick, the owner of the house, and the other she thought must belong to the disapproving woman.

A few minutes later, Mr. Boddick arrived with her coffee and greeted her cordially. His eye was still half upon the door he had come through, however, and his color was high.

"Have I caused you trouble, Mr. Boddick?"

"Rest easy, Miss. My wife's sister's come to 'elp after Mrs. B's confinement, like. She was a mite surprised, like, to realize you weren't the fellow she took you for."

"I am sorry if I distressed your sister-at-law."

"Don't fret, Miss. She ain't been well this sixmonth, and it takes a toll 'pon her temper. I hope you don't take offense by it, Miss."

"Of course not. I hope her health is improving."

Boddick shook his head. "Sorry to say it ain't, Miss. Susan used to be plump as a dove, just like my Katie, and now you see 'er."

"Can nothing be done to help her?"

Again, Boddick shook his head. "Ain't no physic for it. A skee-ruse, the surgeon says, nor it isn't one he dast go cutting to find."

Miss Tolerance digested this information. *Scirrhus* was an old-fashioned term for a cancer. "I am very sorry to hear it, Mr. Boddick."

"So you'll see why Sue ain't as cordial as she used to be, and if you could make allowances—"

"By all means. And if there is any way in which I might be of service, you will call upon me?"

Boddick smiled grimly. "That's kind in you, Miss. I'll remember that you offered. I collect you've come wanting a word with Mr. Glebb? He should be here within the hour."

"Thank you, Mr. Boddick. And—" could she extend an offer of assistance without giving offence? "I am quite serious. If there is any way at all that I can assist—"

Boddick gave a curious motion, smile and shrug and ducking of his head. "That's kind in you, Miss T. More coffee?"

In the event, Boddick was optimistic. Joshua Glebb arrived an hour and a half later, by which time Miss Tolerance had drunk more coffee than she strictly required and had made a trip to the necessary. Glebb took his place at his customary table, waved two fingers at Boddick in lieu of an order, and looked about him. When his eye fell on Miss Tolerance, he inclined his head magisterially and gestured her forward. Several others in the room looked crestfallen.

"Good morning, sir. I trust I see you well?"

"Tolerable, Miss T. And you?"

"Well, and in search of enlightenment."

Glebb raised his handkerchief to mop at the dew at the end of his nose. "How can I enlighten you?"

Miss Tolerance sketched in the background of her

question. "What bank, or banks, might there be which would likely participate in such a scheme?"

Glebb shook his head. "I can't think of one. Them as is flourishing wouldn't risk their reputation. Them as is not—well, the sort of money you're talking about ain't sufficient for the risk."

"Is there anything other than money that a bank might gain from such a scheme?"

Glebb scowled. "Bankers live by money and reputation, Miss T. What else could be offered?"

A glimmer of an idea came to Miss Tolerance. "What about custom, sir?"

Glebb weighed the idea, then shook his head. "The sort of custom they'd be gaining ain't the sort they would be bragging about—elderly impures—nor the sort with a fortune to bring with 'em. I can't see any reason for a banker to fall into it, Miss T."

Miss Tolerance found herself unable to entirely relinquish the notion. "Of all the banks in London, which might be the ones most likely to succumb to the idea? Are there any whose positions are precarious enough that they might be vulnerable?"

Mr. Glebb plainly considered the notion unworthy of his time, but "You can rule out the big houses: Coutts' and Child's and Rothschild and Drummond's and Snow's."

"But the smaller houses—I see that Retifer and Bolt—"

"Oh, if that's the sort of establishment you mean. Retifer inherited half the bank from his old uncle and went straight off to gamble it away."

"One does prefer to think that bankers are not given to such weaknesses."

"Might prefer it, but that's not the way of things. Mind, the uncle was a fine fellow. Only thing he did wrong was to leave the bank to young Mark. The second generation's always a question, ain't it?"

"Are there other banks with *second generation* owners who might be similarly troubled?"

Glebb stared at an invisible point in the air, as if summoning intelligence. At last, "You might look into Jones and Wilkes, and perhaps Joss Hambly of Wheelock and Sons. I can't think of any others. Young Tom Walpole was born and bred to the bank, so was Andrew Pennantine. Neither of them is what I'd call unsteady. Holly married into Portenham's Bank, but that ain't recent, and he's so straight they might stick a pole up his—" The old man stopped, reddened, and apologized.

Miss Tolerance waved away his embarrassment. "Jones and Wilkes, and Wheelock. If it happens you think of any other firms—" she reached for her purse and slid a half-crown across the table. "I can see there are others who wish your attention, sir. Thank you very much for your assistance."

Glebb bid her farewell cordially, already beckoning to his next client.

The pocket watches on view in the window of a clock-maker on the Strand informed her that it lacked an hour until noon. She had told Mr. Kent-Marvell that she would return at that time, and now an inconvenient amount of time lay before her; it was too cold to dawdle and peer into shop windows. In the end, she walked briskly to Stafford Street and ordered soup at the tavern across the street. From the look of it, the Goat was a long-established house favored by locals. She took up a seat by the window and was pleased to see Bart, the leader of her Jermyn Street boys, standing at the corner of Albemarle Street, stamping his feet and wringing his hands in the cold before making a great show of sweeping the crossing for a large matron with a small child.

The soup, when it came, was a welcome change from

coffee: thick, savory, and very hot. Miss Tolerance looked idly out the window and sipped, thinking that perhaps her meeting with Marvell today would render further investigation into banks and bankers unnecessary. In the street, a wagon collided with a pushcart and spilled its contents—stools and other small wooden movables—across the sidewalk. The wagon driver climbed down and looked for the owner of the cart.

The cartman emerged a moment later from Marvell's building, and he and the wagoner began to argue furiously while passers-by stepped carefully over and around the furniture in their path. There was something familiar about the owner of the cart, but he was so thoroughly wrapped against the cold that, between the scarf that muffled him up to his nose and the hat which was drawn over his brow, it was impossible to be certain what he looked like.

Then two women—one elderly and neatly dressed, the other large, shabby, and much younger—made common cause in belaboring both driver and cartman, and after a minute, the men retreated, the wagoner to climb back on his perch and back his horses away, and the cartman to gather up his wares and return them to his pushcart. *Who needs the Opera when any London street affords such drama?*

When the bells of St. Margaret's and St. George's tolled the hour, Miss Tolerance went across to meet with Mr. Kent. She permitted Bart to sweep the street for her, gave him ha'penny, and asked if he or his mates had seen anything worth reporting.

"Nah, none of us seen 'ide nor 'air of im since yestidday. Others come and gone, but yer man ain't been in nor out."

"Well done. Are you frozen through? Do you wish to warm yourself up?"

The boy nodded vigorously. "That'd be fine, miss." He held out his hand as if in hopes that Miss Tolerance would provide wherewithal for the warming. After a moment, she shook her head at her own foolishness and added another ha'penny to the one she had already provided.

The building door was opened by the same elderly man as yesterday. Miss Tolerance climbed to the second floor and knocked.

"Mr. Marvell?"

No answer came. She called again, again received no reply, and tried the door. The latch moved easily: when she pushed the door it swung open. Marvell—George Kent, as he had been in life, lay dead on the floor.

Blood pooled around him, puddled by his head and on one side where a wound of some sort had soaked through his shirt, waistcoat, and coat. The ugly, dapper little man lay on his back, eyes wide, his tongue protruding from between his odd, peg-like teeth. Miss Tolerance swallowed hard against the coppery smell of blood, circled the body so as not to step in the gore, and crouched down to examine his wounds. The blood at his head and his side appeared to have arisen from the same cause: a fireplace poker lay half hidden under Kent's body, coated with gore.

Miss Tolerance removed her glove to probe gently at Kent's throat, where she saw signs of bruising. Throttling again?

She rose, put her glove back on, and went downstairs to give the alarm.

As she waited for the Watch, whom the elderly porter had scuttled off to find, Miss Tolerance reflected that this was the third time she had come upon a person dead, or near death, in less than a week. And odd Mr. Kent, with his peculiar flat face and lively manner, had been so earnest in his insistence that the fund was legitimate, so certain that he would greet her with proof of it. The only one with motive to kill must be the little man's partner, whom he had promised to summon to meet her. With Kent dead, her link to that partner was gone.

The Watch arrived, with the porter panting behind him,

and then a familiar face: Mr. Penryn, the younger of the two Bow Street investigators who most commonly worked with Sir Walter Mandif. He met Miss Tolerance's eye and ducked his head in acknowledgment before he invited all—Watch, porter, and Miss Tolerance—to Marvell's rooms. The porter declined, citing poor wind; the rest ascended.

The Watch, who had taken Miss Tolerance as she seemed, asked over his shoulders, "You discovered the corpus, sir? And what time you come to find 'im? Noon? You certain of the time?" They reached the second floor at the point the third question was asked and answered, and the Watch stood back to let Mr. Penryn precede him through the door. For a few moments, Penryn and the Watch circled round Marvell's body, as careful as Miss Tolerance had been to avoid stepping into the blood.

"He was laid out loike this when you found 'im?" Penryn asked.

Miss Tolerance agreed that the deceased had not moved.

"An' what was yor business wiv the deceased, sir?" That was the Watch again.

"I had asked him about a business venture in which he was involved, and he had bid me come to look at proof of its legitimacy and profitability." Close enough. The last thing she wanted to do was suggest to the Law that she might have reason to have murdered the man. "Did the porter say that anyone else had visited Mr. Marvell?"

The Watchman shook his head. "'E was back in the necessary half the morning, though. A rumpus in 'is bowels, 'e says. Anyone could ha' been in or out."

"Aye, but a man meanin' murder couldn't count on that," Penryn said.

Miss Tolerance agreed and resolved to speak with Bart again. "Perhaps whoever did this did not come with intent to kill. The use of the fire-iron—it's a weapon of opportunity. Perhaps there was a sudden provocation."

"Well, Coroner'll be summoned and likely call a jury. Body can't be moved 'til then." Penryn dispatched the Watch to the nearest magistrate's station in Great Marlborough Street. The man looked relieved to have someone in higher authority make the decision, and was gone in a moment.

Alone with the Runner, Miss Tolerance noted. "I should tell you I had discovered that the deceased's true name is George Kent. He used the name Marvell for his business."

Penryn licked the rounded point of his pencil and made a note in the pocket-book in which he had taking down details of the scene. "Anything else, miss?"

"It is possible that his mother is a Mrs. Kent of Hans Place." She watched as he wrote that as well. "It is very convenient that you were so near by."

Penryn tucked his chin like a boy caught out in mischief. "Sir Walter said you was meeting up with this 'un. He was concerned, loike. As I was in the neighborhood—"

"I see." She was not certain how to feel: Sir Walter had made his concern plain, and she had made equally plain her intention to go alone. However she felt, it was not Penryn's fault that he had, as she suspected, followed her to her rendezvous. "Do I need to stay for the Coroner, do you think?"

Penryn shook his head. "I know fine where to locate you should it prove needful, miss."

She spared a last, regretful, look at Marvell's body, then made her way downstairs.

Bart was nowhere in evidence, but another boy—she could not recall his name—was neatly sweeping a pile of horse dung from the path of a gentleman and lady. When he had been paid for the service, he dodged across the street to her, narrowly escaping death under the wheels of a dray.

"Sweep for ye, lady?" He grinned up at her.

"Please." When the traffic paused, he stepped into the street and swept the path before Miss Tolerance with admirable energy. At the far side, as she paid him, "I know I set you all the task of watching for a little man with bowed legs and a head of curly fair hair. Bart told me he had not left the building. But what about comings and goings?"

"Wot, you mean other blokes goin' in or out?"

"I mean that exactly."

He stuck his lip out, an aid to memory. "I only been 'ere since this mornin', trading off with Bart. There's the old man as sits by the door—only saw him once. And a man brought in a cupboard—brung it in a barrow, carried it up. Dunno 'ow 'e coulda—it was that big. But I dunno if 'e brung the cupboard up to your man wiv the curly thatch."

Miss Tolerance remembered the hostilities she had witnessed between the wagoneer and the carter. "Just a little before noon?"

The lad nodded. "That's the one. Wrapped up against the cold, but no 'at, and 'is 'air all blown about. I din't see 'im come out—Bart come and tol' me to get warmed. It's that cold today."

She agreed that it was indeed very cold.

"You still want us 'ere, miss?"

She weighed the possibility of more information against the cost, recalled to herself that Marvell's rooms would likely have the coroner and his hastily gathered jury in and out of them for the rest of the day, and told the boy that he was relieved of duty. "Tell Bart as well. And thank you."

Then she left and turned her steps toward Bow Street.

Chapter Thirteen

Bow Street court was in recess; the clerk at Bow Street said Sir Walter had stepped out to a pie shop down the road. As she regained the street, Miss Tolerance felt a tug at her coat. Without turning, she put a hand out and grasped the shoulder of a scrawny child. The boy, most of his forearm vanished into the deep front pocket of Miss Tolerance's Gunnard coat, attempted a smile that was spoiled by the panic in his eyes and the rivulets of snot on his upper lip. Miss Tolerance guided the boy's hand out of her pocket, turned it over, and made a great show of examining it before she returned it to its owner. The boy turned and ran.

A voice behind Miss Tolerance said mildly, "He has pluck, to attempt robbery on the courthouse steps." Sir Walter had come up beside her. "Did you come seeking me? Let us go in —perhaps you will share my very humble luncheon?" He carried a parcel wrapped in newspaper, oil-spotted and fragrant of onion and pork.

If she was going to remonstrate with him—and she thought she must—perhaps it would go easier over a meal. And the pie smelled very good.

Settled in Sir Walter's office, and the pie cut into two neat halves between them, Miss Tolerance and Sir Walter spent some time upon refreshment. When she was at last ready to speak, "You set Penryn to follow me?"

Sir Walter captured a piece of pie crust that had fallen to the side. "I told him it was possible he might be needed in the area of Stafford Street." His expression was so much like the guilty grimace she had seen on Penryn's face earlier that Miss Tolerance could not find the heart to scold.

"As it turned out, you were right, but not on my account. Mr. Marvell—whose name was really George Kent—was dead when I arrived to see him."

"Dead. Murdered?"

"Penryn has reported it to you?"

"No. But under the circumstances, I am not surprised. I am certain I will hear from Penryn shortly."

"In the event, it was fortunate he was there," Miss Tolerance said, grave. "Poor Marvell—I think his death must be laid at my door. He told me he would talk to his partner and get me proof that his Fund was licit."

"And you think the partner killed him as a result. What of the other deaths? Do you absolve him of those?"

"I do not know. He seemed genuinely distressed to hear of Mrs. Pouter's death. He insisted that the Fund was legitimate—"

Sir Walter's expression was one of polite disbelief. "And you believed him."

"Not entirely—that is, I believe that *he* believed it. I know reason is against it, Sir Walter, and what Marvell believed is now very much beside the point. Stirring up this business has led to two deaths since Mrs. Pouter first came to me, and an attack on another—"

"Thus, you cannot let the matter rest."

"How can I? If Marvell—Kent—whatever! If *he* was not the criminal, certainly there is one. And if that person is not found, he may start the whole business anew."

Sir Walter swept the last crumbs of pie crust on his desk together in a tidy pile.

"I take it, then, that no blame attaches to Mother Ella's folk? Joe Boswell will be pleased to hear it."

"No blame that I can think of. I had not expected to do so, but I like your Mr. Boswell, Sir Walter—although the same cannot be said for the staff at Tarsio's."

"Kept him out?" Sir Walter's tone was sympathetic.

She nodded. "The landlord at the Duke of Sussex is, fortunately, not so high."

"And Joe was able to give you some assistance. He or Mother Ella."

"He was. He and Mother Ella were—a surprise."

"How so? Did you like Mother Ella?"

"They are hardly the Travelers my nursery maid warned me against when I was naughty. And I should as soon say I *liked* the Queen. Admire her is, perhaps, closer to the mark. She's a very salty, clever old woman. I know she makes tonics and tells fortunes, but what does Joe do? Aside from Mother's bidding?"

"Not what you may imagine. He's a joiner. Quite a fine one, and does handsome work, but many of the people who could pay him what his work is worth will not do so for fear of having him in their homes."

"Cabinetry. I should not have guessed that. How did you come to know them?"

"In the course of my work." Sir Walter steepled his fingers and regarded them. "It is very easy to accuse folk who have no fixed home or work, but I've found that many of the Travelers who are brought before me are no more dishonest than any other citizens. I admit that Joe and Mother Ella both seem to take a little delight in tweaking the common notion of what they—what the Travelers are."

Somewhere outside the room, a clock struck the hour.

"Time for court to reconvene?" Miss Tolerance asked.

Sir Walter looked over the remains of their luncheon regretfully. "It is. This was an unexpected pleasure. Perhaps some other time we might meet for a glass of wine."

Miss Tolerance was not certain what to say. Did he propose to resume the friendship that his proposals had interrupted?

"We are, I hope, still friends," he added.

She did not give him an indication of the pang this sentiment gave her. Instead, "Indeed, I hope we shall always be."

Sir Walter got to his feet and offered his hand to Miss Tolerance. "I shall hope to see you soon. And I condole with you on the death of Mr. Marvell." He bowed over her hand and, upon straightening, shook his shoulders as if assuming the mantle of magistrate again, and returned to the courtroom.

Miss Tolerance occupied herself on the walk back to Manchester Square by considering the degree to which she was complicit in Marvell's death. The questions she had asked had, surely, spurred his confederate to murder.

By the time she reached her cottage, however, common sense had reminded her that, had she taken Kent to the Bow Street or Great Marlborough Public Office she would have had no evidence to offer, only inference and suspicion. Kent would doubtless have protested his blamelessness before the magistracy. And—for all his peculiarity—he was a man, she and her client were women and Fallen. If the matter as it had stood the day before came before a magistrate, even one as sympathetic as Sir Walter Mandif, Miss Tolerance was not at all sure but that the entire issue would be dismissed from the court.

The only way to find the author of Mrs. Pouter's financial ruin and her death, as well as the deaths of Mrs. Black and

Kent himself, and of the near death of Mrs. White, was to continue to pursue the matter.

Miss Tolerance found herself wishing that a woman of good family and fortune with a straying husband might appear, demanding an uncomplicated inquiry into her husband's amours. A simple matter with no unsettling issues of responsibility for what happened as a result of her own action in stirring a pot.

She put the kettle on, then decided she wanted something stronger and took the decanter down from the dresser where she kept her dishes. As she turned away she felt a tickle, a familiar impression that she had failed to notice some important detail, information that would make all clear. Except that, in her experience, information that should make an investigation clear often turned out to be the thing that muddied the waters.

She poured wine and returned to her seat, looking idly at the footstool by the settle.

Footstool, settle, table, dresser. Carpenter. Joiner. Joinery. A pushcart had spilled its contents—stools and tables and chairs—across the sidewalk in front of Marvell's door. A man had come from the building only a few minutes before she entered it, wrapped up in a scarf and hat so that his face could not be seen. Reasonable on a day as cold as this. Miss Tolerance kicked idly at the footstool. She had thought the man looked familiar. That his gait put her in mind of—

She sat upright and almost knocked her glass from the table. Joe Boswell. The pushcart man had put her in mind of Joe Boswell. Who was a joiner. He might have had a delivery to make in Stafford Street, someone in the same building. There were several rooms on each floor, and three floors above the street.

A respect for the forces of coincidence kept Miss Tolerance from concluding that the man she had seen was Joe Boswell, and that he had been there to do harm to a man whose antics appeared to slander the Travelers. But once raised, the question demanded an answer.

Could he have murdered George Kent?

Reluctantly, Miss Tolerance pulled on the boots she had shed upon arriving home, wrapped a muffler twice around her throat, pulled her Gunnard coat down from its peg, and stepped from her house to return to Stafford Street.

The hue and cry that commonly accompanied the discovery of a body had receded. The street was busy but not choked with ghoulish onlookers; likely the coroner had brought his jury, then adjourned to some more cordial surrounding—a tavern, by tradition—to bring in a verdict. Miss Tolerance looked about for Bart or the boy she had encountered earlier, but of course, she had dismissed them. The porter at Number 12 had clearly been treating the cold, or the shock of a murder upon the premises, with a good deal of gin. When she asked him if he remembered a man who made a delivery of furniture that morning, he shook his head sloppily. "'Appen I was at the necessary. Din't see 'im leave neither, if you was going to ask." He peered at her closely. "You was 'ere this mornin' too, wasn't you?"

Unfortunately, no amount of bribery seemed to loosen the porter's memory or his tongue. "Me bowels—" he began.

Miss Tolerance thanked him and left.

After a few minutes in the street, she was able to hire a hackney carriage which she directed to Highbury.

From the little she knew of him Miss Tolerance did not believe that Joe Boswell would kill in cold blood, nor did she believe that Mother Ella would countenance murder. If Joe Boswell had visited Kent and struck him down it was most likely a spontaneous act born of anger or panic.

Clouds rolled in and dusk was falling. On her previous

visit to Mother Ella, she had thought the field where the old woman and her people lived to be curiously warm and welcoming. Today few lamps had yet been lit; approaching on a road where torches provided the only illumination, she now found the prospect of visiting Mother Ella uninvited rather daunting. Miss Tolerance was not in the habit of being daunted. She paid the driver to wait for her and picked her way toward Mother's dwelling.

Before she could call out or knock on the tent's wooden frame, a stripling with nascent mustachios appeared before her, arms folded upon his chest, clearly attempting a ferocious demeanor.

"Wot you want?"

"I'd like a few words with Mother Ella, if she is available." Something about the lad's belligerence provoked adamantine politeness in Miss Tolerance. "Will you tell her that Miss Tolerance has called?"

"D'I look like yer catchfart man?"

"You look like a boy standing in front of Mother Ella's home, and one who will very likely catch a scolding if Mother is kept waiting."

The boy glared at her for a moment, then called over his shoulder. "Lora!"

A moment later, a girl poked her head around the boy's shoulder. "Aye, Johnny?" She looked at Miss Tolerance, first quizzically and then, as she realized that the gentleman at the door was, in fact, a woman she'd encountered before, grinned. "Evening, miss."

"Good evening, Ellora. Would you ask Mother if she will see me for a few moments?"

The girl elbowed the lad aside and took Miss Tolerance's hand. "You come along of me, miss. Johnny, you prat, go fetch the kindlin'."

Miss Tolerance was led through to the large chamber she had visited before. It was far warmer than she had expected:

the hangings and curtains that, doubled and trebled, lined the walls, had the effect of cutting the wind and retaining the heat from the brazier. The air was smoky but not unpleasantly so. Mother Ella was again in the chair at the center of the room. She had a board across her lap and a sharp little knife in her sinewy hand.

"Lora, I'll need more burdock," she said. "Ain't enough here for—" she stopped. "It's young Joe's friend, ain't it? Do ye commonly dress like that for calls upon an ol' woman, girl?"

"I apologize for my appearance, but it is cold this afternoon and I had a long drive to get here."

"I've seen more to offend me than a pair o' knees." Mother Ella gestured to Ellora and handed her the cutting board. "Bring us a little drink, 'Lora, there's a child. And you, set yourself." She gestured toward the stool that Miss Tolerance had occupied upon her first visit. "Set and tell me why you're calling."

"I wanted to thank you and Joe for your effort in unearthing Mr. Marvell. I spoke with him yesterday, and thought you would want to know that he chose the name he used without any desire to throw suspicion upon your people."

"And you believe 'im when 'e says it?"

Miss Tolerance nodded. "Of everything he said to me, that is perhaps the one thing I believe without hesitation."

"Lied about other matters?" Mother Ella went through a fussy process of cleaning and filling her pipe, then catching it from the flame of her candle.

"I am sorting out the truths from evasions."

Ellora returned with two wooden goblets and an earthenware jug, and while Mother Ella and her visitor watched, poured out a small amount of amber-red liquid into each of them. First Mother, then Miss Tolerance, raised their glasses and tasted the wine, which was sweet.

"Elderberry?" Miss Tolerance asked.

"Current. Wiv' a little lavender." Mother Ella took another sip.

Miss Tolerance examined the finely turned stem of her goblet. "Is this Joe's work? It's very handsome."

"Aye. He's a talented lad, our Joe. So ye've come all the way to Highbury—an hour's drive it might be—just to say thank you? That's very pretty manners. Where's the rest of it?"

"The rest of it, ma'am?"

"Don't try to cozen an ol' woman, girl. You an't come out to Highbury on a cold night to do the pretty. You 'ave more questions for me, or for Joe. Din't you say you'd found yer Marvell?"

"Unfortunately, before he could tell me much, Mr. Marvell —Joe told me his true name was Kent—was murdered. Which, you will appreciate, has made finding any more information out from him impossible."

"You don't expect to get none from me, do ye? Being as it was you told us about the fellow—" Mother Ella tilted her head and gulped the last of her wine, then licked a drop from the lip of the cup with a sly dart of her tongue. She looked at Miss Tolerance thoughtfully, her expression darker. "That an't why you come. You're here to find out if one of our folk is responsible for the murder being done."

Miss Tolerance said nothing.

"I thought a friend of Sir Walter'd be better than that. A death been done and it's the Travelers what must ha' done it, aye?"

Despite a strong feeling that she ought to apologize, Miss Tolerance stood her ground. "I've come as part of an inquiry, ma'am. Not to make an accusation. I should be very poor at my work if I did not investigate all the possibilities that present themselves."

"What possibilities is that?"

"I wanted to ask Joe if it was he who delivered a cupboard to the building on Stafford Street this morning. I thought I saw —"

"*Thought* you saw."

"—a man who put me in mind of Joe. I came to discover whether it was he, and if so, what his business was there." She added, as if to soften the information, "Whoever it was, I don't believe Marvell was struck down in cold blood."

"Us'ns being so hot-blooded. Whoever it was, it weren't Joe. He was on my business today."

"And that business would have kept him away from Stafford Street?"

Abruptly, Mother Ella leaned forward and grasped Miss Tolerance's hand, pulling her half off the stool she was perched on. As she had before, the old woman peeled the glove from her visitor's hand and peered at it, her face so close that Miss Tolerance could feel her hot, damp breath on the skin of her palm. At last, she released the wrist she held, tossing the hand aside. "Ye believe what yer saying. Ye may even believe ye mean no mischief. But hear this, miss. I never sent Joe to murder no one."

"I did not say you had done so. And it was not Joe in the building?"

"I carn't say. But if 'e was there, I don't doubt 'e was deliverin' a movable someone'd bought from 'im."

"To Mr. Marvell?"

"I got no idea. Joe does work all over the city. I don't ask who for."

"And you gave him no instruction upon the matter?"

Mother Ella frowned. "Ye won't be satisfied no matter what I say, will you? Joe may 'a been in Stafford Street, but I told 'im to mind 'is business and keep well away from that Marvell." A chilly smile lit her eyes. "It's easy enough to blame the Travelers. Why would Joe or any other of mine do aught to bring the Law down in that fashion? Makes no nevermind the stories yer mam tol' you about the Travelers when you was in leadin' strings." The old woman tapped hard on the side of her cup with one long fingernail. "Ye have yer answer and it's time ye leave."

Miss Tolerance collected her glove, which had fallen to the floor, and stood to go. "I will not ask you to forgive me, ma'am. My employment sometimes requires that I ask questions I had much rather not ask. I will say that, if I were seeking the murderer of one of your people, I would not scruple to ask questions of a duke if it meant an answer and the culprit brought to justice."

Mother Ella was not mollified. "Ye can tell yerself so, but when it comes to it—"

"When it comes to it? Ask," Miss Tolerance said. "Ask Sir Walter Mandif about the circumstances of our meeting, and what I did to bring a murderer to justice." She had no idea why she invoked the history of her connection to, and betrayal of, the Earl of Versellion. Perhaps she was stung by the old woman's view that any question or suspicion constituted a betrayal. Miss Tolerance bowed to Mother Ella and left. When she parted the walls of the tent she found Ellora waiting to lead her out. The smiling child of earlier must have heard the change in Mother Ella's manner to her guest; she scowled as she took Miss Tolerance to the door, and snapped the canvas behind her with a gesture as good as banishment.

She was very glad that she had paid for her carriage to wait.

On the ride to Manchester Square, Miss Tolerance examined her sense of ill-use. There had been many times in her work as an agent of inquiry when persons it was quite reasonable to question had resented it. Why did Mother Ella's outrage provoke the desire to defend herself? Miss

Tolerance had encountered thieves, murderers, even spies. She knew as well pickpockets, whores, fences, and crossing-sweeps who were kind and honorable in their way. She thought she had seen Joe Boswell in Stafford Street; that was reason enough to question him, was it not? It galled to be accused of easy prejudice when she was simply doing her work.

In Manchester Square, Miss Tolerance alit from the carriage, paid the driver, and ascended the steps to Mrs. Brereton's door. Almost before Cole had admitted her, Marianne Touchwell appeared behind him.

"Where have you been? You will find your door covered in notes—"

Irritation was at once replaced by anxiety. "What has happened?"

Mrs. Touchwell steered Miss Tolerance down the hallway. "Your aunt." She kept her voice very low. "You recall we spoke of encouraging her to come downstairs, to let herself be seen, let her be social—"

"Did she over-exert herself? I do wi—"

"Sarah, listen."

Miss Tolerance favored her friend with an attentive expression. "Yes, Marianne?"

"No! *Listen*!" Marianne made a gesture toward the smaller of the two saloons at the front of the hall. The doors to both were closed, but Miss Tolerance could hear, now her attention had been called to it, the sound of an energetic voice raised in song and not a rustic air or German *lied*, but a bouncy, jovial, and very vulgar song.

"Good God." Miss Tolerance regarded Mrs Touchwell with horror. "Aunt Thea—" Without waiting for a response she made for the saloon.

The scene was what she had feared. Several gentlemen sat at leisure, glasses to hand and their chosen female companions beside them, watching in amazement as Mrs. Dorothea Brereton performed.

"…A cunning clockmaker did court me as well
And promised me riches if I'd ring his bell.
So I looked at his clockwork and said, with a shock
Your pendulum's far too small for my clock!
My thing is my own, and I'll keep it so, still!
Other young ladies may do as they will—"

Mrs. Brereton sang with animation, gesturing, nodding, winking knowingly. It was a display of the sort she generally would not have permitted in the house unless at a revel, and then not until well into the evening when everyone—girls and guests alike—were struck with drink and appetite. The final indignity: Mrs. Brereton, speaking, possessed a rich, musical voice. In song, she could not find a tune that had been placed in her hand.

The performance was dreadful. That her aunt seemed unaware of the figure she made was appalling.

At her shoulder, Marianne murmured, "She's been singing for a quarter hour. I don't know what to do." Indeed, the audience seemed rivetted to their seats.

Without thought, Miss Tolerance plowed forward, hands outstretched as if in congratulation. "Why Aunt, I am so pleased to see you heeded my suggestion and came downstairs!"

Mrs. Brereton's voice faltered, attempted to return to the song, then faltered again. The lady regarded her niece as if she had wakened from a daze.

"Sarah! What are you wearing in my drawing room!" She looked around her at the gentlemen, several of whom were smiling uncomfortably, and her whores, who universally regarded their employer with dismay. "Good evening! Good evening to all of you."

This could have been taken as a greeting or farewell; Miss Tolerance did not give her aunt or the audience the time to decide which. She linked her arm in her aunt's and began to steer her toward the door. "I'm delighted you joined your guests for a time, but we must guard your strength. It is time to retire."

Mrs. Brereton did not resist, but at the door, she turned back and called another good evening. The gentlemen in the room had, by now, risen to their feet to bow to her.

"I think I *am* a little tired," Mrs. Brereton confided. "Where is Frost?"

"Here, ma'am dear." Miss Frost was at her elbow. "You come upstairs and we'll make you comfortable directly."

It would be too much to say that the look Frost gave to Miss Tolerance was full of gratitude, but there was an acknowledgement of common purpose.

Mrs. Brereton ascended the stairs on Frost's arm, her stately bearing gone. She looked her age despite all the magic that dress and maquillage could accomplish.

From the room Mrs. Brereton had quitted, a portly young man with a spill of auburn curls down his forehead emerged, his arm around the waist of Susana, who looked an apology at Marianne.

'Ah, well," Marianne said in a philosophic tone. "Poor Mr. Peel waited quite long enough to have what he'd come for. I don't blame him finding it elsewhere, nor Suze for taking it."

"I am sorry," Miss Tolerance offered. The loss of one tumble's income would not hurt her friend, so long as the man did not decide he preferred Susana's charms.

"Oh, Suze won't poach him from me. But it's been a hard afternoon."

"I can see. When she's herself again, Aunt Thea won't like it if she becomes meat for the gossips of London."

"Come talk with her," Marianne urged. "She'll listen to you."

Miss Tolerance reflected that her last conversation with her aunt—when she had urged her to spend more time downstairs—had yielded decidedly mixed results. But she climbed the stairs, and at Mrs. Brereton's door was confronted by Frost in a manner that suggested the dresser had been lying in wait for her there. She looked, from the banded black muslin of her gown to the kerchief crumpled in her hand, like a woman in mourning.

She began without ceremony. "You must do something, Miss Sarah. I know that Marianne, she thinks I'm fretting at trifles, but I ain't. "

That Marianne stood not two feet away, studying the paper on the wall. Miss Tolerance bit, hard, upon the impulse to note that yesterday Frost had accused Marianne of fretting at trifles.

"I am sorry to have been away when so much was happening, Frost. Have you any idea why Aunt Thea decided that today was a day for a recital?"

"Not a scrap! In her right mind, your aunt would rather die than make such a guy of herself."

"Is she settled now?"

"She's still dressed for the salon, and—"

"And I am dressed for the tavern. Frost, perhaps you can persuade Aunt Thea to become more comfortable? I will join you directly I have washed and put myself in order."

Miss Tolerance made for the back stairs, down which she could run at a clip. Once in her cottage, she doffed her Gunnard coat and boots, donned a woolen round gown and slippers, and, refreshed by the application of hot water and a hairbrush, returned to make her way up to her aunt's suite.

Mrs. Brereton's favorite costly scent floated on the air but did not mask a stale smell of illness. The lady herself lay propped upon pillows on the divan; she still wore her day dress. Frost, seated to her right, held her mistress's hand in her own and patted it anxiously. That Mrs. Brereton did not pull her hand away and instruct Frost to stop behaving like a nursery maid told Miss Tolerance how unsettled she was.

"Well, aunt, how do you do?" Miss Tolerance turned to the maid with as much matter-of-factness as she could muster. "Frost, may I sit with my aunt for a moment?"

Mrs. Brereton looked panicked at the thought of losing the dresser's company.

"Don't worry, Frost will be here. You know she does not like to be apart from you." Miss Tolerance took the seat that Frost vacated and her aunt's hand likewise. "You were very merry in the salon this afternoon."

Mrs. Brereton looked sidewise at her niece. "I only wanted—" She broke off and pursed her lips.

"Wanted, ma'am?"

Words spilled from Mrs. Brereton's lips. "All the others have beaux! And none of them are any prettier than I am! I only wanted—"

"A little attention?" Miss Tolerance suggested gently.

Mrs. Brereton looked like a sulky child. "No one admired me."

"Aunt Thea, you are still the chief ornament of the house."

"And Frost left me."

"Frost's place is not in the drawing room. But look, here she is."

"But why did she leave me?"

"I asked her to, not two minutes ago, so I could sit with you in her place. And the things for tea have been brought up: Frost must have gone to give the orders. Now she is back, do you not think you will be very much more comfortable in a dressing gown?"

Miss Frost, recognizing a cue, went to the wardrobe. As she approached with a lavishly laced bed-gown in her arms, Mrs. Brereton reached out, as if the sight of the gown gave her comfort.

"My favorite saucepot. Frow goose endown." The crisply spoken words made no sense.

"Aunt Thea?"

"Frownin sauzu, Sahhsza." Mrs. Brereton slurred. "Tira, tira. Mahaseca." She rose to her feet and stood shakily. "Wrong," she said clearly, and looked blindly about her. Miss Tolerance and Frost were on either side of her, working with rare accord to settle Mrs. Brereton onto the divan.

Miss Frost looked over her mistress's head at Miss Tolerance.

Mrs. Brereton's feelings be damned. "Send for Sir George Hammond at once. *Now*."

Chapter Fourteen

Sir George Hammond arrived with half-a-dozen of Mrs. Brereton's employees following close on his heels. Mrs. Touchwell closed the door firmly behind him; he went at once to his patient, and nodded, businesslike, to Miss Tolerance, who ceded her seat to him. He took Mrs. Brereton's wrist between his fingers to count her pulse.

"Well, ma'am. What's to do?" His tone was pleasant and encouraging.

Mrs. Brereton did not stir.

"Have you salts?"

Miss Frost passed a vinaigrette to the physician and he waved it under Mrs. Brereton's nose. Miss Tolerance was about to say that this remedy had already been tried to no effect, but now Mrs. Brereton stirred and raised a hand toward her face.

"Aunt Thea!" "Ma'am!" "Mrs. B!" All three of women around the divan spoke at once.

Sir George's tone remained the same. "There you are, then. Open your eyes, ma'am, and tell us how you do."

"Vi-viley." Mrs. Brereton's voice was a guttural slur.

The doctor took from his coat pocket a curious tube of

horn. "If you will permit me to examine you, we will do our best to restore you to yourself, hey?" He put one end of the tube on her chest and his ear to the other end. "Will you breathe for me, ma'am?"

Mrs. Brereton drew a loud, rattling breath. "I *am* breathing. If I were not, my niece would have sent for the undertaker." One corner of her mouth was drawn down, and the words came strangely mangled.

The doctor motioned for her to breathe again. She complied, her pulse jumping visibly in her throat.

"Have you any pain?"

Mrs. Brereton's head slipped to one side. "Not… now."

"She's had a griping in her belly," Miss Frost said before her mistress could demur.

"Any disturbances of vision? Hearing? No? If you would be so kind as to open your mouth. Ah. Aha. Yes."

"*Yef?*"Mrs. Brereton spoke around the doctor's probing finger. Whatever difficulties she was experiencing in speech, her tone was acid.

Sir George stepped back and looked around the room as if to gauge whether he could safely speak. "I believe it was an apoplectic stroke. Brought on, perhaps, by a recurrence of your old infection." The word was weighted with meaning. "Did you consult a surgeon as I suggested?"

"She did not," Miss Frost answered.

"That was yearsh ago. I took the cure."

"And you had no other exposure since?" With each question, Miss Tolerance felt both dread and exasperation. It was clear that the sickness around whose name Sir George circled was a disease of venery.

"None I know of. And you may trusht I know the shign of pocsh."

Sir George pressed on, asking when Mrs. Brereton had been treated, and by what method. Between the lady and her dresser, the facts were revealed: fifteen years earlier, with a treatment consisting of blue pills and a mercury douche.

"Made her sick as the pox itself," Frost recalled. Mrs. Brereton glared.

Sir George put the little horn tube back in his coat pocket and wiped his hands on a kerchief. "If you were treated with mercury then you likely were cured, but given your profession, I cannot say that it is a certain thing, and an illness like that can disturb the balance of the brain and bring on apoplexy. I will send a surgeon—the fellow I recommended to you in the past, Mr. Warringe—to make an examination. Until then—" he raised a hand to cut off any protest by his patient. "In the meantime, I will proceed upon the belief that we must seek another cause. Your pulse is not as strong as I would like, and there is some weakness on the left side of your body. I will send a tonic for you to take before bed. I want you to eat beefsteak and drink a pint of porter tonight and tomorrow. Your pallor concerns me. Beyond that, you must rest. And do not turn Mr. Warringe away when he arrives."

Miss Tolerance saw a distinctly mulish expression on her aunt's face, but Mrs. Touchwell took his arm and promised that Mr. Warringe would be brought to Mrs. Brereton at once.

"Rest, red meat, porter. And the powder I'll give to you, to be drunk in wine, morning and night. I'll return tomorrow to see how you go along."

He bowed generally to the room and permitted Mrs. Touchwell to escort him out.

"*Porter!*" The word came explosively from Mrs. Brereton's lips.

"If that is what the doctor says, then porter it will be," Miss Tolerance said firmly. Sir George's matter-of-fact manner had relieved her considerably. Her aunt's slide from incoherence to unconsciousness had scared her badly, and she had clenched around that fear, unwilling to let it be seen lest it encourage fear in others of the household.

"And a shurgeon!"

"To rule out your… your earlier indisposition. If nothing is wrong there, then Sir George can focus his attention on other causes."

"You listen to Miss Sarah, my lady." Frost looked anxiously at employer.

"I wishh—" Mrs. Brereton began. What she wished was left unsaid. Esther, an upstairs maid, entered the room at that moment bearing a tray with glass, decanter, and a twist of apothecary's paper.

"I will leave you to Frost's ministry, ma'am." Miss Tolerance kissed her aunt's hand. "Please let me know when the surgeon visits," she urged Frost.

Mrs. Brereton watched her go. "Lishten to Miss Sharah, indeed. I never thought to hear shuch a phrashe from you, Frosht."

It was, by the light, late afternoon when a knock woke Miss Tolerance from a deep nap. It was Esther with news that Mr. Warringe had arrived to see Madam.

Miss Tolerance found Mrs. Brereton sitting up in bed, entertaining Mr. Warringe with a string of amusing mots. As it was not generally her aunt's custom to waste small talk on a man not a client, Miss Tolerance surmised that she was anxious to put off an examination as long as she could.

The surgeon was all ruddy and rounded: short, bullet-headed, and fat; his green coat yawned across his waistcoat and his riding boots appeared to barely contain his calves. Miss Tolerance thought idly that if he were to be knocked down on a hillside he would roll as roundly as a billiards ball. Warringe turned to nod a greeting to Miss Tolerance, showing a red-cheeked, snub-nosed face and a voluptuary's full lips; his eyes—as round as the rest of him—were shrewd.

"Now, ma'am," he broke into Mrs. Brereton's stream of chatter. "You do not want to waste your charm on an old fellow like me. Let us see what there is to discover—likely nothing at all—and then I shall be on my way, hey?"

With a skill and deftness that surprised Miss Tolerance, Warringe put aside Mrs. Brereton's demurs and began his inspection: her eyes, the inside of her mouth, the skin on the insides of her arms and—after some negotiation and reassurance—her back and legs. Miss Tolerance, at her aunt's request, guarded the door, while Frost helped the surgeon by revealing, one at a time, each area to be examined. Like Sir George Hammond, he had brought a tube—this one of brass rather than horn—that he used to listen to Mrs. Brereton's heart and breathing. At last, when the lady had been restored to order and Frost had been dispatched to order refreshment for all the parties involved, Mr. Warringe took a seat and sighed gustily.

"Well, ma'am, I cannot say that I am entirely pleased by what I see. Sir George informed me that you had taken the cure for syphilis some years ago and been assured of its success?"

Mrs. Brereton nodded.

Warringe blew noisily through his full lips. "It appears that the cure was less effective than you had been told."

At the speaking of the word *syphilis* Miss Tolerance felt a deep flush of dismay. It seemed impossible that her commanding, assured aunt could be stricken by this hazard of the profession.

"Can I say that for certain?" Mr. Warringe was replying to Mrs. Brereton's immediate negative. "Nothing in life is certain. There may have been a later exposure, but in either case, the signs are here, and of a long infection. I understand that you had an apoplectic stroke recently?"

Mrs. Brereton nodded again. "But the treatment—that

wretched treatment—put paid to the pox-shign years ago. I *cannot* be—"

"Syphilis is a deceiver," Warringe said. "And it appears that you were, indeed, deceived. It can lie dormant for many years, only to reappear. I am sorry to say that seems to be what has happened here."

"Can it be treated now?" Miss Tolerance spoke to keep her aunt's distress, and her own, from growing further.

"Treatment must be essayed." Warringe looked grave. "In so established a case—and one which has eluded earlier treatment—I cannot be entirely reassuring, but certainly it is worth—"

"Will I go mad?" Mrs Brereton interrupted. Her voice was steady, but Miss Tolerance recognized what it cost her aunt to make it so.

Again, Warringe pursed his lips, again blew through them. "The disease takes many courses. Not all of them end in madness. I cannot say what will happen with complete certainty. We must be as optimistic as we can. Now, ma'am, there are several remedies I wish to offer you."

What those remedies were, Miss Tolerance was not certain her aunt heard. She nodded her head and agreed with everything the surgeon suggested, but her gaze was inward, as if the horrors of her imagination were far too powerful for the mere suggestions of a medical man to penetrate.

Warringe left after an hour, with assurances that he would send pills and a salve, and instructions for treatment that he hoped would resolve Mrs. Brereton's symptoms.

Sick at heart, Miss Tolerance followed the surgeon from the room. "Truthfully, what chance is there of a cure?"

"Truthfully, miss, we must hope, but we may not promise. It is all I can say to you."

"If my aunt should… Should go mad? What then?"

"Syphilitic madness is generally intermittent. She may

have years of good health and clarity before her. And the disease may not take that form."

"But you think that it will." Horror mingled with pity in her: was Mrs. Brereton, clever, beautiful, and fastidious, to become a babbling madwoman?

Warringe shook his head and planted his hat on his head with sad finality. "When I learn, by your description and her own, that there has already been some apparent derangement of wits, it seems likely. To be frank, though, madness is a far gentler fate than some other outcomes of the pox. Your aunt is a handsome woman—I need not tell you how corrosive the illness can be to beauty." He shook his head briefly as if to dispel an unwelcome image. "Now: I will send the materials I promised, Miss Tolerance. Good evening."

Returning to Mrs. Brereton's side required, on Miss Tolerance's part, all the bravery and obedience to duty she could summon. *But if this news is so horrifying to me, what must it be to her? And how much will she detest pity!* She put on a demeanor of brisk sympathy.

"Well, aunt, it appears that in addition to the porter and beefsteak Sir George prescribed, there will now be a regimen of pills and an ointment prescribed by Mr. Warringe. Tiresome, I know—"

Mrs. Brereton reached to take her niece's hand and pat it. "I appreciate your effort to put a good face on the thing, Sarah, but if it is true that the pox has returned, I shall likely die of it. But not today. Nor tomorrow, I think."

Miss Tolerance nodded in agreement. "I assume you will not want the staff to know."

"Not yet," Mrs. Brereton agreed. "When—*if* my mind is affected."

"It may not be, Aunt Thea. If there is anything I have gleaned from Mr. Warringe's comments, it is that this disease is unpredictable."

Mrs. Brereton turned away. "Frost! Wine, please. Some of

the burgundy from '04. Bring glasses for four, and invite Mrs. Touchwell to join us."

Frost, pleased to have a concrete task, vanished at once.

"Now, Sarah, whatever Warringe or Sir George say, if this wretched disease affects my mind—as I unhappily suspect it will—I know exactly what lies ahead for me."

"Aunt, you cannot—"

"I *can*. When I was just begun on my career—well, gone from my first to second keeper—I had a friend named Eliza Holdem. She was some years older than I, and advised me when I was making my way, and very well I have done. But when she was younger than I am now, Lizzie began to show signs, obvious ones, of the disease. Of course, her custom fell off, and to live in comfort, with a woman to nurse her in a pair of rooms that were not too squalid, ate up her savings very quickly. In the end, I and one of her old lovers paid to keep her." Mrs. Brereton's eyes were focused somewhere in memory. "The last time I saw her, she was utterly disfigured, who had been such a handsome woman. But worse, her mind was quite gone: she wept, she muttered, she... wet herself. She did not recognize me, and when she spoke—"

Miss Tolerance dropped to her knees at her aunt's side and took both her hands in her own. "Dear Aunt Thea, do not distress yourself. We will see you through, whatever comes."

Mrs. Brereton's gaze returned to her niece's face. "I know you will, my dear. And here are Frost and Marianne, and our wine. Set that down, please, Frost. Sarah, will you pour for all of us?"

Miss Frost looked mildly scandalized. "You don't want me drinking with you, ma'am—"

"Indeed I do. Don't stand on your dignity with me." Mrs. Brereton's tone was dry but affectionate. "I put up with quite enough of your airs as it is."

Miss Tolerance offered glasses of wine to Mrs. Touchwell,

Frost, and her aunt. "Now, aunt, I collect we are to drink your health."

"On the contrary, Sarah—I drink to the three of you, for I will need to rely upon each of you, and I do not promise to be as grateful for it as I should be." Mrs. Brereton raised her glass, first to her niece, then to Marianne, then to Frost. "I am sorry for the trouble I shall put you to." She drank deeply from her glass. "For now, however, while I appear to be in possession of my wits, I am still the owner and manageress of this establishment. Unless—" she quirked an eyebrow. "Unless, of course, I attempt to sing again."

Miss Tolerance, Mrs. Touchwell, and Frost all raised their own glasses, pledging to do all that was needful for Mrs. Brereton, and never, on any account, to permit her to sing.

It was full dark when Miss Tolerance at last returned to her cottage. She had been prevailed upon to dine with her aunt, and to read her the news afterward while she struggled through the prescribed pint of porter. Miss Tolerance was through the Dueling Notices and begun on the Court news when an unusual noise suggested to her that Mrs. Brereton was not only asleep but snoring. She had gestured to Frost, who seemed less jealous and more in charity with her mistress's niece than she had ever been before. Miss Tolerance made her departure.

At home, she stirred up the fire, changed into her dressing gown, put the kettle on the hob, changed her mind and took down the decanter from the shelf, only to decide that was not what she wanted either. At last, she dipped some water from the cistern and drank it thirstily. The temptation to dwell on the scenes of the day was strong. Instead she put it in her mind to remember what she had been doing before her thoughts had been consumed by Mrs. Brereton.

Mother Ella and Joe Boswell. Had she made enemies there? It occurred to her that since it was Sir Walter Mandif who had vouched for her and arranged an introduction to Joe and Mother, she should tell him what had followed. She took out her writing desk and a piece of paper, inked her pen, and began to write.

My dear Sir Walter:

I write because you may hear a report of me from Mother Ella or her people which will cast me in an unfriendly light; I do not want to it to discredit you as well. I am afraid I had reason to inquire….

I n the morning, when she crossed the garden to visit her aunt, Miss Tolerance found Mrs. Gordon directing the hand-over to Keefe and Cole of an elaborate array of serving vessels intended for the buffet in the smaller salon. Miss Tolerance had seen this performance before and wanted only to remain out of the line of bustle.

"Package come for you last night, miss." Keefe spoke over a domed dish. "I can bring it across when the service is done."

As Miss Tolerance had hoped to be on her way long before the coffee had cooled in the cups of Mrs. Brereton's patrons, "May I not fetch it myself, Keefe?"

"If you like, Miss. It's in our office upstairs."

Miss Tolerance spoke her thanks to Keefe's departing back.

"Our office" was a room—not much more than a large cloakroom, furnished with a chair, lamp, and cupboard—where Mrs. Brereton's menservants could store the outerwear and incidentals of visitors, hold packages and other sundries for collection, leave instructions for each other and, on the unusual occasion when there was a moment of quiet, take their ease. Miss Tolerance had passed the door any number of times but had never ventured inside. As no patrons cooled their heels waiting for coat or walking stick, Miss Tolerance made bold to enter the office, seeking a package whose size and description were unknown to her.

Perhaps a dozen men's coats hung neatly on pegs, and almost as many hats, brushed to shining and ready for their wearers, lined a shelf above. On the cupboard, there was a miscellany of small parcels and objects, and one very large, wrapped in smudged newspaper and tied with dingy twine. It was perhaps three hands-width in height and two in width. A card had been affixed to it, heavy and of good ivory-tinted stock; written on it in Keefe's deliberate, old-fashioned script, *Miss Sarah*.

She turned the card over—one of her aunt's calling cards. Miss Tolerance took the card and a stub of pencil and in her less ornamented hand wrote, *I have taken the parcel, with thanks, ST*.

She left the house and summoned a chair for Henry Street with the parcel under her arm.

At this hour of the morning Tarsio's Ladies Salon was empty. Miss Tolerance ordered coffee and bread, then seated herself at a desk near the fireplace. It had required some patience not to tear the package open in the chair, but now she could avail herself of a pen knife and cut the twine. The contents proved to be a book, half-bound in yellow calfskin, the marbled boards smirched with inky fingerprints. Tucked between the cover and front papers was a note, penned carefully—which gave her a notion of where those inky prints had originated—and imaginatively spelled.

Miss—Ellora is writin for me. I found this book at Mr. Murvills place yesstiddy and thot twould be of use. I was in the bildin to deliver a cabinet and found his door open and him with no futher use for it. Mother don't know I sent it. This makes us square.

Joe Boswell

*A*nd him with no further use for it. Did Joe Boswell mean that he had found Marvell already dead, or that he had killed the man? By rights she should not touch the thing, should turn it over to Sir Walter, or to the Great Marlborough Street magistracy.

Her curiosity was powerful. She opened the book.

It was a ledger, ruled in pencil. The entries had been made over nearly two dozen pages, in two different hands. The first dozen or so pages were writ in a neat clerk's hand, the latter ones in a large, loopy, eccentric hand that slanted, now forward, now back. She suspected that without the lines to guide him, the second writer's words would have wandered widely across the page.

There was Mrs. Black's name, a date some four years past, the amount of her investment, a notation of how often she was to be paid, and what that payment should be. First payment, then a date. Second payment, then a date. Seventeen entries of payments made, and the book up to date to the last quarter.

But Mrs. Black had died almost a year ago, and received no payments for several quarters before her death. Why continue to mark payments if none had been made?

There were records for nineteen investors in all, each with entries with details, amounts, a schedule of dividends, and notations of payment. Somewhere in the second half of the list, Annie Pouter and her eighteen hundred pounds were recorded. The sums invested varied widely—in some cases no more than thirty or forty guineas, in others, several hundred— but the total was nearly eleven thousand pounds.

By the testimony of the ledger, the scheme had been

working for almost twenty years. Three of the women listed she knew were dead; how many others had died for wanting a little comfort in their old age?

"Excuse me, miss." Hengsman, Tarsio's morning porter, approached with a note on a tray. "This just come for you."

Irritation at the interruption warred with a momentary thought of paying employment, work that would license her to cease her involvement in Mr. Marvell's matter. Instead, she recognized Sir Walter Mandif's hand. The note had been written the day before, evidently in response to her own:

I have cause to thank you: because you had divulged Mr. Marvell's true name, Penryn was able to make a notification of the death to Mrs. Kent, the deceased's next of kin. He described the meeting as peculiar, but I am not certain why.

Of greater interest to you, perhaps: the doctor determined that Mr. Marvell died some hours before your arrival, most probably last night. With regard to your meeting with Mother Ella, I can relieve you on one point. Joe Boswell, on the evidence of several dozen people, including a barman and potboys, was at a public house in Chiswick last night for a meeting. He was there until well past midnight. He is at this point not a suspect in Marvell's death.

It was a relief. She had not realized until this moment how the idea had weighed upon her that she might have sat, drinking coffee in the tavern across the street, while Marvell was murdered.

Miss Tolerance folded the note and put it in her reticule, then returned to her study of the ledger.

Date Name Address
1793 Mrs. Stone (fmly Sal Fondler) Charyn Street, Greenwich
1795 Mrs. Jones (fmly Polly Quim) Adam Street, Rotherhithe
1796 Mrs. White Gt. Quebeck St, Lisson Grove
1798 Mrs. Wood (fmly Dolly Clutchem) Adam Street, Rotherhithe

1799 Mrs. Thom (fmly Annie Belter) Greenwich
1801 Mrs. Johnson (fmly Peg Plumbob) Limehouse
1801 Mrs. Smith (fmly Bessie Baller) Adam Street,
Rotherhithe
1804 Miss H. Kerrwood Cheval Place, Knightsbridge
1804 Mrs. Martin (fmly Lou Licker)
1806 Mrs. Smithson (fmly Liza Crumpet) Black Horse Inn,
Deptford
1807 Mrs. Collins (fmly Betsy Tightly) Black Horse Inn,
Deptford
dec
1809 Mrs. Cook (fmly Nan Birchaboy) Saffron Street, Saffron
Hill
1809 Annie Pouter Castle Street, Seven Dials
1809 Mrs. Black (Belle ??) Dog and Tiger, Bermondsey
1809 Mrs. Green (fmly Mary Swallow) Thames Street,
Broken Wharf
1810 Nell Finger Seven Dials
1810 Alice Cummer ??
1810 Becky Swiving Clerkenwell
1811 Cora Clinger Belton Street

Her plans for the day changed. Miss Tolerance intended to call on as many of the women appearing in the ledger as she could find.

R apid perusal of the list suggested that, if she approached the women in the order of their appearance in the ledger, she would be running from one end of London to the next. Instead, she grouped them geographically: the first in the list, Mrs. Stone, lived in Greenwich, as did Mrs. Johnson, professionally Peg Plumbob and the sixth on the list. Liza Crumpet, now called Mrs. Smithson, was listed at the same address as Mrs. Collins, formerly Betsy Tightly, at an inn in Black Horse Square in Deptford. And a cluster of women (numbers 2, 4, and 7) were housed in Adam Street, Rotherhithe. All south of the river and to the east. Miss Tolerance would start in Greenwich and work her way back to the city.

Mrs. Stone's home was a short walk from the Royal Hospital in rooms above a haberdashery on Charyn Street. When Miss Tolerance presented herself, a dour woman with a starched cap and apron stood across the door as if to bar her way.

"What do you mean with her?" The woman's speech was genteel but strongly northern in accent.

"Only to ask a question or two. Is Mrs. Stone's health so fragile that she cannot entertain a visitor for a brief moment?" Miss Tolerance had thought to provide herself with several bottles of wine, now waiting in the carriage she had hired for the day. "I thought this might be welcome for an invalid."

The woman took the bottle and turned away, not shutting the door in Miss Tolerance's face but neither inviting her in. "Wait here," she ordered, and vanished.

A moment later, she returned, no less disapproving but with the heartening news that Miss Tolerance was to walk through to Mrs. Stone. Even then, the attendant did not actually step out of the way, which forced Miss Tolerance to push past her. She did not beg her pardon.

The room in which she found Mrs. Stone was comfortably but plainly furnished and kept very warm, even for the chill of the day. The lady herself sat with her feet on a footstool and a robe across her lap. The only sign of a former life of frivolity was the lacy cap she wore; the skull over which she wore it was nearly bald, and the woman herself so withered and sunken she seemed nearly skeletal.

"Mrs. Stone?"

"Sit and tell me your business, miss." For all her

sepulchral appearance, Mrs. Stone had a pleasingly musical voice.

Miss Tolerance explained her errand. "I am seeking to learn about others who were part of this business, ma'am. I am delighted to find you—" she paused.

The old woman laughed. "To find me still drawing breath?" She coughed gummily, and the stern attendant was suddenly beside her with a basin and kerchief. Mrs. Stone spat, permitted herself to be dabbed at with the cloth, and patted the hand of her nurse. "Thank you, Dora. You're a great comfort."

Color painted the nurse's cheeks for a moment before she turned away. Mrs. Smith returned to her conversation. "I'm not so old as I look, girl. I imagine *delighted* must mean *surprised*."

"If I am surprised, it is because a number of women who were involved in this Fund have died by violence or been violently attacked."

"Good heavens. But that cannot have anything to do with the Fund."

"I think it must, as the women who were attacked had all complained when their payments ceased."

"Perhaps you have me on that list wrongly, then, miss. I have not been catched in some scheme, as you have it. In all the years I was put in the Fund, the money has appeared in my bank, faithful as love, every quarter, thanks to dear Mr. Kent. If it had not—" she reached into the air and her nurse took her hand. Mrs. Stone patted the attendant's hand. "If it had not I should not have my dear Dora to take care of me. I think you have been given very wrong information."

There was no purpose to argue the point or alarm Mrs. Stone further. Miss Tolerance took her leave and parted, wondering what she was to make of this. The first of the women on the list, and inscribed in the fund for almost twenty years, Mrs. Stone had continued to receive the money due to her.

By the end of the afternoon, Miss Tolerance had spoken to Mrs. Stone and Mrs. Johnson, Mrs. Jones, and Mrs. Wood. The other three she had hoped to speak with were deceased, but of natural causes (one of dysentery and two of influenza). The four surviving women insisted that they had been entered into the Fund as a parting gesture at the end of their liaison with a gentleman they each declined to name, and had continued to receive the money due them since that time. One —Mrs. Smithson (formerly Liza Crumpet)—had appeared a trifle anxious when questioned, but Miss Tolerance was not ready to ascribe a sinister motive to what might well have been nerves. She had made a point of telling Miss Tolerance more than once that it had been she who notified the Fund of Mrs. Collins's death, "though I din't 'ave to, and might'a kept the money meself and none the wiser."

In fact, it appeared that Mrs. Smith of Rotherhithe, whom her friend Mrs. Jones said had died of influenza in 1809, was also still receiving payments three years later. Either the clerk was attempting to make the fund look on the square, or someone was lying to the clerk.

Rattling back to Manchester Square in her hired carriage, Miss Tolerance considered. The eleven first investors had been listed in that clerical hand: the first in 1793, the last in 1807. But all the entries in the book had been scrupulously kept up to date in that later hand, with records of payments to all but one of them (payments to Mrs. Collins, formerly Betsey Tightly, the woman who had died of dysentery in '09, stopped that year).

When she was put down in Spanish Place, Miss Tolerance made for her cottage, lit a lamp, and pored over the ledger again, seeking patterns. Eight names had been entered by the second hand, starting in—Miss Tolerance flipped back to look. In 1809, with a Mrs. Cook (formerly Nan Birchaboy).

Here, too, the record of payments had been scrupulously kept, even to Arabella Black and Annie Pouter, who had not received the last payments that appeared there.

She assumed that the second hand belonged to George Kent—Mrs. Stone had mentioned him by name, she recalled. Which was curious, given that he had later disguised his identity with the name Marvell. At this point, feeling a strong inclination to throw the ledger across the room, Miss Tolerance left off her work and crossed the garden to collect a plate of supper, which she ate in the kitchen with Cook and her helpers. Afterward, much sustained by food, she went up to visit with her aunt, who had passed an uneventful afternoon and was feeling well enough to complain about porter, enforced bed-rest, and the regimen of mercury pills she had been prescribed.

It was several hours later that she returned to her cottage. The ledger was still on the table where she had left it, a reproach of sorts. Perhaps now she would see what had eluded her before. Miss Tolerance spared a momentary, unkind thought for Annie Pouter, who had brought her into this brangle. Then she rubbed the chalk from her slate and began again.

Chapter Fifteen

When the morning had sufficiently advanced to reach the window of Miss Tolerance's sitting room, the dazzle woke her from a very uncomfortable slumber, slouched on the settle where sleep had overcome her. Her slate, she was dismayed to note, had fallen to the floor and cracked down the center.

She sat up, felt a distinct twinge in her back and neck, and swore indecorously. Then she picked up the two halves of slate and attempted to fit them together and remind herself where she had left off in her thinking. What was left was a fractured series of comments.

Who was first clerk, whose was later hand?

Later clerk adds notations to earlier entries. No earlier clerk notations on later.

Did A know B?

Mrs. Stone spoke of Kent, not Marvell

She went upstairs to wash and change and render herself presentable, running through a few fencing drills before she did so to stretch muscles aching from her unorthodox slumber. Then she returned to the ledger.

The eleventh name entered in the book was the last to

have been writ there by the first clerk. She, Mrs. Collins, had died, but by natural causes. Three of the seven women she had sought the day before had died of natural causes, but among names twelve through nineteen, she already knew that two had died violent deaths consequent upon their making inquiries about the fund. She reminded herself again that this was a deadly earnest game; she could not be behind-hand in caution.

Miss Tolerance put the ledger into a drawstring bag together with her pistol, and sought her bonnet.

The address given for Mrs. Anna Cook was in Saffron Street, off the Saffron Hill Road. It was a narrow street with buildings close-built, of ragged brick or plastered wood, the road twisted as the buildings themselves. Number 11 had sunk somewhat, so the dark wood jamb above the door was askew and kept the square-hung door from closing. In the doorway, an elderly person sat, much covered in robes and shawls. It was impossible to guess whether this was male or female, for the face retained no vestige of gender, the mouth was drawn in over missing teeth, and the hair was pulled back and kept beneath a broken and faded tricorne.

"Aye?" The apparition rolled one eye at Miss Tolerance.

"Good morning. I am seeking Mrs. Cook."

The figure cackled. "Nan? Not fer many a year, y'ain't."

"Do I understand she is no longer here? Can you tell me where I might find her?"

"Dunno. When she ran out o' gelt, old Pennyclip turfed 'er out. Ain't been seen round 'ere since. Prolly dead."

From this Miss Tolerance inferred that Pennyclip was the landlord. "Why do you say dead?" The word *ma'am* hung on her lips, but discretion kept her from it.

"An old whore wi' no money?" A rheumy snort. "What

else's left for 'er? She run through it all and kept Pennyclip waitin' for a month, sayin' 'er funds was just delayed." The last words were uttered in sing-song. "Not like 'e'd a give a month to any other female 'ereabouts."

It sounded as though Mrs. Cook had been the Fund's first dereliction. With a murmur of thanks, Miss Tolerance turned away.

"Tha's all? Nuffin' for a poor woman's time?"

The question of gender settled, Miss Tolerance turned to pass a ha'penny to the woman. "Thank you, ma'am."

The next name to appear in the ledger was the late Mrs. Black of Bermondsey. The name after that was Mary Green of Thames Street near the Broken Wharf. The amount noted in the ledger as Mrs. Green's initial investment was meagre enough that Miss Tolerance understood why the woman would have retired to so uncongenial a location. Mrs. Green's address proved to be a whorehouse catering to rivermen and sailors. The doorman, paunchy and unshaven, with a large sore to the right of his nose, sat crossways at the door and eyed Miss Tolerance with an evaluative air.

"Lookin' fer who?"

Miss Tolerance told him. The man pressed one long, dirty finger against his nose, almost upon the site of the sore, and tapped thoughtfully. It was difficult not to stare.

"Mary Green? As might used to been Mary Swaller? Yeh, well, she been gone a few years now. Stayed 'ere for a year or two after she stopped receiving. Mrs. Deeper—Dolly, as runs the place—she's a soft 'eart for some o' the girls. But the pox sign was too clear on Mary for 'er to make even a little, and when 'er mite dried up, well, Dolly'd tell you this ain't work'ouse nor reformatory."

"Her mite dried up?"

The man nodded. "She 'ad some in the bank or some'eres, but then it disappeared, and after a while so'd Mary Swaller."

"You have no idea—"

"Where she went to? None a'tall. Nor I don't think Dolly would, neither. The past's the past, darlin'." Again, an assessing glance at Miss Tolerance from toe to top. "What's a goer like you doin' lookin' for Mrs. Swaller's like, then?"

"Wasting my time, it appears." Miss Tolerance gave the man a ha'penny and left.

By the middle of the afternoon, Miss Tolerance had spoken to only one woman whose name appeared in the ledger. Four were deceased, including Annie Pouter and Mrs. Black, or were assumed to be dead after their money dried up and they departed their last addresses. Of the two who remained, she was directed to the first by the madam of a down-at-heels brothel to a tidy house in Knightsbridge. There was no external marking to suggest what she discovered to be the truth: it was the home of a religious order. The woman who kept the door did not wear the habit familiar to Miss Tolerance from her years on the continent, but a plain black dress and unbleached cap. Anti-Catholic feeling in England was not so far abated that these women could advertise their status, and the Sister was at first suspicious of a request to speak to Mrs. Ellen Jones, formerly Nell Finger.

Finally, "I will ask Mother."

Miss Tolerance waited in a quiet whitewashed room while the nun went to seek guidance from her superior. When the Sister returned, it was with another woman in the same severe gown and white cap.

"I'm Sister Eleanor." She had a small, oval face with a long nose and small mouth; her voice was quiet and low, with the vowels of Cheapside and a notable lisp. "You was wishful to see me, miss? D'I know you?"

Miss Tolerance rose and curtseyed. "No, ma'am. Sister. I was told by Mrs., er, Mrs. Cockrider of a house in Swithin's Lane that you had retired here."

Sister Eleanor gave a tight-lipped smile. "I 'ope you found Mrs. C. in good 'ealth?"

"I believe so. I asked to speak with you because I am attempting to learn what I can about a group of women who made investment with a man called Marvell—"

Two lines appeared between Sister Eleanor's brows, hardly enough to be called a frown. "You ain't—you 'aven't come from Mr. Marvell, 'ave you?"

"No, ma'am. But I am very eager to hear from women who gave him money."

The nun gestured Miss Tolerance to sit and took her chair opposite. "Women 'oo 'ad money stolen by 'im, more like. And now I'll do penance for lack of charity, and pro'lly deserved. Look, miss. When I joined the Order, I made over all I owned as my dowry. Mother kept it in trust until I took me vows, then she was to cashier my investment and add it to the order's accounts."

"Did Marvell refuse to cashier the funds?"

Sister Eleanor's frown deepened. "Mr. Marvell 'ad scarpered. Not t'be found, Mother said. I was 'feared I wouldn't be let to stay. But Mother, she said it were God's will I was 'ere and they wouldn't turn me out. Even w' my past, and all."

"You are fortunate, indeed," Miss Tolerance agreed gravely. "No attempt was made to find Mr. Marvell? Not by you or your Superior?"

The nun looked mildly surprised. "T'weren't—wasn't for me to think about it once Mother'd said I was to stay."

It was entirely possible that Sister Eleanor still lived

because she had not attempted to find Marvell and protest the loss of her investment. "And you are happy here?"

The other woman's face lit with the first full smile since she had entered the room. Miss Tolerance saw now what a pretty girl she must have been. "*Blessed.*"

T he last name on the list was Mrs. Cora Jones of Belton Street. Miss Tolerance found this lady easily; she proved to be one of a cluster of flashy whores sitting on the front steps of Number 6, which she took to be their place of employment.

"Ooo wants to know?" A woman with brassy curls in a knot upon her head looked up at the visitor.

"You tell 'er, Corie," another of the women encouraged.

"My name is Tolerance, Mrs. Jones. I—"

"Tolerance! Come from one of them Reform Shops to make me see the erra' o' me ways?" Mrs. Jones sprawled upon the steps, her blue skirts hiked up to display, not just a set of ankles, but her stockings, garters, and a good deal of plump, unwashed thigh. "I don' need yer conde-whatsit, miss, so you take yerself right off."

Mrs. Jones appeared to be considerably the worse for wine.

"I mean no condescension, Mrs. Jones—"

"I'm Clinger when I'm workin' dearie. Cora Clinger, and clingin's what I do—"

Miss Tolerance interrupted before Mrs. Jones could start on a description of her *spécialités d'amour*. "I need a moment of your time to ask you about an investment you made with a Mr. Marvell."

Mrs. Clinger put her hand down and fumbled among her skirts, rewarded after a moment by the location of a square blue gin bottle. "I'll drink 'is 'ealth," she announced. "Made me a tidy return on me bits and bobs. I mean," she informed the three women who sat with her, "to buy my way into the management of a 'ouse and make them girls work on their backs fer *me*."

"And payments have been made as scheduled, ma'am?"

For the first time, Mrs. Clinger sat up and really regarded Miss Tolerance. "Why woun't they?"

"I gather some investors in the Fund have not been so fortunate. And with Mr. Marvell's death—"

"Dead? That lit'le monkey of a fella? What cause'd 'e to be dead? 'E's younger nor I am."

"You noticed no interruption in your payments?"

"Last quarter come in as es-spected. Next 'un's due at the end of the month. You be certain sure I'd a 'ad 'is balls in me hand if I suspicioned anything was wrong. Whot'd the lit'le fella die of?"

"He was murdered." Miss Tolerance took a very unworthy gratification in the ripple of dismay this caused Mrs. Clinger and her friends. "I do not know who will be administering the Fund now."

"Murdered! And me money?" Mrs. Clinger made to stand, wobbled, and sat down again with a rattling thud. "T'morrow morning, first thing, I'm fer the bank and find out what's what. Thank you fer tellin' me, missy."

Miss Tolerance recognized her dismissal.

As she walked to the nearest corner where she could find a carriage for hire, she reflected that, of the eight women whose names had been inscribed in the ledger by the second clerk, Mrs. Cora Clinger was the first whose funds appeared to be where she imagined they were.

And of the first eleven women in the ledger, those she had spoken to were still receiving money. All disbursed, as the unfortunate George Kent had mentioned, by Pennantine's Bank. Her visit there was overdue.

M iss Tolerance rapped on the roof of her carriage and told the driver to take her to Fleet Street, at the corner of Essex. This corner was assiduously swept by a small, freckled boy with a bad limp. She let the child do his work, gave him a penny, then crossed to find Pennantine's Bank. Unlike some of the longer-established businesses of its type, Pennantine's was not housed in a limestone temple of commerce but rather in a short, modern brick building with large windows looking out on the bustling street. When she reached the door, it was opened by a young black man in livery who bowed her in and asked with low-voiced courtesy where he might direct her.

Miss Tolerance was not certain for whom she might most usefully ask. "I have some questions about an investment fund," she began.

The liveried man pointed her to a white-painted bench along the far wall. "Then you most like to speak with Mr. Pennantine hisself, miss. If you'll take a seat, someone will see you in a few minutes."

Miss Tolerance established herself upon the bench and composed herself to wait. She had not been sitting long when a man approached her.

"What are you doing here?" His voice was an outraged hiss.

It took a long moment for Miss Tolerance to recognize Mr. Walter Hasbrow, nephew of her former client, Mrs. Jones. She had last seen him, stocking-footed and shivering in the cold, when he had ridden in her carriage after having his thefts exposed. Miss Tolerance had not spared the man a thought since then, but noted now that Hasbrow's former extravagances of fashion had been abandoned. He wore a dark broadcloth coat, plain waistcoat, and a neckcloth of moderate height.

"Mr. Hasbrow! Are you employed here?"

"Yes." He looked about him to see whether his conversation with this visitor had been noticed. "Do you mean to tell me you had no idea of it? I took your advice and found occupation, and I don't mean to lose it—"

"Perish the thought that you should do so through any agency of mine, Mr. Hasbrow. I am delighted to see—"

Hasbrow sagged with relief. Miss Tolerance rather thought he would have liked to drop to the bench beside her and give vent to his feelings but dared not. "You have not come here on my account?"

"I have not. I need to ask some questions about an investment fund which I understand made its payments through Pennantine's." She gestured to the bag in which she carried the ledger.

"Investment fund? I have never seen any mention of a formal fund, although there are certainly investments managed—but I have been here only a se'enight. Do you know who managed it? When it was initiated?"

"I have a record of the investors." She took the ledger from the bag and handed it to Hasbrow, realizing as she did so that she felt no qualm in trusting him with it. She knew the limits of Hasbrow's dishonesty. For his part, Hasbrow paged through, making small *hmmms* now and again, before he looked up from the book. "I see no mention of Pennantine's—"

"I was told that all disbursements are made through this bank."

"No mention of Pennantine's," Hasbrow repeated. "But I believe I recognize some of these names as account-holders." In response to Miss Tolerance's look of inquiry, "There are not so many women who are sole owners of accounts not held in trust for them; one remembers them. What is curious is I'd swear the first entries were writ by the old Chief Clerk here."

He handed the book back to Miss Tolerance, who slipped it into its bag again.

Miss Tolerance was conscious of a flare of excitement. "The Chief Clerk?"

Hasbrow nodded. "Do you know the history of Pennantine's, Miss—" a pause while he retrieved the memory of her name. "Miss Tolerance? The founder, Mr. Pennantine, died young, and for almost twenty years the business was managed in trust, and very capably, too, from what I have heard, by his clerk, Mr. Kent. When Mr. Pennantine the younger—"

"Kent?" She found herself rearranging puzzle pieces in her head. "Could you, perhaps, describe this Mr. Kent?"

Hasbrow shook his head as if at some foolishness. "I never had the pleasure to meet him. Mr. Kent has been dead these five years."

Dead these five years? How was this possible? The Mr. Kent she had encountered had been, by her reckoning, in his twenties. "But you believe the first writer to have been this Mr. Kent. Do you recognize the writing of the second?" She took the ledger out and again offered it to him.

Hasbrow flipped through the latter pages but shook his head. "It is no hand I recognize, Miss Tolerance. It is not a—" she watched him make an effort at tact. "It is not a clerical hand."

Miss Tolerance nodded. Hasbrow was still speaking. "But I'm sure Mr. Pennantine can assist you. And—" Hasbrow turned at the sound of approaching steps. "Here he is. Miss." He bowed to Miss Tolerance, then to the gentleman who had joined them, and took himself away.

"I understand you wished to ask some questions about the bank, madam? I am Andrew Pennantine."

Miss Tolerance, distracted by her thoughts, greeted this new arrival mechanically and agreed to his suggestion that they adjourn to his office, where they might speak privately.

Kent five years dead? She followed the banker to an office built out at the back of the room, windowed to permit light. Pennantine made polite conversation until he saw his guest seated. He was very, tall, golden-haired and blue-eyed, and almost unsettlingly handsome, and carried himself with the unconscious assurance of a man whose wealth and good looks had always smoothed his way.

When Mr. Pennantine had taken his own chair, he regarded her with an air of polite inquiry.

Miss Tolerance recalled herself to the moment and introduced herself. "You may think my errand unusual, but I have been asked to determine what I can about a fund of investment which appears to have some connection to Pennantine's."

"Asked by whom, madam?" If Pennantine was concerned that, by the evidence of her name, the woman before him was Fallen, he gave no sign of it. Business, clearly, was business.

"By a retired woman who invested in it."

"And what makes you believe that this fund has anything to do with my bank?"

"I was told by the fund's late manager that all payments were made from Pennantine's. Further, I have some evidence that suggests that the chief clerk of the bank may have been involved with it."

"Our chief clerk? Mr. Williams?" Pennantine looked out at the bank floor, his gaze alighting upon a swarthy, square-set man of middle years. His tone was one of bewilderment, but it did not convince.

"I beg your pardon, sir. I should have said, your late chief clerk, a Mr. Kent."

"Ah!" Pennantine drew the word out as if enlightened. "I cannot answer for Mr. Kent—he died in '07. Nor can the bank take any responsibility for actions so far in the past." That was a very quick denial of a problem Miss Tolerance had yet to state. "Pennantine's, as you may imagine, makes a number of payments to a number of people. May I inquire as to the name of this manager?"

"He called himself Marvell, but his name was actually George Kent."

"*George* Kent? Perhaps that is the occasion of the confusion. Our Mr. Kent was Mr. *Albion* Kent."

Albion Kent, with whose wife she had had such a peculiar interview several days past. As Miss Tolerance digested that, she heard in memory one of the retired women she had spoken to. "*The money appeared in my bank, every quarter, thanks to dear Mr. Kent—*" Of course, George Kent would have been in the nursery when Mrs. Stone's entry into the ledger had been made.

"Is it possible, then, that Albion Kent was involved in the fund before his death, and Mr. George Kent took up that involvement afterward?"

A shadow of some strong emotion—anger, perhaps—chased across Andrew Pennantine's striking face before he shook his head. "I understand Kent's son was a half-wit," as if the matter was settled. "I cannot imagine him able to manage anything, let alone something as complex as an investment fund."

"The Mr. George Kent I met was—" she paused for the just word. "He was a curious young man, and not, perhaps, inordinately clever. But—"

"I cannot account for your impression, miss. But George Kent, the son of our late head clerk, was as imbecile as he was repulsive." Pennantine's face twisted in an expression of disgust and then, as if he realized he had been too forceful, he smiled at her. "Is there anything else I can do to assist you?"

He is very certain that smile will redeem any mis-step, Miss Tolerance thought uncharitably. "You can give me no idea how to find the person or persons who are managing this fund?"

"Not the least in the world. You said you had evidence of

Mr. Kent's involvement beyond the coincidence of payments being made through my bank?"

Where five minutes before she had offered up the ledger to Hasbrow without demur, Miss Tolerance now found herself loath to do so. Something about this decorative young man did not sit well with her. She kept the book in its drawstring bag. "I have paperwork going back more than twenty years, written in his hand."

"May I see it?"

"You do not think I carry it with me? It has—" she sought the term. "It has *probative value*, I believe the solicitors would call it."

"Are solicitors involved? Does the woman for whom you act expect some business in court?"

"At the moment, sir, all my client wants to know is who controls her investment. Not an unreasonable question."

For the third time, Pennantine smiled. Miss Tolerance was now confirmed in her dislike of the man.

"Well, until I see this evidence you speak of, I do not think I can assist you further. Is there any other business you would like to discuss?"

Was there anything further to be gained from this meeting? Miss Tolerance shook her head. "No, Mr. Pennantine. I thank you for your time."

She rose to go. The banker bowed and ushered her as far as the door to his office. As she crossed to the street door, Miss Tolerance saw Mr. Hasbrow watching her. She smiled and nodded. He nodded in return, apparently secure that his job was in no danger from her.

In nearly six years practice of her unorthodox profession, Miss Tolerance had learned to trust her instincts but to be wary of a quickly-felt prejudice. As she turned her steps toward the Wheat Sheaf, she considered whether her dislike of Pennantine—based largely upon the man's smug reliance on his power to please—might color her response to his information. She thought again that she trusted Walter Hasbrow, whose sort and level of dishonesty was known to her, more than she did Pennantine.

A beam of sunlight illuminated the well-laundered folds of Joshua Glebb's neckcloth and the sloping, half-shaven wobble of the chin that nestled therein. Mr. Glebb was looking a trifle liverish. Miss Tolerance expected that jollification at his daughter's wedding had caught up with him. More, Mr. Glebb was nursing a mug of coffee instead of his usual ale, and the smile that crossed his face when Miss Tolerance seated herself was more pursed than usual.

"I hope I see you well, Mr. Glebb."

Glebb winced and took a sip from his mug. "Good day, Miss T."

"May I hope you have news for me?" Mr. Boddick put a mug before her, and Miss Tolerance drank a little of her coffee, disposing herself to wait upon Glebb's pleasure.

"You asked me to look into Pennantine's, and I admit I didn't expect much in the way of scandal there—Albie Kent was a rough diamond, to be sure, but he loved that bank like he'd birthed it hisself, and it prospered while 'e had the management of it. Taught young Pennantine well, from what I hear."

"This you have told me before, Mr. Glebb. Do I detect some reservation now?"

"Not about the bank. I tell you plain, Pennantine's is solid and has been. But the men theirselves! Albie Kent was fond of a tumble, fancied the rougher sort of girl, if you'll pardon my mentioning of it. Nor that didn't stop with 'is marriage. It comes clear, do you ask into the matter, that he caught the pox. I find it was an open secret that was what kilt 'im five year ago."

Miss Tolerance spared a thought for her aunt. This information also shed light upon the widow Kent's extreme distaste for women of easy virtue. "His poor wife."

"You might say so, Miss T. But he took care of the bank, as I said, and trained 'is step-son up to it as well, whatever else his failings might 'a been as a husband. Brought young Andrew into the bank—"

"Wait—" Miss Tolerance extended a hand to stem Glebb's words. "Do you mean to tell me that Kent's wife—"

"The widow Pennantine," Glebb said, with the air of a man playing a trump card.

"The bank was left to young Andrew on 'is father's death, with the widow and Kent as his guardians, so after 'er year of mourning I 'spose it makes sense that Kent married 'er. Though I'll say I think she got the raw end of that bargain."

"George Kent was Pennantine's step-brother?" She thought of the curl of Pennantine's elegant lip when he spoke of George Kent as imbecile.

"George? Was that 'is name? Aye, they did 'ave a son, but I didn't hear much about 'im. Frankly, Miss T., I was under the impression 'e'd died. But about that fund—"

"Yes. The fund." Miss Tolerance forced herself to attention.

"As I said, Kent was a square dealer in 'is way. Regardless of where 'e was dippin' 'is pen, if you'll forgive the expression, Miss T., Kent took as good care of the bank as if it were 'is own name on the door. The pox didn't seem to have gone to 'is brain like it does for some."

"A prince among men," Miss Tolerance murmured. Glebb's sympathy, it seemed, was all for the money Kent had shepherded.

"You might say so. 'E was kinder to 'is mistresses than most, as well. Kent started up that little fund for some of the ladies 'e patronized, if you take what I mean. Fair rate, a little below the Navy Fund, and for 'is bits, once 'e'd 'ad done with 'em, he'd sweeten the fund with a couple of pounds to start it off. Not a money-making proposition, in course, but not a losing one. Meant to provide 'em something to retire upon."

"It may have started that way, but from what I have found, it did not continue."

Glebb cleared his throat gummily and spat into a large spotted handkerchief. "Well, the best idee may not outlast a man's death. But young Pennantine would 'ave to have known of this fund—by the time he come to learn the business, it'd been going for years." Glebb performed a complicated realignment of his head and neck and, at the last, produced a fragrant belch. "'Pologies, Miss T."

"Please continue, sir." Miss Tolerance's patience was wearing thin.

"So five years ago, Albie Kent met 'is maker." Glebb took a sip of his coffee and pushed the mug aside, grimacing.

"And Mr. Pennantine took over its management?"

Glebb shook his head. The wattles of his neck swayed gently in the negative. "That's where I can't say, Miss T. For certain sure 'e takes control at the bank. As for the Fund? Not dissolved—you dissolve a fund and there's payments and records and such. Record of this fund just… vanished into the air."

"But it did not. That is, I know that some of those women —the ones whose involvement pre-dated Mr. Albion Kent's death—are still receiving payment."

"Then someone hid those payments in some other instrument at the bank." Glebb was adamant. "No bank just sends out money without they keep a record. What about the women as signed on after Kent's death, with that Marvell what started this whole brangle?"

"Most of them dead. Murdered. As is Marvell—whose name was George Kent."

Joshua Glebb regarded Miss Tolerance with disbelief, and then his expression slowly transformed into what appeared at first to be a grimace of pain but at last became a broad grin. "Marvell is Pennantine's brother!" He began to chuckle.

In the years Miss Tolerance had been acquainted with Joshua Glebb, she had never seen him overcome by amusement. It was an unsettling display.

"So it ties up neat like a bonnet string!" he said at last. "Ain't that a thing!"

"I suppose it is, sir. So *all* of the women—the ones in the first group—were Mr. Kent's connections?" When she considered the prolificacy of Albion Kent's *amours* it was difficult not to regard his widow's bitterness with more sympathy.

"I imagine so. It'd be how they got referred to the fund, after all."

"But after his death, whoever was managing the fund decided to recruit elsewhere, and to—steal the money of elderly whores? Surely there are easier ways to make greater sums of money."

"I'd say so, Miss T. Why do it, is what I want to know. Make an old woman think 'er money's safe and 'er future's cared for, then take that away? That's cruel, when I come to think on it."

Miss Tolerance considered the women on the latter part of the list and agreed. "Perhaps that was the point?"

"Cruelty?" Glebb shook his head. "There's no money in it, Miss T."

Miss Tolerance thanked Mr. Glebb for his time with the thanks she knew he most valued: a brace of shillings. Information danced in her brain in patterns that refused to settle. She needed quiet time and her slate—which, she recalled, was broken. Sighing, she turned her steps toward Manchester Square, reflecting that there might not be money in cruelty, but that did not rule it out as a motive for murder.

Chapter Sixteen

Mrs. Brereton was feeling enough restored to chafe against the prescriptions that the doctor and surgeon had directed. When she dined with her aunt that evening, Miss Tolerance was entertained with an hour's discourse on the iniquities of porter and the treatments that Mr. Warringe had ordered. At last, "Aunt, I believe you have exhausted the topic," she said.

Mrs. Brereton regarded her niece with surprise. After a moment, she chuckled. "Am I becoming a prosy invalid? I apologize, Sarah. It is all I have had on my mind these last days. Except when Marianne comes up to report on how the house goes on. Divert me. Tell me what you have that keeps you so busy. Did you ever find anything more about Annie Pouter's business?"

Miss Tolerance unrolled the whole of what she had learned; it was not a surprise to hear that Mrs. Brereton knew of Albion Kent and his affairs. "I had not known he was so considerate of his long list of doxies as to set them up for a comfortable old age."

"The women who joined the fund before his death, certainly," Miss Tolerance acknowledged.

"And you have talked with them all?"

"All but the ones who had died—of causes quite natural, I am relieved to say. The other in that group—" she ran down the list in her head. "All are receiving the money they are due —" she paused. "No, there's one I have not found."

"Perhaps she is dead, as well." Mrs. Brereton examined the fingernails on her left hand critically.

"Perhaps. But the name is the only one without a *nom d'amour* attached. Which is peculiar, for Mr. Kent's tastes appear to have run to the professional." She visualized the page. "Miss Helen Kerrwood, of Cheval Place, Knightsbridge. Rather a better part of town than the rest as well. She was enrolled in the list in '04."

"Why did you ignore her?"

"I hadn't meant to do. I started with the names on the eastern side of London, and then looked at the more recent ones, and—"

"Knightsbridge is not in the east," Mrs. Brereton finished. "It would be awkward if this Miss Kerrwood was the one who knew everything, would it not?"

Miss Tolerance suspected that her aunt was attempting to tease. She agreed gravely that that would be very awkward, indeed.

In a dense, cold fog, Miss Tolerance left for Knightsbridge the next morning. The year of Miss Kerrwood's enrollment in the fund was recent enough that she had at least some hope of finding the woman still in residence.

Her carriage left her at the corner of Montpelier Street and Cheval Place. The houses here were respectably kept, but there was an air of clinging to respectability rather than moving upward. Number 7 was a small wooden house, two storeys high, with dirty ivory plaster chipped around the doorsill. When she knocked at the door, it was opened almost immediately by a woman who seemed prepared for a wholly different visitor but was not dismayed. Miss Tolerance suspected an expected visit by the landlord.

"Miss Kerrwood?"

The woman was of middle years and middle height, dressed in a brown stuff gown and apron. She looked over Miss Tolerance's shoulder and, satisfied that no one more sinister lurked there, turned her gaze to the visitor on her doorstep. "Which one?"

There was more than one? "Miss *Helen* Kerrwood."

"Not lived in this house for years. The family did live here, but the widow died and the girls got married—one of 'em not before time, if I'm a judge. Both of 'em moved east. I think Miss Jane bought a house in Bethnal Green."

Miss Tolerance was aware of a new snapping-together of puzzle pieces. "Did Miss Jane Kerrwood marry a Mr. Pilgrim, ma'am?"

"Captain Pilgrim, I think. Navy man."

"Thank you, ma'am. You have been very helpful."

Miss Tolerance returned to her waiting carriage, aware that the woman in the door of Number 7 was staring after her.

A return to Bethnal Green was clearly indicated, but first —as it was only half-an-hour's walk—she meant to stop again in Hans Place. Miss Tolerance believed that the second writer in the ledger must be George Kent, but it would be a good thing to confirm it with someone of Mrs. Kent's household. Perhaps the man's mother had a scrap of his writing somewhere. At least, she could offer her condolences.

The house in Hans Place displayed none of the outward signs of a household in mourning: no mourning wreath over the door, the knocker unmuffled, and the liveried porter who opened the door was without a black arm band. Had she not known from Sir Walter that the Runner Penryn had notified the family of George Kent's death, she would have thought the household unaware.

When she gave her name, the porter looked apprehensive. Had instructions been given, after her last visit, to turn her away?

"I only wished to give my condolences to Mrs. Kent on the death of her son."

Cates's discomfort redoubled. "Mr—" he paused. "Mrs. Kent is not accepting condolences." He moved to close the door, but Miss Tolerance put her hand on the man's wrist to stay him—very few well-mannered servants are willing to actually close a door on the arm of a woman.

"Not accepting condolences? I am sorry to hear it. Is there no one in the household who might remember Mr. George Kent with kindness, and be willing to speak with me?"

The porter hesitated. "Most of us ain't been here long enough to know Mr. Kent particular. Except Mrs. Whettle," he suggested. "Used to be in the nursery. She might. But madam won't like it."

Miss Tolerance was sympathetic, having seen Mrs. Kent's rage. "Could you give her a message? That I would be very glad to speak with her, perhaps away from this house? If she would meet with me at Tarsio's Club in Henry Street this morning—"

The sound of bustling from the upper hallway made the porter look over his shoulder, alarmed.

"Will you tell her?" Miss Tolerance asked again.

With the air of a man who will do anything to end an interview, Cates nodded emphatically. Miss Tolerance loosed his wrist and withdrew her hand. He closed the door.

She was on the pavement a few houses down when the door of Mrs. Kent's house opened and the woman herself, attended by a maid, issued forth with the pomp of a royal procession. A carriage pulled up before, and the women were taken up and vanished within a minute.

Miss Tolerance retreated to Henry Street and Tarsio's Club.

At Tarsio's, she found a letter waiting for her in which, Miss Tolerance rejoiced to find, was a bank draft for a piece of work she had done a month before. On the strength of this, she ordered tea and a plate of current cake and read the newspapers. She hoped that the Kent's nursery maid would come to talk with her while her mistress was out, and was willing to spend the morning waiting upon that chance. After noon she would go to Bethnal Green.

She had not long to delve into the details of Court news. A few minutes after her refreshments were brought, a woman arrived in the door of the Ladies Salon.

"I beg your pardon. Are you Miss Tolerance?"

As there was no one else in the room at that hour, the inquiry seemed a matter of formality. Miss Tolerance rose and gestured the woman to come in. The words "in the nursery" had led her to expect a sturdy country maid with rosy cheeks. But the woman who approached was so tall and narrow that, had she been a man, Miss Tolerance might have described her as cadaverous.

"Please sit, ma'am. I am Miss Tolerance. Am I correct that you are Mrs. Whettle?"

The woman nodded. She was closer to sixty than thirty, dressed in a gown of so dark a shade of puce that it might have been taken for black, with a plain bonnet and black gloves. Miss Tolerance found herself thinking that a hoop, dropped over her head, would meet with no impediment as it fell to the ground. Certainly, she could do with a slice of cake.

"May I offer you some refreshment? " Miss Tolerance asked. "Will you join me in a dish of tea?"

Her guest was breathing heavily, as though she had run from all the way from Hans Place. "Tea would be very welcome. I could not come away at once, and I must return before Mrs. Kent is aware that I have gone."

Miss Tolerance signed to a waiter, and a cup and fresh hot water were provided. Miss Tolerance refreshed the pot and cut a slice of currant cake.

The tea, heavily sugared, appeared to restore the woman to equilibrium. "Thank you," she said at last. "You are very kind to a stranger met under such circumstances."

Miss Tolerance shook her head. "It is you who is kind to come to me, and a stranger who has made such an effort must be restored to her ability to speak." She smiled. "I *am* correct that you are Mrs. Whettle? And that you knew the late Mr. George Kent?"

The narrow woman nodded. "I am. I was—I suppose I am Mrs. Kent's secretary these days. But when he was young, I was George's—Mr. Kent's—governess. He was a very sweet child. It is very distressing to think he came to such a cruel end."

"I am sorry to occasion painful memories," Miss Tolerance said gently. Mrs. Whettle's grief was the more stark in contrast with the apparent disinterest of the rest of Mrs. Kent's household. "But I assure you that my reason is not idle curiosity. What can you tell me of him?"

The smile that crossed the narrow woman's face softened its harsh planes, and her eyes—large and dark—lit with affection. "I met him when he was a wee lad—no more than three or four, still in smocks and capering about on his poor legs. I was not meant to teach him, really. Mrs. Kent only desired me to keep the child as far away from her as possible; Mr. Kent as well, but men so rarely take interest in the nursery that I did not expect it to be otherwise. George—Mr. Kent—

was a sweet, loving boy, brighter than I had expected when I realized his...his condition."

"And what was that condition, ma'am?"

The skin over Mrs. Whettle's taut cheekbones flushed. "Did you meet him in life, Miss—?"

"Miss Tolerance," she reminded gently. "And yes, I did."

"Did you not remark something unusual about his form, his visage? I recognized it at once—"

"He was certainly an odd-looking man," Miss Tolerance said carefully.

"My sister married a sailor." From the way that Mrs. Whettle said it, it was clear that there was a connection. "In the way of some sea-going men, he brought back an infection with him that neither she nor he suspected, and by the time they understood what had happened, their little girl was born: the same peg teeth and curved legs. Only Araminta hadn't Georgie's health. She died young."

"You are saying that Mr. Kent was born syphilitic?"

Mrs. Whettle nodded. "He had the physical markers, but he was a sweet, gentle lad, and far cleverer than I had expected when first I met him. He rewarded patience or affection with the most absolute devotion—but I am afraid he never received that from either his mother or his father."

"I suppose I can understand how that might be." What would it mean to a woman to have a child and know that she had given it, not only life but a disease that would mark him for life? What would it mean to a man who had brought the infection home to wife and then child?

"Whatever you might understand, the circumstances were no fault of George's. He had kindness only from myself, a few of the maids, and... sometimes... his brother. Oh, his brother could do no wrong, George thought. *I* never thought the boy cared for George except as another person to admire and worship him."

Miss Tolerance could very easily imagine this of the Andrew Pennantine she had met.

"Mrs. Whettle, you say that Mr. Kent was cleverer than you had anticipated. Could he read and write?"

The woman bridled at the perceived slight to her favorite. "Of course, he could. I taught him myself. George was… slow of apprehension, but he rewarded patience."

"Then you would recognize his handwriting?" Could she return home, fetch the ledger, and return with it in time for Mrs. Whettle to return to Hans Place before her mistress arrived?

"I would. He used to write me a letter every month—directed in care of my church, so that his mother did not know of it. I have one here with me." Mrs. Whettle rifled through her reticule until she found what she sought. "You must forgive—" she gestured at several spots easily recognizable as tear-stains. "I am afraid I made the ink run."

The letter, cross-written and on inexpensive paper, was difficult to decipher, although its opening and closing salutations were made in terms of the greatest affection. And as Mrs. Whettle had said, there were spots where the ink had run. It was sufficient to confirm for Miss Tolerance that the second handwriting in the ledger had been George Kent's.

Mrs. Whettle spoke a little about her late charge's childhood as she finished her tea and current cake. "I had hoped Mr. Pennantine might give Georgie a job there when he reached manhood—he could not cipher at all, he would have been no use in a counting house, but despite his peculiarity of looks, he had great charm. But of course, neither Mr. Kent nor, after he died, Mr. Pennantine would let him near the business. Still, I believe Mr. Andrew had put Georgie in the way of employment, selling shares to distressed gentlewomen to improve their income."

Miss Tolerance had taken a sip of tea; now she coughed and very nearly spat it out.

"That is one way of describing Mr. Kent's occupation."

"It was Georgie himself who told me so, and whatever faults he had, he could not lie. He turned as red as Cornish apple!"

"Might he have been cozened into an occupation that *seemed* licit, ma'am?"

"Are you saying it was not?" The narrow woman nodded; the skin over her cheekbones was mottled red-and-white. "He might. I said he could not cipher, and certain kinds of reasoning were beyond him: taking two facts to deduce a third." She reached out one dry, cold, long-fingered hand and took Miss Tolerance's own in it. "But if the person was someone whom he loved, he could be persuaded to almost anything. What do you believe he was doing?"

"Your description was not far off: he was engaged in selling investment in a bogus fund to retired women."

"To prostitutes." Mrs. Whettle coughed into her kerchief. "You may use the word—I hear it often enough on Mrs. Kent's lips when the mood is upon her. But a *bogus* fund? How would he ever have become connected to such a thing?"

Miss Tolerance trod gently. "At the bank?"

"I have told you, he was not brought into the bank because—"

"I do not say that he worked for, or in the bank, Mrs. Whettle. But I wonder if perhaps someone at the bank might have inveigled Mr. George Kent into this work—"

"You mean his brother." Mrs. Whettle pressed her lips together as if to contain the worst of her opinion. "It is not impossible," she said at last. "As I said, George could be persuaded to anything by someone he loved, and he did love his brother, no matter how little that love was earned. You say that you met him, Miss? When you saw him, how did he look? His chest was always weak, and this autumn has been so blowy—" she stopped, as if remembering that the child she loved had been slain.

Miss Tolerance tried not to think of George Kent as she had last seen him, lying in a puddle of his own gore.

"You will think me very silly, I imagine," Mrs. Whettle went on. "But I never had a child, so my feelings toward George—and he was such a sweet, dear little fellow—"

Miss Tolerance listened politely and agreed that George Kent had been a very agreeable man, whatever his peculiarities. She agreed, as well, that he had likely been cozened into promoting the fund; she was convinced that he had never understood its criminal intent.

At last, "I must return home before Mrs. Kent does." Mrs. Whettle thanked Miss Tolerance for the refreshment. In her turn, Miss Tolerance desired Steen to find—and pay for—a carriage to take Mrs. Whettle back to Hans Place. She was certain the woman would accept no payment for her assistance; the least Miss Tolerance could do was see she did not arrive home panting.

The question of Andrew Pennantine's involvement in the Fund having been answered to her own satisfaction, Miss Tolerance settled with Steen for Mrs. Whettle's carriage fare and desired him to hail another carriage for herself. It was time to make her much-delayed return to Bethnal Green.

When she knocked at the door in Paradise Row, it was Mrs. Graham who opened to her. She greeted the visitor politely but with some curiosity. "Mrs. Tolerance? No, Miss," she corrected herself. "I had not thought we should see you here again."

Miss Tolerance agreed that she had not intended to return. "But your name occurred again in connection to my inquiries and I wished to understand it—and perhaps to give you a warning."

"A warning?" Mrs. Graham's eyebrows rose. "I think you must come in and explain, Miss Tolerance."

Seated again in the pleasant front room, Miss Tolerance described the ledger. "And a Helen Kerrwood was among the women listed there. I believe that was your maiden name?"

"It was. But I am quite sure I am unacquainted with any of those women whose names you mention. They seem—" Mrs. Graham paused delicately. "They all appear to have been women of—"

"They were all Fallen," Miss Tolerance confirmed. "As you are clearly not, I came to wonder how your name would be among them."

"I—" Mrs. Graham blushed. "I was fortunate enough to have a small sum invested for the maintenance of myself and my son, but as to how my name came to be among that group — And you say you brought a warning, as well?" She looked alarmed. "I hope that income is not imperiled. It is all that Martin and I have."

"A number of the women on the list have lost that income, ma'am. The Fund appears to have been a scheme devised to swindle them out of their savings. And a number of those women have met with untimely deaths."

Mrs. Graham put her hand to her lips. "No, no. This cannot be the same fund! Mr. Pennantine said—"

"Mr. Pennantine knows of the fund?" Whatever she had believed, this was the first direct evidence Miss Tolerance had encountered of it.

Mrs. Graham looked distressed. "Of course, he does. His step-father began it."

"And Mr. Pennantine continues it."

"It is a charitable enterprise. He wanted to help women— it is his mother's specific wish. A very generous lady, as he spoke to me about her."

Whatever Mrs. Graham believed, it was so totally in

opposition to what Miss Tolerance knew as to defy belief. "Mr. Pennantine's mother, Mrs. Albion Kent?"

"Why, yes. I believe Kent is her name. She married again after Andr—after Mr. Pennantine's father died."

Feeling that a few more bits of information would at last make the whole of the case plain to her, Miss Tolerance asked with as much kindness as she could summon, "Mrs. Graham, what is the relationship between you and Mr. Pennantine?"

Mrs. Graham dropped her eyes to her fingers, knotting in her lap. "There *is* no—when I was young, I thought—I believed we would marry."

"But you did not."

Mrs. Graham shook her head. "We were both terribly young. His step-father thought it would not serve. I hadn't much of a dowry, and they were ambitious for him. And, too —" she leaned forward to confide. "I thought that Jane must come to live with us when we wed, and I do not think Andrew cared for the idea. But our mother was ill so much of the time, I thought if Jane stayed with her, she would have no chance of marrying herself. And when we had children, how very useful she would have been."

Mrs. Graham's concern for her sister did not seem to admit of the notion that *being useful* in her own household might be a bar to marriage as well.

She was speaking still. "When Andrew's father was so very opposed—well, I could not marry him in such a case. Even when I found myself..." her voice lowered. "*Embarrassed.* My mother—you can imagine what she would have said, but then she died, and Jane married Captain Pilgrim, and he had a friend, Mr. Graham. Who had a sadly weak chest, and here we are—" she waved a hand to indicate the room in which they sat. "I have Martin to console me. And Mr. Pennantine has been so considerate. Which is why I cannot believe that he would have anything to do with a scheme such as you describe. I am very sorry to hear that these women have lost their money, but it must be a different fund. You cannot persuade me that I should be troubled about my money, or that Mr. Pennantine could have been a part of something criminal."

At this moment, Mrs. Pilgrim entered the room. There was a brief flurry of greetings before Mrs. Pilgrim inquired what had occasioned Miss Tolerance's return to their house.

"I was just telling her—Mrs.—*Miss* Tolerance—" Mrs. Graham spoke very loudly, as if accustomed to overcoming her sister's deafness. "I was telling her about the kindness of Mr. Pennantine in assisting me to my small income."

Mrs. Pilgrim came close to rolling her eyes. "Were you? Oh he was kind indeed, once he was prodded to it."

Mrs. Graham was thrown into confusion. "Jane, how can you say such a thing? When you consider how very—"

Mrs. Pilgrim rose from her chair, stepped forward, and turned her back upon her sister. It was clearly done to make it difficult for her to hear what Mrs. Graham might say to interrupt or distract her. "If I had not insisted that I would tell his mother—please recall, Helen, that it was she, and not Andrew's stepfather who objected to your match—and if his stepfather had not come forward in a very handsome way, you and Martin would be living in poverty."

Behind Mrs. Pilgrim's back, Mrs. Graham was saying, unhappily, "But Andrew—Mr. Pennantine—he would have— you are being very unfair to him—"

If Mrs. Pilgrim heard her sister's protests, she did not heed them.

"I cannot say whether Mr. Pennantine meant when he and Helen were courting to—to abandon her. I would like to think he did not; he was rather a spoiled young man and used to getting his way. I believe he expected his mother to yield to his wishes in this as she did in everything else."

From behind her, Mrs. Graham cried out in shrill protest.

"*Of course,* he did not intend it! When he came to tell me—after his mother—he raged and raged!"

Mrs. Pilgrim had heard that and turned back to her sister; her ear-trumpet was clenched tightly in her fist. "He raged to you because his will was thwarted, not on your behalf. He was not so enraged as to stand up to his mother's demands, was he? He raged, and then he abandoned you."

"You wouldn't have him dishonor his mother's wishes!"

"Had I known that you were with child? I would have had him honor *you*, Helen. I would have had him honor your son."

"And the Fund?" Miss Tolerance urged. This was clearly an old quarrel between the sisters, much repeated. She did not care to hear any more of it. "The Fund," she said again, more loudly.

Mrs. Pilgrim turned back to her, the ear trumpet raised. "The what?"

"The Fund. Who added Mrs. Graham's name to the Fund?"

"Ah. After Pennantine left, and her condition became clear to us, Helen married Lieutenant Graham. He died before even seeing action and left her with his name, Pennantine's son, and barely enough to live upon. I had married Captain Pilgrim by that time and would have brought them to live with us, only the Captain could not be persuaded to it. So I went to the bank to see Pennantine—"

"To the bank!" Mrs. Graham was round-eyed at the enormity of her sister's shamelessness. "You never told me! How could you?"

"My letters went unanswered. What else was I to do? I went to see him and laid the matter out before him, and this time I threatened to go to his mother if he did not take some responsibility for the life he had created. Oh, that threw him into a panic, you may imagine." Mrs. Pilgrim smiled grimly. "Mr. Kent, his step-papa, came to see what the ado was. And that is how Helen—and later I—came to be beneficiaries of the Fund. Mr. Kent saw to it all."

"But *Andrew*—" Mrs. Graham said faintly.

"Mr. Kent ordered him to provide some money, then locked it away in the Fund where it could not be touched, and bless him for that. He gave me to understand that he had done as much for a number of his own lovers over the years—" she ignored Mrs. Graham's protest at being lumped in with the long list of Kent's courtesans. "It was a simple thing to add us to the fund, and he promised that no one—I collect that included Mr. Pennantine himself—could touch that money. Does this answer your questions, Miss Tolerance?"

"It does, indeed." It also explained why none of the women who were installed in the Fund prior to Kent's death had lost their investment. "When did this all happen?"

"It must have been in '05. Yes, for my poor Captain Pilgrim died at Trafalgar, and I requested that Mr. Kent put some money away for me in his fund."

"It was genuine, then?"

"It was, and as my sister is still being paid from it, I think it must be still."

"For those who were invested while Mr. Kent was still alive. But for those who enrolled subsequent to his death, it appears to have been managed for fraudulent purposes only."

"But why?" Mrs. Graham had come forward and stood at her sister's side. "Why would anyone do such a thing, even to —even to—"

"Retired whores?" Miss Tolerance's tone was dry. "Because he saw the cost to his mother of his step-father's *amours*? Because it was a way to relatively easy money, with a scheme that could be laid off upon his poor brother?"

"Andrew had no brother," Mrs. Graham said. Perhaps she hoped that this would serve to put these crimes all at some other Andrew Pennantine's doorstep.

"He did have a brother, the son of Mr. Kent and his

mother. He was—" Mrs. Graham was an unworldly idiot; Mrs. Pilgrim, for all her shrewdness, might be no more sophisticated. How to explain George Kent's condition? "He was not a clever man, and I believe Pennantine thought he would not understand what he had been made part of."

"And did he?" Mrs. Pilgrim asked, with genuine curiosity.

"I believe he did at the last, and upbraided his brother, and was killed for it."

Mrs. Graham put her face in her hands and sank into a chair. "Not by Andrew's hand. Surely not."

"If not by his hand, I am convinced that it was at his order."

"What do you mean to do now?" Mrs. Pilgrim sat down, fidgeting with the ear trumpet in her hand.

"I mean to tell what I know to a magistrate of my acquaintance who will, I hope, take the steps necessary to bring Pennantine and any confederates to justice."

Mrs. Pilgrim extended her hand to take her sister's. "Will we be needed to testify?"

Helen Graham pulled her hand away, horrorstruck. "I could *never*."

"I cannot say. It is possible. But as you, Mrs. Pilgrim, are the one who actually spoke to Albion Kent, perhaps the Law will only require to hear from you."

"There, Nell. I shall manage it for you." Miss Tolerance wondered how often in their lives Mrs. Pilgrim had made that same promise.

Miss Tolerance had one more matter to settle to her satisfaction. "Mrs. Pilgrim, when I visited you last, I asked if you had received any letters asking for references, addressed to a Mrs. Brown, and written reference letters. You provided proof that you had not done so."

"I recall." Mrs. Pilgrim, her face turned perforce to her visitor, had contrived to turn her back on her sister.

"Mrs. Graham, was it you who wrote to Mrs. Pouter and Mrs. Black?"

Tearstained and pathetic, Mrs. Graham nodded. "Andrew asked if I would be so kind as to recommend his business manager, Mr. Marvell, and I was happy to do so! He has been so very generous to us!"

"It was his stepfather who was generous, Nell." Mrs. Pilgrim said. "If Mr. Pennantine had aught to do with it, you'd have had a hungry road, you and Martin."

"You never liked him," Mrs Graham shot back. "And I—" she turned back to Miss Tolerance. "I had no idea that the Fund—I still cannot believe—"

"Quite so," Miss Tolerance said. Her tone was dry.

Mrs. Pilgrim's lips were pressed tightly together, as if to contain an unflattering judgment upon her sister's naivete. Miss Tolerance rose and curtsied to the two sisters. Mrs. Graham barely looked up from where she sat, curled over her distress and weeping quietly. Mrs. Pilgrim escorted their visitor to the door and, rather than an exchange of curtsies, extended her hand to shake Miss Tolerance's own.

"I am sorry my sister is not wiser," she said. "I hope she may not have been the cause of some great harm to—to someone."

Miss Tolerance could give no reassurance on this point, so thought it best to stay silent.

She left the house in Paradise Row, unhappily aware that she had deranged the peace of that household, perhaps beyond repair. That the damage done had begun years before was no comfort to her.

Chapter Seventeen

As little sympathy as Miss Tolerance had for the late Albion Kent, she had to admit that he had dealt, not just fairly but generously with his lemans as well as with Helen Graham. Based upon her brief acquaintance with Andrew Pennantine and despite whatever pressure Mrs. Pilgrim might have brought to bear, she agreed that relying upon him for any kindness would have yielded nothing but disappointment.

A thought occurred. Miss Tolerance looked about her for a place to sit. There were no benches; she walked a little way into the park, sat upon the trunk of a fallen tree not yet cleared away, and took the ledger from the bag in which she carried it. Mrs. Graham's entry, under the name Helen Kerrwood, was written in Albion Kent's clear, even hand. As Mrs. Pilgrim had said, it had been the dissolute Mr. Kent who had arranged for the payments, and not Andrew Pennantine.

"Well, then. Proof clear that Pennantine's Bank is entangled with this fund—and that Andrew Pennantine knows of—" Her murmured thoughts were interrupted by the crack of a branch trod underfoot. She looked up to see a man, tall and broad-built, in a heavy gray topcoat and a sagging tricorn hat pulled low over his face. A man the size of the fellow who had assaulted her in Hans Place the week before. The man was approaching, at speed and with an expression of intent which Miss Tolerance did not like.

She reached into the bag again and produced her pistol. She was happy to note that the powder was still in place. She laid the pistol flat on the ledger and looked directly at the oncomer.

"Good afternoon, sir."

The man did not speak. Closer to, she noted dark hair, a chin covered in coarse black and gray stubble, and a long scar running from his eye to his lip, which was pulled back on one side to display a couple of filmy yellow teeth; the expression was, she felt certain, intended to make him look ferocious.

"Good afternoon," she said again. This time, she raised the pistol so it was plainly visible.

As if that had been a signal, the man charged at her. Miss Tolerance fired.

Although she was seated and the pistol not large, she was still almost knocked from her place on the branch by the force of the recoil. Miss Tolerance's ears rang, and the taste of gunpowder choked her for a moment. She had not expected to hit her man—pistols, particularly when fired at a moving target, were notoriously inaccurate, and she had barely had time to aim. But the man who a moment before been running toward her was now on the ground. Miss Tolerance took a moment to reload the pistol, then, with it trained upon her attacker, approached him.

The bullet had struck him in the side a little above his hip. It had been her assailant's misfortune that his coat hung open and had offered no resistance to the ball. After a moment of shock, the man began to scream profanely. Miss Tolerance looked about her for any source of assistance; in the distance, a woman was shepherding a trio of children, but resolutely turned away when she saw Miss Tolerance wave. A moment later, however, a manservant from one of the houses on Paradise Row emerged from the brush, his expression a mingling of curiosity and suspicion.

"Thank God!" Miss Tolerance said. "Will you run for the Watch, sir? And a surgeon. This man attacked me and I was forced to defend myself." If the fellow had enough imagination to ask what a woman was doing in a park, alone but armed with a flintlock pistol, he did not stop to argue but hared off at once.

The yells of the man on the ground subsided; he curled around the pain from his wound, hand clenched over it. Blood seeped between his fingers.

Miss Tolerance fumbled left-handed with her reticule and produced a handkerchief. "Use this," she instructed. "I've sent for help." She took a shaky breath. Her hands were trembling, although she did not loose her grip on the pistol she held. She was careful to stay out of her assailant's reach.

"Bitch." The word was forced from between clenched teeth, but he took the kerchief and pressed it to the wound

"You may think so, sir." Her heart was beating very fast, and there was a lump in her throat, but she kept her tone cool and even. "But what was your intention in charging toward me in that fashion? I defended myself; 'tis your bad luck that you did not consider a woman alone might be capable of something other than victimhood. What was your intent: to throttle me as you did Mrs. Pouter and Mrs. White?" It was a shot in the dark: the man might have been a mere footpad intent upon robbery. But she did not believe that.

At the mention of those names, her assailant, who had been white with shock before, paled still more until his face in the sunlight was distinctly green. He pressed his lips tight, whether in response to pain or her question Miss Tolerance could not tell. Before he could produce an answer, the footman returned, followed close by the Watch and a clerical-looking man with a surgeon's case. Both men went to work, and Miss Tolerance retired to sit on the branch again, return her pistol to her reticule, and allow her hands and her breathing to steady, now that the worst of the crisis was done.

When the Watch, having gotten no useful response from the man on the ground, came to ask her to explain why she had shot him, Miss Tolerance gave him a brief summary of the event, then referred him to Sir Walter Mandif or, failing that, to Messers Hook and Penryn of Bow Street. As she had hoped, these names provided as much *bona fide* as the man required.

"Bow Street! And they'll speak for ye?" The man was young for the Watch, but the deep limp on his left side suggested that while he was not elderly, his Nation had shown its gratitude for his injury at war with employment.

"They should. If you wish me to write a note—"

The man shook his head. "You'll be wanting to go 'ome, then." As if the matter was concluded, he began to turn away.

"Wait!" Miss Tolerance made bold to physically stop him with a hand to his arm. "I have some questions for him once the surgeon is done."

This seemed so unlikely to the Watchman as to be incomprehensible. "Questions, miss?"

"Why did he attack me?"

"You *was* a woman all alone in the park," the Watch said, as if that must explain all. A note of suspicion crept into his voice. "You're sure 'e ain't known to you? You wasn't having a h'assignation?"

Do I appear the sort of woman who has noon-time assignations in a public park? Miss Tolerance did not ask this aloud, but after a moment's speaking silence, the Watch shook his head. "I beg pardon, miss, but ye'll admit it's a odd circumstance."

"Precisely why I want to know why he attacked me. And at whose behest."

"Beh—You think someone sent 'im to attack you? Whyever for?"

Here Miss Tolerance debated unpacking her profession for the man or creating a fiction which skated truth as it disarmed further inquiry. Expedience won. "I have been apprehensive for some time that I was being followed—" inspiration struck. "Why else would I have a pistol with me? Bow Street advised me to provide for my safety."

The Watch nodded sagely. "Well, if Bow Street said it—"

"Even so. But sir, I truly would like to ask the fellow a question or two."

Whether the Watch would eventually have yielded to her persuasions, Miss Tolerance was not to know, for at that moment a square, grizzled figure appeared, coming over the rise in the park. Mr. Hook, of Bow Street. When the Runner took command of the scene Miss Tolerance was, albeit discreetly, urged to ask what questions she would of her attacker.

"'Is name's Williams, Miss. An' 'e won't say what 'e was doin' comin' atter you. Fact o' the matter, 'e says you shot at 'im out of the blue, like, while 'e was strollin' on the green."

Miss Tolerance raised her eyebrow. Hook nodded. In perfect agreement at the stupidity of the criminal class, the two approached Mr. Williams, who had been propped against a tree following the surgeon's ministrations. A large bandage girdled his torso, and his coat had been removed and draped over him like a blanket against the chill. He was tall and heavily built, and an expression of sulky defiance sat oddly upon his coarse features. Just below a general stink of sweat and unwashed man there was a reek of alcohol—rum, not gin —which appeared to have been applied liberally to the wound and patient alike.

"How do you do?" Miss Tolerance knelt out of reach but on her assailant's level.

"No thanks to you. 'Pears I'll live. Providin' that 'ole you put in me don't go sour."

"I did give you an opportunity to stop," Miss Tolerance pointed out.

"I didn't think you'd shoot. Nor you could hit nowt with that little popgun."

"I was surprised myself," Miss Tolerance allowed. "Who sent you to kill me?"

The man reared back against the tree so hard that the thud of impact was audible. "I never—"

"Mr. Williams, let us be plain. I believe this is the second attempt you have made on my life—the last was near Hans Place last week. You had better luck with Mrs. White, Mrs. Pouter, and Mrs. Black, did you not? But of course, they were unwarned and elderly. I am neither. You did not decide to attack all of us on a whim, so who paid you to do it? And as importantly, why?"

Here Mr. Hook saw fit to interject, "'Appen it'll go easier for ye if ye peach on the man as 'ired you."

Williams groaned, looked from right to left to avoid the attention from his interlocutors, and finally dropped his head and said, "What if no one 'ired me?"

"You will be charged, tried, and I imagine you will be convicted. But I do not believe it; to my knowledge, I had never encountered you before the last week, yet you attempted twice to kill me. And killed—what? Four elderly women? Five? And it was all your idea? Where is the sense in it? Perhaps if they press you you'll have an answer for them."

Williams's head dropped lower. "Leave me 'lone. You're the one 'alf kilt *me*."

Miss Tolerance and Mr. Hook exchanged glances. "If you wish to hang alone, I suppose you must be allowed to do so.

But if you were to help the prosecution, perhaps the judge might be moved to consider transportation instead."

Mr. Williams clenched his jaw as mulishly as a toddler in the nursery. Miss Tolerance got to her feet. "Well, we have tried. I shall leave him to you."

"You can do that, Miss. We know 'ow to 'andle 'is like." Mr Hook followed Miss Tolerance as she started away.

"Let him consider his fate a little, Mr. Hook. Perhaps he'll be more reasonable when the rum has worn off." Already she was considering where best to find a hired carriage to return her to Manchester Square.

From behind them, Williams cried out. "'Old there!"

Hook turned back with Miss Tolerance at his heels. Williams made a show of ignoring Miss Tolerance and speaking only to Hook. "You think judge'll make it easier if—"

"Can't say, but I know you'll get nothin' if you stand mute. 'Cept perhaps pressin' to wring the truth out you. Nor I don't think he'll wait until that wound's fully healed."

Williams shifted, moaned, and began to talk. He had been hired by a swell to give a warning to a few old whores as was being troublesome—but when the first one was killed by accident, his client had been delighted and asked that any other of the troublesome old whores to which Williams was dispatched receive the same treatment.

"And the name of this swell?" Miss Tolerance asked.

Williams again made it plain he was ignoring Miss Tolerance and speaking only to Hook. "Runs a money house in the City. The pay was good, but 'he treated me like what 'e'd scrape off 'is shoe. Sent word by a street-sweep when 'e wanted me, 'ad me meet in 'is rooms in Stafford Street."

Miss Tolerance felt a familiar sensation as several pieces slid into place. "*The name.*"

"The name," Hook echoed, and kicked at the sole of

Williams's boot, which action appeared to send a shudder of anguish through the man.

"Penny-time!"

"Pennantine," she echoed. "And the other man, the one who also used those rooms?"

"Other man? The little poxy chap? 'E was only there the once, come in while Penny-time and I was finishin' our business. Little fellow got reg'lar glimflashy, scoldin' and carryin' on. I took me gelt and scarpered and left 'em to it."

Hook nodded as if in comprehension, but asked from the side of his mouth, "that make any sense to you?"

She nodded. "All the sense. I—"

She was interrupted by the arrival of a brace of carters carrying a plank stretcher. While they wrestled Williams onto the board and started off toward Paradise Row, where they had apparently left their wagon, Miss Tolerance and Mr. Hook devised a plan. He must take Williams to Bow Street and see him properly written in and locked up. She would follow them there and tell Sir Walter the whole of what they had learned. Then it would be in the hands of the law, although Miss Tolerance hoped with unladylike relish that she would be permitted to be present when Andrew Pennantine was arrested.

"Uh, Miss, you going to come to Bow Street like—" Hook made a comprehensive gesture at Miss Tolerance's torso.

"I beg your—" she looked down and realized unhappily that she had knelt in a pool of mud and Williams's blood, and a patch of gore disfigured the front of her coat. She contained a heartfelt profanity. "No, I will go home and change. I hope I can salvage this coat."

Hook nodded. "Vinegar," he suggested. "Wife swears by it. 'Appens she's 'ad more'n one occasion to test it out."

"Not salt?" The thought of a Mrs. Hook was distracting, but one should never pass up the opportunity to learn a new professional secret.

Hook shook his head. "Vinegar, 'at's the trick. Well, I'll meet you at Bow Street, then?"

Miss Tolerance agreed and took herself off to find a carriage to Manchester Square.

She arrived home and went directly to the gate on Spanish Place, lest her aunt's patrons be affronted by the sight of her gore. To her dismay, she found, upon inspection, that the blood had soaked not only through the coat and its lining but into the fabric of the gown she wore. Unconstrained by witnesses, this time she *did* swear. Then went across the garden to beg a beaker of vinegar from the kitchen, and returned to disrobe and dab carefully at her stained garments until they reeked but the worst of the stains were lifted. All the time she labored, she fretted that she would miss the moment when Andrew Pennantine met Bow Street, but she could not afford to replace a coat and a gown, and Mrs. Brereton's laundress, while expert at removing the sort of stains common to a brothel's linens, was not so adept with significant bloodstains.

At last, her cleaned clothes hanging to dry, she dressed in what was to hand—breeches and boots, with her Gunnard great coat over all—and went out to summon a chair for Bow Street.

There, as always, she found chaos. It seemed half of London had business with the magistracy or had come along to gawk at those who did. The clerk at the desk was not one familiar to Miss Tolerance nor she to him, and in the press of people around her, it took several moments for her to identify herself and ask for Sir Walter Mandif.

"Might be 'e's still in court?"

"Is that certain, or simply a hazard?" The clerk looked blank. "A guess?"

The clerk—he was a grizzled, stocky fellow with a snuff stain upon one drooping collar, and no interest in answering the questions of a person of no discernible consequence—shrugged and returned his attention to the ledger on his desk.

Miss Tolerance persisted. "Where are Mr. Hook and his partner?"

"Hook's down the lock-up. Brought a right criminal in an hour past—"

"I know. Mr. Hook told me to meet with him and Sir Walter—"

"Told *you?*" The clerk looked expressively from head to toe as if to divine what a woman such as herself—by accent identified with the gentry but wearing a man's caped coat and trousers—might be doing with two Runners and a Magistrate. His conclusion did not appear savory. "And you'll be doin' *what* wiv the three of 'em?"

She was saved from the necessity of schooling the clerk in manners when a clout from behind very nearly knocked him off his stool. "Moind yer manners, Franks," Mr. Penryn said. "This lady 'az business 'ere, loik she said. She's a friend of Zor Walter's—nor not that zort of friend, neither," he added before Miss Tolerance could. "Professional, loik. You coom along away from the din, miss."

She followed him through the crowd, which parted in deference to his red waistcoat, the badge and signifier of his office. He had a crease between his brows. "Thought you'd already be on your way."

"On my way to—have Sir Walter and Mr. Hook gone before us to Stafford Street?"

"Zor Walter 'ad a stop to make, miss, and Hook and me, we's to foller along direct we got that Williams locked away. In a right frenzy he was, even with a 'ole in 'im—blacked Hook's eye proper, and—"

"Sir Walter went ahead?"

"Well, yes, miss. But 'e 'ad an errand to do first, loik I

zaid. 'E won't a' got there yet. And even did he get there first, Zor Walter's no fool, 'e can 'andle 'isself with one gullgroper. We thought as 'ow you'd be meeting with 'im there once you saw 'is note," he added. He must have read incomprehension in her expression, for he added, "The which you ain't seen? Well, 'e's only ten minutes ahead, miss, and if you can wait for another ten, Hook and me can coome along of ye."

Miss Tolerance had no reason to be anxious on Sir Walter's behalf; he was, as Penryn said, no fool and very familiar with the ways of the criminal classes. "No harm done, I suppose. I will go now to meet him. You will follow as soon as you are done here?"

Penryn called his agreement to her retreating back.

The carriage she hired became immediately mired in traffic: two carters had collided at the corner of Cranbourn Street and Charing Cross Road, and had descended at once to fisticuffs. It appeared that others of the drivers caught in the mess were likely to join in a general melee. When her driver began to roar advice to the combatants, Miss Tolerance decided it was a matter of moments before he would descend from the perch to join in the fighting. She slipped out of the carriage and started toward Stafford Street on foot; a look behind her made it clear that her driver had given in to temptation and begun to brawl.

The sun had gone behind a cloud, and the wind picked up. The most unpleasant autumn she could remember, she thought, and pulled the collar of her coat closer. She walked briskly along Leicester Street and Piccadilly, finally turning on to Stafford Street. A glance at her watch assured her that she had made good time. The old man who had opened the door to her on her last two visits was not in evidence, but the building door was not locked. Miss Tolerance entered the dim hallway and made her way by guess and touch to the second floor, running her fingers along the wall until she reached the door she knew to be the rooms used by Mr. Marvell—poor, dead George Kent.

Should she knock and enter, or wait until Sir Walter joined her?

The decision was made when she heard profanity and a crash from within. The door swung open at her touch to reveal Andrew Pennantine, disheveled, panting, and in a rage, staring at her. He had evidently pitched a bottle of wine against the wall to his left: long fingers of burgundy trailed down the whitewashed plaster.

Miss Tolerance looked first at Pennantine, then from one side to the other to make sure he had no assistance. No one loomed on either side of the door, but a few feet to her left, she saw the form of a man slumped against the wall, his plain waistcoat and neckcloth soaked with blood.

Sir Walter Mandif.

His head had fallen forward, and she could see a welt on his brow where he had been struck. But the volume of blood she saw could not have come from that injury, She realized, with rage and anguish: his throat had been cut.

Panic flooded her: her hands shook. She wanted to ignore Pennantine and go to Mandif's side. But the room was still full of threat and that threat must be tamed, no matter the acid rage and grief that filled her.

She bit down hard upon those feelings. Charles Connell had told her, when first he taught her to fence, that it was a fatal error to enter a fight with a hot head. It was her task to make sure that Andrew Pennantine paid for Sir Walter's death, as well as for the others already laid to his account. She would have a lifetime to weep later. After. She took one long, steadying breath.

"You have been busy, I see," she said coolly. She returned

her gaze to Pennantine. "As this man is neither a woman nor elderly, I wonder at your nerve."

"What was I to do?" Pennantine temporized. "He accosted me! Came accusing me of murder and theft. Clearly out of his mind."

"So you answered the accusation with another murder? Surely that was a bit precipitate. He was not a madman but a magistrate." *Was.* Her throat tightened on the word.

The smug expression flickered on Pennantine's face. "Magistrate?" He visibly sought his show of confidence. "I suppose magistrates are as prone to insanity as anyone else. He attacked me—"

"I see no weapon. And you cut his throat. Not so easy to do to an attacker. Did he throw himself upon your blade?"

"He attacked me," Pennantine said again.

"You will not be believed when I tell of how I found you and him."

As if she had suddenly come into focus for him, Pennantine straightened where he stood. "You will not tell." Pennantine had no weapon in his hand, but his menace was plain.

Miss Tolerance felt for the pistol in her pocket. "I shall, you know."

"Not after I—"

"Murder me? I am not so easy a target." She drew the pistol out and aimed it at him, eying the pan to make sure it still held the charge.

Pennantine had stopped his advance and looked at the pistol as if upon an asp. "Unfair." The word came out as a whine; he sounded like a boy balked of a win at cricket.

"Step back, Mr. Pennantine. I do not intend to blow a hole through you unless I must. I was forced to do that to Mr. Williams an hour ago, and it gave me no pleasure. Now, take that seat, if you will." She gestured with the pistol.

Pennantine groped behind him to find the chair and

lowered himself into it, his gaze fixed upon Miss Tolerance's weapon. Neither the name of his confederate nor the news that she had apparently shot the man seemed to have any effect upon him.

"Please put your hands upon the arms of your chair," she directed. From her pocket, she retrieved a kerchief, which she tossed to him. "Use that to tie your left hand to the arm." While he did so, Miss Tolerance looked about her for another ligature. At the window, she saw a strip of fabric meant to tie back the curtain. She circled around Pennantine, ripped the thing from its tack, and used it to tie Pennantine's right wrist to the chair. Then she pocketed her pistol and went to the door.

"Downstairs! Help! Someone run for the Watch! Here's murder done!" She cried it several times and was about to go to the window and call into the street when a ropy, grizzled man appeared at the bottom of the stairs, swearing bitterly.

"What in Christ's name are ye about callin' a man fro—"

"Get the Watch," she said again. "Murder's been done. I've the murderer tied up here."

"Murder?" Rather than departing at once for the Law, the man heaved himself up the stairs, hand over hand on the bannister. He had, she realized, a twisted foot. "Who's dead, then?" He peered past Miss Tolerance to goggle at the captive Pennantine and then, at Sir Walter's bloody body. "'E done that?"

"He did. Send for the Watch." She no longer expected the man to run, but if he did not take himself down the stairs to dispatch someone she felt likely to do murder herself. She had withdrawn her pistol from her pocket and looked down at it. At its sight, the grizzled man turned and left with haste.

Now she had a moment for Sir Walter.

She approached the body gingerly and dropped to one knee. "My dear, foolish friend, what were you thinking?" She reached to stroke back the sandy hair that had fallen over his brow, heedless of the blood. His skin was still warm. "What were you thinking?" Her voice caught.

Under her hand, the head tilted up and Sir Walter regarded her. "Didn't think." The words came out in a grating whisper, followed by a grunt of pain.

In her shock, Miss Tolerance rocked backward onto her backside. Pennantine yelped.

As carefully as she could, Miss Tolerance knelt again and moved Sir Walter's head to see the wound she had believed to be fatal. Straight across the throat, a little above the Adam's apple. She put her ear down to listen but heard no whistle of air from the wound. The cut had not been deep enough to sever the windpipe.

For a very long moment, Miss Tolerance knelt in shock and gratitude, eyes closed, unable to move. Then she got to her feet and went again to the head of the stairs, calling, "Help! Fetch a surgeon! A shilling to the one who first brings a surgeon to me."

When she turned back to the room Pennantine was scowling. "He is dead! I killed him!"

"*He lives*. It is Sir Walter's good fortune that you are a banker and not a butcher. Which makes it your good fortune as well."

She went back to Sir Walter's side and, rather than kneeling, sat beside him, heedless of the gore, to support his body with her own. "You gave me a fright," she murmured. When his lips moved to make a retort, she laid a finger across them. "Don't speak. At least not until a surgeon has seen to you." There were a dozen questions she wanted to ask him, but she sat mute. She had no idea if the gash in his throat would open wider with talking, and had no desire to find out.

Minutes went by with no sign of either a surgeon or the Watch. The man with the twisted foot had left what seemed an age ago, and Miss Tolerance could not be certain that anyone had heard her and gone to fetch a surgeon. Reluctantly, and with care not to jostle Sir Walter, she moved from her spot against the wall, rose, and circled around Pennantine to reach the window behind him. She threw up the sash and leaned out over the street.

"Hi! Down there!" At the sound of her voice, several people looked around them blindly. "Up here!" She waved. Two boys—too well turned-out to be street sweeps, but not young gentlemen, either—looked up. "A shilling to the first one of you to bring a surgeon to the second floor!" At the mention of money, not only the boys but several passers-by had looked up to see her waving half out the window. Then the two boys ran off, with an aproned man just after them.

She pulled her head in and turned back to Sir Walter. Her way was blocked by Pennantine, who had somehow freed his left hand—the one he had tied—and come up behind her dragging the chair by his right. Without a word, he charged at her, his free arm outstretched to push her out the window, his body half-turned to pull the chair along. Miss Tolerance dodged to her right, not far enough to avoid Pennantine's lunge but enough that both of them smashed against the window sill. The wood did not give, but she heard a splintering noise by her ear and pushed away quickly. The next push, she thought, might break the sill entirely.

Again Miss Tolerance attempted to circle to her right, away from Pennantine and the window. But the man threw his free arm heavily over her shoulder and attempted to push her down and through the window. In the struggle, the lower sash came out of its rails and the window fell inward, knocking her upon the head and breaking glass indiscriminately over her and Pennantine. The banker moved his head as if to shake the shards away but only succeeded in cutting his jaw and chin.

Pennantine's right wrist was still lashed to the chair, but the chair itself was coming apart, the carved wood of the arm pulling from the seat and back. If once he regained the use of both hands, she did not think she could stand against him—

and with her hands occupied in keeping herself from being tossed out the window, the pistol in her pocket might as well be at home on her mantel.

Pennantine continued to push her to the right and downward until her head and his were out the window. The half-splintered upper window sash looked from her vantage point like the blade of the French guillotine, ready to drop and kill them both. She could feel the man pulling at the chair, yanking on the arm of the chair to break it away. His weight was on her, making it impossible to move; all she could do was push and strike her assailant.

With shocking suddenness, the arm of the chair gave way and Pennantine's weight came forward, pushing Miss Tolerance further out the window, his body atop hers and his head outside, just above her own.

Miss Tolerance reached upward desperately, caught the sash, and pulled it down hard.

The blow was not hard enough to kill, but for a moment Pennantine was stunned. Miss Tolerance heaved at his weight and rolled awkwardly away and back into the room, bleeding from a dozen small cuts, but free. She fumbled for her pistol as Pennantine rolled onto his back and straightened—surged —upward, only to slam into the splintered upper sash of the window, which broke, sending wood and glass flying.

Miss Tolerance stepped back. "It's done, sir." She had her pistol in hand now and pointed it with tolerable steadiness at Andrew Pennantine.

The banker pitched forward onto his knees. As Miss Tolerance watched, he put his hand to his neck. It came away bloody. He sat back on his heels, pawing at a splinter of whitewashed wood that had skewered his throat. Blood seeped around the splinter and Miss Tolerance cried out "Don't!" as Pennantine raised his hand to pull it away. Miss Tolerance grabbed for his hand and kept it from his throat.

"Pull that out and you'll be dead in a minute," she said.

She looked about her for something to stanch the blood still seeping from the wound. The piece of curtain tie which had secured Pennantine to the chair was now on the floor. Miss Tolerance pushed Pennantine's hand away and pressed the fabric to the wound, uncertain she was doing any good but unwilling not to try. He leaned against her, aware now of his mortal peril, oddly trusting in her willingness to keep him alive.

It was thus that the Watch and the surgeon found them.

Chapter Eighteen

All was chaos for a time.

The officer of the Watch, seeing Miss Tolerance nearly as bloodied as Pennantine, dragged her away from the body and loudly offered to arrest her in the name of the Law for willful murder. The surgeon, pushing past the Watch, observed the splinter of wood still in Pennantine's neck and pointed it out to the Law as an unlikely murder weapon, but the officer was unmoved by this testimony. Miss Tolerance's only concern was to get the surgeon to leave Pennantine's side and attend upon Sir Walter. The arrival of the two lads who had fetched the surgeon, suing for the promised shilling, added a final piquant touch to a scene that would have done credit to the satires of George Cruikshank.

The surgeon fussed over Andrew Pennantine for some minutes, making clucking noises, as if he disapproved of gentlemen who found themselves impaled upon window frames. At last, he pronounced that Pennantine was fit to be carried away, and rose to shift his attention to Sir Walter. Miss Tolerance, who had been placed in a chair by the officer and instructed on no account to move, dug out her pocketbook and paid the boys half of the promised shilling each, then settled to watch anxiously as the medico examined Sir Walter's wound.

"A very near thing, but if infection can be avoided, I believe you will do well enough, sir," he said. Mandif whispered something hoarsely. "No, no more of that, sir. You will mend much more quickly if you do not speak. That blow to your head will have you dozy as well. What?" The surgeon bent his head to listen. "I understand." He turned to the officer. "This man says that the other fellow attempted to murder him, then made a similar attempt upon this—" he sought a word suited to the occasion. "This person," he finished, indicating Miss Tolerance.

Just as the Watch drew breath to refute this testimony, Mandif's Runners, Messers Hook and Penryn, appeared in the doorway.

"Zor Walter told us—" Penryn stopped, electrified by the sight of his superior, soaked in blood and with a fresh bandage being wrapped about his throat.

"What 'appened 'ere?" Hook asked Miss Tolerance. By his tone, he was ready to assign blame to her for not taking proper care of his senior.

The Watch bustled forward to intercede, evidently much impressed by the red waistcoats that identified the new arrivals from the Bow Street magistracy. "I arrested 'er—'im —'er for the murder of—"

"The man is *not* dead!" The last word was almost a yelp—and the groan of pain that followed made the surgeon scold Sir Walter exceedingly.

"Zor Walter don't seem to think that's right," Penryn said over his shoulder. He had dropped to one knee next to Mandif and was having a low-voiced conversation with the surgeon.

"It is *not* right." Miss Tolerance took advantage of the arrival of the Runners to give again her version of the events just transpired, speaking to Hook rather than the Watch.

Pennantine, the splinter in his neck still held in place with gauze and bandages, said nothing; he sat, propped against the wall, staring listlessly at Sir Walter, the man he had failed to murder.

When Miss Tolerance had finished her recital, the Watch opined that the story was ridiculous. How could a woman, attacked by a man of Pennantine's size, keep from being killed if he was bent upon it? And wasn't stabbing a man in the neck the sort of treachery one might expect of a woman?

"You can't 'ave that both ways," Hook said firmly. "If she weren't strong enough to keep that 'un from killing 'er, ow'd she manage to 'alf kill '*im*?"

"She's knoown to us, and odd as her dress may be, she's not a killer." Penryn agreed. "Zor Walter says the man attacked him first, then wounded hisself in the breaking of the window. Anyroad, no one's been murdered 'ere."

The officer scowled balefully at Miss Tolerance, whom he seemed determined to find guilty of something worse than offending his sense of decorum. If he dreamt of being celebrated as the man who'd caught a dastardly murderer, he had been undone by a witness who was not only a victim but a man of the Law.

The surgeon insisted that he would accompany Sir Walter to his home and do any suturing necessary there. Penryn went down to hire a carriage and returned a few minutes later with help to begin, gingerly, moving Sir Walter down the stairs. It cost Miss Tolerance considerable effort to stay where she was, reciting again the events of the afternoon. Mr. Hook appeared sympathetic to her anxiety—her friendship with the magistrate was well known to him and his partner—but would not dismiss her until "I 'as a tol'able understanding of what 'appened ezzakly." He was particularly curious as to why Sir Walter would have come up without waiting for his Runners, and seemed to find Miss Tolerance's assertion that she did not know hard to credit.

"Mr. Penryn told me we were all to meet here, so I came

straight away and found him as you saw. All I can imagine is that Sir Walter decided to address Pennantine first as a way of keeping me safe."

Hook raised an eyebrow like a sinister caterpillar. "*Sir Walter* meant to keep *you* safe? Did 'e mean to *think* yon villain to death?"

"He is not incompetent!" Miss Tolerance was hot in her friend's defense. "Nor is he a fool!"

"But nor 'e's no fighter, miss. Should 'ave waited for Penryn and me."

Miss Tolerance could not dispute it.

Even with the assurances of Mr. Hook as to her innocence and reliability, Miss Tolerance was not able to depart from the rooms for more than an hour after Sir Walter was carried forth, accompanied by Penryn, the doctor, and two staunch stretcher-men. She had stood by the splintered window as the party attained the street and Sir Walter was conveyed with care into a waiting carriage. When the vehicle wheeled away she turned back to the room to answer again the Watchman's repeated questions.

At last, resentfully, the man agreed that she was likely not a party to attempted murder. There were other matters that required her assistance, however. Once she had identified Pennantine and briefly sketched in the reason for his murderous attack upon Sir Walter and herself, there was the question of who to notify of the arrest.

"'Im bein' a gentleman and all, there's like to be a wife at 'ome will be wonderin' where 'e got to."

"I do not believe he is married. You might speak with his mother, a Mrs. Kent, who lives in Hans Place." Hook made notes in a small pencil-ruled book with the stub of a pencil he had rescued from the pocket of his red waistcoat. "It will be difficult enough to tell her. She is not... not well. I believe Mr. Penryn spoke with her once."

Hook sighed gustily. "I s'pose there's no time the news'll come easier. We'd be grateful if ye'd come along o' one of us to notify that'un's mother, miss," Hook said. "In the ord'nary way Sir Walter'd ha' done it, but—"

Miss Tolerance agreed before she had a moment to think. "Now? I suppose I—well, I must go home first and change—" she gestured at her clothes, stiff with Sir Walter's blood and Andrew Pennantine's as well.

"I can take you home, miss, and then—"

"It must be done today?" She knew it must—Pennantine would be taken into custody, and whichever gaol he arrived at, he would not be made comfortable—indeed, he might not survive if his family did not provide payment for care and accommodation. Feeling resentful, she muttered, "I would have liked to see that Sir Walter arrived safely at his house."

Hook looked sympathetic. "It ain't required, miss, but it's like to be better to get it over with. And it would come better with a woman there. Specially as the prisoner's a gentleman and all."

She saw his logic: Pennantine's mother was a gentlewoman and a widow; even if her son was a villain, she deserved some kindness along with this distressing news. Perhaps more because her son *was* a villain.

"If we can return to Manchester Square, I will turn myself out respectably and we will call upon poor Mrs. Kent."

"Thankee, miss." Hook looked about the room and his eye settled on the Watch. "Oi, you! There's a pair o' fellows comin' soon from Bow Street to take this 'un away. You'll wait for 'em, aye?"

The Watch waved them off. Miss Tolerance took a last look at Pennantine, now staring at the toes of his boots, then was happy to lead the way out of the apartment and down to the street.

As appearing in her gore on Mrs. Brereton's doorstep seemed needlessly melodramatic, Miss Tolerance let herself into the garden from Spanish Place. Hook had agreed to wait for her in the carriage, so Miss Tolerance made as short work as possible of stripping off her sullied clothing, for a second time that day sponging with vinegar before putting it all to soak and dressing herself in respectable feminine attire. The whole took her less than half an hour, and she emerged into the garden ready to make an uncomfortable call upon Mrs. Kent.

Instead, she found the boy Harry sitting on her doorstep, chin on his fists, scowling at a clod of dirt at the toe of his shoe. *Good God, what now?*

"Marianne set me to watch for you, Miss Sarah. Wasn't sure you were to home. Mrs. B was taken badly this afternoon."

"Taken badly how?"

"I don't know exactly, but Miss Frost and Miss Marianne are looking like thunderheads."

Miss Tolerance took off her bonnet, turned back to her cottage to put it there, and dispatched Harry to tell the waiting Mr. Hook that she would not be able to accompany him to Mrs. Kent. "Tell him if the matter can wait until tomorrow, I will go with him then, but if time is of the essence, he had better go without me."

With Harry gone, she made her way to the kitchen and past Mrs. Gordon and her helpers, noting the crease of anxiety on each brow: if Mrs. Brereton was ailing, all the staff worried.

Keefe, exhibiting that same preoccupied frown, directed her to Mrs. Brereton's rooms.

"Oh, thank God you've come, Sarah."

Marianne Touchwell sat on the right of Mrs. Brereton's bed, holding the madam's hand. Miss Frost, lips pursed, sat on the left of the bed, her eyes upon her mistress.

"What happened?" Miss Tolerance murmured. It was the sort of sickroom that seemed to compel whispered voices.

"We were talking about the inventory of linens. She seemed quite as usual, asking how many sheets could be repaired—the custom does tend to rip through 'em. Then she spilled her tea. Her arm dropped as if the cup weighed too much to hold, and when she tried to scold—you know how she does—the words came out all jumbled. I called the doctor and we put her to bed—we've seen this before, but this, this seems worse."

"Worse in what way?" Miss Tolerance asked, but it was almost needless that she do so. One look at her aunt's face, the features on the right side drooping like melted tallow, made it clear that this was a far worse apoplectic fit than the last. "Is she unconscious?"

"She's sleeping." Miss Frost was fierce. "She'll wake in her own good time, ma'am will."

Miss Tolerance did not argue. "I'm sure you know best." To Marianne, "When did you send for the doctor?"

"Near on an hour ago, but he wasn't at home when we sent. I'm in hope he'll come shortly. Sarah, can you stay?"

"Of course. You have things to do? Go, Marianne. Frost and I will take care of Aunt Thea; she'd want to make sure everything else is in hand."

Over the next hours, as she sat with her aunt, then welcomed Sir George Hammond and stood by during his examination, heard the doctor's opinion, and sat again at Mrs. Brereton's side, Miss Tolerance thought of Sir Walter, and felt the sullen stiffening of her muscles, outraged in the fight with Andrew Pennantine. Could it have been only that afternoon?

Some time after three in the morning, Marianne, having seen a late caller out the door, returned. "You ought to get some sleep, Sarah." Miss Frost was asleep in her chair, snoring softly.

"Have you slept?"

Marianne smiled. "Good as. My last caller was an older gent, comes more for conversation and a cuddle. I'm quite refreshed. You go up to the yellow room and sleep for a while. And yes—" before Miss Tolerance could make the request. "When Mrs. B wakes, I'll send for you at once."

Grateful, Miss Tolerance put a hand on her friend's shoulder by way of thanks and took herself upstairs to lie, fully dressed, on the luxurious bed of the yellow room.

When she woke, the sun shone in at the window. Miss Tolerance put her hair to rights, shook what wrinkles she could from her gown, and went downstairs to her aunt's apartment. The house was quiet: it was late enough that some of the night's clients were up and about, but not so late that new clients were arriving for a morning visit.

Miss Frost was awake and had been so long enough to put a fresh cap over her mistress's short curls and to plump the pillows behind her. Marianne sat with a ledger in her lap, going over figures.

"How does she?" Miss Tolerance asked.

At the sound of her voice, Mrs. Brereton's eyes opened. The frightening droop of her features was still there, but there was sense in the eyes that regarded her niece. Miss Tolerance went at once to sit upon the bed and take her aunt's hand. "Good morning, Aunt Thea! What a scare you have given us!"

"Sa—" The syllable was drawn out enough that Miss Tolerance realized it might be meant to be her own name.

"I am here, aunt. Don't press yourself to speak if you had rather not. "

"Here, ma'am dear." Miss Frost held a cup of tea to Mrs. Brereton's lips, tilting it just enough that the liquid did not dribble down the slack side of the older woman's lips. "Just as you like it, with milk and sugar."

Mrs. Brereton's eyes lit upon her dresser with an expression of gratitude that Miss Tolerance had never before seen there.

Marianne rose, put aside the ledger, and beckoned to Miss Tolerance. They stepped away a few paces, and Mrs. Touchwell explained that the doctor was due to call at any moment. "I'll stay until he does. Then, if you don't mind, Sarah, I'll get some sleep."

"What do you think?" Miss Tolerance asked.

"I don't know, and that's a fact. Mrs. B's come back from these strokes before, but there ain't been one as bad as this before. Still, she's none so old, she may come around of it. I wonder, though, if she'd want to live with her face—" Marianne drew a line down her own cheek. "She's that proud of her looks."

"Nonsense," Miss Tolerance made her tone brisk. "Aunt Thea has far too much commonsense to be ruled by so small a disfigurement." She would not admit that she wondered the very same thing.

The doctor arrived an hour later to find Mrs. Brereton breakfasting on thin porridge being spooned for her by Miss Frost, and Miss Tolerance eating rashers and toast. He was hearty with the patient, assuring her that he expected to see her up and about in no time. He was, however, less sanguine with Miss Tolerance and Mrs. Touchwell.

"I cannot disguise that this was a very grave episode, and not one I expect her to make so smart a recovery from. The weakness in her arm and in her face, we must expect to be permanent—"

"But she will live?"

The doctor shrugged. "A point comes, Mrs. Touchwell, when the best a doctor may do is encourage sound care—and prayer. I *think* she will live, but—"

"But she may not," Miss Tolerance finished.

He nodded.

The doctor prescribed beef tea and porter and rest. Miss Tolerance listened, all the while trying to imagine a world without her aunt's astringent, affectionate, hard-headed presence. "We will do all that may be done," she promised.

When he left and Mrs. Touchwell had gone off for her own rest, Miss Tolerance returned to her aunt's side and held the older woman's hand as she dozed.

It was some time after one in the afternoon when Mr. Cole came to the door with a message.

"Mr. Hook's compliments, Miss. He is wondering if you might be able to make a *call of notification* with him?" The man raised an eyebrow dubiously.

Miss Tolerance recalled what she had promised, the day before.

"I had best do it now. Marianne?" The other woman had returned from her nap half an hour earlier. "I will be back in an hour or so. I promised yesterday that I would—"

"It's business, Sarah. I don't need to know more than that." Marianne made a shooing motion with her hand. "We'll do very well for an hour. Go."

Miss Tolerance dispatched Cole to tell Hook she would join him as soon as she had her bonnet and coat. In the carriage to Hans Place, before all else, she demanded any news the Runner had of Sir Walter.

"Seen 'im, an 'e looks the worse for wear, but 'e's comfortable and surgeon says 'e'll do." Mr. Hook gave a sympathetic grimace before he turned to business. He produced his little notebook and thumbed through it, smearing pencil lead across the pages, until he came to the notation he sought.

"The family name is Kent, Miss?" Miss Tolerance nodded. "Then 'ow's it the man in custody's name was Pennantine?"

"He was her son from a first marriage."

"But then—" Hook read further, put his finger down to

hold his place, and read again. "Ain't one of the ones 'e killed a Mr. Kent?"

"It appears that Mr. George Kent was his brother."

"Well, that's a nasty thing, in'it? Killin' your own flesh and blood. Not but what we see some of it, but it ain't usually bankers and such."

"I expect that even among bankers, fratricide is not unheard of." Miss Tolerance thought of the odd, cheerful Mr. Marvell with sadness.

Cates, the footman who opened the door to Mr. Hook and his companion, attempted to close it again immediately, but the Runner inserted his staff into the door, preventing its closure.

"I've business with Mrs. Kent, me lad, and ye'd do well to let me be about it."

The footman let Hook—and then Miss Tolerance—in the door, but stood between them and the stairway as if he feared they would charge upstairs to accost his mistress.

"We must speak to Mrs. Kent," Miss Tolerance said gently, in her most depressively genteel voice. "I am afraid we have... news for her."

"News?"

"About Mr. Andrew Pennantine," Hook announced.

There was a stir upon the landing, as if that name had unfrozen a mechanism. After a moment, a maid trotted down the stair and murmured into the manservant's ear. "Madam says let them come."

The footman, his back rigid with disapproval, acquiesced. The maid—Milston, Miss Tolerance recalled—led them up the stairs and into the same sitting room where she had previously spoken with Mrs. Kent. Mr. Hook might have pride of office, but Miss Tolerance preceded him into the room upon the Runner's murmured suggestion that the news might come better-like from a female.

"Miss Tolerance and..." Milston let her voice trail off before pronouncing the Runner's name.

Miss Tolerance curtsied. "I beg you will not rise, ma'am."

As before, Mrs. Kent was expensively dressed, but there was a curious disorder about her person, as if the work of her day had been to subtly undo the efforts of her maid that morning. Her gaze was unfocused, and in her hand, she held a broidery frame that trailed a length of floss without a needle.

"You have called upon me before, I think." Mrs. Kent's speech was as unfocused as her gaze. "You are—Miss Ben—Miss Benjamin?"

What alias had she used on her last visit? Miss Tolerance could not recall. "You may not remember my name is Tolerance, ma'am." She did not introduce Hook, and Mrs. Kent appeared to overlook her second visitor.

"You did come before."

"I did, inquiring for your son."

The woman's lips pursed, and Miss Tolerance detected a sudden suspicion. "Which son?"

"Mr. Kent, ma'am."

"Oh." Mrs. Kent's dark brows raised in an expression of dismissal. "George. Oh yes. He is dead."

Her tone was so untroubled that both Miss Tolerance and Mr. Hook exchanged looks of surprise. Was the woman drunk? Under the influence of laudanum or some other drug?

"Are you quite well, ma'am?"

Mrs. Kent smiled. "I am very well, indeed. Thank you for asking. But as I told you, George is dead, so there is no need for you to inconvenience yourself—"

"I am sorry to say—that is, Mr. Hook and I must be the bearers of sad news beyond even that, ma'am."

"Mr.— that man." Mrs. Kent's nod was a scant acknowledgment of the third person in the room.

Hook, who a few minutes before had been happy to have Miss Tolerance give the news of her elder son's arrest to Mrs. Kent, appeared now to have lost patience with the pace of the interview.

"Hook, of Bow Street, ma'am. I regret to inform you that your son is in custody and 'is life is despaired of." He delivered the information as if he meant to break through the woman's distracted manner, but the news barely seemed to register.

"If there is nothing else you need—" Mrs. Kent's gaze returned to her broidery frame.

Hook was disturbed. "Ma'am, did you 'ear me?"

"George is dead, yes. I know."

"Not Mr. George Kent. Mr. Andrew Pennantine. Taken to Newgate on suspicion of fraud and murder."

"No, you are confused." Mrs. Kent was polite but adamant, speaking over Hook as he began a recitation of Pennantine's crimes. "You are mistaken. It is not kind to say such things to a mother."

If it had been within the power of that denial to have achieved it, Miss Tolerance would have been unsurprised to see Andrew Pennantine walk through the door. There was no anger in Mrs. Kent's voice, only absolute certainty.

"Mrs. Kent," Miss Tolerance spoke gently. "George Kent is dead. Your older son has been taken into custody for his murder. Mr. Pennantine was gravely injured, and his survival is not certain—" That, she thought, would bring the woman to her senses. Her favored son wounded and in gaol for the murder of his brother? That must break through the fog that seemed to surround the woman.

"Andrew was at his office," she said after a moment. "I saw him after." Her tone was one of dreamy reflection. "George had to die. It was kinder so." She looked up at Miss Tolerance. "You met him? It would have been better if he had died in his cradle. A monster. I should have stayed a widow." It was not a non sequitur. "Andrew is such a beautiful boy."

"Mr. Andrew Pennantine—" Hook began again, but Mrs. Kent was far from attending.

"My beautiful clever boy. Imagine my feelings with a son like Andrew, and then... Kent's get. Ruining everything. I couldn't let him."

It was clear to Miss Tolerance that Mrs. Kent was telling a story to herself, unheeding of her visitors.

"I did my duty. I raised him up, kept him clothed and fed and shod—even after Kent died, I did my duty. I couldn't love him, that would have been impossible. Not when there was Andrew."

"Ma'am," Miss Tolerance urged. The woman's confession of preference made her deeply uncomfortable, as though she had chanced upon the secrets of the woman's bed. "Mrs. Kent, I beg you will attend what this man has to say to you." Unasked, Miss Tolerance sat on the settee next to Mrs. Kent and took her hand.

"He was determined to oppose his brother," Mrs. Kent went on. "He meant to scold Andrew! He threatened to inform upon him—I couldn't permit it."

Hook was showing signs of losing patience, shifting from one foot to the other. He leaned forward to Miss Tolerance and murmured, "We done what we come for. Best to go now—"

"Wait." Something niggled at Miss Tolerance. "How did you know I had met Mr. Kent, ma'am? When we last spoke I had not discovered his location."

"He told me." Mrs. Kent made an impatient motion as if to brush the conversation away. "Said you came asking him about some whore's pension and put him on to a matter of Andrew's business. As if George could understand business; it was through Andrew's kindness that he had employment at all."

"When did he tell you this, ma'am?"

"He sent a message to me, asked to call here. Asking for advice. I don't want him coming here—once he left the house —well, that's not to the point. I went to him. In rooms above a shop! And he told me a woman had been snooping about. He said *he* was disappointed in Andrew! Said he'd believed he had been doing good. Said that now he knew differently, he would stop and make Andrew do, too. Said he would tell the Law if Andrew didn't heed him. I knew what I must do and I did it. I never had the strength to do it when he was a babe, but a mother protects her son."

Hook made a noise of exhalation, as if the breath had been pushed out of him all at once. "Which son was this you was protectin', ma'am?"

"*My* son." Mrs. Kent smiled upon something that was not visible to her visitors. "My beautiful boy. George said that Andrew was running a—a swindle, he called it. That was the word—I had to ask what it meant. He raved about protecting innocent old women— He would have taken the *whores'* side over his brother's."

"Taken the Law's side," Hook said. "So Kent was meaning to give evidence 'gainst Mr. Pennantine?"

"*He* felt wronged, said he had believed the Fund was meant to do good. Said he gave his word to them. To the *whores*."

The lamps in the room did not flicker, but it was as if a shadow had fallen over Mrs. Kent and her auditors.

"What did you do?" Miss Tolerance made her voice as passionless as she could.

"I took a ribbon from my cap—not this one." She reached up a hand to touch the cambric that framed her face. "It was easier than I should have thought. Perhaps his neck was always weak."

Hook squared his shoulders, aware that his errand had become something else. "Mrs. Kent, I arrest you—"

Miss Tolerance held a hand up to stop him. "A moment, I beg you." She turned back to the older woman. "You throttled him with a ribbon?"

Mrs. Kent nodded. "Oh, yes. I should have done it when he was in the cradle. It would have been kinder."

Miss Tolerance called to her memory the sight of George Kent, face blackened and tongue protruding, the marks of hands around his neck. Hands, not a single narrow line. But she must be certain.

"You left him there in his blood?"

"There was no blood," Mrs. Kent said. "I cannot abide it."

Miss Tolerance rose and went to whisper in Hook's ear. "I saw Kent's body—there was a great deal of blood from a wound to the head. And the throttling left hand-marks, not marks from a ribbon. She could not have done the murder."

"Then why'd she admit of it? She might ha'—"

Miss Tolerance had no answer. "You know the day that George Kent died. Ask her servants where Mrs. Kent was that day. Did she leave the house?"

A moment's thought and Hook nodded and turned upon his heel. As he left the room Miss Tolerance sat again beside Mrs. Kent, who smiled gently.

"You have called upon me before, have you not?"

"I have, ma'am."

"And your name is Miss Benjamin?"

Miss Tolerance gave way to the misapprehension. "It is, ma'am."

"And you are a friend of my son's?"

"I suppose I am, ma'am."

They were silent then until Hook returned to the room and nodded. Miss Tolerance rose.

"I will take my leave of you, Mrs. Kent." She curtsied.

"It was kind in you to call." But already Mrs. Kent's thoughts were elsewhere; she picked up her broidery frame and plucked idly at a loose thread.

Outside the room, he confirmed what Miss Tolerance had thought. "Both maid and footman say she were to home all that day, but Mr. George did call."

"And told her he meant to inform upon Pennantine."

Hook nodded but waited until they had left the house before he asked, "But why tell us the other? Why say she'd killed 'er own son?"

"She said it, did she not? A mother protects her son. She would not let Andrew Pennantine be accused of fratricide—"

"What of all the other charges that was fixed upon him?"

"Did we mention them? And I do not think Mrs. Kent would call them crimes. She had no sympathy for the women Pennantine cheated. But what will happen to her now? She is clearly—"

"Mad as a March hare," Hook nodded. "And both 'er sons is gone. Someone will 'ave to look to her welfare, but that's none of my affair. Must be someone in this 'ousehold I should give the news to, though. Pennantine'll still need garnish if 'e's to 'ave any chance of survivin' to trial."

Miss Tolerance suggested he ask for Mrs. Whettle and explained her position in the household.

"Whettle. Very good. Well, my thanks for coming along of me." He put a finger to the brim of his hat in salute and dismissal. "I don't suppose you wish to stay for that interview?"

Miss Tolerance owned she had rather not.

"Very well. Ask the porter to hail you a carriage, shall I?"

"Please."

But once inside the hired carriage, Miss Tolerance gave the direction, not of Manchester Square, but of Gracechurch Street and Sir Walter Mandif's house.

The sun was low over the rooftops, and she realized it might be late in the afternoon for such a call, but "Sir Walter will want to see you, certain," Sir Walter's manservant said. Michael had, six months before, been a boy, snub-nosed and puppyish, with a clear admiration of his master. In half a year, he had grown half a head, his voice had dropped, and he had a new sense of importance about him. Miss Tolerance was careful to treat him as his height and gravitas demanded, not in accordance with his age.

She had expected that the magistrate would be upstairs in his chamber and was surprised when Michael led her to the parlor. She had, herself, spent some time in that room, lying on the sofa, recovering from concussion. Now it was Sir Walter who occupied that place. His eyes were closed. Miss Tolerance took a chair from beside the fire, moved it to the head of the sofa, sat, and removed her bonnet.

"Sir Walter?"

His breathing did not vary nor did his eyes open. Miss Tolerance regarded him for several moments until, with a sense both of hazard and certainty, she reached to take one of his hands in her own.

The tick of the clock on the mantel, and Sir Walter's soft, even breathing, made a quiet contrapuntal rhythm. In the stillness of the room, she let go a fear that had knotted in her breast, and tears leaked from between her closed eyes. She was wracked with silent sobs that were part relief, part anger, and, at the last, part wonder. She wept until she was exhausted, finally passing from weeping to a doze.

She was wakened by a murmur. "It is good of you to call."

Miss Tolerance straightened in her chair. She would have loosed her hold on his hand, but Sir Walter tightened his own.

"I came to confirm for myself the surgeon's assurances." Her tone was as mild as his own.

"Are you reassured?" His voice was a raw whisper; a

grimace suggested that the effort to speak was painful; at its sound, Miss Tolerance felt tears well up again, so powerfully that she did not dare to speak. She swallowed hard. "O'Leary tells me that I will recover," Sir Walter said. "I am fortunate that Pennantine was an untutored cut-throat."

He was very pale; his sleek, sandy hair was disarranged, falling down on either side of his face rather than in its usual sweep back from his brow. His gory clothes had been exchanged for clean, and the fresh linen bandage wrapping his throat displayed only a few sinister spots of rusty brown; the cut in his throat had ceased to bleed.

Miss Tolerance swallowed again. "Please do not speak if you are under orders not to—" Lest more gentle feeling overcome her, she took refuge in outrage. "But if you *do* intend to speak, perhaps you will tell me what possessed you to confront Pennantine without Hook or Penryn or myself? Confront a man who was a presumed murderer—"

"Of elderly women," Sir Walter whispered. "I did not think it much of a risk."

Miss Tolerance was in no mood to smile. "A man cornered? Who might do anything to save himself and his position? Sir Walter, you are not a stupid man, but that was stupidly done."

The magistrate's smile was crooked. "So it appears."

"Your friends—*your friends* will tell you it were better that a man like that be lost entirely than that you..." Her voice faltered.

"I am sorry if I frightened you," he whispered.

"Well, you did! And Hook and Penryn as well. And likely Michael and your cook!" Words failed her. The clock ticked steadily, and Miss Tolerance focused her attention upon a spot on Sir Walter's quilt, rubbing at it irritably with her free hand. Sir Walter seemed happy to wait as they were, handfast and silent.

At last, "What am I to do?" she asked, low.

"Do?"

She scowled. Did he mean to make her declare her feelings as he had once declared his own? Did her tears not make ample declaration?

"I seem," she said at last, with dignity, "to have discovered my heart."

"All it required was to have someone slit my throat?" Mandif's smile made a jest of his words.

"A rather drastic solution, I admit." She returned the smile. With her free hand, she pushed a lock of hair back from his forehead.

"I apprehend that if I were to renew my offer of the Spring—"

"You did *not* offer," Miss Tolerance corrected. "You gave me the reasons why I was unlikely to accept if you *did* offer."

When Sir Walter attempted to nod, a spasm of discomfort crossed his face. He waited to continue. At last, "Very well, then—if I were to make the offer to you now that I did not *quite* make then, what would your answer be?"

"I am stubborn and used to going about my own business. I would bring you no credit—"

"Allow me to disagree. You cannot know the credit you would bring me—but we will pass upon that."

"I have spent the last six years mixing in the worst company possible—my aunt runs a brothel, my work brings me—as you well know—into commerce with the worst of London's criminals—"

"As does mine," Sir Walter noted.

"We would clash—you know we would. I am too used to occupation—"

"You like your work. As I do mine. It is a thing we have in common."

"A thing you would permit me to continue?" She allowed misgiving to creep into her voice.

"*Permit?*" There was a dry rasp of amusement. "I cannot

imagine the trouble you could cause if you were not *permitted* to follow the dictates of your conscience and your wit. It would require the running of a ducal establishment to fully occupy your wit—and as I cannot offer that, following your own profession seems the safest choice."

Miss Tolerance was startled into a laugh. "But how will we—"

"We will learn that as we go along."

She was silent for a few moments imagining. Again, tears started in her eyes.

At last, "You might ask for much more than a Fallen woman past her youth."

Sir Walter raised Miss Tolerance's hand to his lips. "Are you quite done listing your inadequacies?"

"I suppose I am."

"Very well, then. Sarah, will you do me the honor to marry me?"

She did not speak at once, still weighted with a sense that to do so would be to accept a prize she had not earned, or at least did not deserve.

"Sarah?" Sir Walter urged her.

"You deserve better," she said.

"Allow me to know my best deserts," he whispered. "Say yes."

"Yes."

When she had said the word Miss Tolerance felt a lightness she had not felt since the early days of her romance with Charles Connell. This must have shown in her countenance, for Sir Walter again raised her hand to his lips.

"So little a word."

She nodded. "But heavily freighted."

Unmoved by the scene playing before it, the mantel clock chose that moment to chime the hour.

"Seven o'clock! I had no notion it was so late. I promised Marianne that I would be gone no more than an hour!"

Sir Walter choked on a laugh, winced, and whispered, "You mean to leave me?"

Miss Tolerance nodded. "I must. For now. My aunt is ill again and I stole an hour to look in upon you. I promised..."

"I would not have you foresworn. I will let you leave me now. But in future—"

Miss Tolerance leaned forward to press her lips very gently to Sir Walter's. "In future," she agreed. "I will call upon you tomorrow."

"I look forward to it," he said gravely, but his eyes were amused.

Miss Tolerance took up her bonnet and went to the door to desire Michael to summon a hackney carriage. She could feel Sir Walter's gaze upon her as she left.

Chapter Nineteen

Miss Tolerance dined with her aunt that evening. With a sense that her own news was fresh and tender, she did not speak of Sir Walter and their affiancement. However sympathetic Mrs. Brereton might feel, Miss Tolerance was certain her aunt would be acerbic on the topic. Instead, she read the court news aloud. Mrs. Brereton's sense of humor did not appear to have been affected by the apoplectic stroke. Her comments on the Duke of Kent's interest in Canadian unification were arch and dismissive, despite the slur in her words. Regarding the presentation at court of three young ladies whose fathers had been lovers of hers: "No chin, no waist, no gumption. Like their fathers." Mrs. Brereton dabbed at the drooping corner of her mouth with a handkerchief balled in her good hand.

"Poor girls."

"Not at all; their fathers will buy them nice husbands and they will produce mild, chinless children."

Laughing, Miss Tolerance kissed her aunt and went blamelessly to sleep in the yellow room, where she had taken to sleeping lest she be needed in the night.

Morning came far too soon. Priscilla, one of the maids, clattered in to catch the fire—a piece of clumsiness Miss Tolerance had never before encountered in her aunt's household.

"What is it?"

The girl looked up from the hearth, eyes red-rimmed. "Miss Marianne said not to wake you—"

"Never mind that." Miss Tolerance felt a flicker of anxiety. "What is the matter, Priscilla? Mrs. Brereton—"

Tears rolled down the girl's cheeks to drop on the hearthstones. "Gone in the night, miss. Miss Marianne says—"

She did not wait to hear what Marianne said. Miss Tolerance, barefoot and disheveled, was tying her wrapper as she left the room.

In Mrs. Brereton's apartments, the sitting room was empty; she went through to the bedroom and found there a tableau of Marianne, Miss Frost, and the doctor, all arranged around her aunt's still form. In life, Dorothea Brereton had been a tall woman; in death, wearing a lacy cap and robe, settled among laced and beribboned pillows, she looked like a wax doll. The vitality which even in sickness had radiated from her was gone, startlingly and abruptly.

"What happened?" she asked.

Marianne advanced to her, took her hand, and drew her to the side of the bed. "She woke Frost—"

Miss Frost interrupted. "I lay down on the sofa to rest me eyes, just for a moment or so, then I heard ma'am coughing, as I thought it was. A horrid harsh noise, like she couldn't catch 'er breath. And stock still, like she couldn't move a hair."

"Frost called for me and I sent Keefe for Sir George at once, but— it all was so quick, Sarah."

"It sometimes happens so," Hammond agreed. "After

several strokes, it is not surprising that one would carry her off. A blessing, really." As he spoke, he was packing his tools —the horn stethoscope, a watch, an ivory wand meant to hold the tongue down—into a small bag. "I condole with you upon your loss," he said to the room in general. "If there is any way in which I can be of service to you?"

Miss Tolerance and Marianne both murmured their thanks, and Marianne escorted Sir George out. Miss Tolerance took the place her friend had vacated. She had been present at deaths and deathbeds before; the un-reality of loss was familiar to her. Had her Aunt Thea sat up and scolded her for taking a little ruse so seriously it would not have surprised her; she had felt the same when Charles Connell had died. Tears, she knew from experience, would come later.

Marianne returned. "He'll talk to the undertaker," she said. "Sarah, do you want some time alone?"

Miss Tolerance shook her head. "I had rather be doing something." She did not believe, in any case, that it would be possible to prise Miss Frost from her mistress's side. "Perhaps we should make a list?"

First, according to Miss Frost, came the necessity to decide what Mrs. Brereton would wear to be buried in. There was a certain amount of discussion—to her surprise, Frost sided with her in preferring a plain morning gown of violet merino, against Mrs. Touchwell's suggestion of one of the opulent dresses Mrs. Brereton had commonly worn when presiding in the salon.

"Ma'am would want to dress appropriate," the dresser insisted. "I'll put her in her new cap, as well." Frost made it clear that no one but herself would be permitted to wash and dress the body, which left Mrs. Touchwell to manage the household and Miss Tolerance to attend to all those other duties required by a death—even a natural death with no whiff of criminality about it.

But first she had a personal task. She had promised Sir Walter that she would visit. That would have to wait, but she wanted—*needed*—to let him know what had happened, that her neglect was not a reflection of any doubt on her part. In the yellow room, once she dressed for the day, she drew a sheet of paper to her and took up her pen.

My dear Sir Walter—

I fear I must begin our... she paused here, hesitant to write the word, then shook her head at her foolishness. *I fear I must begin our engagement by reneging upon my promise of yesterday. I will not be able to visit today: my aunt Dorothea died last night, and I am, as you will imagine, much taken up with the work of notification and arrangement. Please believe that I would not be apart for any reason less grave. I will hope to see you soon. In the meantime, if you will let me know that you continue to mend, it would give more pleasure than you can imagine to*

—your Sarah

Sanded, folded, sealed, and addressed, Miss Tolerance took the tray downstairs to Cole for dispatch.

She spoke with the undertaker, then called upon the minister at All Souls to set the time and date for the funeral. Although she suspected that her aunt would have disapproved mightily, Keefe and Cole were instructed to tell gentlemen that there had been a death in the house and none of the ladies of the house would be receiving tonight.

"Should it be generally known, do you think?" she asked Mrs. Touchwell. "Outside of the household?"

"Oh, I think so." Marianne was engaged in hemming black ribbon armbands for the staff. "Put notices in the newspapers. There are those will want to pay their respects... old followers, girls as worked here in the past. Will you tell your brother?"

Miss Tolerance realized with some dismay that she had

not thought of Adam at all. "I ought. I know he will not want to make a public show of mourning, but she was our aunt."

Marianne bit a thread off neatly and looked up from her work. "Sarah, how do *you* do?"

"I?"

Marianne put a hand on her shoulder. "*You*. She was your aunt. I know there was affection between you, however *peculiarly* it was sometimes expressed. I worry."

It took a moment for Miss Tolerance to answer. She was sorrowing—that her aunt's astringent, intelligent presence was gone forever, seemed impossible. "I loved Aunt Thea and I am deeply grieved, but you know it's not my way to wear my heart upon my sleeve. I appreciate that you ask, but —"

Marianne shook her head. "That is why I worry. Always keeping to yourself what any other of us here would share without a thought. All right, if you promise me that you will speak up when you are needful, I shan't fret about you until you tell me 'tis time to do."

Miss Tolerance smiled at her friend and both she and Marianne went back to their chores. In fact, Miss Tolerance was unhappily aware that as she went about drafting a death notice for the newspapers, her thoughts drifted to Sir Walter. Despite the note she had written, she wanted badly to sneak away from her aunt's house and reassure herself that the surgeon Mr. O'Leary had been right, that Mandif was recovering apace, that her affiancement was not a dream.

"What do you think of this?" She turned at last to Marianne. "*BRERETON, Mrs. Dorothea Elinor, London, 27 October inst. aet 55. A skilled businesswoman and considerate mistress, her management provided work and safety for many; died after a brief illness. Service to be held at All Souls Church.*"

"Oh, that's lovely, Sarah. Your aunt would laugh to hear it."

"What else should I have said? Obituaries are for the folk

left behind to grieve and remember. Don't you think Mrs. Gordon or Cole or Frost would rather hear my aunt written of with respect, rather than as a way of twitting society?"

"Nothing about humility and Christian faith?" Marianne took the paper from Miss Tolerance's hand to read it again. "Very dignified and just as it should be."

Miss Tolerance nodded. She had already begun a brief letter to her brother.

Dear Adam,

I know you will wish to know that our Aunt Dorothea died yesterday after a short illness. You will not want to come for the service, I imagine, but I thought it only right that I share the news with you. Please know that we are doing everything in the style she would have wanted. My best love to Clarissa and yourself—

She blotted the paper, folded, addressed, and sealed it, and put it on a tray with the rest of the correspondence to be mailed. *How is Sir Walter?* She itched to be out of her aunt's house.

"Sarah, did you write to the solicitor?"

"No. I had not—"

"There's her will to be read, and if it's of small matter to you, the others will want to know if Mrs. B remembered them in any way—a few bob, or a bit of finery, like. Particularly as your aunt made such a point about changing her will so recently—"

"Of course." Miss Tolerance sat again, opened the inkwell, put another piece of laid paper on the blotter, and began a note to Mrs. Brereton's solicitor. "Do you think we can put the reading of the will off until after the funeral?"

Marianne nodded slowly. "I think that's what is generally done—I've never been concerned with a death where there was property—women so often haven't anything to leave, nor do men leave property to women except it's handed over to other men in keeping."

Miss Tolerance nodded, added another sentence to her letter, then signed, sanded, and sealed it, and gathered up the letters already written. "I will ask Cole to post these."

"Can you wait just a moment? I'm copying the notice for the *Times*."

"Of course." Miss Tolerance sat again, thinking of Sir Walter.

The house was uncannily quiet. As she passed the salon she saw four of Mrs. Brereton's whores sitting quietly, sewing black ribbons onto hats and dresses. Cole wore a black armband over his livery. Miss Tolerance realized she had not given a thought to her own mourning clothes. She had a black gown, but it was shabby and most often used as the basis for a costume for an imposture. Perhaps if she wore black ribbons and gloves?

How Aunt Thea would laugh at me, Miss Tolerance thought. And with that, she went into the salon to speak with the ladies there.

"Oh, Miss Sarah, I'm so sorry," Anne-Josephe said softly.

Chloe, Lisette, and Jane murmured much the same.

"Thank you all—but this is your loss as much as mine. It occurred to me to ask you all: do you think my aunt would have wished the whole house to go into mourning?"

"Not if it kept the custom away," Lisette said firmly. Then her hand went to her mouth and she looked at the others guiltily.

"I was thinking the same myself," Miss Tolerance agreed. "You all knew my aunt well. She would be mightily pleased to know the fondness you had for her, but I do not think she would require too deep or too long a mourning. This house is her best monument, and Aunt Thea would want it to be as it has been, a lively place. So," she said with decision. "Once the funeral is over, let us put away the blacks as a way of honoring her memory."

"Not even a little black ribbon?" Anne-Josephe asked, plaintive.

Miss Tolerance held back a laugh. "I would never stop anyone from wearing what they wished."

Later, when she told Marianne what she had decreed, her friend smiled and nodded and said it was very clever. "Very nice for your first order in the house, Sarah."

Miss Tolerance shook her head. "I have no desire—"

"Nor you do," Marianne agreed. "But what you desire and what you get do not always march together. Any girl here would tell you that."

On the following day, Miss Tolerance visited the vicar of All Souls to choose the hymns for her aunt's funeral, then spoke with the sexton; the funeral was set for three in the afternoon. That errand done, with a guilty sense of truancy, she stole an hour to visit in Gracechurch Street.

At her entrance, Sir Walter attempted to sit up. She gently —but ruthlessly—pressed him back into his pillows.

"Don't stir yourself," she scolded. "Has the surgeon said you may sit up? What does—"

Sir Walter pressed a finger to her lips. "Pynt says I am a damned lucky fool," he whispered.

"Lucky that Andrew Pennantine was not an experienced cutthroat!" Miss Tolerance took a seat at his side. She was pleased to see his color much improved, and the bandage around his neck spotlessly clean. Mrs. Yarrow and Michael had clearly been scrupulous in Sir Walter's care.

"Among other things, yes." Sir Walter's voice was still close to a whisper. "You will like to know that it appears that Pennantine will survive to stand his trial. He was lucky you kept him from bleeding to death. Not so fortunate as I, of course. And lucky to have you visit, with all that has happened. I am so very sorry about your aunt, Sarah."

"Thank you. I—I forget, did you ever meet her?"

"Only through your stories. She sounded a remarkable woman."

"She was. For all the souls that occupy it still, the house seems very empty without her." She told him the plans for the funeral, "so I shall not likely be able to visit again for a day or two."

"And then?" Sir Walter had possessed himself of her hand and held it firmly in his own, as if he would keep her there.

"After the funeral? I don't—my aunt threatened to leave me the house, but my ambitions don't lean that way."

"Then you will stay in the garden cottage until we marry."

Miss Tolerance found herself blushing. "I suppose—I had not had time to think."

Sir Walter smiled. "You said *yes*. I shall not allow you to cry off. As it appears that you might lose your home, I hope you will not require a long engagement. It will give me very great pleasure to make a home for you."

To her horror, Miss Tolerance found tears running down her cheeks. She was not certain if they were for her aunt or for herself. Sir Walter relinquished her hand, but only to pull her head down upon his shoulder.

"I would offer you my kerchief, but I don't know where Mrs. Yarrow has put it." he murmured.

"You are not to move," she said. "This must be uncomfortable." She made to sit up. Instead, Mandif moved so that her head rested upon his chest.

"Sarah, listen to me. I do not want to take from you the independence you prize. But I do want you to know… Since Connell died you have made your own way alone. I hope you understand that you are not—that you will never be alone so long as I have breath in my body."

She listened to the steady beat of his heart under her ear.

After a few minutes, she gave a damp, rueful laugh. "I am not certain I know how to be not-alone."

"I expect it will be difficult for you at first. But you are a very clever woman; I have faith."

"You're laughing at me!" Now she sat up.

"Only a little." He took her hand again. "At the risk of being indelicate, how long a period of mourning must you observe before you will marry me?"

"At least long enough so that I do not worry that your wound will open up in the church!"

"I will put my mind to mending," he said firmly.

Mrs. Dorothea Brereton was laid to rest on the afternoon of the third day after her death, in the churchyard adjacent to All Souls' Church. The service was, as Marianne Touchwell had predicted, widely attended, not only by the members of her household but by the proprietors of many competing brothels and a number of men of varying ages and in varying stages of disguise. It was fortunate for those men who did not wish to be identified that it was cold enough to make the swathing of one's face in a muffler a reasonable thing.

In discussion with the funeral furnisher, Miss Tolerance and Mrs. Touchwell had balanced the need to, as Mrs. Touchwell might have said, do the thing properly for the sake of the members of the household against a sense that Mrs. Brereton herself would have disliked the spending of money on wagons and horses draped in black, formal mourners, and the more outlandish funerary excesses of the upper classes. The velvet-draped coffin was borne by the men of her household: Cole and Keefe, Harry and Frank, an old employee of the house, Tim from the kitchen, old Gurgin, the gardener.

"One of the advantages of being Fallen," Mrs. Touchwell had noted, "is one may give vent to one's feelings without being ashamed." Most of the women and a few of the men in attendance wept unself-consciously.

The anthems were sung, the psalms recited, the responses given, Communion taken, and at last, the soul of Mrs. Dorothea Brereton was committed to the care of her creator. Miss Tolerance, for whom faith was a real but often unconsidered thing, found herself silently repeating the words as the celebrant said them: *Give rest, O Christ, to thy servant with thy saints, where sorrow and pain are no more, neither sighing, but life everlasting.*

Folded in the pocket of her coat like a charm against too great grief, Miss Tolerance had the note she had received from Sir Walter, regretting that he was not yet recovered enough to stand with her at the graveside. *I can only hope that my love, and the knowledge that I am with you in your grief, will be of some comfort until I can be with you again.* She found herself clutching the slip of paper as she might have held its author's hand.

When the service had finished, Miss Tolerance, in a black gown and coat Frost had found among her aunt's wardrobe, stood with the minister at the door of the church, receiving the condolences of those in attendance. Then the hardiest of the party followed the coffin to the graveside, where it was committed to the earth. Miss Tolerance felt tears hot in her eyes, but it was not in her nature to make a display of the sort that seemed to come easily to others from the household. When the funeral was done and the fees duly paid for the service, the burial, and the ringing of bells, the party returned to Manchester Square, and Miss Tolerance went at once to her cottage and to bed.

At Miss Tolerance's urging, Marianne had instructed Cole to turn patrons away the next day until the solicitor had finished his visit. With the entire household—whores and servants alike—assembled in the Salon, Miss Tolerance appreciated anew what a large establishment it was. Ten girls, including Marianne, as well as young Harry, who was kept on for those gentlemen whose tastes were not of the usual sort. Frost, Cole, Keefe, and Cook, Jess and Tim from the kitchen, Mrs. Shattuck, the laundress, and her two daughter-assistants, Jim Gurgin, the gardener, four maids, and two running boys. Miss Tolerance had been told that her presence was necessary, but she felt in some wise as though she was intruding upon another family's grief. She had loved her aunt—as much as Mrs. Brereton would permit such an emotion—but had set up her life so that she did not depend upon her.

Mr. McBride, the solicitor, had been given the prime seat, near the fire but not too near, with the household ringed around him. Miss Tolerance had taken a chair to the side of the room and waited with the rest while the man shook out his cuffs, took a sip at the wine Keefe had poured for him, and cleared his throat.

"Shall I read the will entire or simply tell you what Mrs. Brereton's wishes were?"

"Read it all, please," Mrs. Touchwell instructed. "In case Mrs. B. left any messages or instructions we'd ought to have."

McBride, a tall, doughy man with thin ginger hair, younger than Miss Tolerance would have expected, re-settled the eyeglasses upon his nose and nodded. "Very well." He began to read.

I, Dorothea Elinor Brereton, spinster of this parish, do leave this Last Will and Testament to my wishes and designs as in life.

To each of the persons currently employed by me or my establishment at the time of my death, the sum of £15, in the hope that this provides the kernel of savings which will keep them from want in their age, together with my thanks for their constant service and goodwill.

To Hiram Cole, in particular, as well, the choice of one from the case of pistols in the library which have been kept here for the defense of the ladies employed here. To Patrick Keefe, in particular, the remaining pistol, ditto.

To Ellen Frost, my attendant and maid for many years, £100 and her choice of any among the clothing of which I die possessed, excepting only the Valenciennes lace. Any clothing which Frost does not wish to take away may be distributed among the women of the establishment as they see fit.

To my dear niece, Sarah Brereton, also known as Tolerance, all other money and property of which I die possessed after payment of my lawful debts and the cost of my funeral, with the following conditions:

1) That the business which has been my life's work to establish shall continue to operate as it has done for the period of at least one year from the proving of this Will;

2) That Miss Brereton continue to reside upon the premises during that time;

3) That she retain and consult Marianne Touchwell as the manageress of this establishment, as being the one who most closely understands its operation;

4) That, should she refuse to abide by these first conditions, my establishment shall close at once, the building be sold at once, and all the proceeds distributed to the charities I have listed below.

At the end of the year mentioned in the first condition, Miss Brereton shall be free to sell or otherwise convey whatever part of this property and money to others.

I appoint Miss Sarah Brereton and Mrs. Marianne Touchwell as executrices of this Will, believing that they will provide sage counsel, one to the other.

McBride looked up from the paper in his hand and blinked

nearsightedly. "Do you wish me to read the names of the charities?"

Several women, hearing of Mrs. Brereton's largesse (and the shares to which they were each liable) had begun to weep again.

"That will not be necessary, I think." Mrs. Touchwell thanked Mr. McBride, who took another sip from the glass at his elbow, then asked if there were any questions.

The solicitor noted, with a tone of concern, "In particular, I pointed out to Mrs. Brereton the—the *unconventional* nature of her will, leaving two women as executrices without the benefit of a man's advice. Should you ladies require assistance, I am of course happy to—"

Miss Tolerance, feeling very much as if a thunderbolt had struck her from a clear sky, interrupted. Her voice shook despite her attempt to steady it. "Am I to understand that if I do not accept this legacy then everyone in this household immediately loses their home and livelihood?"

All eyes trained again upon Mr. McBride, who cleared his throat and agreed that that was Mrs. Brereton's intention.

"What in the name of God could she have thought to accomplish by this?"

"I imagine her hope was that in the passage of a year you might come to value —" McBride began.

"Good God." Miss Tolerance, aware that she was now responsible for the immediate future of every single person in the room, barring the solicitor, felt as though there was no air. She rose and stumbled from the room into the hallway.

For the love of God, Aunt Thea, what were you thinking? Lightheaded, she clung to the newel post of the great stairway and, realizing that she was panting, attempted to slow her breathing. Had her aunt had any idea this news would throw her into such a panic? For that matter, had *she*? Mrs. Brereton had always spoken as if someday the house would be her niece's, but— "I never believed it," she said aloud. The words were very loud in the empty hallway.

"Never believed she meant you to have the business?"

Marianne Touchwell stood by the parlor door as if wary of coming too close. Like all the others in the house, she still wore funereal black; one of her ribbons had come untied.

"She told you often enough, even if you thought she was only needling you. You may not like it, but whether you like it or not, folk will be looking to you now. And I don't mind telling you that you running from the room like that, white as a sheet, has put a right scare into the others in the house. I think they're all expecting to be shown the door in the morning."

"I wouldn't—" Miss Tolerance, more in control of herself now, sat without dignity on the bottom stair. "But surely I can have a day or so to understand—to decide what I must do. If you and I are executrices, that power must be in our hands."

Marianne sat next to her, a comforting, sensible presence. "Why not give her the year she wanted?" Miss Tolerance shook her head. "No, see, Sarah. How would it be any different than the way things have gone on since you returned to England six years ago? You might like to move into the house; Lord knows it's warmer in the winter, and the bath water will be hot when it reaches you."

Miss Tolerance laughed weakly. "It isn't the house, Marianne... it's...Before Aunt Thea died I had—my life was going to be different—"

"Different or the same. I know it isn't what you wanted—"

"You don't *understand*—"

"Why, because I'm a whore?" Marianne's tone cooled.

Miss Tolerance turned to regard her friend. "No! Oh, my God, Marianne, that was not said to hurt you—"

Marianne shrugged. "You haven't done, though you might hurt one of the others with your delicate notions. You've lived on the grounds, known precisely what went on here. You've had it both ways, not quite a part of the house but not quite on your own. Your Aunt saw it. P'raps this was her way of making you see it, too."

Miss Tolerance put her head in her hands. "I would have no idea how—"

"That's why she required you to retain my services as Manageress," Marianne reminded her. "I can teach you—"

"Teach me to manage a brothel?" Miss Tolerance raised her head. "Had you asked me a week ago, I should have said my future lay in putting by enough money to live upon quietly when I was too old to do the work I do now. In the last four days I've seen my future change and change again—"

"You could refuse the inheritance—in course, you'd have to find a new place to sleep, but then, so will we all."

Miss Tolerance shook her head. "I cannot casually throw away the livelihood of two dozen souls—my aunt knew it."

"There's many—your aunt included—who'd do so in a heartbeat did it go against what they wanted. Mrs. B. was kind in her way and made a point to treat all of us decent, but that was business for her: a happy whore pleases the custom better than a sullen one. But the minute it went against her own inclination—"

"Even if that were true—I am not my aunt."

"No. But Sarah—" Marianne put her arm about Miss Tolerance's shoulders. "If you decide to stay, it's but a year. Can a year matter so much?"

Miss Tolerance thought of Sir Walter. "He has been so patient," she murmured to herself.

"He?" Marianne took in a sharp breath. "The magistrate? Oh, Sarah!" As if a star had risen above her, Mrs. Touchwell appeared to be struck by light. "Did you and he *finally*—"

Miss Tolerance nodded and gave a sad little laugh. "The day Aunt Thea had the stroke, I entered into an engagement."

"But Sarah, that's lovely!" the other woman swept Miss

Tolerance into an embrace. "I'm so glad—" And then the import of this news struck her. "*Oh, Sarah.*"

Miss Tolerance pulled gently out of her friend's arms. "Precisely." She leaned back against the baluster. "If it had not been a secret from her, I should have suspected my aunt of setting matters so deliberately, just for the trouble it would stir up."

Mrs. Touchwell nodded matter-of-factly. "She liked to stir things up, it's true. Although perhaps not to such an extent as this. What will you do?"

"What *can* I do?" Miss Tolerance looked at the salon door. "I shall visit Sir Walter and lay the situation before him and hope—with my whole heart—that he will consent to wait a while for me."

"As you say, he's waited this long," Marianne said.

Miss Tolerance shook her head. "Should he wait longer? Will he do so? I've no right to ask."

"By that token, we've no right to ask you to stay with the house. But you mean to do so because—"

"Because I cannot do anything else." Miss Tolerance gave a watery laugh.

"There you go. And that's why he will wait for you."

"I hope you are right."

Marianne nodded but said nothing, as indeed there was little to say.

"I suppose I should go reassure them," Miss Tolerance said at last. She rose and straightened the folds of her dress. She let Marianne precede her into the room and stood in the doorway for a long moment, poised between duty and a pardonable desire for flight. Then, aware of the weight of regard turned upon her, Miss Tolerance squared her shoulders and went in to talk to her people.

The Fate of Fallen Women* ... and Thank Yous

So what really became of the aging "Fallen" of Regency England? Over the course of writing the Sarah Tolerance mysteries I've created various "retired" courtesans, but how realistic is that? Retirement itself is a relatively modern concept: as you aged, if you became too infirm to do the work you'd done all your life, your care became the responsibility of your family. If you had no family, or your family would have nothing to do with you, you might find yourself confined to an Almshouse. But most people just kept working until they died.

In 1811 England the average lifespan—across all social classes—was about 40 years. But this figure is skewed: adjusted for high mortality rates for infants and children, life expectancy for women was closer to 62 years. But longevity depended on a number of factors, including how hard your life was. The employees of Mrs. Brereton's establishment are lucky: they're well fed and protected from some of the brutal hazards of their occupation. Most sex workers were *not* lucky; to the normal hazards of life in 1810, add sexually transmitted disease, alcoholism and drug use, brutality, hunger, and poverty. Prostitution is in most cases a young-person's game, and when youth and looks were gone, income (and therefore food and shelter) followed.

Courtesans working at the highest level did not take money for services so much as expect to be provided with a *lifestyle*. And most of these women spent money lavishly while they could: then as now, being beautifully dressed and bejeweled was an advertisement. What most successful courtesans did *not* do was keep money for a rainy day, or for their "retirement". Even the most successful courtesans of their day had a hard time of it. Consider Emma, Lady Hamilton and Harriette Wilson.

Hamilton, in her early teens, became an actress and dancer and mistress to a string of men, until in 1791 she married Sir William Hamilton, the British Envoy to Naples. To all accounts they were happy, and Emma, despite uncouth manners, became a confidante and advisor of Queen Maria Carolina of Naples. Then, in 1798, Horatio Nelson arrived in Naples in the wake of his victory at Aboukir. He and Lady Hamilton became friends, and then lovers. The fact of their relationship was well known in Naples and later in London (to the outrage of Nelson's wife, Fanny; Sir William appears to have been philosophical, once writing to Nelson, when Emma was being pursued by the Prince of Wales, to assure him that his wife was still faithful to Nelson!). Emma bore Nelson's child, Horatia; Sir William died (Fanny, Lady Nelson, remained stubbornly alive, defeating what almost certainly would have been a marriage between Nelson and Emma), and then in 1805, Nelson died at Trafalgar. Nelson had literally consigned care of Emma and Horatia to a grateful nation mourning its hero, but the nation turned its back on her. Ten years after Nelson's death, Emma Hamilton died in Calais, whence she had fled to escape her creditors, at 49 years of age.

Unlike Emma Hamilton, who was a serial courtesan, Harriette Wilson was the real deal: even when she was a man's mistress that didn't keep her from taking other clients. Wilson's solution, when she grew too old to draw clientele, was to write a memoir, and offer to redact the names of the men she name-checked in it... at £200 a pop. Famously, the Duke of Wellington told her "publish and be damned!" She did—and to no one's surprise her memoirs included some humiliating comments on the Hero of Waterloo. But even with some money coming in—Wilson took to writing novels and poetry—she did not manage her finances well. She too died penniless, just after her 59th birthday.

And these were highly successful courtesans. What did the rank-and-file sex workers do? In Miss Tolerance's world those who have saved up enough over the years strive to retire respectably. For many working poor (among whom most prostitutes would emphatically have numbered) any money they put by was likely locked up in a box under the bed, or perhaps deposited in a bank. The business-minded might invest in the Navy Fives, government stock that provided a 5% annual return (Jane Austen had £600 in the Navy Fives, earning an annual return of £30).

Much of what we think of as normal financial practice was different in 1810. For one thing, private banks in Great Britain and Ireland could issue their own banknotes, which circulated the same way as notes issued by the Bank of England. What started out as hand-written IOUs drawn on a given bank (rather like a check) became, in time, preprinted blanks with details handwritten and signed by the issuing clerks. But for most people hard cash—that is, coins—were the preferred unit. The guinea—made with a quarter ounce of gold—varied in value depending on the price of gold. In 1811 England was still using guineas; in 1816 the guinea was replaced with the sovereign.

An English laborer in 1811 made about £58 a year (a woman made about £32 a year). When you consider this, Miss Tolerance's fee of three guineas a day plus expenses is deliberately high (after all, she has to cover times when she has no work). With sex work the price was whatever the traffic would bear—but in the poorer parts of town, the traffic didn't bear much. Subtract lodging, drink, and food and there would be precious little to save for one's old age. If one lived that long.

Many sex-workers didn't live long enough to retire. Syphilis was rampant, and until the 20th century the cures for it were hit or miss at best. Like Mrs. Brereton, many sufferers who sought treatment were deceived by the nature of the disease—which can go dormant for years, even decades—into believing they had been cured, only to have the disease come roaring back later. It's an ugly disease that takes many forms, and it's very transmissible; I've said elsewhere that I'm still surprised that anyone in 18th and 19th century Europe didn't have the pox. I am grateful to live in a time when medical science has made this, and so many other diseases, curable.

This book took a long time to write. I must thank, first, the many people who have contacted me over that very long time, asking for more of Miss Tolerance, and being encouraging. Never think a writer doesn't care that you want more, or that she's created something that resonated with you! So I apologize that it so long; I can only plead the distractions of family and a day job.

On that note, I want to thank my co-workers at the American Bookbinders Museum in San Francisco, who provided huge amounts of information and enthusiasm. Writers live by picking up stray morsels of information; over eight years at the ABM I was stuffed full of information about bookbinding, the history of literacy, and the history of work. Some of that has definitely made its way into Miss Tolerance's world.

As always, I thank my stage combat teachers: TJ Glenn, Richard Rizk, J. David Brimmer, and M. Lucie Chin, who taught me to think of mayhem in three dimensions (at the very least)! Miss Tolerance and I thank them every day.

Then there are the people who helped bring this book into the world. Deborah J. Ross, herself a writer of considerable note, took time away from her work to edit the book and make it tighter and better, for which she should have not only my thanks, but those of the reader! As I forged (slowly) into the brave new world of indie- and micro-press publishing, Laura Anne Gilman, Burdock Broughton, Lyn Forester, and Kate Larking held my hand, explained things, and never lost patience with my nine hundredth question. I am grateful to the folks at Plus One (Deborah and Nic Grabien and the late and much missed Jacqueline Smay); and at Tor/Forge (Patrick Nielsen Hayden and Anna Genoese, and a raft of others) for their help in bringing *Point of Honour*, *Petty Treason*, and *The Sleeping Partner* into the world.

I am blessed with many friends and colleagues who have been helpful on this book and on the series over the years. Jennifer Stevenson and Brenda Clough, Sherwood Smith, Kris Smith, Chaz Brenchley, Steven Popkes, Marissa Doyle, Ellen Kushner and Gillian Polack at various times have provided information, help, encouragement, even proof-reading! I owe you all. Victor Raymond pitched in with an onerous marketing task that might never have got done, except for his cheery confidence and enthusiasm. Finally the members of my writing group, including Katherine Kerr, Nancy Jane Moore, Cliff Winig, Karen Brenchley, Jeannie Warner, Denise Tanaka, and Berry Kercheval, saw chunks of this book often, in different combinations of events and words, and yet were able to provide helpful, *useful* feedback. There aren't enough Thank Yous in the world.

As usual, the last word in the love and appreciation goes to my husband, Danny Caccavo, and our daughters, Jules and Rebecca, for being the best things in my life, hands down.

About the Author

Madeleine E. Robins has been a nanny, an administrator, an actor, and a swordswoman; has trafficked book production, edited comics, and repaired hurt books. She's also the author of the *New York Times* Notable urban fantasy *The Stone War*; *Daredevil: The Cutting Edge*; historical novel *Sold for Endless Rue;* and alt-Regency-noir mysteries *Point of Honour*, *Petty Treason*, *The Sleeping Partner*, and *The Doxies Penalty*. A lifelong fan of cities, urban infrastructure, and English history, she lives in San Francisco with her husband, and owns more baking paraphernalia than is strictly legal.

instagram.com/Madeleine.robins

facebook.com/MadRobins

bsky.app/profile/madrobins.bsky.social

threads.com/@Madeleine.robins

mastodon.social/@MadRobins@norcal.social

www.ingramcontent.com/pod-product-compliance
Lightning Source LLC
Chambersburg PA
CBHW071229300726
48975CB00002B/339